PENGUIN CLASSICS

NEWS FROM NOWHERE
AND OTHER WRITINGS

WILLIAM MORRIS (1834–1896), designer, craftsman, poet, prose writer, translator, socialist, conservationist and publisher, was one of the most influential thinkers and artists of his time. At Oxford, with the painter Burne-Jones, he fell under the influence of Ruskin and Rossetti. Pre-occupied with the poverty of modern design, he taught himself at least thirteen crafts and founded his own design firm, Morris & Co. In 1858 *The Defence of Guenevere and Other Poems* was published; his other books of verse include *The Earthly Paradise* (1868–70) and *Sigurd the Volsung* (1876). In the late 1870s he became active in political and environmentalist matters, announcing his conversion to Socialism in 1883. In 1884 he helped to found the Socialist League. His prose works include lectures on art and politics, as well as several romances, among them the Utopian dream *News from Nowhere* (1890). He translated verse and prose from several languages, notably a series of Icelandic sagas. In 1891 he started the Kelmscott Press. Morris married Jane Burden in 1859 and was deeply devoted to their two daughters.

CLIVE WILMER was born in 1945, grew up in London and read English at King's College, Cambridge. He works as a freelance poet, critic, lecturer and broadcaster. He has also edited John Ruskin's *Unto This Last and Other Writings* for Penguin Classics and Dante Gabriel Rossetti's *Selected Poems and Translations*. His books of verse are *The Dwelling-Place* (1977), *Devotions* (1982) and *Of Earthly Paradise* (1992). He has translated poetry from several languages, including two books from Hungarian. Formerly an editor of the magazine *Numbers*, he was from 1989 to 1990 the chief presenter for BBC Radio 3's *Poet of the Month*. He has two children and lives in Cambridge.

William Morris

* * *

NEWS FROM
NOWHERE
and Other Writings

Edited with an Introduction and Notes by
CLIVE WILMER

PENGUIN BOOKS

PENGUIN BOOKS

Published by the Penguin Group
Penguin Books Ltd, 27 Wrights Lane, London W8 5TZ, England
Penguin Books USA Inc., 375 Hudson Street, New York, New York 10014, USA
Penguin Books Australia Ltd, Ringwood, Victoria, Australia
Penguin Books Canada Ltd, 10 Alcorn Avenue, Toronto, Ontario, Canada M4V 3B2
Penguin Books (NZ) Ltd, 182–190 Wairau Road, Auckland 10, New Zealand

Penguin Books Ltd, Registered Offices: Harmondsworth, Middlesex, England

This edition first published 1993
5 7 9 10 8 6

Introduction and Notes copyright © Clive Wilmer, 1993
All rights reserved

Filmset in 10/12.5pt Monophoto Janson
Typeset by Datix International Limited, Bungay, Suffolk
Printed in England by Clays Ltd, St Ives plc

To my sister

VAL

Radical and Traditionalist

... thinking of their passed-away builders I can see through them very faintly, dimly, some little of the medieval times, else dead and gone from me for ever; voiceless for ever. And those same builders, still surely living, still real men and capable of receiving love, I love no less than the great men, poets and painters and such like, who are on earth now; no less than my breathing friends whom I see looking kindly on me now.

Shadows of Amiens (1856)

CONTENTS

* * *

vii

LETTERS

INTRODUCTION

* * *

When William Morris died in 1896 at the relatively early age of sixty-two, one doctor had no doubt about the cause of death. 'I consider the case is this,' he commented: 'the disease is simply being William Morris, and having done more work than most ten men.' The doctor was hardly exaggerating. Looking over Morris's career, one is indeed struck by the quantity of his work, but even more so by its range and variety.

He is best known today as a designer and craftsman. In the view of at least one major art historian, Morris must be regarded as the greatest European pattern-designer since the end of the Middle Ages, one moreover who revived several long-forgotten crafts and skills. He achieved major success in at least thirteen fields of decorative art: stained glass, ceramics, painted or stencilled decoration, embroidery, wallpapers, chintzes, printed fabrics, woven materials, tapestries, carpets, illuminated manuscripts, typography and book design. He had no formal training in any of these fields and often had to teach himself forgotten skills by studying ancient artefacts or reading the primers of medieval craftsmen. His concern extended beyond the methods of design and production to his raw materials themselves: dyes, papers, inks and so on. By all these means, he became a major authority on textile design in medieval Europe and the Middle East, as well as on illuminated manuscripts and early printed books.

In his own day Morris was thought of as primarily a poet. His most popular work, however, a book-length poem called *The Earthly Paradise*, may strike the modern reader as prolix, over-decorative and escapist. In general his poetry has not worn well, though the best of his lyric verse and his epic, *Sigurd the Volsung*, are unlikely to be forgotten. He also translated verse and prose from Greek, Latin,

Danish, Icelandic, Old English and Old French. His versions of Icelandic sagas represent a literary treasure he may be said to have discovered for the English-speaking world. According to his daughter May, he was a natural story-teller, a talent that emerges in his many prose romances, most of which have roots in northern folklore. Out of this habit of romancing came his two great political fictions, *A Dream of John Ball* and *News from Nowhere*. During the last two decades of his life, the years of his political activism, he also became a noted lecturer and journalist on subjects that ranged from practical skills in the field of design to the kind of society he hoped for as a Socialist.

The co-existence in Morris's work of revolutionary politics and nostalgic romance is puzzling to the reader unfamiliar with his range. It has provoked some mockery and the charge of sentimentality. Yet Morris was a practical man and anything but an armchair Socialist. He worked virtually full time for, successively, the Eastern Question Association, the National Liberal League, the Social Democratic Federation and the Socialist League, which he helped to found and lead. It is estimated that, between 1884 and 1890, he spoke or lectured at, on average, three meetings a week. This involved him in extensive travelling, as well as participating in demonstrations, chairing his branch of the League, attending executive meetings and running the League's remarkable newspaper, the *Commonweal*. Many of the skills he brought into politics he had learnt in the world of business. Inheriting shares in a copper-mining company, he served for several years on the board of directors. He also ran his own successful design firm and, at the end of his life, the Kelmscott Press as well. He was a very rich man: at twenty-one he came into an inheritance that earned him £900 a year. in 1884 he was earning £1,800 a year from his firm alone, and he died leaving an estate worth £62,118.*

His political activity extended outside the world of party politics to consumerist and environmental lobbying. He founded the Society for the Protection of Ancient Buildings, and inspired and supported the conservationist bodies that have led in our day to the Council for the Protection of Rural England, the National Trust and others.

*For an approximation to today's values, these figures should probably be multiplied by 200.

A few months before he died he addressed the first meeting of the Society for Checking the Abuses of Public Advertising. His influence has been enormous, particularly at the intersection of politics, art and the environment. He inspired the Garden City and Arts and Crafts movements, the landscape gardener Gertrude Jekyll, the Modernist architect Walter Gropius, the town-planner Lewis Mumford; and his thought has had its effect today on the Green movement and the various campaigns for alternative technologies.

THE LIFE OF WILLIAM MORRIS

Morris was born in Walthamstow in 1834. The area was still rural at the time, though it began to be built on in the course of his life. The story goes that as a small boy he was often to be seen dressed in a miniature suit of armour, riding his pony through Epping Forest. Always an omnivorous reader, he is said to have worked his way through the novels of Sir Walter Scott by the age of seven. Both these legends convey the necessary image of a child steeped in Romantic medievalism from his earliest years.

They also remind us of the wealth that underpinned all Morris's dreams. His father was a wealthy bill-broker in the City, who died when Morris was thirteen, leaving him the wherewithal for the schemes and experiments of a lifetime. At the age of fourteen he was sent to Marlborough College in the early days of the public school system. He claimed to have learnt nothing from the school, which he despised as a 'boy-farm', except for what he found in the well-stocked library and on solitary excursions into the surrounding countryside. For that region of Wiltshire is crammed with prehistoric monuments and remains, which stimulated his passion for the past in general and for the heartland of rural England in particular.

These passions were more than confirmed by his experience of Oxford, still today the most medieval of English cities and part of the landscape he had learnt to love. Oxford in 1853, when he went up to Exeter College, was the centre of the Anglo-Catholic and Ritualistic revival in the Church of England, a movement closely related to the Gothic Revival in architecture, both tendencies ultimately deriving from Romantic medievalism. Almost immediately Morris met a kindred spirit who was to remain his closest friend for the rest of his life. This was the painter Edward Burne-Jones, whose adolescent dream was to set up a quasi-monastic brotherhood of art and learning, its members dedicated to a 'crusade and holy warfare against the age'. Together these young men discovered the work of their medievalizing older contemporaries: Tennyson, Kingsley, Carlyle and, most important of all, John Ruskin, whose great book *The Stones of Venice*, with its central chapter on 'The Nature of Gothic', was to shape the course of Morris's subsequent life. That chapter not only defines the beauties of the style Morris valued most; it explains it in terms of the labour conditions that made it possible, specifically contrasting them with life in a modern factory. Creative freedom, for Ruskin, is the source of all human happiness; soulless drudgery a crime against humanity. Thus begins the nineteenth-century alliance of decorative artist and campaigner for social justice.

In 1855, with Ruskin fresh in their minds, the young men toured the cathedrals of northern France. For Morris, the experience of large-scale Gothic buildings, often in broadly medieval settings and with most of their sculpture and stained glass intact, was visionary in its intensity. It stayed with him for the rest of his life: an image of how things might be. He and Burne-Jones had previously aspired to holy orders; now, in the shadow of Rouen Cathedral, they vowed themselves to the life of art – a calling, as they saw it, no less holy. For Morris it was to be architecture and he was soon articled to the neo-Gothic architect G. E. Street, in whose office he met another life-long friend, Philip Webb, whose first building was to be Morris's house. By this time Morris had begun writing poems and prose romances. With the wealth he came into at the age of twenty-one he set up a magazine in which to publish his writings alongside work of a similar character, Keatsian and medievalist. It drew Morris and his circle to the attention of the newly famous Dante Gabriel Rossetti, under whose spell they now fell. Before long Morris had abandoned architecture for painting and was working with Rossetti and his associates on a cycle of frescos in the Oxford Union building. There, in the typically Pre-Raphaelite atmosphere of lofty idealism and boyish horseplay, he fell in love with a 'stunner' whom Rossetti had invited to model for them. Jane Burden was a groom's daughter and one of the most beautiful women of the age. In 1859 she became Morris's wife.

The experience of communal creativity now began to give form to Morris's aspirations. In need of a home and wealthy enough to make one that fulfilled his artistic ideals, he commissioned Webb to design a modern house in the medieval manner. The Red House in north Kent is something more than pastiche or Gothic fantasy. The Morrises found it impossible to furnish, given the degeneracy of contemporary taste, and so decided to make their own things. The whole circle contributed: Rossetti, Burne-Jones, Webb, Ford Madox Brown and the young couple themselves. (Jane was an accomplished embroiderer, needlewoman and wood-engraver.) The satisfaction Morris derived from this confirmed the truth of all he had learnt from Ruskin: the superiority of handicraft to mass production, the pleasure of creative work, and much else besides. As a result, in 1861, the friends launched what Morris ever after called 'the Firm': Morris, Marshall, Faulkner & Co., 'Fine Art Workmen in Painting, Carving, Furniture, and the Metals'. Success came quickly in terms of reputation and important commissions, though it was not until the mid seventies that the Firm began to make really substantial profits.

The great mass of their early commissions came from churches. The best of Morris's stained glass, most of it from cartoons by Burne-Jones, towers above any other contemporary product. But the real greatness of Morris as a designer emerged later when he began to concentrate on domestic work. He had early adopted a motto from Jan van Eyck: *Si je puis* – 'If I can'. It proved more than appropriate. Whenever a craft he needed proved dead or degenerate, he would simply settle down to learn it himself. So, for example, when in 1879 he began high-warp tapestry weaving, he studied an eighteenth-century French primer, 'one of the series of *Arts et Métiers*', set up a loom in his bedroom and spent several hours a day – 516 in all – weaving his first tapestry alone. He also visited the Gobelins factory in France to see the *hautelisse*, or vertical loom, in use.

During the 1860s Morris became famous as a poet. His first (and best) book, *The Defence of Guenevere and Other Poems* (1858), had been a critical disaster. The poems are precisely detailed medieval fantasies, which typically drew the charge of affectation. What the critics missed was the compensating realism, vigorous sometimes to the point of brutality. There was always something full-blooded about Morris to counter what he was later to condemn as 'the more maundering side of medievalism'. The violence is even more marked in the prose romances of this period, where, allied to sexual adventures, it perhaps points to a deep emotional turmoil that in maturity he was able to sublimate in industry. The poems of his middle years, *The Life and Death of Jason* (1867) and *The Earthly Paradise* (1868–70), are mostly less disturbing. As a result, they are easy reading but, in the end, lack depth and substance. E. P. Thompson calls this work 'The Poetry of Despair':* for the successes of Morris's middle life conceal considerable depression and discontent. By the late 1860s, though he was now a father with two daughters, Morris's marriage had effectively died and Jane was involved with Rossetti. He had, moreover, lost his religious faith – with little anguish by Victorian standards – but it had left him obsessed with death and futility. His very success as a designer, paradoxically, intensified his feelings of guilt and impotence, for his achievement was thrown into harsh relief by the predominant ugliness of modern life, while the pleasure he derived from his own labours contrasted painfully with the drudgery endured by the great mass of people just as a matter of course.

With hindsight it is not difficult to see how Morris became a Socialist, but as early as 1856 he had written to a friend: 'I see that things are in a muddle, and I have no power or vocation to set them right in ever so little a degree. My work is the embodiment of dreams in one form or another.' Dreams, for the author of *The Earthly Paradise*, were a mode of escape, as indeed was poetry itself:

> Forget six counties overhung with smoke,
> Forget the snorting steam and piston stroke,
> Forget the spreading of the hideous town;
> Think rather of the pack-horse on the down,
> And dream of London, small and white and clean,
> The clear Thames bordered by its garden green.

* *William Morris: Romantic to Revolutionary*, revised edition, London (Merlin Press) 1977, pp. 110–150.

But already present in this forgetting is a protest against the filth and misery of capitalist society. For the Morris of *News from Nowhere* in 1890, to dream of such a London had revolutionary implications.

Morris's road to Socialism, oddly enough, begins in his personal tragedy. In 1870 his main concern was how to deal with the failure of his marriage. Reading between the lines one can only suppose that he resolved to accept the relationship between Jane and Rossetti, thereby preserving a stable home for his children and perhaps maintaining friendship with the lovers. Two things helped him through the consequent loneliness: Icelandic literature and Kelmscott Manor.

Morris had long been interested in the folklore and mythology of northern Europe and had begun to recognize in himself an innate preference for the northern and Teutonic over the Latin and Italianate. In 1868, in collaboration with an Icelander living in London, Eiríkr Magnússon, he began translating the sagas, an activity he was to keep up for the rest of his life. Shortly afterwards, seeking a refuge from work and the horrors of London, he lit upon a living earthly paradise.

Kelmscott Manor is a handsome sixteenth-century farmhouse, unostentatious and modest in proportions. It is situated on the edge of a small Oxfordshire village near the upper reaches of the Thames. It is built, like most of the village, of a fine grey local stone. Even today, the idyllic but unsensational countryside seems cut off from the main routes; in the late nineteenth century the labours of agriculture still went on there very much as they had for countless centuries. The tiny Norman church, where Morris is buried, has escaped the hand of the Victorian 'restorer', though that achievement was due to Morris himself. When he found the place, it must have struck him immediately as a chance to turn dream into tangible reality.

In 1871 Rossetti and Morris took on the joint tenancy of the house, thus setting up a decorous *ménage à trois* that was scarcely noticed till long after their deaths. That summer Morris set sail for his first visit to Iceland, leaving Jane and Rossetti to Kelmscott and intimacy. Two years later he visited Iceland again and otherwise seems to have kept as far away from Rossetti as possible. Then, in 1874, Rossetti suffered a nervous breakdown and attempted suicide. As a result he left Kelmscott for good and severed most of his links with the Morrises.

About Rossetti's relationship with Jane Morris no certain information can be found. All parties behaved with extreme discretion, no doubt in order to protect Jane from the disgrace that attached to erring wives in Victorian times. Morris's natural bravery and stoicism were now enhanced by his experience of Iceland. He contrasted Icelandic values and mores with the luxury and self-indulgence of the English middle class. He admired the natural egalitarianism of the social arrangements he found there, the sense of continuity with an ancient past, the easy intimacy with nature and, above all, 'the religion of the Northman . . . the worship of Courage'.

His growing distaste for Rossetti – hardly surprising in the circumstances – was intensified by Nordic contempt for the older man's self-pity. Morris now decisively rejected the 'maundering' aestheticism of his old associates too. It is surely significant that, directly after the breach with Rossetti, the Firm (in which Rossetti had been a partner) was reconstituted as Morris & Co., with Morris as sole proprietor. Free of the old despair, he now composed a heroic poem in the Nordic manner, *Sigurd the Volsung,* and moved into a new phase of creativity edged with activism. For Iceland had also politicized him. It had helped him to distinguish between ineluctable laws of nature and an unjust social order which, made by human beings, can be unmade by them too.

His emergence as a political activist was quite sudden. In 1876 he fired off a letter to the *Daily News* in protest at the Conservative government's policy in the Balkans. The Turks had massacred 12,000 Bulgarians after an uprising against Ottoman rule. The Russians, who had long craved naval access to the Mediterranean, were threatening to intervene on behalf of their fellow Slavs and fellow Christians. It was this possibility that troubled the British government, who saw the Ottoman Empire as a bulwark against Russian expansionism. To protect their interests in the Near East, they offered the Turks their military support.

A significant section of British public opinion, mostly Liberal in persuasion, was outraged by this cynical demonstration of *realpolitik.* Morris's letter, which gave voice to their feelings, thrust him suddenly into the public sphere. In a matter of weeks he had been elected Treasurer of the Eastern Question Association, formed to campaign against the prospect of war. By 1879 he had broadened his activities to become Treasurer, too, of the largely working-class National Liberal League. This early association with working people is significant. Morris had always voted Liberal as a matter of instinct, but he now became aware of the party's inescapably false position. It had come into being to represent the people enfranchised by the 1832 Reform Bill: the middle classes, whose enterprise was responsible for the nation's wealth and power. When the franchise was further extended in 1867 to large sections of the working class, it succeeded – as the party of progress and reform – in attracting the new voters too. It was, in other words, running with the hare and hunting with the hounds. The Eastern Question campaign very soon enlightened Morris in this regard, for when Gladstone and the Liberals returned to power, they seemed to him no different to the Tories. A genuinely radical policy, anti-imperialist and independent of all financial interests, could be achieved (in Morris's view) only with the will and support of the working class. In 1883, therefore, he took the plunge, declared himself a Socialist and joined the Democratic (later, Social Democratic) Federation.

By this time activism had become a habit. In 1877 he had also founded what we should now call a conservationist pressure group. The Society for the Protection of Ancient Buildings, or 'Anti-Scrape' as its adherents called it, was formed to resist the fashion for 'restoration'. The fashion was heavily promoted by the new Ritualists in the Church of England. It was usually a case of some successful architect throwing out medieval stonework in need of repair to replace it with what he and the incumbent imagined the scheme of the building to have been at an earlier and liturgically more favoured stage of development. A visit to the churches at Kelmscott and nearby Inglesham, both of which Morris rescued from proposed restoration, will give the clearest idea of the Society's achievement. These are buildings of genuine antiquity, not preserved in aspic but parts of a living continuum, kept alive by use, their imperfections inseparable from their charm. When he launched the Society, Morris wrote, 'our ancient buildings are not mere ecclesiastical toys, but sacred monuments of the nation's growth and hope'. The force and precision of the language typify Morris's writing of this period: *growth*, because human society grows as nature does; *hope* – a key word in his vocabulary – because art grows into the future out of deep roots in the past. His objection to the art of his day, even to work he admired, was that it had 'no root'. Having no source in a people's sense of its wholeness, art had become merely individual, disconnected from society.

Such thoughts run through a series of lectures on which Morris embarked in 1877, originally in order to raise funds for Anti-Scrape. The great master of the public lecture at the time was John Ruskin, who treated it as a kind of secular sermon. In lecture after lecture Morris acknowledges the influence of Ruskin, who as far back as 1849 had been drawing attention to the loss incurred through misguided restoration; and who in his work from that time onward had insisted on the links that bind a nation's art to the health or otherwise of its economic and social arrangements. To read the first six of Morris's lectures (published as *Hopes and Fears for Art* in 1882) is to follow the progression of his mind through despair for art in the modern world to hopes for a new society. A further collection of lectures, *Signs of Change* – all broadly Socialist in content – was published in 1888. These two books, central to Morris's work, must count among the finest of his achievements.

When the SDF was formed in 1881, it was the only Socialist movement in the country. In the earlier nineteenth century, at the time of Robert Owen and then of the Chartists, Britain had been at the forefront of political innovation. But after 1848, the year of revolutions, all that had changed. This was partly due to some genuine improvements: the extension of the suffrage in 1867, the rise of the trades unions, increasing prosperity and liberal reforms. Continental Europe, by contrast, had experienced major political ferment, which found theoretical expression in the writings of Karl Marx. Ironically, in the 1870s, the calm of liberal England had provided Marx and Engels with a safe haven in which to develop their 'scientific' theories of social change. Their observations suggested to them that Britain, as the most advanced of the capitalist countries, with its extremes of urban poverty in a context of political freedoms, was the most likely setting for the coming revolution.

So it seemed, too, to the founders of the SDF, who regarded

themselves as Marxists. Indeed, when Morris joined in 1883, he did so on the assumption that the inevitable revolution was only a few years off and that it might still be peaceful. By the time he published *News from Nowhere* – only seven years later – his view had changed almost beyond recognition.

The founder and leader of the SDF, H. M. Hyndman, was hardly the obvious candidate for the job. A stockbroker by profession and a Tory, he had been quite suddenly converted on first reading a book by Karl Marx. He was an ambitious politician of autocratic tendency, and it was by no means clear that in foreign policy he differed from the imperialists. Morris distrusted him from the start but accepted his leadership because there was no alternative. Within eighteen months, however, Morris and his circle – which included the prophet's daughter, Eleanor Marx – had left the SDF to set up the Socialist League. The parties continued more or less in parallel until 1890, when the League also split and Morris resigned from its executive. All commentators seem now to agree that the split in the SDF had been disastrous: an error of judgement that set British Socialism back at least ten years. The fissiparousness of radical movements, of course, is now a familiar feature of political life. It is surely to Morris's credit that, though he lamented it, he could also see the funny side of it, as is clear from the League meeting in *News from Nowhere*: 'there were six persons present, and consequently six sections of the party were represented, four of whom had strong but divergent Anarchist opinions'.

It was the Anarchists in fact who split the League, though some of the orthodox Marxists had already begun to drift back towards the SDF. This latter group more or less shared the SDF commitment to what Morris calls State Socialism. That is to say, they wanted a Socialist party to fight both local and national elections and believed that Socialism would be achieved by means of, for instance, nationalization. The third group, to which Morris adhered, were also Marxists, but in their view the purpose of the League was to agitate, educate and organize; that is, to prepare the workers for the coming revolution. In their view participation in the parliamentary process would inevitably compromise their leaders, committing them to palliative measures and indefinitely postponing genuine change. Morris's group believed in what he called (in the title of a series of articles) 'Socialism from the Root Up' — fundamental change brought about by spontaneous popular revolution. Morris lost this argument: most subsequent varieties of Socialism have accepted some form or other of the State Socialist solution. Since the fall of Soviet Communism, however, and with the decline of Social Democracy, his position has acquired a renewed relevance. Could equality imposed from above ever have satisfied the desire of working people for autonomy? Could it ever have been other than an imposition?

On the other hand, Morris and his faction were quite incapable of seeing 'how to combine the struggle for Socialism with the struggle for immediate demands'.* This led them into conflict with the trades unions, and it was not until the collapse of the League that the various radical movements in the country began to draw together. Before he died, Morris was reconciled to the SDF, had recognized the achievements of the London County Council and was prepared to go along with Parliamentary action. One suspects that he was never wholly convinced but saw that the essential thing was to hold the movement together. In 1893 the West Yorkshire branch of what had been the League announced the formation of the Independent Labour Party and, in 1900, within four years of Morris's death, the modern Labour Party came into being.

It would be hard to overestimate the disappointment Morris must have felt as sectarian bickering became the order of the day. He treated his work for the League as a full-time job, which entailed a good deal of hardship. Such things could be borne if there was hope, but as the movement developed and resistance to it developed too, the probability of early change retreated. The later 1880s were dominated by the Free Speech campaign, in which the Socialists of both parties struggled for the right to demonstrate and propagandize in public places. In the course of this campaign Morris was twice arrested and fined, and hopes for a peaceful solution collapsed in 1887 at the Trafalgar Square demonstration known as Bloody Sunday, when without provocation the police attacked the crowd. Ranks closed against the Socialists after this: the enlightened middle class,

* A. L. Morton in his edition of *The Political Writings of William Morris*, revised edition, London (Lawrence & Wishart) 1984, p. 220.

the radicals, the press, even at times the trades unions. Bloody Sunday convinced Morris, first, that change would never come by peaceful means and, secondly, that the struggle would be longer and harder than he had anticipated.

It was in this context, and as the Socialist League drew nearer disintegration, that Morris wrote *News from Nowhere*, a book that combines continuing trust in a Socialist future with a need to re-charge the batteries of an imagination near exhaustion. For many years it was asserted that the onset of violence in the streets and the break-up of the League gave Morris second thoughts about revolu-tion. Thanks largely to E. P. Thompson, we now know that events such as Bloody Sunday and the successful dock strike of 1889 made Morris *more* certain that revolution was necessary and inevitable. Though he ceased to be an especially prominent figure, he continued to work wholeheartedly for the Socialist movement in all its aspects. The difference was he now knew he would never live to see the change to which he had given so much of his life.

One effect of this relative disengagement was that he now returned to his creative work with renewed invention. Not that he had ever stopped: many of his finest designs, notably the carpets, date from the 1880s. But the foundation in 1891 of the Kelmscott Press was an entirely new venture. Morris had always been interested in the problems of book production. Medievalist that he was, he had always really longed for a return to the days of the illuminated manuscript. Yet it is perhaps the secret of his genius that he could usually find a *practical* outlet for his dreams. An enthusiast for early printed books, which he collected, he saw the history of printing as a long process of decline, accelerating through the eighteenth and nineteenth centu-ries. In 1889, under the influence of a printer and fellow Socialist, Emery Walker, he began studying the craft of fine printing and in 1891 started producing books. In the five years of life left to him, Morris was responsible for designing and printing some fifty-two volumes, ranging from small books of pamphlet length (such as his reprint of Ruskin's *The Nature of Gothic*) to the 564 folio pages of the incomparable Kelmscott *Chaucer*, described by W. B. Yeats as 'the most beautiful of all printed books'.

This last creative venture, however, highlights the central contradiction of Morris's career. As a designer he always aimed at the best, and the best for him was always work by hand. His purpose was to improve public taste and, more importantly, to motivate a happier society through the satisfactions of creative work. As he says in his preface to *The Nature of Gothic*, 'the lesson which Ruskin here teaches us is that art is the expression of man's pleasure in labour.' Thus, changed conditions of labour would not only produce better art but happier individuals more capable of enjoying it. He was not opposed to machines as a matter of principle. Contrary to popular belief, he was in favour of labour-saving devices where hardship or mere dullness were concerned. He argued, though, that, under capitalism, machines were primarily used to increase production, thereby increasing the worker's drudgery, since machine production is mindless and repetitive. But here is the contradiction: in a modern competitive society, hand-made goods are inevitably more expensive than those made by machine. They are therefore available only to the rich and privileged, so the worker remains deprived. This contradiction is especially glaring in the case of publishing, for a Socialist, it might be argued, should aim at producing books the poor have some chance of reading.

Morris was not unaware of these contradictions and could to some extent have answered the criticisms. He would have argued that while we live under the capitalist system we cannot escape the laws of the market. That being the case, the creation of beautiful furnishings and so on is part of a process of public education, providing a model of good production methods and pioneering a return to higher standards of design. The Kelmscott Press, strangely enough, has something in common with Morris's all-or-nothing politics: his rejection of palliatives. Rather than compromise with commercial publishing, he preferred to show the world a possible alternative.

His literary activities at this time are even more contradictory. Between 1885 and 1890 he wrote three political narratives for serialization in the *Commonweal: Pilgrims of Hope*, a verse tale about the Paris Commune, was followed by two prose romances, *A Dream of John Ball* and *News from Nowhere*, arguably the best of his literary works. Around the same time, however, he returned to romancing of a purely escapist kind and, between 1888 and 1896, wrote six prose tales set in imaginary heroic societies. His characters, simpler people from a simpler time, owe something to the Icelandic sagas and something also to Grimm's fairy-tales. The language is not merely coloured with archaism, as it is in *A Dream of John Ball* or *Sigurd the Volsung*: it is an artificial language that insulates the tales from the touch of reality. In their escapism they come close to the long-discarded 'poetry of despair'. Yet they can also be seen as complementary to the political romances. Like so many of Morris's creations – the stained glass, the carpets, the decorated initials – they are visionary accounts of an ideal world. To dream of the impossible and disregard reality is to question the inevitability of existing circumstances.

There is a simple explanation for Morris's partial retreat in his last years. By 1890 he was exhausted. He had suddenly begun to look old, and his health was breaking down. He put as much work into the rest of his days as most people put into a lifetime. But it is perhaps not surprising that he allowed himself to look to the work for comfort. Though he had a genius for friendship and seems to have been a strong and loving father, he was a deeply lonely man. His wife, though she stuck to him, had never loved him; one can only assume, for instance, that there had been no sexual relations between them for something like thirty years. The fault undoubtedly lay within himself; even Burne-Jones, who knew him better than anyone, was often frustrated by Morris's self-sufficiency. With his powerful will, his energy and the range of all his talents, Morris seemed not to need people – and yet he felt their lack. His daughter May, who made herself responsible for his memory, tells how in June 1896 he handed her his last great achievement, a copy of the Kelmscott *Chaucer*: 'the look of profound melancholy that (perhaps unconsciously) he turned on me in smiling tenderly seemed like a glimpse into a very far country ... it was the look of an intensely lonely man – never to be forgotten while memory serves'.* Just over three months later, on 3 October 1896, he died. The funeral was just as he would have wished it. Garlanded with willow-boughs and bullrushes, his coffin was borne on a haycart to Kelmscott

* *The Introductions to the Collected Works of William Morris*, Vol. II, New York (Oriole Editions) 1973, p. 710.

churchyard, the spiritual centre of his earthly paradise. 'You can lose a man like that by your own death,' wrote Bernard Shaw, 'but not by his.'

EARTHLY PARADISES

Morris called *News from Nowhere* 'A Utopian Romance'. *Utopia*, the title of Sir Thomas More's great satire, is derived from a Greek word meaning 'nowhere'. Both More and Morris clearly intend an irony. Utopia/Nowhere is a country that does not and cannot exist – at best a dream, at worst an irrelevance. On the other hand, a dream set in a real or possible place may invite attention to the short-comings of contemporary reality. It may thus promote discontent and, through it, the hope for change. Morris's Nowhere is unmistak-ably England; equally unmistakably, it is a much happier place than we or his contemporaries have known.

Morris was not certain, though, that something rather like it had not existed before. His preoccupation in the latter part of his life with possible futures is a condition of his earlier feeling for the past: both his personal past, as a boy growing up in an unspoilt rural Essex, and the historical past of the Middle Ages, poignantly recalled in surviving artefacts. In both cases the past is Arcadian: a paradisal world from which humanity has since fallen.

His personal past is evoked in Chapter XXIII of *News from Nowhere* in a lyrical description of his childhood landscape. This feeling for the physical substance of rural England, blighted by industrial capital-ism, is at the core of all Morris's work. It recurs with a still greater emotional charge at the end of the book when the protagonist reaches the goal of his journey, 'the old house by the Thames' we recognize as Kelmscott Manor. 'It seems to me,' says Ellen, 'as if it had waited for these happy days, and held in it the gathered crumbs of happiness of the confused and turbulent past.' And she continues: 'Oh me! Oh me! How I love the earth, and the seasons, and weather, and all things that deal with it, and all that grows out of it, – as this has done!' 'This' is the house itself, which, built in vernacular style out of local stone, embodied for Morris a way of living, building and working in harmony with nature. Because it had once been, he reasoned, it might be again too.

So Morris's sense of a rural paradise unites, in 'the old house by the Thames', with his dream of an ideal past. Romantic medievalism, in which Morris had his roots, was a way of by-passing the rationalistic ethos of eighteenth-century life. Aesthetically, this meant an alternative to Neo-Classicism, which Morris detested with a vehemence it is hard for a modern person to understand. Gothic buildings were mysterious and atmospheric; organic in form, they seemed to grow out of nature; their lofty aspirations and dark recesses are resonant with the complexities of human nature. What is more, Gothic is a northern European style, functionally related to the climate, materials and conditions of northern life; it therefore seems more intimate with nature than Neo-Classicism does. The latter struck Morris as cold, impractical and snobbish. The attempt to emulate Roman imperial power, the acceptance of a cultural hierarchy, the concern with propriety – to Morris these conveyed a particular social message. No one, in his view, built such buildings because they liked them; they merely sought to aggrandize themselves.

We are accustomed today to hearing the words 'feudal' and 'medieval' used as terms of abuse, as 'Gothic' itself originally was. It is therefore essential to stress that, even as a Socialist, Morris thought feudalism superior to capitalism. He found his reasons originally in Ruskin and Ruskin's master, Thomas Carlyle. The freedom of expression and the feeling for natural beauty that Ruskin identified in Gothic revealed a culture in which arts and crafts, art and work, were one. The delight the workman took in the physical world was expressed in his own physical workmanship, and his workmanship returned his delight to the human world. If feudalism was hierarchical, it at least created a society with clearly defined roles and responsibilities, not an individualist jungle in which only the ruthless and greedy could survive. For greed is the natural enemy of the fulfilment Ruskin celebrates. Medieval culture, as he describes it, died with the advent of mercantilism at the end of the fifteenth century – when the pursuit of material gain superseded the love of God and the beauty of his handiwork.

It is easy to scoff at this view of the Middle Ages as idealized and historically incomplete. As Morris developed, in fact, he grew more critical of the period and of the Ruskinian myth. But by the time he became a Socialist, his knowledge of medieval life was deep and wide. What it taught him was, quite simply, that a society based on self-interest is not the only possible form of society. Medieval England, as he increasingly realized, had its brutalities and injustices, but it was rarely guilty of the specifically social and economic evils that deform the industrial world. According to the sociologist T. H. Marshall,* Carlyle, Ruskin and Morris were quite right to believe that feudal society, characterized as it was by rigid stratification, guaranteed a dignified role for those in its lowest stratum. Marshall quotes a report of 1797, Sir Frederick Eden's *The State of the Poor*: 'To the growth of civilization and *the development of commerce* may be ascribed the introduction of a new class of men, henceforward described by the Legislature as the Poor' (italics mine). 'The relation of the poor to those on whom they depended,' Marshall comments, 'was a durable one, governed as to its terms by custom and the principle of the "just wage" and the "just price".' The modern concept of a fixed social class 'permanently at risk of severe poverty' was established by the Poor Law of 1601, which none the less – through its imposition of a Poor Rate – continued to acknowledge the responsibility of society for those overtaken by economic disaster. But the New Poor Law of 1834, in abolishing this responsibility, created a new under-class of social outcasts. In the notorious workhouses it provided, in effect, prisons for the punishment of poverty, as if failure in the struggle for survival should be regarded as a crime.

When Morris became a Marxist, he must have felt bound to reconcile the medievalism that had shaped his adult life with the 'progressive' politics to which he now assented. It cannot have been easy. Marx had been contemptuous of thinkers like Carlyle, whom he classed as 'feudal Socialists'. The implication was that they were too timid to face the future. Marx admired many aspects of capitalism – its inventiveness, its energy, the freedom of thought it encouraged – and saw it as a necessary stage in the process of social evolution.

*T. H. Marshall, *The Right to Welfare and Other Essays*, London (Heinemann) 1981, pp. 29–32.

Morris gave his assent to this analysis – rather too dutifully, it might be thought – but continued to dream of the Middle Ages.

Yet now there was a difference. In a lecture like 'The Hopes of Civilization' (1885) he looks at the past with a Marxist's eye. The medieval world is no longer a refuge from the present; it helps him, rather, to understand the present and construct, in imagination, an alternative future. From the Romanticism of Keats and Scott, Morris had learnt the power and value of dreams. Pre-Raphaelite art had seemed to take his dreams of an ideal rural England and the Middle Ages and make them palpable – in paint or sensuous verse. The Morris of, say, 'The Story of the Unknown Church' (1856) is a dreamer of this kind, inward-looking, withdrawn and ultimately impotent. He evokes the type in *The Earthly Paradise*:

> Dreamer of dreams, born out of my due time,
> Why should I strive to set the crooked straight?

And yet there are different kinds of dream. As his early writings show, the escapist dream is sometimes continuous with nightmare; pleasant illusions may end by evoking the very fears they sought to escape. Other dreams, though, may embody hopes of a possible future. *Hopes* and *fears* are key words in Morris's vocabulary:

> To what a heaven the earth might grow
> If fear beneath the earth were laid,
> If hope failed not, nor love decayed.

The earth *is* a paradise, though marred by tears and death. By middle life the Rossettian palace of art had become for Morris a frustrating and claustrophobic habitation. Probably, aestheticism had never satisfied him. What he wanted was the real world with its prelapsarian glow restored to it. By the mid 1870s he began to feel that this was attainable.

It was in his work as a decorative artist that Morris first achieved this blend of the actual and the paradisal. His designs represent his medievalism at its most fruitful. Art historians call him a 'historicist', but his work always exceeds mere imitation. As he argues in the lecture 'Gothic Architecture' (1889), some historical styles provide an opening to the future while others close it off; you need to go back in order to go forward. The architecture and design in the imagined future of *News from Nowhere* is often compared to medieval work, yet it is always seen to be a new development, and the same is true of Morris's designs, once he got past the stage of emulation. This is where the feudal world as model of a possible future became operative in his creative work. There was nothing theoretical about it. In his desire to learn from medieval design, he came to understand the conditions of its production and to see how removed they were from anything possible in the modern world. To take an obvious example: no modern person would devote a lifetime of creative endeavour to a building he or she could never hope to see completed and in use, yet that is what the masons did who worked on the great cathedrals. Such people must have derived satisfaction from creative work executed on behalf of a community and a way of life that extended far beyond one person's allotted span. 'Therefore, when we build,' wrote Ruskin, 'let us think that we build for ever.'*

Nikolaus Pevsner makes the point when he says, 'What raises Morris as a reformer of design above the [best of his contemporaries] is not only that he had the true designer's genius and they had not, but also that he recognized the indissoluble unity of an age and its social system, which they had not done.'† Morris's desire to improve design was inseparable from his desire to improve society. Where the beauties of his verse represent a withdrawal from social reality, his designs constitute an engagement with it. Take the fresh simplicity of the early wallpaper known as 'Daisy' (1861) or, by contrast, the witty and sophisticated fabric called 'Strawberry Thief' (1883). These are images of paradise that bring the hope of its attainment nearer. But the paradise is earthly. Critics have observed that the secret of Morris's designs lies in his understanding of the patterns of natural growth and his obedience to them. Such natural patternings, admitted to the circumstances of domestic life, confer a kind of blessing on it. In Morris's terms, they bring *hope* and *rest*. And rest is the reward for labour – labour which should, in a just society, bring pleasure through fulfilment.

For the great mass of people, as Morris was all too aware, these

* *The Seven Lamps of Architecture*, Ch. VI, § X.
† *Pioneers of Modern Design*, revised edition, Harmondsworth (Penguin) 1960, p. 48.

ideals were not even unattainable dreams. The example the Firm provided was an achievement but it could never be enough, especially as it meant that he earned his living by 'ministering to the swinish luxury of the rich', which pricked his conscience. From the mid 1870s on, the problem was how to realize the world he had long dreamt of, in which 'art is the expression of man's pleasure in labour'.

The turning-point came in 1876. In his letter on the Eastern Question, Morris uses a characteristic metaphor in an uncharacteristic context. He imagines falling asleep after the Bulgarian massacre and waking up three weeks later to find that Britain is going to war. He would have rejoiced at this possibility, he says: having slept, he would have assumed that his country was about to fight for justice. '... but alas, though I have not slept, *I have awakened*, and find the shoe quite on the other foot' (italics mine). The image of dreaming could hardly be more significant. No longer a form of escape, it becomes the means whereby a different order is conceived and then becomes possible in the process of awakening. The awakening, moreover, is not only to the facts of political life but also to his own long-suppressed awareness. It anticipates in this way the momentous dreams and awakenings that provide the structure of *A Dream of John Ball* and *News from Nowhere*.

UTOPIA

Morris was not much interested in the main traditions of European literature – in classical poetry or realist fiction. What he valued most was 'the kind of book which Mazzini called "Bibles"; they cannot always be measured by a literary standard, but to me are far more important than any literature. They are in no sense the work of individuals, but have grown up from the very hearts of the *people*.' Among the books of this kind which he names are the Greek, Indian, Persian and Anglo-Saxon epics, the Old Testament, Hesiod, the Norse *Eddas* and Grimm's fairy-tales. In other words, he was not concerned with the faithful analysis of character and motive – the thinness of the personages is the most glaring weakness of *News from Nowhere* – or in the exact representation of social conditions. He looks to literature for the timeless and symbolic patterns of human experience which we find in myth, in folk literature and in dreams.

Writings of this sort often include records of paradise, usually envisaged as an earlier state of the world now lost through human corruption. The Garden of Eden and the classical Golden Age are for Western man the two that first come to mind. These ideal pastoral states stand outside time, before the beginning of history in effect. Other works, especially common during the Middle Ages, refer us to supposed periods of history when humans lived in an ideal social order. Such periods are not free from the ravages of sin, death, war and natural disaster, but the social order is governed in truth and justice. An obvious instance of this would be Malory's *Le Morte d'Arthur* (1485), a story particularly relevant to Morris, not only because of the Pre-Raphaelite obsession with the Arthurian myth, but because the pattern of history he argued for is reflected in it: a past era of justice and beauty, now dead, but sure to return before the end of time. The legend is common to many cultures – 'the king over the water' – but it does seem to be an especially British obsession. Thus, at the most sophisticated level, it is implicit in *Hamlet*, the knightly honour of the dead king set against the corruption of the entire body politic under Claudius, though Shakespeare offers no hope of a return. It is also the essence of the Robin Hood legend, which Morris alludes to once or twice. Indeed, Robin is a highly Morrisian figure: a medieval rebel who, in the name of justice, sustains the betrayed values of a past order in his natural and egalitarian retreat.*

Morris was also affected by consciously Utopian texts. The first-century historians Plutarch and Tacitus both depicted societies in which simpler cultural values brought about a way of life conducive to virtue and decency. In the *Life of Lycurgus* Plutarch looks back to the origins of Sparta, a time later than the dawn of history but only recorded in tradition. The *Germania* of Tacitus, by contrast, deals with contemporary ways of life beyond the fringes of the Roman

---

*A similar point is made by Timothy Hilton in *The Pre-Raphaelites*, London (Thames & Hudson) 1970, p. 126. The modern idea of Robin Hood was created, to all intents and purposes, by Sir Walter Scott in his novel *Ivanhoe* (1819), a book Morris adored from earliest boyhood.

Empire. He expresses admiration for these German communities, unaffected by the decadence of his own society. Both writers use their subjects as sticks with which to beat their fellow countrymen, and it is clear they gave Morris a hint of how he might do likewise. Both, for instance, describe societies which, like Morris's Iceland, set a high premium on personal courage, value good craftsmanship, are unaffected by social distinctions and care little for material wealth or luxury, preferring good health or closeness to nature. Lycurgus, according to Plutarch, abolished money, thus removing both the need to enforce laws and the main index of social superiority. Among the Germans, Tacitus tells us, exploitation and usury are unknown. In both cases, as in *News from Nowhere*, people naturally want what they really need or what really brings them happiness; there is no market and no social ladder to stimulate false desires. To the modern reader familiar with Stalinism or the Hitler youth, it must be added, both of these books have a slightly ominous ring, which Morris mostly avoids.

The Iceland Morris visited was probably the last of the old Germanic societies to survive into modern times. It must have reminded him of the *Germania* and Tacitus's implicit critique of imperial Rome. The relevance to imperial Britain was obvious. The Roman historian's sense of a nearly ideal society contemporary with his own also informed a number of utopias that sprang up during the Renaissance. There was More's *Utopia* (1516), Campanella's *City of the Sun* (1602), Bacon's *New Atlantis* (1629) and Harington's *Oceana* (1656), to say nothing of several works (such as *The Tempest*) that include utopian motifs. All these writers were influenced by the discovery of the New World and the often simpler societies encountered there – sometimes on islands cut off from the corrupting influences of larger civilizations. The notorious unreliability of the traveller's tale provided many of these moralists with an occasion for depicting ideal or fantastic societies that reflect on our own. Sometimes, as in a later work like *Gulliver's Travels* (1726), they show the evils and follies of the reader's own community in a distorting mirror. This is probably the case with More's *Utopia*.

Morris admired *Utopia* so much that he published a beautiful edition of it at the Kelmscott Press and wrote an eloquent foreword for it. He takes the book very much at face value – as a portrait of an ideal communistic society, critical by implication of early Tudor England. This view of it has not been universally accepted, but it is one possible interpretation which provides us with a useful perspective on *News from Nowhere*. The traveller–narrator of More's tale, Raphael Hythloday (the name means 'nonsense-talker'), is a man of uncertain nationality whose travels have brought him to England as well as to the Americas and the unknown island that gives the book its title. As a foreigner, he has found much to criticize in Tudor England: usury, mercantilism, land enclosures and so on. The defamiliarized picture is more than usually important, since Utopia, where a form of communism prevails, is praised from an identical point of view. Morris sees this, rightly or wrongly, as More's attempt to preserve certain medieval values in the teeth of the new commercialism. There are many things, it should be said, that Morris dislikes in More's ideal society, though he recognizes most of them as inescapable parts of medieval life. Thus More's book points to the limitations of medievalism for Morris, while indicating the dangers of regarding any utopia as a blueprint for the future. Its value for Morris lies in More's sense of a dying social order which he evidently prefers to the one developing round him. The loss of it provokes in him a *longing*, as Morris understands him, 'for a society of equality of condition'.

Hesiod, Malory, Plutarch, Tacitus, Chaucer, More and Plato: all these had their effect on *News from Nowhere*. But the immediate inspiration probably came from two contemporary works: Morris's own *A Dream of John Ball* (1886–7) and Edward Bellamy's *Looking Backward* (1887).

The former begins as a dream of the Middle Ages. Morris (or his narrator) falls asleep and dreams that he wakes in fourteenth-century Kent. The scene, by contrast with the dismal present, is fresh, clean, vigorous and brightly coloured. One is reminded of the idealized use of architecture as social criticism in the writings of Ruskin and the Gothic Revival architect A. W. N. Pugin. Yet almost immediately there is a difference, for this is 1381, the year of the Peasants' Revolt, and the dissident priest John Ball is inciting the Kentish people to rise up against their overlords. After a brief skirmish in which the rebels are victorious, Ball begins to feel foreboding about the future. Recognizing the narrator as a time-traveller and seeking reassurance, he questions him about the ages to come, only to learn with growing horror of the Industrial Revolution and the triumph of capitalism. He is pulled back from the brink of despair by the assurance that his exemplary role will in the end contribute to the overthrow of all forms of economic oppression.

The final impact of *John Ball*, truth to tell, is unintentionally ambiguous. It is hard to accept the narrator's assurances about a future that he cannot know, when the intervening time has been so discouraging. It is also the case that his account of history, touched as it is with a residue of his old romanticized medievalism, comes close to celebrating the social order that could produce a hero like Ball. The real value of the story lies, perhaps, in what it has to say about the lives of those who commit themselves to the class struggle. The narrator puts it in these memorable words: 'I pondered ... how men fight and lose the battle, and the thing they fight for comes about in spite of their defeat, and when it comes turns out to be not what they meant, and other men have to fight for what they meant under another name.' For a generation that has seen the collapse in Eastern Europe of a tyranny that called itself Socialist, these words possess an unmistakable resonance.

It has been said that Morris's most significant contribution to Socialist thought is to be found in his reconciliation of Karl Marx with John Ruskin. Looking back over his life in 1894, Morris was to write: 'how deadly dull the world would have been twenty years ago but for Ruskin! It was through him that I learned to give form to my discontent, which I must say was not by any means vague. Apart from the desire to produce beautiful things, the leading passion of my life has been and is hatred of modern civilization.' This strange marriage is especially evident in *John Ball*, where the Ruskinian view of medieval labour blends with the Marxist dialectic of history. Ruskin's 'The Nature of Gothic', indeed, anticipates Marx's doctrine of alienated labour point for point. Where Morris runs into difficulty, though, is in squaring Marx's progressive optimism with the profoundly lapsarian philosophy of history that runs through all the writings of Ruskin. John Ball's glimpse into the future (by way of our past) draws heavily on the historical parts of *Capital*, which Morris read in 1883. This sense of a dialectic culminating in revolution, an improved social order and the Communist millennium provides Morris with a structure, almost mythical in its simplicity, for *News from Nowhere*, but it is vital to note that the later book would have been impossible without, first, a Ruskinian journey back into the past.

Bellamy's *Looking Backward*, which Morris reviewed in 1889, is a journey into the future. Didactic though it is, it was hugely (if briefly) successful both in Britain and Bellamy's native America. It tells the story of a young man named Julian West, who is awakened from a hypnotic trance to find himself living in the year 2000. He finds a new and perfect order which has been achieved by what Morris contemptuously describes as 'machinery': both the literal mechanization of all production and the rationalization of society by bureaucratic control. This transformation has been effected by the evolution of monopoly capitalism into a corporate state run for the benefit of all. Work is now so regulated as to be free of pain, or so we are told, and the great goal of life seems to be leisure, which comes to everyone with superannuation at the age of forty-five.

This was precisely *not* what Morris was fighting for. He concedes that it might be an improvement on the capitalist system, less brutal and more efficient, but 'organized with a vengeance' and utterly soulless. Indeed, society remains competitive in Bellamy's world — there are rewards for labour — and it is almost totally urban. Worst of all, work — far from being a source of happiness — is severely regimented and still basically thought of as something to be endured. Such a society would be, though Morris refrains from saying so directly, even more meaningless than a capitalist one, ruled by impersonal diktat and the laws of supply and demand, with no true community, no art, no nature, no sense of the past and nothing to hope for but freedom from work.

To the modern reader Bellamy's world is chillingly familiar. Morris puts his finger on it with prophetic insight: it may be described, he says, 'as State Communism, worked by the very extreme of centralization'. It brings to mind not only Soviet Communism but all the statist bureaucracies that, in dream or reality, have haunted the modern age. One thinks especially of *dystopia* – of the anti-utopian fables so characteristic of the twentieth century: E. M. Forster's *The Machine Stops*, Aldous Huxley's *Brave New World*, George Orwell's *1984*.

Morris's conception of the ideal society was valuably deepened by his response to *Looking Backward*. For one thing, it helped him to formulate his dislike for one major part of Socialist tradition. It also helped him to see how important to his view of Socialism was the largely Ruskinian idea of pleasure in work: how else in a post-Christian world was human life to acquire purpose and significance? And the failure of Bellamy's parable encouraged him to formulate an ideal world of his own. 'The only safe way of reading a Utopia,' he writes in his review of the book, 'is to consider it as the expression of the temperament of its author.' We are thus warned not to read *News from Nowhere* as either blueprint or prediction. It is first of all an expression of discontent and, secondly, a personal vision, born from one man's passions and preoccupations, of how different the world might be. It asserts the possibility of a better world. We are not expected to swallow Morris's dream. On the contrary, we are encouraged to dream for ourselves.

NEWS FROM NOWHERE

When Morris wrote *News from Nowhere*, he could not have anticipated its importance, for he had little time to plan it. It was serialized in the Socialist League's newspaper, the *Commonweal*, between January and October 1890. Morris, who was extremely busy and wrote a good deal of the paper anyway, composed his instalments week by week. As a result there are several inconsistencies and improbabilities, none of them important. The story is plainly written for a League audience. It begins at an executive meeting of the League and there are one or two obvious in-jokes. The reader is clearly meant to recognize the protagonist as an ironic self-portrait and to identify Morris's two homes: Kelmscott House in Hammersmith, which he bought in 1878, and Kelmscott Manor itself.

When it was published in book form the following year, Morris tidied it up a little, adding a chapter and a few paragraphs, but he made no fundamental changes. The only difference worth noting concerns his projected dates. In the serialized version, for instance, the revolution takes place in 1910. In the book, revised for publication less than a year later, the date has been put forward to 1952: evidence, surely, of Morris's growing pessimism.

The book is not without its weaknesses. There is the thinness of the characters, to begin with, and there are times when the plot flags under the weight of didactic purpose. It remains, none the less, a compelling tale. Like the river that dominates the plot, it gathers in force and substance as it proceeds. As it does so, it blends and unites the various currents of Morris's thought and writing. It is, in the medieval sense, a romance – two journeys through a moralized landscape, culminating in a vision half bestowed and half denied: the hero, like Malory's Lancelot, sees the light of his Holy Grail but not its substance. As romances often are, it is also a dream, but unlike the dreams in Morris's earlier writings, it presents no occasion for terror. It has all the pleasures of escapist writing but, since its whole purpose is to criticize the present, it does not turn away from painful realities. Though it draws on the medieval world, it looks to the future for answers to the ills of modern times. It thus reconciles two fundamentally different kinds of narrative: the timeless and schematic mythical tale, and the nineteenth-century realist novel with characters and events embedded in history. As political parable, it invites comparison with, say, the contemporary fables of H. G. Wells; but there is a closer family resemblance to *Three Men in a Boat* (1889) or *The Wind in the Willows* (1908). On the other hand, if the ideal world of the action is reminiscent of Hesiod or Malory, the intellectual debate at the centre of it is surely based on Plato's *Republic*. It is, on the face of it, an odd confection.

The book's structure, though, is very simple. It consists of two journeys framing a long discursive conversation. The protagonist, William Guest – choleric and prematurely ageing – is a piece of engagingly ironic self-portraiture. (One might compare the similarly self-mocking persona adopted by Chaucer in *The Canterbury Tales*.) Guest wakes one morning in his Hammersmith home to find himself in the year 2102. He gradually realizes that England has undergone a revolution that has utterly transformed it. A young boatman named Dick volunteers to guide him through the new society, and they set off on a journey into central London, now a set of urban villages strung together by gardens, woodlands and patches of green countryside. In the British Museum they meet Dick's 105-year-old uncle, old Hammond, an historian with a special interest in the nineteenth century and the revolution of 1952. Hammond, who also in some sense mirrors the author, agrees to treat Guest as 'a visitor from another planet' and explain to him the order of this new society. He concludes his long exposition with an account of 'How the Change Came', the story of the revolution, which springs from events very similar to those experienced by Morris on Bloody Sunday. In Hammond's section, fictional history takes over from myth; we feel how revolution, generated by the struggles of Morris's day, has given birth to a new society that seems as timeless as the Golden Age. Then, in the final section, Dick and his wife Clara take Guest on a boat-trip up the Thames, rowing from Kelmscott House to Kelmscott Manor, as Morris had done with a group of friends in 1881. Their object is to join in the year's haymaking in Oxfordshire, that annual necessity of those who dwell on the land having become in the new England an occasion for festival. On the way they meet an unconventional and glamorous young woman named Ellen, with whom Guest falls in love. The tale ends with their arrival at the old house, which now typifies this revived nation whose present is in harmony with its past.

The first of the two journeys, which brings the protagonist knowledge and understanding, is a Marxist inquiry into the historical process. The second involves all his instinctual life, leading him into the past, the heart of England and the sources of human happiness. The language of the book, as E. P. Thompson has stressed, is dominated by expressions of longing and desire. In the last phase of the narrative Guest is overtaken by passionate desire for Ellen, so that by the final chapter the possible fulfilment of such sexual want becomes a metaphor for the whole complex of human fulfilments that the daily grind for profits has stultified. In the balmy summer landscape – there has been a striking improvement in the English weather! – we are reminded of Hammond's words, spoken in an historical context: 'The spirit of the new days ... was to be delight in the life of the world; intense and overweening love of the very skin and surface of the earth on which man dwells, such as a lover has in the fair flesh of the woman he loves ...'

Desire of that kind is intrinsic to our nature. To deny or suppress it is to stifle our humanity. Morris was motivated by the perception that industrial capitalism separates us from our real desires by diverting our longings into 'sham wants'. The citizens of Nowhere, by contrast, have 'cast away riches and attained to wealth' – preferred well-being to the cash nexus.* Morris was well aware that his good fortune in being born rich had granted him, in effect, a privileged perception. The liberty bestowed by money had enabled him to learn of the pleasure good work may give and the blessings conferred by a beautiful environment. In *News from Nowhere* he describes a society in which good fortune like his own is common to all. Social revolution has restored to mankind those things which, after all, are merely the gifts of nature.

In constructing his ideal society Morris surveys a variety of questions. Sometimes he takes us by surprise: learned, literate and antiquarian though he was, he appears to argue for the abolition of schools, while few of his characters have much time for books or knowledge of the past. Sometimes he may disappoint us, as when the women at the Hammersmith Guest House 'bustled about on our behoof', as if the service of men was enough to satisfy the deepest desires of women – though to be sure the female 'master' mason in Chapter XXVI and Ellen's sun-tanned eroticism go some way towards making up for this particular limitation. There are obvious blindnesses: Morris's general indifference to machinery makes him incapable of imagining any sort of technological advance. There is something rather comic about his picture of the forces of repression in 1952 with nothing more sophisticated than the Gatling gun to crush a revolution. Moreover, to the post-Freudian (or indeed to the Christian) mind, his eminently sensible solutions to problems of sexual conflict and violent crime are, to say the least, incomplete.

Yet when at the end of the book Morris puts in a plea for his

* This well-known phrase is from Thomas Carlyle's *Chartism* (1839): 'cash payment has become the sole nexus of man to man'.

personal dream to be recognized as a vision, it is hard to dissent. Indeed, to many in the 1990s his vision has seemed more relevant than ever. Why should this be?

There are several answers to this question, the first of which we have already touched upon. That is that in harnessing the power of myth to a vision of the future which makes no claims to being anything but personal, Morris recalls to life the dormant longings for a better world, juster and more beautiful, which we all share with him. We do so because to dream is to be human. And as Stephen Coleman has recently observed: 'The enemy of the dreamer of better times to come is the ideologist of the present, armed in defence of the existing miseries with the claim that the prevailing relationships of oppression are immutable.' And yet, he goes on, 'History can explode. And when it does it is ignited by those who have dared to dream, who have the courage to take on seemingly unbeatable odds, who are brave enough to demand the impossible.'*

For sometimes the impossible does happen. It did, as Coleman points out, in 1989, when the Socialist tyrannies of Eastern Europe collapsed like so many packs of cards. This should remind us of those planks of Morris's argument that have stood the test of time. He lost the debate, it will be remembered, about State Socialism. In *News from Nowhere* he depicts a country where the state has 'withered away' (to use the Marxist terminology) and individual communities are free to run their own affairs. This is the millennial condition which, in Marxist theory, will come to pass once 'the dictatorship of the proletariat' has done its work. But Morris plainly envisages Socialism, even in its early stages, as a form of decentralized popular democracy: precisely the opposite of the Socialist states that have now been so decisively rejected. It is important therefore to see that those who agreed with Engels when he called Morris 'a settled sentimental Socialist'† were far more mistaken in the long term than was Morris himself.

Still more impressive is Morris the environmentalist. When the

---

* Preface to *William Morris and News from Nowhere: A Vision for Our Time*, edited by Stephen Coleman and Paddy O'Sullivan, Bideford (Green Books) 1990, p. 11.
† *Frederick Engels, Paul and Laura Lafargue: Correspondence*, vol. I, London (Lawrence & Wishart) 1959, p. 370.

Communist governments in Eastern Europe fell, the world discovered the full extent of the ruin they had wrought on their natural environments. Irony of ironies: the pollution caused by the selfish and bloated West seems insignificant beside the achievements of those apostles of brotherly love. Here again, back in the 1880s, it had been Morris who dissented from the 'progressive' view about the expansion of industry for the increase of social wealth. As early as 1878, in 'The Lesser Arts', he reflected on the role of 'disinterested' Science in our wealth-creating societies; 'what will she do?' he asks.

I fear she is so much in the pay of the counting-house, the counting-house and the drill-sergeant, that she is too busy, and will for the present do nothing. Yet there are matters which I should have thought easy for her: say for example teaching Manchester how to consume its own smoke, or Leeds how to get rid of its superfluous black dye without turning it into the river, which would be as much worth her attention as the production of the heaviest of black silks, or the biggest of useless guns. Anyhow, however it be done, unless people care about carrying on their business without making the world hideous, how can they care about Art?

The world depicted is so sadly familiar that there is no word for the writing but 'prophetic'. Compare Marx at his most optimistic:

Subjection of nature's forces to man, machinery, application of chemistry to industry and agriculture, steam-navigation, railways, electric telegraphs, clearing of whole continents for cultivation, canalization of rivers, whole populations conjured out of the ground – what earlier century had even a presentiment that such productive forces slumbered in the lap of social labour.

A generation under threat from global warming, a phenomenon brought about by precisely these instances of progress, may find the pastoral nostalgia of *News from Nowhere* marginally less sentimental than *The Communist Manifesto*. The originating myth of the book *is* pastoral and, to that extent, nostalgic; yet closer examination will reveal a vision of society based on a practical and sustainable relationship with nature. One cannot imagine Morris approving, for instance, of the clearing of the Amazon rainforest.

Yet, in the end, romances are not meant to be manifestos. Morris observes of *Looking Backward* that the romance is only there to sugar the didactic pill. The dull utopia – and there are many of them – is dull either for lack of sugar or for too much of it. Morris avoids dullness by maintaining the sense of romantic enchantment and refracting his personal vision through a self-deprecating lens. His blundering persona provides many occasions for humour and he even, through the person of Ellen's crusty old grandfather, presents us with some of the more telling objections to his version of paradise. The successful utopia achieves its effect not by sermonizing but by creating a compelling dream-world to stand in opposition to the world we know. In that sense the genre shares something with its acidulous cousin, the satirical fable – with *Gulliver's Travels*, say, or *1984*. Morris's New Jerusalem may be impossible, inconceivable, even in some respects undesirable (as More's utopia was to Morris). Nevertheless, its emotional power reminds us of the wretchedness of much of modern life, insisting that the way we live is not inevitable. Industrial capitalism, as he learnt from his medieval studies, is not a law of nature and, for that reason, William Guest's journey into the future is also a journey into the past, back into the depths of England, towards the physical roots from which life might begin again.

In making this selection, I have concentrated on two things: I have tried to enlarge on some of the themes of *News from Nowhere*, while illustrating something of the range of Morris's concerns. It may therefore strike the reader as odd that of the eighteen texts selected, only one, 'The Story of the Unknown Church', belongs to the earlier half of Morris's life. This is mainly because Morris wrote very little prose before the late 1870s, though it also reflects my view that his political involvements dramatically affected the quality of his writing. I decided at the outset to exclude Morris's poetry, the best of which (with a few important exceptions) belongs to his early life, on the grounds that it needs a volume of its own; and I have included nothing from the later heroic romances, partly because their value seems to me slight, and partly because it is difficult to extract from them. Morris's expository writing is in my judgement superior to his 'imaginative' prose: a general rule to which *News from Nowhere* is a glorious exception.

Cambridge, 1991

CHRONOLOGY

* * *

1834   24 March, Morris born at Elm House, Walthamstow, the third child and eldest son of William Morris, a bill-broker in the City, and Emma (née Shelton), his wife.

1840   Family moves to Woodford Hall, near Epping Forest.

1847   Father dies, leaving a fortune.

1848   Family moves to Water House, Walthamstow (now the William Morris Gallery). Morris sent to Marlborough College.

1851   Involved in school 'rebellion'. Leaves school for private tuition.

1853   Exeter College, Oxford. Meets Burne-Jones. Beginnings of 'The Brotherhood'. Reads *The Stones of Venice*.

1854   Visit to Belgium and northern France; sees Amiens, Beauvais, Rouen.

1855   Begins writing poetry. Annual income of £900 on attaining majority. Second tour of French cathedrals with Burne-Jones leads to resolution to become architect.

1856   Launches *Oxford and Cambridge Magazine*. Articled to architect G. E. Street in Oxford. Meets Philip Webb in Street's office. Takes B A. Meets Rossetti. Moves to London, taking rooms in Red Lion Square with Burne-Jones. Begins painting under Rossetti's influence and gives up architecture.

1857   Designs settle for Red Lion Square. Meets Ruskin. With Rossetti and others, paints frescos in Oxford Union. Meets Jane Burden and paints her as 'La Belle Iseult'.

1858   *The Defence of Guenevere and Other Poems* published.

1859   Marries Jane Burden. Work begins on the Red House, Upton, designed by Webb; this leads to plans for the 'Firm'.

1860   The Morrises move into the Red House. Burne-Jones marries Georgiana Macdonald.

1861   Jane Alice (Jenny) Morris born. Foundation of Morris, Marshall, Faulkner & Co.

1862   Mary (May) Morris born. First wallpapers. Firm exhibits at the Second Great Exhibition.

1864   Ill with rheumatic fever. Financial difficulties.

1865   Move from Red House to Firm's premises in Queen Square, Bloomsbury.

1866   Firm decorates room in St James's Palace.

1867   *The Life and Death of Jason* published. Firm decorates Green Dining-Room in South Kensington (now Victoria and Albert) Museum.

1868–70 *The Earthly Paradise* published.

1868   Studies Icelandic with Eiríkr Magnússon.

1869   *The Eyrbyggja Saga* and *The Story of Grettir the Strong* (translated by Morris with Magnússon) both published.

1870   Translation of *The Story of the Volsungs and Niblungs* published. Begins making illuminated manuscripts.

1871   With Rossetti, acquires lease of Kelmscott Manor, Oxfordshire. First trip to Iceland.

1872   Moves from Queen Square to Horrington House, Turnham Green. *Love is Enough* published.

1873   Visits to Tuscany (with Burne-Jones) and Iceland.

1874   Rossetti suffers nervous breakdown and gives up Kelmscott tenancy. Morris visits Belgium with family.

1875   The Firm reorganized as Morris & Co. with Morris as sole proprietor. He takes up dyeing and carpet weaving. *Three Northern Love Stories* and *The Aeneids of Virgil* published.

1876   Appointed Examiner at the School of Art, South Kensington. Diagnosis of daughter Jenny's epilepsy. *Sigurd the Volsung* published. 12,000 Bulgarian Christians massacred by the Turks; Morris attacks government support for Turks in *Daily News*, his first letter to the press on a political topic; becomes Treasurer of Eastern Question Association.

1877   Writes manifesto *To the Working Men of England*. Founds Society for the Protection of Ancient Buildings ('Anti-Scrape'). Gives first public lecture on decorative arts, later published as pamphlet, *The Lesser Arts*. Rejects nomination as Oxford

Professor of Poetry. Firm opens show-room in Oxford Street.

1878   Beginning of political disillusionment with regard to the Eastern Question Association. Writes first political poem. Visits the Veneto with family. Buys Kelmscott House, Hammersmith.

1879   Begins high-warp tapestry weaving. Becomes Treasurer of National Liberal League. Launches campaign to save the west façade of St Mark's, Venice, from 'restoration'.

1880   Continuing political disenchantment. Firm decorates the Throne Room at St James's Palace. First boat-trip, Hammersmith to Kelmscott.

1881   Removal of Morris & Co. works to Merton Abbey.

1882   Works for Iceland Famine Relief Committee. *Hopes and Fears for Art* published. Gives evidence before Royal Commission on Technical Education. Death of Rossetti.

1883   Honorary Fellow of Exeter College, Oxford. Joins Democratic (later Social Democratic) Federation; elected to executive committee. Death of Karl Marx. Reads *Das Kapital* in French translation. Lectures on 'Art under Plutocracy' in University Hall, Oxford, Ruskin in the chair; declares for Socialism. Begins travelling around the country to speak on behalf of the SDF.

1884   Begins financing and writing for SDF newspaper, *Justice*. Forms Hammersmith branch of SDF. A split in SDF leads to the resignation of Morris and associates, who then set about founding the Socialist League. Foundation of Art Workers' Guild.

1885   Edits, finances and writes for SL newspaper, the *Commonweal*: *Pilgrims of Hope* serialized in it (1885–6). Several Socialists arrested after Free Speech Demonstration, Limehouse; Morris arrested after disturbances in court but later discharged. Suffers from gout and fatigue.

1886   More arrests after Free Speech Demonstrations; Morris fined. Unemployed demonstrate in Trafalgar Square.

1886–7   *A Dream of John Ball* serialized in the *Commonweal*.

1887   Translation of the *Odyssey* published. Socialists campaign in support of miners' strike in the north. 'Bloody Sunday' (13 November): a demonstration in Trafalgar Square broken up by the police with considerable brutality. Acts as pall-bearer and speaks at funeral of Alfred Linnell, killed by police the day after the demonstration; writes a 'Death Song' for the occasion. Arts and Crafts Exhibition Society founded.

1888   *A Dream of John Ball* and *A King's Lesson* published in book form. Also *Signs of Change*, lectures and addresses, and *The House of the Wolfings*, the first of a series of prose romances. Lectures at the first Arts and Crafts exhibition on tapestry-weaving. Delegate at Socialist Congress in Paris.

1889   London Dock Strike. Begins study of printing with Emery Walker. *The Roots of the Mountains* published. Lectures on dyeing and Gothic architecture to Arts and Crafts Exhibition Society. Reviews Edward Bellamy's *Looking Backward*. Attends Second Socialist International, Paris.

1890   Dismissed from editorship of the *Commonweal*, though continues to serialize *News from Nowhere* in it. Resigns from SL; Hammersmith branch of League renamed Hammersmith Socialist Society. Kelmscott Press founded.

1891   Kelmscott Press publishes its first book, Morris's *The Story of the Glittering Plain*. Serious illness begins; with Jenny, holidays in France. *News from Nowhere* published in book form; also *Poems by the Way* and first volume of the Saga Library.

1892   Writes preface to Kelmscott edition of Ruskin's *The Nature of Gothic*. Elected Master of Art Workers' Guild. Makes it known that he would reject offer of Poet Laureateship. Second volume of Saga Library.

1893   Third volume of Saga Library. In collaboration with E. Belfort Bax, publishes *Socialism, Its Growth and Outcome*, a collection of articles. Helps to draft *Manifesto of English Socialists* with Bernard Shaw and Sidney Webb.

1894   Death of his mother, Emma Morris. *The Wood Beyond the World* published. Reconciliation with SDF.

1895   With Magnússon, completes translation of *Heimskringla*. *The Water of the Wondrous Isles* and translation of *Beowulf* published. Death of Engels.

1896   *The Well at the World's End* published. Last public speech at meeting of Society for Checking the Abuses of Public Advertising. Kelmscott *Chaucer* published. Advised to go on sea-voyage for health; goes to Norway. Dies 3 October. Buried in Kelmscott Churchyard.

1897   *The Sundering Flood* published.

1898   Burne-Jones dies.

1900   Ruskin dies.

1902   *Architecture, Industry and Wealth*, articles and lectures, published.

1910–15 *The Collected Works of William Morris* published in twenty-four volumes, edited by May Morris.

1913   Purchase of Kelmscott Manor by Jane Morris.

1914   Jane Morris dies.

BIBLIOGRAPHICAL NOTE

* * *

The texts used in this selection are those established by May Morris in her beautifully printed edition of *The Collected Works of William Morris*, twenty-four vols., London, 1910–15, and in a subsequent compilation, *William Morris: Artist, Writer, Socialist*, two vols., Oxford, 1936, which also includes Bernard Shaw's memoir 'Morris as I Knew Him'. May Morris's introductions to each volume of her edition have since been published as a separate work: *The Introductions to the Collected Works of William Morris*, two vols., New York, 1973. Several writings which eluded May Morris's researches are now obtainable, notably *The Unpublished Lectures of William Morris*, edited by Eugene LeMire, Detroit, 1969. The others include *Icelandic Journals*, Fontwell, 1969, and an unfinished fiction, *The Novel on Blue Paper*, London, 1982.

Morris wrote splendid letters. There is a selection of them that is now only available in the United States: *The Letters of William Morris to His Family and Friends*, edited by Philip Henderson, New York, 1978. The scholarly edition, three volumes so far and not yet complete, is *The Collected Letters of William Morris*, edited by Norman Kelvin, Princeton, 1984–7.

A number of individual works are still in print. Notable among them are two books edited by A. L. Morton for the Marxist publishers Lawrence & Wishart: *Three Works by William Morris* (*News from Nowhere*, *Pilgrims of Hope* and *A Dream of John Ball*), London, 1968, and *Political Writings of William Morris*, revised edition, London, 1984. Two of the prose romances are published by Dover Publications: *The Wood beyond the World*, New York, 1972, and *The Story of the Glittering Plain*, New York, 1988. *Selected Poems*, edited by Peter Faulkner, Manchester, 1992, is a substantial selection of short poems only.

Morris's activity as an artist and designer has received much more attention in recent years than his literary work. Monographs are too numerous to mention, and the same is true of critical and historical studies. The best study of Morris's work as a whole and in all its aspects is Paul Thompson's *The Work of William Morris*, London, 1967 (paperback 1977).

There are two outstanding biographies. *The Life of William Morris*, two vols., London, 1899, is by Burne-Jones's son-in-law, J. W. Mackail; in theory the official biography, it far outclasses the general run of pious Victorian monuments, though its account of Morris's political career is misleading. This last is rectified by E. P. Thompson in his *William Morris: Romantic to Revolutionary*, revised edition, London, 1977; this is a passionately committed political biography, more than half of which deals with Morris's Socialist years. A worthy but much more run-of-the-mill study, a good deal shorter than Thompson or Mackail, is Philip Henderson's *William Morris: His Life, Work and Friends*, London, 1967 (paperback 1973).

ROMANCE

* * *

THE STORY OF
THE UNKNOWN CHURCH

* * *

Published in
the *Oxford and Cambridge Magazine*,
January 1856

I was the master-mason of a church that was built more than six hundred years ago; it is now two hundred years since that church vanished from the face of the earth; it was destroyed utterly, – no fragment of it was left; not even the great pillars that bore up the tower at the cross, where the choir used to join the nave. No one knows now even where it stood, only in this very autumn-tide, if you knew the place, you would see the heaps made by the earth-covered ruins heaving the yellow corn into glorious waves, so that the place where my church used to be is as beautiful now as when it stood in all its splendour. I do not remember very much about the land where my church was; I have quite forgotten the name of it, but I know it was very beautiful, and even now, while I am thinking of it, comes a flood of old memories, and I almost seem to see it again ... that old beautiful land! Only dimly do I see it in spring and summer and winter, but I see it in autumn-tide clearly now; yes, clearer, clearer, oh! so bright and glorious! yet it was beautiful too in spring, when the brown earth began to grow green: beautiful in summer, when the blue sky looked so much bluer, if you could hem a piece of it in between the new white carving; beautiful in the solemn starry nights, so solemn that it almost reached agony – the awe and joy one had in their great beauty. But of all these beautiful times, I remember the whole only of autumn-tide; the others come in bits to me; I can think only of parts of them but of all autumn; and of all days and nights in autumn, I remember one more particularly. That autumn day the church was nearly finished, and the monks, for whom we were building the church, and the people, who lived in the town hard by, crowded round us often-times to watch us carving.

Now the great Church, and the buildings of the Abbey where the monks lived, were about three miles from the town, and the town stood on a hill overlooking the rich autumn country: it was girt about with great walls that had overhanging battlements, and towers at certain places all along the walls, and often we could see from the church yard or the Abbey garden the flash of helmets and spears, and the dim shadowy waving of banners, as the knights and lords and men-at-arms passed to and fro along the battlements; and we could see too in the town the three spires of the three churches; and the spire of the Cathedral, which was the tallest of the three, was gilt all over with gold, and always at night-time a great lamp shone from it that hung in the spire midway between the roof of the church and the cross at the top of the spire.

The Abbey where we built the Church was not girt by stone walls, but by a circle of poplar trees, and whenever a wind passed over them, were it ever so little a breath, it set them all a-ripple; and when the wind was high, they bowed and swayed very low, and the wind, as it lifted the leaves, and showed their silvery white sides, or as again in the lulls of it, it let them drop, kept on changing the trees from green to white, and white to green; moreover, through the boughs and trunks of the poplars we caught glimpses of the great golden corn sea, waving, waving, waving for leagues and leagues; and among the corn grew burning scarlet poppies, and blue corn-flowers; and the corn-flowers were so blue, that they gleamed, and seemed to burn with a steady light, as they grew beside the poppies among the gold of the wheat. Through the corn sea ran a blue river, and always green meadows and lines of tall poplars followed its windings.

The old Church had been burned, and that was the reason why the monks caused me to build the new one; the buildings of the Abbey were built at the same time as the burned-down Church, more than a hundred years before I was born, and they were on the north side of the Church, and joined to it by a cloister of round arches, and in the midst of the cloister was a lawn, and in the midst of that lawn, a fountain of marble, carved round about with flowers and strange beasts; and at the edge of the lawn, near the round arches, were a great many sun-flowers that were all in blossom on that autumn day; and up many of the pillars of the cloister crept passion-flowers and roses. Then farther from the Church, and past the cloister and its buildings, were many detached buildings, and a great garden round them, all within the circle of the poplar trees; in the garden were trellises covered over with roses, and convolvulus, and the great-leaved fiery nasturtium; and specially all along by the poplar trees were there trellises, but on these grew nothing but deep crimson roses; the hollyhocks too were all out in blossom at that time, great spires of pink, and orange, and red, and white, with their soft, downy leaves. I said that nothing grew on the trellises by the poplars but crimson roses, but I was not quite right, for in many places the wild flowers had crept into the garden from without; lush green briony, with green-white blossoms, that grows so fast, one could almost think that we see it grow, and deadly nightshade, La bella donna, oh! so beautiful; red berry, and purple, yellow-spiked flower, and deadly, cruel-looking, dark green leaf, all growing together in the glorious days of early autumn. And in the midst of the great garden was a conduit, with its sides carved with histories from the Bible, and there was on it too, as on the fountain in the cloister, much carving of flowers and strange beasts.

Now the Church itself was surrounded on every side but the north by the cemetery, and there were many graves there, both of monks and of laymen, and often the friends of those whose bodies lay there, had planted flowers about the graves of those they loved. I remember one such particularly, for at the head of it was a cross of carved wood, and at the foot of it, facing the cross, three tall sunflowers; then in the midst of the cemetery was a cross of stone, carved on one side with the Crucifixion of our Lord Jesus Christ, and on the other with Our Lady holding the Divine Child.

So that day, that I specially remember, in autumn-tide, when the church was nearly finished, I was carving in the central porch of the west front (for I carved all those bas-reliefs in the west front with my own hand); beneath me my sister Margaret was carving at the flower-work, and the little quatrefoils that carry the signs of the zodiac and the emblems of the months: now my sister Margaret was rather more than twenty years old at that time, and she was very beautiful, with dark brown hair and deep calm violet eyes. I had lived with her all my life, lived with her almost alone latterly, for our father and mother died when she was quite young, and I loved her very much, though I was not thinking of her just then, as she stood beneath me carving. Now the central porch was carved with a bas-relief of the Last Judgment, and it was divided into three parts by horizontal bands of deep flower-work. In the lowest division, just over the doors, was carved the Rising of the Dead; above were angels blowing long trumpets, and Michael the Archangel weighing the souls, and the blessed led into heaven by angels, and the lost into hell by the devil; and in the topmost division was the Judge of the world.

All the figures in the porch were finished except one, and I remember when I woke that morning my exultation at the thought of my Church being so nearly finished; I remember, too, how a kind of misgiving mingled with the exultation, which, try all I could, I was unable to shake off; I thought then it was a rebuke for my pride, well, perhaps it was. The figure I had to carve was Abraham, sitting with a blossoming tree on each side of him, holding in his two hands the corners of his great robe, so that it made a mighty fold, wherein, with their hands crossed over their breasts, were the souls of the faithful, of whom he was called Father: I stood on the scaffolding for some time, while Margaret's chisel worked on bravely down below. I took mine in my hand, and stood so, listening to the noise of the masons inside, and two monks of the Abbey came and stood below me, and a knight, holding his little daughter by the hand, who every now and then looked up at him, and asked him strange questions. I did not think of these long, but began to think of Abraham, yet I could not think of him sitting there, quiet and solemn, while the Judgment-Trumpet was being blown; I rather thought of him as he looked when he chased those kings so far; riding far ahead of any of his company, with his mail-hood off his head, and lying in grim folds down his back, with the strong west wind blowing his wild black hair far out behind him, with the wind rippling the long scarlet pennon of his lance; riding there amid the rocks and the sands alone; with the last gleam of the armour of the beaten kings disappearing behind the winding of the pass; with his company a long, long way behind, quite out of sight, though their trumpets sounded faintly among the clefts of the rocks; and so I thought I saw him, till in his fierce chase he leapt, horse and man, into a deep river, quiet, swift, and smooth;

8

and there was something in the moving of the water-lilies as the breast of the horse swept them aside, that suddenly took away the thought of Abraham and brought a strange dream of lands I had never seen; and the first was a place where I was quite alone, standing by the side of a river, and there was the sound of singing a very long way off, but no living thing of any kind could be seen, and the land was quite flat, quite without hills, and quite without trees too, and the river wound very much, making all kinds of quaint curves, and on the side where I stood there grew nothing but long grass, but on the other side grew, quite on to the horizon, a great sea of red corn-poppies, only paths of white lilies wound all among them, with here and there a great golden sun-flower. So I looked down at the river by my feet, and saw how blue it was, and how, as the stream went swiftly by, it swayed to and fro the long green weeds, and I stood and looked at the river for long, till at last I felt some one touch me on the shoulder, and, looking round, I saw standing by me my friend Amyot, whom I love better than anyone else in the world, but I thought in my dream that I was frightened when I saw him, for his face had changed so, it was so bright and almost transparent, and his eyes gleamed and shone as I had never seen them do before. Oh! he was so wondrously beautiful, so fearfully beautiful! and as I looked at him the distant music swelled, and seemed to come close up to me, and then swept by us, and fainted away, at last died off entirely; and then I felt sick at heart, and faint, and parched, and I stooped to drink of the water of the river, and as soon as the water touched my lips, lo! the river vanished, and the flat country with its poppies and lilies, and I dreamed that I was in a boat by myself again, floating in an almost land-locked bay of the northern sea, under a cliff of dark basalt. I was lying on my back in the boat, looking up at the intensely blue sky, and a long low swell from the outer sea lifted the boat up and let it fall again and carried it gradually nearer and nearer towards the dark cliff; and as I moved on, I saw at last, on the top of the cliff, a castle with many towers, and on the highest tower of the castle there was a great white banner floating, with a red chevron on it, and three golden stars on the chevron; presently I saw too on one of the towers, growing in a cranny of the worn stones, a great bunch of golden and blood-red wall-flowers, and I watched the wall-flowers and banner for long; when suddenly I heard a trumpet blow from the castle, and saw a rush of armed men on to the battlements, and there was a fierce fight, till at last it was ended, and one went to the banner and pulled it down, and cast it over the cliff into the sea, and it came down in long sweeps, with the wind making little ripples in it; slowly, slowly it came, till at last it fell over me and covered me from my feet till over my breast, and I let it stay there and looked again at the castle, and then I saw that there was an amber-coloured banner floating over the castle in place of the red chevron, and it was much larger than the other: also now, a man stood on the battlements, looking towards me; he had a tilting helmet on, with the visor down, and an amber-coloured surcoat over his armour; his right hand was ungauntleted, and he held it high above his head, and in his hands was the bunch of wall-flowers that I had seen growing on the wall; and his hand was white and small, like a woman's, for in my dream I could see even very far-off things much clearer than we see real material things on the earth: presently he threw the wall-flowers over the cliff, and they fell in the boat just behind my head, and then I saw, looking down from the battlements of the castle, Amyot. He looked down towards me very sorrowfully, I thought, but, even as in the other dream, said nothing; so I thought in my dream that I wept for very pity, and for love of him, for he looked as a man just risen from a long illness, and who will carry till he dies a dull pain about with him. He was very thin, and his long black hair drooped all about his face, as he leaned over the battlements looking at me: he was quite pale, and his cheeks were hollow, but his eyes large and soft and sad. So I reached out my arms to him, and suddenly I was walking with him in a lovely garden, and we said nothing, for the music which I had heard at first was sounding close to us now, and there were many birds in the boughs of the trees: oh, such birds! gold and ruby, and emerald, but they sang not at all, but were quite silent, as though they too were listening to the music. Now all this time Amyot and I had been looking at each other, but just then I turned my head away from him, and as soon as I did so, the music ended with a long wail, and when I turned again Amyot was gone; then I felt even more sad and sick at heart than I had before when I was by the river, and I leaned against a tree, and put my hands before my eyes. When I looked again the garden was gone, and I knew not where I was, and presently all my dreams were gone. The chips were flying bravely from the stone under my chisel at last, and all my thoughts now were in my carving, when I heard my name, 'Walter', called, and when I looked down I saw one standing below me, whom I had seen in my dreams just before – Amyot. I had no hopes of seeing him for a long time, perhaps I might never see him again, I thought, for he was away (as I thought) fighting in the holy wars, and it made me almost beside myself to see him standing close by me in the flesh. I got down from my scaffolding as soon as I could, and all thoughts else were soon drowned in the joy of having him by me. Margaret, too, how glad she must have been, for she had been betrothed to him for some time before he went to the wars, and he had been five years away, five years! and how we had thought of him through those many weary days! how often his face had come before me; his brave, honest face, the most beautiful among all the faces of men and women I have ever seen. Yes, I remember how five years ago I held his hand as we came together out of the cathedral of that great, far-off city whose name I forget now; and then I remember the stamping of the horses' feet; I remember how his hand left mine at last, and then, some one looking back at me earnestly as they all rode on together – looking back, with his hand on the saddle behind him, while the trumpets sang in long solemn peals as they all rode on together, with the glimmer of arms and the fluttering of banners, and the clinking of the rings of the mail, that sounded like the falling of many drops of water into the deep, still waters of some pool that the rocks nearly meet over; and the gleam and flash of the swords, and the glimmer of the lance-heads and the flutter of the rippled banners, that streamed out from them, swept past me, and were gone, and they seemed like a pageant in a dream, whose meaning we know not; and those sounds too, the trumpets, and the clink of the mail, and the thunder of the horse-hoofs, they seemed dream-like too – and it was all like a dream that he should leave me, for we had said that we should always be together; but he went away, and now he is come back again.

We were by his bed-side, Margaret and I; I stood and leaned over him, and my hair fell sideways over my face and touched his face; Margaret kneeled beside me, quivering in every limb, not with pain, I think, but rather shaken by a passion of earnest prayer. After some time (I know not how long), I looked up from his face to the window underneath which he lay; I do not know what time of the day it was, but I know that it was a glorious autumn day, a day soft with melting, golden haze: a vine and a rose grew together, and trailed half across the window, so that I could not see much of the beautiful blue sky, and nothing of town or country beyond; the vine leaves were touched with red here and there, and three over-blown roses, light pink roses, hung amongst them. I remember dwelling on the strange lines the autumn had made in red on one of the gold-green vine leaves, and watching one leaf of one of the over-blown roses, expecting it to fall every minute; but as I gazed, and felt disappointed that the rose leaf had not fallen yet, I felt my pain suddenly shoot through me, and I remembered what I had lost; and then came bitter, bitter dreams – dreams which had once made me happy – dreams of the things I had hoped would be, of the things that would never be now; they came between the fair vine leaves and rose blossoms, and that which lay before the window; they came as before, perfect in colour and form, sweet sounds and shapes. But now in every one was something unutterably miserable; they would not go away, they put out the steady glow of the golden haze, the sweet light of the sun through the vine leaves, the soft leaning of the full blown roses. I wandered in them for a long time; at last I felt a hand put me aside gently, for I was standing at the head of – of the bed; then some one kissed my forehead, and words were spoken – I know not what words. The bitter dreams left me for the bitterer reality at last; for I had found him that morning lying dead, only the morning after I had seen him when he had come back from his long absence – I had found him lying dead, with his hands crossed downwards, with his eyes closed, as though the angels had done that for him; and now when I looked at him he still lay there, and Margaret knelt by him with her face touching his: she was not quivering now, her lips moved not at all as they had done just before; and so, suddenly those words came to my mind which she had spoken when she kissed me, and which at the time I had only heard with my outward hearing, for she had said: 'Walter, farewell, and Christ keep you; but for me, I must be with him, for so I promised him last night that I would never leave him any more, and God will let me go.' And verily Margaret and Amyot did go, and left me very lonely and sad.

It was just beneath the westernmost arch of the nave, there I carved their tomb: I was a long time carving it; I did not think I should be so long at first, and I said, 'I shall die when I have finished carving it,' thinking that would be a very short time. But so it happened after I had carved those two whom I loved, lying with clasped hands like husband and wife above their tomb, that I could not yet leave carving it; and so that I might be near them I became a monk, and used to sit in the choir and sing, thinking of the time when we should all be together again. And as I had time I used to go to the westernmost arch of the nave and work at the tomb that was there under the great, sweeping arch; and in process of time I raised a marble canopy that reached quite up to the top of the arch, and I painted it too as fair as I could, and carved it all about with many flowers and histories, and in them I carved the faces of those I had known on earth (for I was not as one on earth now, but seemed quite away out of the world). And as I carved, sometimes the monks and other people too would come and gaze, and watch how the flowers grew; and sometimes too as they gazed, they would weep for pity, knowing how all had been.

So my life passed, and I lived in that Abbey for twenty years after he died, till one morning, quite early, when they came into the church for matins, they found me lying dead, with my chisel in my hand, underneath the last lily of the tomb.

A KING'S LESSON

* * *

Published in the *Commonweal*,
18 September 1886,
under the title 'An Old Story Retold'

Published in book form with
A Dream of John Ball,
London, 1888

KING'S LESSON

It is told of Matthias Corvinus, king of Hungary[1] – the Alfred the Great of his time and people – that he once heard (once *only?*) that some (only *some*, my lad?) of his peasants were over-worked and under-fed. So he sent for his Council, and bade come thereto also some of the mayors of the good towns, and some of the lords of land and their bailiffs, and asked them of the truth thereof; and in diverse ways they all told one and the same tale, how the peasant carles[2] were stout and well able to work and had enough and to spare of meat and drink, seeing that they were but churls; and how if they worked not at the least as hard as they did, it would be ill for them and ill for their lords; for that the more the churl hath the more he asketh; and that when he knoweth wealth, he knoweth the lack of it also, as it fared with our first parents in the Garden of God. The King sat and said but little while they spake, but he misdoubted them that they were liars. So the Council brake up with nothing done; but the King took the matter to heart, being, as kings go, a just man, besides being more valiant than they mostly were, even in the old feudal time. So within two or three days, says the tale, he called together such lords and councillors as he deemed fittest, and bade busk them for a ride; and when they were ready he and they set out, over rough and smooth, decked out in all the glory of attire which was the wont of those days. Thus they rode till they came to some village or thorpe of the peasant folk, and through it to the vineyards where men were working on the sunny southern slopes that went up from the river: my tale does not say whether that were Theiss, or Donau, or what river. Well, I judge it was late spring or early summer, and the vines but just beginning to show their grapes; for the vintage is late in those lands, and some of the grapes are not gathered till the first frosts have touched them, whereby the wine made from them is the stronger and sweeter. Anyhow there were the peasants, men and women, boys and young maidens, toiling and swinking; some hoeing between the vine-rows, some bearing baskets of dung up the steep slopes, some in one way, some in another, labouring for the fruits they should never eat, and the wine they should never drink. Thereto turned the King and got off his horse and began to climb up the stony ridges of the vineyard, and his lords in like manner followed him, wondering in their hearts what was toward; but to the one who was following next after him he turned about and said with a smile, 'Yea, lords, this is a new game we are playing to-day, and a new knowledge will come from it.' And the lord smiled, but somewhat sourly.

As for the peasants, great was their fear of those gay and golden lords. I judge that they did not know the King, since it was little likely that any one of them had seen his face; and they knew of him but as the Great Father, the mighty warrior who kept the Turk from harrying their thorpe. Though, forsooth, little matter was it to any man there whether Turk or Magyar was their over-lord, since to one master or another they had to pay the due tale of labouring days in the year, and hard was the livelihood that they earned for themselves on the days when they worked for themselves and their wives and children.

Well, belike they knew not the King; but amidst those rich lords they saw and knew their own lord, and of him they were sore afraid. But nought it availed them to flee away from those strong men and strong horses – they who had been toiling from before the rising of the sun, and now it wanted little more than an hour of noon: besides, with the King and lords was a guard of crossbowmen, who were left the other side of the vineyard wall, – keen-eyed Italians of the mountains, straight shooters of the bolt. So the poor folk fled not; nay they made as if all this were none of their business, and went on with their work. For indeed each man said to himself, 'If I be the one that is not slain, to-morrow I shall lack bread if I do not work my hardest to-day; and maybe I shall be headman if some of these be slain and I live.'

Now comes the king amongst them and says: 'Good fellows, which of you is the headman?'

Spake a man, sturdy and sunburnt, well on in years and grizzled: 'I am the headman, lord.'

'Give me thy hoe, then,' says the King; 'for now shall I order this matter myself, since these lords desire a new game, and are fain to work under me at vine-dressing. But do thou stand by me and set me right if I order them wrong: but the rest of you go play!'

The carle knew not what to think, and let the King stand with his hand stretched out, while he looked askance at his own lord and baron, who wagged his head at him grimly as one who says, 'Do it, dog!'

Then the carle lets the hoe come into the King's hand; and the King falls to, and orders his lords for vine-dressing, to each his due share of the work: and whiles the carle said yea and whiles nay to his ordering. And then ye should have seen velvet cloaks cast off, and mantles of fine Flemish scarlet go to the dusty earth; as the lords and knights busked them to the work.

So they buckled to; and to most of them it seemed good game to play at vine-dressing. But one there was who, when his scarlet cloak was off, stood up in a doublet of glorious Persian web of gold and silk, such as men make not now, worth a hundred florins the Bremen ell. Unto him the King with no smile on his face gave the job of toing and froing up and down the hill with the biggest and the frailest dung-basket that there was; and thereat the silken lord screwed up a grin, that was sport to see, and all the lords laughed; and as he turned away he said, yet so that none heard him, 'Do I serve this son's son of a whore that he should bid me carry dung?' For you must know that the King's father, John Hunyad, one of the great warriors of the world, the Hammer of the Turks, was not gotten in wedlock, though he were a king's son.[3]

Well, they sped the work bravely for a while, and loud was the laughter as the hoes smote the earth and the flint stones tinkled and the cloud of dust rose up; the brocaded dung-bearer went up and down, cursing and swearing by the White God and the Black; and one would say to another, 'See ye how gentle blood outgoes churls' blood, even when the gentle does the churl's work: these lazy loons smote but one stroke to our three.' But the King, who worked no worse than any, laughed not at all; and meanwhile the poor folk stood by, not daring to speak a word one to the other; for they were still sore afraid, not now of being slain on the spot, but this rather was in their hearts: 'These great and strong lords and knights have come to see what work a man may do without dying: if we are to have yet more days added to our year's tale of lords' labour, then are we lost without remedy.' And their hearts sank within them.

So sped the work; and the sun rose yet higher in the heavens, and it was noon and more. And now there was no more laughter among those toiling lords, and the strokes of the hoe and mattock came far slower, while the dung-bearer sat down at the bottom of the hill and looked out on the river; but the King yet worked on doggedly, so for shame the other lords yet kept at it. Till at last the next man to the King let his hoe drop with a clatter, and swore a great oath. Now he was a strong black-bearded man in the prime of life, a valiant captain of that famous Black Band that had so often rent the Turkish array; and the King loved him for his sturdy valour; so he says to him, 'Is aught wrong, Captain?'

'Nay, lord,' says he, 'ask the headman carle yonder what ails us.'

'Headman,' says the King, 'what ails these strong knights? Have I ordered them wrongly?'

'Nay, but shirking ails them, lord,' says he, 'for they are weary; and no wonder, for they have been playing hard, and are of gentle blood.'

'Is that so, lords,' says the King, 'that ye are weary already?'

Then the rest hung their heads and said nought, all save that captain of war; and he said, being a bold man and no liar: 'King, I see what thou wouldst be at; thou hast brought us here to preach us a sermon from that Plato of thine; and to say sooth so that I may swink no more, and go eat my dinner, now preach thy worst! Nay, if thou wilt be priest I will be thy deacon. Wilt thou that I ask this labouring carle a thing or two?'

'Yea,' said the King. And there came, as it were, a cloud of thought over his face.

Then the captain straddled his legs and looked big, and said to the carle: 'Good fellow, how long have we been working here?'

'Two hours or thereabout, judging by the sun above us,' says he.

'And how much of thy work have we done in that while?' says the captain, and winks his eye at him withal.

'Lord,' says the carle, grinning a little despite himself, 'be not wroth with my word. In the first half-hour ye did five-and-forty minutes' work of ours, and in the next half-hour scant a thirty minutes' work, and the third half-hour a fifteen minutes' work, and in the fourth half-hour two minutes' work.' The grin now had faded from his face, but a gleam came into his eyes as he said: 'And now, as I suppose, your day's work is done, and ye will go to your dinner, and eat the sweet and drink the strong; and we shall eat a little rye-bread, and then be working here till after the sun has set and the moon has begun to cast shadows. Now for you, I wot not how ye shall sleep nor where, nor what white body ye shall hold in your arms while the night flits and the stars shine; but for us, while the stars yet shine, shall we be at it again, and bethink ye for what! I know not what game and play ye shall be devising for to-morrow as ye ride back home; but for us when we come back here to-morrow, it shall be as if there had been no yesterday and nothing done therein, and that work of that to-day shall be nought to us also, for we shall win no respite from our toil thereby, and the morrow of to-morrow will all be to begin again once more, and so on and on till no to-morrow abideth us. Therefore, if ye are thinking to lay some new tax or tale upon us, think twice of it, for we may not bear it. And all this I say with the less fear, because I perceive this man here beside me, in the black velvet jerkin and the gold chain on his neck, is the King; nor do I think he will slay me for my word since he hath so many a Turk before him and his mighty sword!'

Then said the captain: 'Shall I smite the man, O King? or hath he preached thy sermon for thee?'

'Smite not, for he hath preached it,' said the King. 'Hearken to the carle's sermon, lords and councillors of mine! Yet when another hath spoken our thought, other thoughts are born therefrom, and now have I another sermon to preach; but I will refrain me as now. Let us down and to our dinner.'

So they went, the King and his gentles, and sat down by the river under the rustle of the poplars, and they ate and drank and were merry. And the King bade bear up the broken meats to the vine-dressers, and a good draught of the archer's wine, and to the headman he gave a broad gold piece, and to each man three silver pennies.

But when the poor folk had all that under their hands, it was to them as though the kingdom of heaven had come down to earth.

In the cool of the evening home rode the King and his lords. The King was distraught and silent; but at last the captain, who rode beside him, said to him: 'Preach me now thine after-sermon, O King!'

'I think thou knowest it already,' said the King, 'else hadst thou not spoken in such wise to the carle; but tell me what is thy craft and the craft of all these, whereby ye live, as the potter by making pots, and so forth?'

Said the captain: 'As the potter lives by making pots, so we live by robbing the poor.'

Again said the King: 'And my trade?'

Said he, 'Thy trade is to be a king of such thieves, yet no worser than the rest.'

The King laughed.

'Bear that in mind,' said he, 'and then shall I tell thee my thought while yonder carle spake. Carle, I thought, were I thou or such as thou, then would I take in my hand a sword or a spear, or were it only a hedge-stake, and bid others do the like, and forth would we go; and since we would be so many, and with nought to lose save a miserable life, we would do battle and prevail, and make an end of the craft of kings and of lords and of usurers, and there should be but one craft in the world, to wit, to work merrily for ourselves and to live merrily thereby.'

Said the captain: 'This then is thy sermon. Who will heed it if thou preach it?'

Said the King: 'They who will take the mad king and put him in a king's madhouse, therefore do I forbear to preach it. Yet it *shall* be preached.'

'And not heeded,' said the captain, 'save by those who head and hang the setters forth of new things that are good for the world. Our trade is safe for many and many a generation.'

And therewith they came to the King's palace, and they ate and drank and slept, and the world went on its ways.

Two extracts from
A DREAM OF JOHN BALL

* * *

Serialized in the *Commonweal*,
13 November 1886 to 22 January 1887

Published in book form with
'A King's Lesson',
London 1888

[*In a dream, the narrator finds himself in the Kent countryside during the Peasants' Revolt of 1381. He is drawn into the rebellion by a burly longbowman named Will Green, who gives him hospitality, and he hears the dissident priest John Ball addressing the insurgents at the village cross. Much moved by Ball's words, he then witnesses a skirmish in which the rebels are triumphant, though several men on either side are killed. Recognizing the narrator as a time-traveller, Ball asks him to come that night to the village church, where the bodies of the day's dead have been laid out.*]

We entered the church through the south porch under a round-arched door carved very richly, and with a sculpture over the doorway and under the arch, which, as far as I could see by the moonlight, figured St Michael and the Dragon. As I came into the rich gloom of the nave I noticed for the first time that I had one of those white poppies in my hand; I must have taken it out of the pot by the window as I passed out of Will Green's house.

The nave was not very large, but it looked spacious too; it was somewhat old, but well-built and handsome; the roof of curved wooden rafters with great tie-beams going from wall to wall. There was no light in it but that of the moon streaming through the windows, which were by no means large, and were glazed with white fretwork, with here and there a little figure in very deep rich colours. Two larger windows near the east end of each aisle had just been made so that the church grew lighter toward the east, and I could see all the work on the great screen between the nave and chancel which glittered bright in new paint and gilding: a candle glimmered in the loft above it, before the huge rood that filled up the whole space between the loft and the chancel arch. There was an altar at the east end of each aisle, the one on the south side standing against the outside wall, the one on the north against a traceried gaily-painted screen, for that aisle ran on along the chancel. There were a few oak benches near this second altar, seemingly just made, and well carved and moulded; otherwise the floor of the nave, which was paved with a quaint pavement of glazed tiles like the crocks I had seen outside as to ware, was quite clear, and the shafts of the arches rose out of it white and beautiful under the moon as though out of a sea, dark but with gleams struck over it.

The priest let me linger and look round, when he had crossed himself and given me the holy water; and then I saw that the walls were figured all over with stories, a huge St Christopher with his black beard looking like Will Green, being close to the porch by which we entered, and above the chancel arch the Doom of the last Day, in which the painter had not spared either kings or bishops, and in which a lawyer with his blue coif was one of the chief figures in the group which the Devil was hauling off to hell.

'Yea,' said John Ball, ''tis a goodly church and fair as you may see 'twixt Canterbury and London as for its kind; and yet do I misdoubt me where those who are dead are housed, and where those shall house them after they are dead, who built this house for God to dwell in. God grant they be cleansed at last; forsooth one of them who is now alive is a foul swine and a cruel wolf. Art thou all so sure, scholar, that all such have souls? and if it be so, was it well done of God to make them? I speak to thee thus, for I think thou art no delator;[1] and if thou be, why should I heed it, since I think not to come back from this journey.'

I looked at him and, as it were, had some ado to answer him; but I said at last, 'Friend, I never saw a soul, save in the body; I cannot tell.'

He crossed himself and said, 'Yet do I intend that ere many days are gone by my soul shall be in bliss among the fellowship of the saints, and merry shall it be, even before my body rises from the dead; for wisely I have wrought in the world, and I wot well of friends that are long ago gone from the world, as St Martin, and St Francis, and St Thomas of Canterbury,[2] who shall speak well of me to the heavenly Fellowship, and I shall in no wise lose my reward.'

I looked shyly at him as he spoke; his face looked sweet and calm and happy, and I would have said no word to grieve him; and yet belike my eyes looked wonder on him: he seemed to note it and his face grew puzzled. 'How deemest thou of these things?' said he: 'why do men die else, if it be otherwise than this?'

I smiled: 'Why then do they live?' said I.

Even in the white moonlight I saw his face flush, and he cried out in a great voice, 'To do great deeds or to repent them that they ever were born.'

'Yea,' said I, 'they live to live because the world liveth.' He stretched out his hand to me and grasped mine, but said no more; and went on till we came to the door in the rood-screen; then he turned to me with his hand on the ring-latch, and said, 'Hast thou seen many dead men?'

'Nay, but few,' said I.

'And I a many,' said he; 'but come now and look on these, our friends first and then our foes, so that ye may not look to see them while we sit and talk of the days that are to be on the earth before the Day of Doom cometh.'

So he opened the door, and we went into the chancel; a light burned on the high altar before the host, and looked red and strange in the moonlight that came through the wide traceried windows unstained by the pictures and beflowerings of the glazing; there were new stalls for the priests and vicars where we entered, carved more abundantly and beautifully than any of the woodwork I had yet seen, and everywhere was rich and fair colour and delicate and dainty form. Our dead[3] lay just before the high altar on low biers, their faces all covered with linen cloths, for some of them had been sore smitten and hacked in the fray. We went up to them and John Ball took the cloth from the face of one; he had been shot to the heart with a shaft and his face was calm and smooth. He had been a young man fair and comely, with hair flaxen almost to whiteness; he lay there in his clothes as he had fallen, the hands crossed over his breast and holding a rush cross. His bow lay on one side of him, his quiver of shafts and his sword on the other.

John Ball spake to me while he held the corner of the sheet: 'What sayest thou, scholar? feelest thou sorrow of heart when thou lookest on this, either for the man himself, or for thyself and the time when thou shalt be as he is?'

I said, 'Nay, I feel no sorrow for this; for the man is not here: this is an empty house, and the master has gone from it. Forsooth, this to me is but as a waxen image of a man; nay, not even that, for if it were an image, it would be an image of the man as he was when he was alive. But here is no life nor semblance of life, and I am not moved by it; nay, I am more moved by the man's clothes and war-gear – there is more life in them than in him.'

'Thou sayest sooth,' said he; 'but sorrowest thou not for thine own death when thou lookest on him?'

I said, 'And how can I sorrow for that which I cannot so much as think of? Bethink thee that while I am alive I cannot think that I shall die, or believe in death at all, although I know well that I shall die – I can but think of myself as living in some new way.'

Again he looked on me as if puzzled; then his face cleared as he said, 'Yea, forsooth, and that is what the Church meaneth by death, and even that I look for; and that hereafter I shall see all the deeds that I have done in the body, and what they really were, and what shall come of them; and ever shall I be a member of the Church, and that is the Fellowship; then, even as now.'

I sighed as he spoke; then I said, 'Yea, somewhat in this fashion have most of men thought, since no man that is can conceive of not being; and I mind me that in those stories of the old Danes, their common word for a man dying is to say, "He changed his life."'

'And so deemest thou?'

I shook my head and said nothing.

'What hast thou to say hereon?' said he, 'for there seemeth something betwixt us twain as it were a wall that parteth us.'

'This,' said I, 'that though I die and end, yet mankind yet liveth, therefore I end not, since I am a man; and even so thou deemest, good friend; or at the least even so thou doest, since now thou art ready to die in grief and torment rather than be unfaithful to the Fellowship, yea rather than fail to work thine utmost for it; whereas, as thou thyself saidst at the cross,[4] with a few words spoken and a little huddling-up of the truth, with a few pennies paid, and a few masses sung, thou mightest have had a good place on this earth and in that heaven. And as thou doest, so now doth many a poor man unnamed and unknown, and shall do while the world lasteth: and they that do less than this, fail because of fear, and are ashamed of their cowardice, and make many tales to themselves to deceive themselves, lest they should grow too much ashamed to live. And trust me if this were not so, the world would not live, but would die, smothered by its own stink. Is the wall betwixt us gone, friend?'

He smiled as he looked at me, kindly, but sadly and shamefast, and shook his head.

Then in a while he said, 'Now ye have seen the images of those who were our friends, come and see the images of those who were once our foes.'

So he led the way through the side screen into the chancel aisle, and there on the pavement lay the bodies of the foemen, their weapons taken from them and they stripped of their armour, but not otherwise of their clothes, and their faces mostly, but not all, covered. At the east end of the aisle was another altar, covered with a rich cloth beautifully figured, and on the wall over it was a deal of tabernacle work, in the midmost niche of it an image painted and gilt of a gay knight on horseback, cutting his own cloak in two with his sword to give a cantle of it to a half-naked beggar.

'Knowest thou any of these men?' said I.

He said, 'Some I should know, could I see their faces; but let them be.'

'Were they evil men?' said I.

'Yea,' he said, 'some two or three. But I will not tell thee of them; let St Martin, whose house this is, tell their story if he will. As for the rest they were hapless fools, or else men who must earn their bread somehow, and were driven to this bad way of earning it; God rest their souls! I will be no tale-bearer, not even to God.'

So we stood musing a little while, I gazing not on the dead men, but on the strange pictures on the wall, which were richer and deeper coloured than those in the nave; till at last John Ball turned to me and laid his hand on my shoulder. I started and said, 'Yea, brother; now must I get me back to Will Green's house, as I promised to do so timely.'

'Not yet, brother,' said he; 'I have still much to say to thee, and the night is yet young. Go we and sit in the stalls of the vicars, and let us ask and answer on matters concerning the fashion of this world of menfolk, and of this land wherein we dwell; for once more I deem of thee that thou hast seen things which I have not seen, and could not have seen.' With that word he led me back into the chancel, and we sat down side by side in the stalls at the west end of it, facing the high altar and the great east window. By this time the chancel was getting dimmer as the moon wound round the heavens; but yet was there a twilight of the moon, so that I could still see the things about me for all the brightness of the window that faced us; and this moon twilight would last, I knew, until the short summer night should wane, and the twilight of the dawn begin to show us the colours of all things about us.

So we sat, and I gathered my thoughts to hear what he would say, and I myself was trying to think what I should ask of him; for I thought of him as he of me, that he had seen things which I could not have seen.

[Anticipating his own execution and fearing that the uprising will fail, Ball is anxious to foresee the eventual outcome of the class struggle and questions the narrator about the centuries to come.]

He said: 'Many strange things hast thou told me that I could not understand; yea, some of my wit so failed to compass, that I cannot so much as ask thee questions concerning them; but of some matters would I ask thee, and I must hasten, for in very sooth the night is worn old and grey. Whereas thou sayest that in the days to come, when there shall be no labouring men who are not thralls after their new fashion, that their lords shall be many and very many, it seemeth to me that these same lords, if they be many, shall hardly be rich, or but very few of them, since they must verily feed and clothe and house their thralls, so that that which they take from them, since it will have to be dealt out amongst many, will not be enough to make many rich; since out of one man ye may get but one man's work; and pinch him never so sorely, still as aforesaid ye may not pinch him so sorely as not to feed him. Therefore, though the eyes of my mind may see a few lords and many slaves, yet can they not see many lords as well as many slaves; and if the slaves be many and the lords few, then some day shall the slaves make an end of that mastery by the force of their bodies. How then shall thy mastership of the latter days endure?'

'John Ball,' said I, 'mastership hath many shifts whereby it striveth to keep itself alive in the world. And now hear a marvel: whereas thou sayest these two times that out of one man ye may get but one man's work, in days to come one man shall do the work of a hundred men – yea, of a thousand or more: and this is the shift of mastership that shall make many masters and many rich men.'

John Ball laughed. 'Great is my harvest of riddles to-night,' said he; 'for even if a man sleep not, and eat and drink while he is a-working, ye shall but make two men, or three at the most, out of him.'

Said I: 'Sawest thou ever a weaver at his loom?'

'Yea,' said he, 'many a time.'

He was silent a little, and then said: 'Yet I marvelled not at it; but now I marvel, because I know what thou wouldst say. Time was when the shuttle was thrust in and out of all the thousand threads of the warp, and it was long to do; but now the spring-staves go up and down as the man's feet move, and this and that leaf of the warp cometh forward and the shuttle goeth in one shot through all the thousand warps. Yea, so it is that this multiplieth a man many times. But look you, he is so multiplied already; and so hath he been, meseemeth, for many hundred years.'

'Yea,' said I, 'but what hitherto needed the masters to multiply him more? For many hundred years the workman was a thrall bought and sold at the cross; and for other hundreds of years he hath been a villein⁵ – that is, a working-beast and a part of the stock of the manor on which he liveth; but then thou and the like of thee shall free him, and then is mastership put to its shifts: for what should avail the mastery then, when the master no longer owneth the man by law as his chattel, nor any longer by law owneth him as stock of his land, if the master hath not that which he on whom he liveth may not lack and live withal, and cannot have without selling himself?'

He said nothing, but I saw his brow knitted and his lips pressed together as though in anger; and again I said:

'Thou hast seen the weaver at his loom: think how it should be if he sit no longer before the web and cast the shuttle and draw home the sley, but if the shed open of itself and the shuttle of itself speed through it as swift as the eye can follow, and the sley come home of itself; and the weaver standing by and whistling 'The Hunt's Up!' the while, or looking to half-a-dozen looms and bidding them what to do. And as with the weaver so with the potter, and the smith, and every worker in metals, and all other crafts, that it shall be for them looking on and tending, as with the man that sitteth in the cart while the horse draws. Yea, at last so shall it be even with those who are mere husbandmen; and no longer shall the reaper fare afield in the morning with his hook over his shoulder, and smite and bind and smite again till the sun is down and the moon is up; but he shall draw a thing made by men into the field with one or two horses, and shall say the word and the horses shall go up and down, and the thing shall reap and gather and bind, and do the work of many men. Imagine all this in thy mind if thou canst, at least as ye may imagine a tale of enchantment told by a minstrel, and then tell me what shouldst thou deem that the life of men would be amidst all this, men such as these men of the township here, or the men of the Canterbury gilds.'6

'Yea,' said he; 'but before I tell thee my thoughts of thy tale of wonder, I would ask thee this: In those days when men work so easily, surely they shall make more wares than they can use in one countryside, or one good town, whereas in another, where things have not gone as well, they shall have less than they need; and even so it is with us now, and thereof cometh scarcity and famine; and if people may not come at each other's goods, it availeth the whole land little that one countryside hath more than enough while another hath less; for the goods shall abide there in the storehouses of the rich place till they perish. So if that be so in the days of wonder ye tell of (and I see not how it can be otherwise), then shall men be but little holpen by making all their wares so easily and with so little labour.'

I smiled again and said: 'Yea, but it shall not be so; not only shall men be multiplied a hundred and a thousand fold, but the distance of one place from another shall be as nothing; so that the wares which lie ready for market in Durham in the evening may be in London on the morrow morning; and the men of Wales may eat corn of Essex and the men of Essex wear wool of Wales; so that, so far as the flitting of goods to market goes, all the land shall be as one parish. Nay, what say I? Not as to this land only shall it be so, but even the Indies, and far countries of which thou knowest not, shall be, so to say, at every man's door, and wares which now ye account precious and dear-bought, shall then be common things bought and sold for little price at every huckster's stall. Say then, John, shall not those days be merry, and plentiful of ease and contentment for all men?'

'Brother,' said he 'meseemeth some doleful mockery lieth under these joyful tidings of thine; since thou hast already partly told me to my sad bewilderment what the life of man shall be in those days. Yet will I now for a little set all that aside to consider thy strange tale as of a minstrel from over sea, even as thou biddest me. Therefore I say, that if men still abide men as I have known them, and unless these folk of England change as the land changeth – and forsooth of the men, for good and for evil, I can think no other than I think now, or behold them other than I have known them and loved them – I say if the men be still men, what will happen except that there should be all plenty in the land, and not one poor man therein, unless of his own free will he choose to lack and be poor, as a man in religion or such like; for there would then be such abundance of all good things, that, as greedy as the lords might be, there would be enough to satisfy their greed and yet leave good living for all who laboured with their hands; so that these should labour far less than now, and they would have time to learn knowledge, so that there should be no learned or unlearned, for all should be learned; and they would have time also to learn how to order the matters of the parish and the hundred,[7] and of the parliament of the realm, so that the king should take no more than his own; and to order the rule of the realm, so that all men, rich and unrich, should have part therein; and so by undoing of evil laws and making of good ones, that fashion would come to an end whereof thou speakest, that rich men make laws for their own behoof; for they should no longer be able to do thus when all had part in making the laws; whereby it would soon come about that there would be no men rich and tyrannous, but all should have enough and to spare of the increase of the earth and the work of their own hands. Yea surely, brother, if ever it cometh about that men shall be able to make things, and not men, work for their superfluities, and that the length of travel from one place to another be made of no account, and all the world be a market for all the world, then all shall live in health and wealth; and envy and grudging shall perish. For then shall we have conquered the earth and it shall be enough; and then shall the kingdom of heaven be come down to the earth in very deed. Why lookest thou so sad and sorry? what sayest thou?'

I said: 'Hast thou forgotten already what I told thee, that in those latter days a man who hath nought save his own body (and such men shall be far the most of men) must needs pawn his labour for leave to labour? Can such a man be wealthy? Hast thou not called him a thrall?'

'Yea,' he said; 'but how could I deem that such things could be when those days should be come wherein men could make things work for them?'

'Poor man!' said I. 'Learn that in those very days, when it shall be with the making of things as with the carter in the cart, that there he sitteth and shaketh the reins and the horse draweth and the cart goeth; in those days, I tell thee, many men shall be as poor and wretched always, year by year, as they are with thee when there is famine in the land; nor shall any have plenty and surety of livelihood save those that shall sit by and look on while others labour; and these, I tell thee, shall be a many, so that they shall see to the making of all laws, and in their hands shall be all power, and the labourers shall think that they cannot do without these men that live by robbing them, and shall praise them and wellnigh pray to them as ye pray to the saints, and the best worshipped man in the land shall be he who by forestalling and regrating[8] hath gotten to him the most money.'

'Yea,' said he, 'and shall they who see themselves robbed worship the robber? Then indeed shall men be changed from what they are now, and they shall be sluggards, dolts, and cowards beyond all the earth hath yet borne. Such are not the men I have known in my life-days, and that now I love in my death.'

'Nay,' I said, 'but the robbery shall they not see; for have I not told thee that they shall hold themselves to be free men? And for why? I will tell thee: but first tell me how it fares with men now; may the labouring man become a lord?'

He said: 'The thing hath been seen that churls have risen from the dortoir[9] of the monastery to the abbot's chair and the bishop's throne; yet not often; and whiles hath a bold sergeant become a wise captain, and they have made him squire and knight; and yet but very seldom. And now I suppose thou wilt tell me that the Church will open her arms wider to this poor people, and that many through her shall rise into lordship. But what availeth that? Nought were it to me if the Abbot of St Alban's with his golden mitre sitting guarded by his knights and sergeants, or the Prior of Merton[10] with his hawks and his hounds, had once been poor men, if they were now tyrants of poor men; nor would it better the matter if there were ten times as many Houses of Religion in the land as now are, and each with a churl's son for abbot or prior over it.'

I smiled and said: 'Comfort thyself; for in those days shall there be neither abbey nor priory in the land, nor monks nor friars, nor any religious.' (He started as I spoke). 'But thou hast told me that hardly in these days may a poor man rise to be a lord: now I tell thee that in the days to come poor men shall be able to become lords and masters and do-nothings; and oft will it be seen that they shall do so; and it shall be even for that cause that their eyes shall be blinded to the robbing of themselves by others, because they shall hope in their souls that they may each live to rob others: and this shall be the very safeguard of all rule and law in those days.'

'Now am I sorrier than thou hast yet made me,' said he; 'for when once this is established, how then can it be changed? Strong shall be the tyranny of the latter days. And now meseems, if thou sayest sooth, this time of the conquest of the earth shall not bring heaven down to the earth, as erst I deemed it would, but rather that it shall bring hell up on to the earth. Woe's me, brother, for thy sad and weary foretelling! And yet saidst thou that the men of those days would seek a remedy. Canst thou yet tell me, brother, what that remedy shall be, lest the sun rise upon me made hopeless by thy tale of what is to be? And, lo you, soon shall she rise upon the earth.'

In truth the dawn was widening now, and the colours coming into the pictures on wall and in window; and as well as I could see through the varied glazing of these last (and one window before me had as yet nothing but white glass in it), the ruddy glow, which had but so little a while quite died out in the west, was now beginning to gather in the east – the new day was beginning. I looked at the poppy that I still carried in my hand, and it seemed to me to have withered and dwindled. I felt anxious to speak to my companion and tell him much, and withal I felt that I must hasten, or for some reason or other I should be too late; so I spoke at last loud and hurriedly:

'John Ball, be of good cheer; for once more thou knowest, as I know, that the Fellowship of Men shall endure, however many tribulations it may have to wear through. Look you, a while ago was the light bright about us; but it was because of the moon, and the night was deep notwithstanding, and when the moonlight waned and died and there was but a little glimmer in place of the bright light, yet was the world glad because all things knew that the glimmer was of day and not of night. Lo you, an image of the times to betide the hope of the Fellowship of Men. Yet forsooth, it may well be that this bright day of summer which is now dawning upon us is no image of the beginning of the day that shall be; but rather shall that day-dawn be cold and grey and surly; and yet by its light shall men see things as they verily are, and no longer enchanted by the gleam of the moon and the glamour of the dreamtide. By such grey light shall wise men and valiant souls see the remedy, and deal with it, a real thing that may be touched and handled, and no glory of the heavens to be worshipped from afar off. And what shall it be, as I told thee before, save that men shall be determined to be free; yea, free as thou wouldst have them, when thine hope rises the highest, and thou art thinking not of the king's uncles, and poll-groat bailiffs,[11] and the villeinage of Essex, but of the end of all, when men shall have the fruits of the earth and the fruits of their toil thereon, without money and without price. The time shall come, John Ball, when that dream of thine that this shall one day be, shall be a thing that men shall talk of soberly, and as a thing soon to come about, as even with thee they talk of the villeins becoming tenants paying their lord quit-rent;[12] therefore, hast thou done well to hope it; and, if thou heedest this also, as I suppose thou heedest it little, thy name shall abide by thy hope in those days to come, and thou shalt not be forgotten.'

I heard his voice come out of the twilight, scarcely seeing him, though now the light was growing fast, as he said:

'Brother, thou givest me heart again; yet since now I wot tell that thou art a sending from far-off times and far-off things: tell thou, if thou mayest, to a man who is going to his death how this shall come about.'

'Only this may I tell thee,' said I; 'to thee, when thou didst try to conceive of them, the ways of the days to come seemed follies scarce to be thought of; yet shall they come to be familiar things, and an order by which every man liveth, ill as he liveth, so that men shall deem of them, that thus it hath been since the beginning of the world, and that thus it shall be while the world endureth; and in this wise so shall they be thought of a long while; and the complaint of the poor the rich man shall heed, even as much and no more as he who lieth in pleasure under the lime-trees in the summer heedeth the murmur of his toiling bees. Yet in time shall this also grow old, and doubt shall creep in, because men shall scarce be able to live by that order, and the complaint of the poor shall be hearkened, no longer as a tale not utterly grievous, but as a threat of ruin, and a fear. Then shall those things, which to thee seem follies, and to the men between thee and me mere wisdom and the bond of stability, seem follies once again; yet, whereas men have so long lived by them, they shall cling to them yet from blindness and from fear; and those that see, and that have thus much conquered fear that they are furthering the real time that cometh and not the dream that faileth, these men shall the blind and the fearful mock and missay, and torment and murder: and great and grievous shall be the strife in those days, and many the failures of the wise, and too oft sore shall be the despair of the valiant; and back-sliding, and doubt, and contest between friends and fellows lacking time in the hubbub to understand each other, shall grieve many hearts and hinder the Host of the Fellowship: yet shall all bring about the end, till thy deeming of folly and ours shall be one, and thy hope and our hope; and then – the Day will have come.'

Once more I heard the voice of John Ball: 'Now, brother, I say farewell; for now verily hath the Day of the Earth come, and thou and I are lonely of each other again; thou hast been a dream to me as I to thee, and sorry and glad have we made each other, as tales of old time and the longing of times to come shall ever make men to be. I go to life and to death, and leave thee; and scarce do I know whether to wish thee some dream of the days beyond thine to tell what shall be, as thou hast told me, for I know not if that shall help or hinder thee; but since we have been kind and very friends, I will not leave thee without a wish of goodwill, so at least I wish thee what thou thyself wishest for thyself, and that is hopeful strife and blameless peace, which is to say in one word, life. Farewell, friend.'

For some little time, although I had known that the daylight was growing and what was around me, I had scarce seen the things I had before noted so keenly; but now in a flash I saw all – the east crimson with sunrise through the white window on my right hand; the richly-carved stalls and gilded screen work, the pictures on the walls, the loveliness of the faultless colour of the mosaic window lights, the altar and the red light over it looking strange in the daylight, and the biers with the hidden dead men upon them that lay before the high altar. A great pain filled my heart at the sight of all that beauty, and withal I heard quick steps coming up the paved church-path to the porch, and the loud whistle of a sweet old tune therewith; then the footsteps stopped at the door; I heard the latch rattle, and knew that Will Green's hand was on the ring of it.

Then I strove to rise up, but fell back again; a white light, empty of all sights, broke upon me for a moment, and lo! behold, I was lying in my familiar bed, the south-westerly gale rattling the Venetian blinds and making their hold-fasts squeak.

I got up presently, and going to the window looked out on the winter morning; the river was before me broad between outer bank and bank, but it was nearly dead ebb, and there was a wide space of mud on each side of the hurrying stream, driven on the faster as it seemed by the push of the south-west wind. On the other side of the water the few willow-trees left us by the Thames Conservancy looked doubtfully alive against the bleak sky and the row of wretched-looking blue-slated houses, although, by the way, the latter were the backs of a sort of street of 'villas' and not a slum; the road in front of the house was sooty and muddy at once, and in the air was that sense of dirty discomfort which one is never quit of in London. The morning was harsh too, and though the wind was from the south-west it was as cold as a north wind; and yet amidst it all, I thought of the corner of the next bight of the river which I could not quite see from where I was, but over which one can see clear of houses and into Richmond Park, looking like the open country; and dirty as the river was, and harsh as was the January wind, they seemed to woo me toward the countryside, where away from the miseries of the 'Great Wen' I might of my own will carry on a day-dream of the friends I had made in the dream of the night and against my will.[13]

But as I turned away shivering and downhearted, on a sudden came the frightful noise of the 'hooters', one after the other, that call the workmen to the factories, this one the after-breakfast one, more by token. So I grinned surlily, and dressed and got ready for my day's 'work' as I call it, but which many a man besides John Ruskin (though not many in his position) would call 'play'.[14]

NEWS FROM NOWHERE

or

An Epoch of Rest

being some chapters from a Utopian Romance

* * *

Serialized in the *Commonweal*,
11 January to 4 October 1890

Published in book form and revised,
Boston, 1890, and London, 1891

Chapter I
DISCUSSION AND BED

Up at the League,[1] says a friend, there had been one night a brisk conversational discussion, as to what would happen on the Morrow of the Revolution, finally shading off into a vigorous statement by various friends of their views on the future of the fully-developed new society.

Says our friend: Considering the subject, the discussion was good-tempered; for those present, being used to public meetings and after-lecture debates, if they did not listen to each other's opinions (which could scarcely be expected of them), at all events did not always attempt to speak all together, as is the custom of people in ordinary polite society when conversing on a subject which interests them. For the rest, there were six persons present, and consequently six sections of the party were represented, four of which had strong but divergent Anarchist opinions.[2] One of the sections, says our friend, a man whom he knows very well indeed, sat almost silent at the beginning of the discussion, but at last got drawn into it, and finished by roaring out very loud, and damning all the rest for fools; after which befell a period of noise, and then a lull, during which the aforesaid section, having said good-night very amicably, took his way home by himself to a western suburb, using the means of travelling which civilization has forced upon us like a habit. As he sat in that vapour-bath of hurried and discontented humanity, a carriage of the underground railway,[3] he, like others, stewed discontentedly, while in self-reproachful mood he turned over the many excellent and conclusive arguments which, though they lay at his fingers' ends, he had forgotten in the just past discussion. But this frame of mind he was so used to, that it didn't last him long, and after a brief discomfort, caused by disgust with himself for having lost his temper (which he was also well used to), he found himself

43

musing on the subject-matter of discussion, but still discontentedly and unhappily. 'If I could but see a day of it,' he said to himself; 'if I could but see it!'

As he formed the words, the train stopped at his station, five minutes' walk from his own house, which stood on the banks of the Thames, a little way above an ugly suspension bridge.[4] He went out of the station, still discontented and unhappy, muttering 'If I could but see it! if I could but see it!' but had not gone many steps towards the river before (says our friend who tells the story) all that discontent and trouble seemed to slip off him.

It was a beautiful night of early winter, the air just sharp enough to be refreshing after the hot room and the stinking railway carriage. The wind, which had lately turned a point or two north of west, had blown the sky clear of all cloud save a light fleck or two which went swiftly down the heavens. There was a young moon half way up the sky, and as the home-farer caught sight of it, tangled in the branches of a tall old elm, he could scarce bring to his mind the shabby London suburb where he was, and he felt as if he were in a pleasant country place – pleasanter, indeed, than the deep country was as he had known it.

He came right down to the river-side, and lingered a little, looking over the low wall to note the moonlit river, near upon high water, go swirling and glittering up to Chiswick Eyot; as for the ugly bridge below, he did not notice it or think of it, except when for a moment (says our friend) it struck him that he missed the row of lights downstream. Then he turned to his house door and let himself in; and even as he shut the door to, disappeared all remembrance of that brilliant logic and foresight which had so illuminated the recent discussion; and, of the discussion itself there remained no trace, save a vague hope, that was now become a pleasure, for days of peace and rest, and cleanness and smiling goodwill.

In this mood he tumbled into bed, and fell asleep after his wont, in two minutes' time; but (contrary to his wont) woke up again not long after in that curiously wide-awake condition which sometimes surprises even good sleepers; a condition under which we feel all our wits preternaturally sharpened, while all the miserable muddles we have ever got into, all the disgraces and losses of our lives, will insist

on thrusting themselves forward for the consideration of those sharpened wits.

In this state he lay (says our friend) till he had almost begun to
enjoy it: till the tale of his stupidities amused him, and the entanglements before him, which he saw so clearly, began to shape themselves
into an amusing story for him.

He heard one o'clock strike, then two and then three; after which
he fell asleep again. Our friend says that from that sleep he awoke
once more, and afterwards went through such surprising adventures
that he thinks that they should be told to our comrades and indeed
the public in general, and therefore proposes to tell them now. But,
says he, I think it would be better if I told them in the first person, as
if it were myself who had gone through them; which, indeed, will be
the easier and more natural to me, since I understand the feelings
and desires of the comrade of whom I am telling better than any one
else in the world does.

Chapter II
A MORNING BATH

Well, I awoke, and found that I had kicked my bedclothes off; and
no wonder, for it was hot and the sun shining brightly. I jumped up
and washed and hurried on my clothes, but in a hazy and half-awake
condition, as if I had slept for a long, long while, and could not shake
off the weight of slumber. In fact, I rather took it for granted that I
was at home in my own room than saw that it was so.

When I was dressed, I felt the place so hot that I made haste to
get out of the room and out of the house; and my first feeling was a
delicious relief caused by the fresh air and pleasant breeze; my
second, as I began to gather my wits together, mere measureless
wonder: for it was winter when I went to bed the last night, and now,
by witness of the river-side trees, it was summer, a beautiful bright
morning seemingly of early June. However, there was still the
Thames sparkling under the sun, and near high water, as last night I
had seen it gleaming under the moon.

I had by no means shaken off the feeling of oppression, and wherever I might have been should scarce have been quite conscious of the place; so it was no wonder that I felt rather puzzled in despite of the familiar face of the Thames. Withal I felt dizzy and queer; and remembering that people often got a boat and had a swim in mid-stream, I thought I would do no less. It seems very early, quoth I to myself, but I daresay I shall find some one at Biffin's to take me. However, I didn't get as far as Biffin's, or even turn to my left thitherward, because just then I began to see that there was a landing-stage right before me in front of my house: in fact, on the place where my next-door neighbour had rigged one up, though somehow it didn't look like that either. Down I went on to it, and sure enough among the empty boats moored to it lay a man on his sculls in a solid-looking tub of a boat clearly meant for bathers. He nodded to me, and bade me good-morning as if he expected me, so I jumped in without any words, and he paddled away quietly as I peeled for my swim. As he went, I looked down on the water, and couldn't help saying:

'How clear the water is this morning!'

'Is it?' said he; 'I didn't notice it. You know the flood-tide always thickens it a bit.'

'H'm,' said I, 'I have seen it pretty muddy even at half-ebb.'

He said nothing in answer, but seemed rather astonished; and as he now lay just stemming the tide, and I had my clothes off, I jumped in without more ado. Of course when I had my head above water again I turned towards the tide, and my eyes naturally sought for the bridge, and so utterly astonished was I by what I saw, that I forgot to strike out, and went spluttering under water again, and when I came up made straight for the boat; for I felt that I must ask some questions of my waterman, so bewildering had been the half-sight I had seen from the face of the river with the water hardly out of my eyes; though by this time I was quit of the slumbrous and dizzy feeling, and was wide-awake and clear-headed.

As I got in up the steps which he had lowered, and he held out his hand to help me, we went drifting speedily up towards Chiswick; but now he caught up the sculls and brought her head round again, and said:

'A short swim, neighbour; but perhaps you find the water cold this morning, after your journey. Shall I put you ashore at once, or would you like to go down to Putney before breakfast?'

He spoke in a way so unlike what I should have expected from a Hammersmith waterman, that I stared at him, as I answered, 'Please to hold her a little; I want to look about me a bit.'

'All right,' he said; 'it's no less pretty in its way here than it is off Barn Elms; it's jolly everywhere this time in the morning. I'm glad you got up early; it's barely five o'clock yet.'

If I was astonished with my sight of the river banks, I was no less astonished at my waterman, now that I had time to look at him and see him with my head and eyes clear.

He was a handsome young fellow, with a peculiarly pleasant and friendly look about his eyes, – an expression which was quite new to me then, though I soon became familiar with it. For the rest, he was dark-haired and berry-brown of skin, well-knit and strong, and obviously used to exercising his muscles, but with nothing rough or coarse about him, and clean as might be. His dress was not like any modern work-a-day clothes I had seen, but would have served very well as a costume for a picture of fourteenth-century life: it was of dark blue cloth, simple enough, but of fine web, and without a stain on it. He had a brown leather belt round his waist, and I noticed that its clasp was of damascened steel beautifully wrought. In short, he seemed to be like some specially manly and refined young gentleman, playing waterman for a spree, and I concluded that this was the case.

I felt that I must make some conversation; so I pointed to the Surrey bank, where I noticed some light plank stages running down the foreshore, with windlasses at the landward end of them, and said, 'What are they doing with those things here? If we were on the Tay, I should have said that they were for drawing the salmon-nets; but here—'

'Well,' said he, smiling, 'of course that is what they *are* for. Where there are salmon, there are likely to be salmon-nets, Tay or Thames; but of course they are not always in use; we don't want salmon *every* day of the season.'

I was going to say, 'But is this the Thames?' but held my peace in my wonder, and turned my bewildered eyes eastward to look at the bridge again, and thence to the shores of the London river; and surely there was enough to astonish me. For though there was a bridge across the stream and houses on its banks, how all was changed from last night! The soap-works with their smoke-vomiting chimneys were gone; the engineer's works gone; the lead-works gone; and no sound of riveting and hammering came down the west wind from Thorneycroft's. Then the bridge! I had perhaps dreamed of such a bridge, but never seen such an one out of an illuminated manuscript; for not even the Ponte Vecchio at Florence came anywhere near it. It was of stone arches, splendidly solid, and as graceful as they were strong; high enough also to let ordinary river traffic through easily. Over the parapet showed quaint and fanciful little buildings, which I supposed to be booths or shops, beset with painted and gilded vanes and spirelets. The stone was a little weathered, but showed no marks of the grimy sootiness which I was used to on every London building more than a year old. In short, to me a wonder of a bridge.

The sculler noted my eager astonished look, and said, as if in answer to my thoughts:

'Yes, it *is* a pretty bridge, isn't it? Even the up-stream bridges, which are so much smaller, are scarcely daintier, and the down-stream ones are scarcely more dignified and stately.'

I found myself saying, almost against my will, 'How old is it?'

'Oh, not very old,' he said; 'it was built, or at least opened, in 2003.[5] There used to be a rather plain timber bridge before then.'

The date shut my mouth as if a key had been turned in a padlock fixed to my lips; for I saw that something inexplicable had happened, and that if I said much, I should be mixed up in a game of cross questions and crooked answers. So I tried to look unconcerned, and to glance in a matter-of-course way at the banks of the river, though this is what I saw up to the bridge and a little beyond; say as far as the site of the soap-works. Both shores had a line of very pretty houses, low and not large, standing back a little way from the river; they were mostly built of red brick and roofed with tiles, and looked, above all, comfortable, and as if they were, so to say, alive and sympathetic with the life of the dwellers in them. There was a continuous garden in front of them, going down to the water's edge, in which the flowers were now blooming luxuriantly, and sending delicious waves of summer scent over the eddying stream. Behind the houses, I could see great trees rising, mostly planes, and looking down the water there were the reaches towards Putney almost as if they were a lake with a forest shore, so thick were the big trees; and I said aloud, but as if to myself:

'Well, I'm glad that they have not built over Barn Elms.'

I blushed for my fatuity as the words slipped out of my mouth, and my companion looked at me with a half smile which I thought I understood; so to hide my confusion I said, 'Please take me ashore now: I want to get my breakfast.'

He nodded, and brought her head round with a sharp stroke, and in a trice we were at the landing-stage again. He jumped out and I followed him; and of course I was not surprised to see him wait, as if for the inevitable after-piece that follows the doing of a service to a fellow-citizen. So I put my hand into my waistcoat-pocket, and said, 'How much?' though still with the uncomfortable feeling that perhaps I was offering money to a gentleman.

He looked puzzled, and said, 'How much? I don't quite understand what you are asking about. Do you mean the tide? If so, it is close on the turn now.'

I blushed, and said, stammering, 'Please don't take it amiss if I ask you; I mean no offence: but what ought I to pay you? You see I am a stranger, and don't know your customs – or your coins.'

And therewith I took a handful of money out of my pocket, as one does in a foreign country. And by the way, I saw that the silver had oxydized, and was like a black-leaded stove in colour.

He still seemed puzzled, but not at all offended; and he looked at the coins with some curiosity. I thought, Well after all, he *is* a waterman, and is considering what he may venture to take. He seems such a nice fellow that I'm sure I don't grudge him a little over-payment. I wonder, by the way, whether I couldn't hire him as a guide for a day or two, since he is so intelligent.

Therewith my new friend said thoughtfully:

'I think I know what you mean. You think that I have done you a service; so you feel yourself bound to give me something which I am not to give to a neighbour, unless he has done something special for me. I have heard of this kind of thing; but pardon me for saying, that

49

it seems to us a troublesome and roundabout custom; and we don't know how to manage it. And you see this ferrying and giving people casts about the water is my *business*, which I would do for anybody; so to take gifts in connection with it would look very queer. Besides, if one person gave me something, then another might, and another, and so on; and I hope you won't think me rude if I say that I shouldn't know where to stow away so many mementoes of friendship.'

And he laughed loud and merrily, as if the idea of being paid for his work was a very funny joke. I confess I began to be afraid that the man was mad, though he looked sane enough; and I was rather glad to think that I was a good swimmer, since we were so close to a deep swift stream. However, he went on by no means like a madman:

'As to your coins, they are curious, but not very old; they seem to be all of the reign of Victoria; you might give them to some scantily-furnished museum. Ours has enough of such coins, besides a fair number of earlier ones, many of which are beautiful, whereas these nineteenth-century ones are so beastly ugly, ain't they? We have a piece of Edward III, with the king in a ship, and little leopards and fleurs-de-lys all along the gunwale, so delicately worked. You see,' he said, with something of a smirk, 'I am fond of working in gold and fine metals; this buckle here is an early piece of mine.'

No doubt I looked a little shy of him under the influence of that doubt as to his sanity. So he broke off short, and said in a kind voice:

'But I see that I am boring you, and I ask your pardon. For, not to mince matters, I can tell that you *are* a stranger, and must come from a place very unlike England. But also it is clear that it won't do to overdose you with information about this place, and that you had best suck it in little by little. Further, I should take it as very kind in you if you would allow me to be the showman of our new world to you, since you have stumbled on me first. Though indeed it will be a mere kindness on your part, for almost anybody would make as good a guide, and many much better.'

There certainly seemed no flavour in him of Colney Hatch;[6] and besides I thought I could easily shake him off if it turned out that he really was mad; so I said:

'It is a very kind offer, but it is difficult for me to accept it, unless—' I was going to say, Unless you will let me pay you properly; but fearing to stir up Colney Hatch again, I changed the sentence into, 'I fear I shall be taking you away from your work – or your amusement.'

'Oh,' he said, 'don't trouble about that, because it will give me an opportunity of doing a good turn to a friend of mine who wants to take my work here. He is a weaver from Yorkshire, who has rather overdone himself between his weaving and his mathematics, both indoor work, you see; and being a great friend of mine, he naturally came to me to get him some outdoor work. If you think you can put up with me, pray take me as your guide.'

He added presently: 'It is true that I have promised to go upstream to some special friends of mine, for the hay-harvest; but they won't be ready for us for more than a week: and besides, you might go with me, you know, and see some very nice people, besides making notes of our ways in Oxfordshire. You could hardly do better if you want to see the country.'

I felt myself obliged to thank him, whatever might come of it; and he added eagerly:

'Well, then, that's settled. I will give my friend a call; he is living in the Guest House like you, and if he isn't up yet, he ought to be this fine summer morning.'

Therewith he took a little silver bugle-horn from his girdle and blew two or three sharp but agreeable notes on it; and presently from the house which stood on the site of my old dwelling (of which more hereafter) another young man came sauntering towards us. He was not so well-looking or so strongly made as my sculler friend, being sandy-haired, rather pale, and not stout-built; but his face was not wanting in that happy and friendly expression which I had noticed in his friend. As he came up smiling towards us, I saw with pleasure that I must give up the Colney Hatch theory as to the waterman, for no two madmen ever behaved as they did before a sane man. His dress also was of the same cut as the first man's, though somewhat gayer, the surcoat being light green with a golden spray embroidered on the breast, and his belt being of filigree silverwork.

He gave me good-day very civilly, and greeting his friend joyously, said:

'Well, Dick, what is it this morning? Am I to have my work or rather your work? I dreamed last night that we were off up the river fishing.'

'All right, Bob,' said my sculler; 'you will drop into my place, and if you find it too much, there is George Brightling on the look-out for a stroke of work, and he lives close handy to you. But see, here is a stranger who is willing to amuse me to-day by taking me as his guide about our countryside; so you may imagine I don't want to lose the opportunity; so you had better take to the boat at once. But in any case I shouldn't have kept you out of it for long, since I am due in the hay-fields in a few days.'

The newcomer rubbed his hands with glee, but turning to me, said in a friendly voice:

'Neighbour, both you and friend Dick are lucky, and will have a good time to-day, as indeed I shall too. But you had better come in with me at once and get something to eat lest you should forget your dinner in your amusement. I suppose you came into the Guest House after I had gone to bed last night?'

I nodded, not caring to enter into a long explanation which would have led to nothing, and which in truth by this time I should have begun to doubt myself. And we all three turned toward the door of the Guest House.

Chapter III
THE GUEST HOUSE AND BREAKFAST THEREIN

I lingered a little behind the others to have a stare at this house, which, as I have told you, stood on the site of my old dwelling.

It was a longish building with its gable ends turned away from the road, and long traceried windows coming rather low down set in the wall that faced us. It was very handsomely built of red brick with a lead roof; and high up above the windows there ran a frieze of figure subjects in baked clay, very well executed, and designed with a force and directness which I had never noticed in modern work before. The subjects I recognized at once, and indeed was very particularly familiar with them.

However, all this I took in in a minute; for we were presently within doors, and standing in a hall with a floor of marble mosaic and an open timber roof. There were no windows on the side opposite to the river, but arches below leading into chambers, one of which showed a glimpse of a garden beyond, and above them a long space of wall gaily painted (in fresco, I thought) with similar subjects to those of the frieze outside; everything about the place was handsome and generously solid as to material; and though it was not very large (somewhat smaller than Crosby Hall[7] perhaps), one felt in it that exhilarating sense of space and freedom which satisfactory architecture always gives to an unanxious man who is in the habit of using his eyes.

In this pleasant place, which of course I knew to be the hall of the Guest House, three young women were flitting to and fro. As they were the first of the sex I had seen on this eventful morning, I naturally looked at them very attentively, and found them at least as good as the gardens, the architecture, and the male men. As to their dress, which of course I took note of, I should say that they were decently veiled with drapery, and not bundled up with millinery; that they were clothed like women, not upholstered like arm-chairs, as most women of our time are. In short, their dress was somewhat between that of the ancient classical costume and the simpler forms of the fourteenth-century garments, though it was clearly not an imitation of either: the materials were light and gay to suit the season. As to the women themselves, it was pleasant indeed to see them, they were so kind and happy-looking in expression of face, so shapely and well-knit of body, and thoroughly healthy-looking and strong. All were at least comely, and one of them very handsome and regular of feature. They came up to us at once merrily and without the least affectation of shyness, and all three shook hands with me as if I were a friend newly come back from a long journey: though I could not help noticing that they looked askance at my garments; for I had on my clothes of last night, and at the best was never a dressy person.

A word or two from Robert the weaver, and they bustled about on our behoof, and presently came and took us by the hands and led us to a table in the pleasantest corner of the hall, where our breakfast was spread for us; and, as we sat down, one of them hurried out by the chambers aforesaid, and came back again in a little while with a great bunch of roses, very different in size and quality to what Hammersmith had been wont to grow, but very like the produce of an old country garden. She hurried back thence into the buttery, and came back once more with a delicately made glass, into which she put the flowers and set then down in the midst of our table. One of the others, who had run off also, then came back with a big cabbage-leaf filled with strawberries, some of them barely ripe, and said as she set them on the table, 'There, now; I thought of that before I got up this morning; but looking at the stranger here getting into your boat, Dick, put it out of my head; so that I was not before *all* the blackbirds: however, there are a few about as good as you will get them anywhere in Hammersmith this morning.'

Robert patted her on the head in a friendly manner; and we fell to on our breakfast, which was simple enough, but most delicately cooked, and set on the table with much daintiness. The bread was particularly good, and was of several different kinds, from the big, rather close, dark-coloured, sweet-tasting farmhouse loaf, which was most to my liking, to the thin pipe-stems of wheaten crust, such as I have eaten in Turin.

As I was putting the first mouthfuls into my mouth, my eye caught a carved and gilded inscription on the panelling, behind what we should have called the High Table in an Oxford college hall, and a familiar name in it forced me to read it through. Thus it ran:

GUESTS AND NEIGHBOURS, ON THE SITE OF THIS GUEST-HALL ONCE
STOOD THE LECTURE-ROOM OF THE HAMMERSMITH SOCIALISTS.
DRINK A GLASS TO THE MEMORY! MAY 1962

It is difficult to tell you how I felt as I read these words, and I suppose my face showed how much I was moved, for both my friends looked curiously at me, and there was silence between us for a little while.

Presently the weaver, who was scarcely so well mannered a man as the ferryman, said to me rather awkwardly:

'Guest, we don't know what to call you: is there any indiscretion in asking you your name?'

'Well,' said I, 'I have some doubts about it myself; so suppose you call me Guest, which is a family name you know, and add William to it if you please.'

Dick nodded kindly to me, but a shade of anxiousness passed over the weaver's face, and he said:

'I hope you don't mind my asking, but would you tell me where you come from? I am curious about such things for good reasons, literary reasons.'

Dick was clearly kicking him underneath the table; but he was not much abashed, and awaited my answer somewhat eagerly. As for me, I was just going to blurt out 'Hammersmith', when I bethought me what an entanglement of cross purposes that would lead us into; so I took time to invent a lie with circumstance, guarded by a little truth, and said:

'You see, I have been such a long time away from Europe that things seem strange to me now; but I was born and bred on the edge of Epping Forest; Walthamstow and Woodford, to wit.'

'A pretty place too,' broke in Dick, 'a very jolly place, now that the trees have had time to grow again since the great clearing of houses in 1955.'[8]

Quoth the irrepressible weaver: 'Dear neighbour, since you knew the Forest some time ago, could you tell me what truth there is in the rumour that in the nineteenth century the trees were all pollards?'

This was catching me on my archaeological natural-history side, and I fell into the trap without any thought of where and when I was; so I began on it, while one of the girls, the handsome one, who had been scattering little twigs of lavender and other sweet-smelling herbs about the floor, came near to listen, and stood behind me with her hand on my shoulder, in which she held some of the plant that I used to call balm: its strong sweet smell brought back to my mind my very early days in the kitchen-garden at Woodford, and the large blue plums which grew on the wall beyond the sweet-herb patch, – a connection of memories which all boys will see at once.

I started off: 'When I was a boy, and for long after, except for a piece about Queen Elizabeth's Lodge, and for the part about High

Beech;[9] the Forest was almost wholly made up of pollard hornbeams mixed with holly thickets. But when the Corporation of London took it over about twenty-five years ago, the topping and lopping, which was a part of the old commoners' rights, came to an end, and the trees were let to grow. But I have not seen the place now for many years, except once, when we Leaguers went a-pleasuring to High Beech. I was very much shocked then to see how it was built-over and altered; and the other day we heard that the philistines were going to landscape-garden it. But what you were saying about the building being stopped and the trees growing is only too good news; – only you know—'

At that point I suddenly remembered Dick's date, and stopped short rather confused. The eager weaver didn't notice my confusion, but said hastily, as if he were almost aware of his breach of good manners, 'But I say, how old are you?'

Dick and the pretty girl both burst out laughing, as if Robert's conduct were excusable on the grounds of eccentricity; and Dick said amidst his laughter:

'Hold hard, Bob; this questioning of guests won't do. Why, much learning is spoiling you. You remind me of the radical cobblers in the silly old novels, who, according to the authors, were prepared to trample down all good manners in the pursuit of utilitarian knowledge. The fact is, I begin to think that you have so muddled your head with mathematics, and with grubbing into those idiotic old books about political economy (he he!), that you scarcely know how to behave. Really, it is about time for you to take to some open-air work, so that you may clear away the cobwebs from your brain.'

The weaver only laughed good-humouredly; and the girl went up to him and patted his cheek and said laughingly, 'Poor fellow! he was born so.'

As for me, I was a little puzzled, but I laughed also, partly for company's sake, and partly with pleasure at their unanxious happiness and good temper; and before Robert could make the excuse to me which he was getting ready, I said:

'But, neighbours' (I had caught up that word), 'I don't in the least mind answering questions, when I can do so: ask me as many as you please; it's fun for me. I will tell you all about Epping Forest when I was a boy, if you please; and as to my age, I'm not a fine lady, you know, so why shouldn't I tell you? I'm hard on fifty-six.'

In spite of the recent lecture on good manners, the weaver could not help giving a long 'whew' of astonishment, and the others were so amused by his *naïveté* that the merriment flitted all over their faces, though for courtesy's sake they forbore actual laughter; while I looked from one to the other in a puzzled manner, and at last said:

'Tell me, please, what is amiss: you know I want to learn from you. And please laugh; only tell me.'

Well, they *did* laugh, and I joined them again, for the above-stated reasons. But at last the pretty woman said coaxingly:

'Well, well, he *is* rude, poor fellow! but you see I may as well tell you what he is thinking about: he means that you look rather old for your age. But surely there need be no wonder in that, since you have been travelling; and clearly from all you have been saying, in unsocial countries. It has often been said, and no doubt truly, that one ages very quickly if one lives amongst unhappy people. Also they say that southern England is a good place for keeping good looks.' She blushed and said: 'How old am I, do you think?'

'Well,' quoth I, 'I have always been told that a woman is as old as she looks, so without offence or flattery, I should say that you were twenty.'

She laughed merrily, and said, 'I am well served out for fishing for compliments, since I have to tell you the truth, to wit, that I am forty-two.'

I stared at her, and drew musical laughter from her again; but I might well stare, for there was not a careful line on her face; her skin was as smooth as ivory, her cheeks full and round, her lips as red as the roses she had brought in; her beautiful arms, which she had bared for her work, firm and well-knit from shoulder to wrist. She blushed a little under my gaze, though it was clear that she had taken me for a man of eighty; so to pass it off I said:

'Well, you see, the old saw is proved right again, and I ought not to have let you tempt me into asking you a rude question.'

She laughed again and said: 'Well, lads, old and young, I must get to my work now. We shall be rather busy here presently; and I want to clear it off soon, for I began to read a pretty old book yesterday, and I want to get on with it this morning; so good-bye for the present.'

She waved a hand to us, and stepped lightly down the hall, taking (as Scott says[10]) at least part of the sun from our table as she went.

When she was gone, Dick said, 'Now, guest, won't you ask a question or two of our friend here? It is only fair that you should have your turn.'

'I shall be very glad to answer them,' said the weaver.

'If I ask you any questions, sir,' said I, 'they will not be very severe; but since I hear that you are a weaver, I should like to ask you something about that craft, as I am – or was – interested in it.'

'Oh,' said he, 'I shall not be of much use to you there, I'm afraid. I only do the most mechanical kind of weaving, and am in fact but a poor craftsman, unlike Dick here. Then besides the weaving, I do a little with machine printing and composing, though I am little use at the finer kinds of printing; and moreover machine printing is beginning to die out, along with the waning of the plague of book-making; so I have had to turn to other things that I have a taste for, and have taken to mathematics; and also I am writing a sort of antiquarian book about the peaceable and private history, so to say, of the end of the nineteenth century, – more for the sake of giving a picture of the country before the fighting began than for anything else. That was why I asked you those questions about Epping Forest. You have rather puzzled me, I confess, though your information was so interesting. But later on, I hope, we may have some more talk together, when our friend Dick isn't here. I know he thinks me rather a grinder, and despises me for not being very deft with my hands: that's the way nowadays. From what I have read of the nineteenth-century literature (and I have read a good deal), it is clear to me that this is a kind of revenge for the stupidity of that day, which despised everybody who *could* use his hands. But, Dick, old fellow, *Ne quid nimis!*[11] Don't overdo it!'

'Come now,' said Dick, 'am I likely to? Am I not the most tolerant man in the world? Am I not quite contented so long as you don't make me learn mathematics, or go into your new science of aesthetics, and let me do a little practical aesthetics with my gold and steel, and the blowpipe and the nice little hammer? But, hillo! here comes

another questioner for you, my poor guest. I say, Bob, you must help
me to defend him now.'

'Here, Boffin,'[12] he cried out, after a pause; 'here we are, if you
must have it!'

I looked over my shoulder, and saw something flash and gleam in
the sunlight that lay across the hall; so I turned round, and at my
ease saw a splendid figure slowly sauntering over the pavement; a
man whose surcoat was embroidered most copiously as well as
elegantly, so that the sun flashed back from him as if he had been
clad in golden armour. The man himself was tall, dark-haired, and
exceedingly handsome, and though his face was no less kindly in
expression than that of the others, he moved with that somewhat
haughty mien which great beauty is apt to give to both men and
women. He came and sat down at our table with a smiling face,
stretching out his long legs and hanging his arm over the chair in the
slowly graceful way which tall and well-built people may use without
affectation. He was a man in the prime of life, but looked as happy as
a child who has just got a new toy. He bowed gracefully to me and
said:

'I see clearly that you are the guest, of whom Annie has just told
me, who have come from some distant country that does not know
of us, or our ways of life. So I daresay you would not mind answering
me a few questions; for you see—'

Here Dick broke in: 'No, please Boffin! let it alone for the present.
Of course you want the guest to be happy and comfortable; and how
can that be if he has to trouble himself with answering all sorts of
questions while he is still confused with the new customs and people
about him? No, no: I am going to take him where he can ask
questions himself, and have them answered; that is, to my great-
grandfather in Bloomsbury: and I am sure you can't have anything to
say against that. So instead of bothering, you had much better go out
to James Allen's and get a carriage for me, as I shall drive him up
myself; and please tell Jim to let me have the old grey, for I can
drive a wherry much better than a carriage. Jump up, old fellow, and
don't be disappointed; our guest will keep himself for you and your
stories.'

I stared at Dick; for I wondered at his speaking to such a

dignified-looking personage so familiarly, not to say curtly; for I thought that this Mr Boffin, in spite of his well-known name out of Dickens, must be at the least a senator of these strange people. However, he got up and said, 'All right, old oar-wearer, whatever you like; this is not one of my busy days; and though' (with a condescending bow to me) 'my pleasure of a talk with this learned guest is put off, I admit that he ought to see your worthy kinsman as soon as possible. Besides, perhaps he will be the better able to answer *my* questions after his own have been answered.'

And therewith he turned and swung himself out of the hall.

When he was well gone, I said: 'Is it wrong to ask what Mr Boffin is? whose name, by the way, reminds me of many pleasant hours passed in reading Dickens.'

Dick laughed. 'Yes, yes,' said he, 'as it does us. I see you take the allusion. Of course his real name is not Boffin, but Henry Johnson; we only call him Boffin as a joke, partly because he is a dustman, and partly because he will dress so showily, and get as much gold on him as a baron of the Middle Ages. As why should he not if he likes? only we are his special friends, you know, so of course we jest with him.'

I held my tongue for some time after that; but Dick went on:

'He is a capital fellow, and you can't help liking him; but he has a weakness: he will spend his time in writing reactionary novels, and is very proud of getting the local colour right, as he calls it; and as he thinks you come from some forgotten corner of the earth, where people are unhappy, and consequently interesting to a story-teller, he thinks he might get some information out of you. Oh, he will be quite straightforward with you, for that matter. Only for your own comfort beware of him!'

'Well, Dick,' said the weaver, doggedly, 'I think his novels are very good.'

'Of course, you do,' said Dick; 'birds of a feather flock together; mathematics and antiquarian novels stand on much the same footing. But here he comes again.'

And in effect the Golden Dustman hailed us from the hall-door; so we all got up and went into the porch, before which, with a strong grey horse in the shafts, stood a carriage ready for us which I could not help noticing. It was light and handy, but had none of that sickening vulgarity which I had known as inseparable from the carriages of our time, especially the 'elegant' ones, but was as graceful and pleasant in line as a Wessex waggon. We got in, Dick and I. The girls, who had come into the porch to see us off, waved their hands to us; the weaver nodded kindly; the dustman bowed as gracefully as a troubadour; Dick shook the reins, and we were off.

Chapter IV
A MARKET BY THE WAY

We turned away from the river at once, and were soon in the main road that runs through Hammersmith. But I should have had no guess as to where I was, if I had not started from the waterside; for King Street[13] was gone, and the highway ran through wide sunny meadows and garden-like tillage. The Creek, which we crossed at once, had been rescued from its culvert, and as we went over its pretty bridge we saw its waters, yet swollen by the tide, covered with gay boats of different sizes. There were houses about, some on the road, some amongst the fields with pleasant lanes leading down to them, and each surrounded by a teeming garden. They were all pretty in design, and as solid as might be, but countrified in appearance, like yeomen's dwellings; some of them red brick like those by the river, but more of timber and plaster, which were by the necessity of their construction so like mediaeval houses of the same materials that I fairly felt as if I were alive in the fourteenth century; a sensation helped out by the costume of the people that we met or passed, in whose dress there was nothing 'modern'. Almost everybody was gaily dressed, but especially the women, who were so well-looking or even so handsome, that I could scarcely refrain my tongue from calling my companion's attention to the fact. Some faces I saw that were thoughtful, and in these I noticed great nobility of expression, but none that had a glimmer of unhappiness, and the greater part (we came upon a good many people) were frankly and openly joyous.

I thought I knew the Broadway by the lie of the roads that still met there. On the north side of the road was a range of buildings and courts, low, but very handsomely built and ornamented, and in that way forming a great contrast to the unpretentiousness of the houses round about; while above this lower building rose the steep lead-covered roof and the buttresses and higher part of the wall of a great hall, of a splendid and exuberant style of architecture, of which one can say little more than that it seemed to me to embrace the best qualities of the Gothic of northern Europe with those of the Saracenic and Byzantine,[14] though there was no copying of any one of these styles. On the other, the south side, of the road was an octagonal building with a high roof, not unlike the Baptistry at Florence in outline, except that it was surrounded by a lean-to that clearly made an arcade or cloisters to it: it also was most delicately ornamented.

This whole mass of architecture which we had come upon so suddenly from amidst the pleasant fields was not only exquisitely beautiful in itself, but it bore upon it the expression of such generosity and abundance of life that I was exhilarated to a pitch that I had never yet reached. I fairly chuckled for pleasure. My friend seemed to understand it, and sat looking on me with a pleased and affection-ate interest. We had pulled up amongst a crowd of carts, wherein sat handsome healthy-looking people, men, women, and children very gaily dressed, and which were clearly market carts, as they were full of very tempting-looking country produce.

I said, 'I need not ask if this is a market, for I see clearly that it is; but what market is it that it is so splendid? And what is the glorious hall there, and what is the building on the south side?'

'Oh,' said he, 'it is just our Hammersmith market; and I am glad you like it so much, for we are really proud of it. Of course the hall inside is our winter Mote-House;[15] for in summer we mostly meet in the fields down by the river opposite Barn Elms. The building on our right hand is our theatre: I hope you like it.'

'I should be a fool if I didn't,' said I.

He blushed a little as he said: 'I am glad of that, too, because I had a hand in it: I made the great doors, which are of damascened bronze. We will look at them later in the day, perhaps: but we ought to be getting on now. As to the market, this is not one of our busy days; so we shall do better with it another time, because you will see more people.'

I thanked him, and said: 'Are these the regular country people? What very pretty girls there are amongst them.'

As I spoke, my eye caught the face of a beautiful woman, tall, dark-haired, and white-skinned, dressed in a pretty light-green dress in honour of the season and the hot day, who smiled kindly on me, and more kindly still, I thought, on Dick; so I stopped a minute, but presently went on:

'I ask because I do not see any of the country-looking people I should have expected to see at a market – I mean selling things there.'

'I don't understand,' said he, 'what kind of people you would expect to see; nor quite what you mean by "country" people. These are the neighbours, and that like they run in the Thames Valley. There are parts of these islands which are rougher and rainier than we are here, and there people are rougher in their dress; and they themselves are tougher and more hard-bitten than we are to look at. But some people like their looks better than ours; they say they have more character in them – that's the word. Well, it's a matter of taste. – Anyhow, the cross between us and them generally turns out well,' added he, thoughtfully.

I heard him, though my eyes were turned away from him, for that pretty girl was just disappearing through the gate with her big basket of early peas, and I felt that disappointed kind of feeling which overtakes one when one has seen an interesting or lovely face in the streets which one is never likely to see again; and I was silent a little. At last I said: 'What I mean is, that I haven't seen any poor people about – not one.'

He knit his brows, looked puzzled, and said: 'No, naturally; if anybody is poorly, he is likely to be within doors, or at best crawling about the garden: but I don't know of any one sick at present. Why should you expect to see poorly people on the road?'

'No, no,' I said: 'I don't mean sick people. I mean poor people, you know; rough people.'

'No,' said he, smiling merrily, 'I really do not know. The fact is, you must come along quick to my great-grandfather, who will understand you better than I do. Come on, Greylocks!' Therewith he shook the reins, and we jogged along merrily eastward.

Chapter V
CHILDREN ON THE ROAD

Past the Broadway there were fewer houses on either side. We presently crossed a pretty little brook that ran across a piece of land dotted over with trees, and awhile after came to another market and town-hall, as we should call it. Although there was nothing familiar to me in its surroundings, I knew pretty well where we were, and was not surprised when my guide said briefly, 'Kensington Market'.

Just after this we came into a short street of houses; or rather, one long house on either side of the way, built of timber and plaster, and with a pretty arcade over the footway before it.

Quoth Dick: 'This is Kensington proper. People are apt to gather here rather thick, for they like the romance of the wood; and naturalists haunt it, too; for it is a wild spot even here, what there is of it; for it does not go far to the south; it goes from here northward and west right over Paddington and a little way down Notting Hill: thence it runs north-east to Primrose Hill, and so on; rather a narrow strip of it gets through Kingsland to Stoke-Newington and Clapton, where it spreads out along the heights above the Lea marshes; on the other side of which, as you know, is Epping Forest holding out a hand to it. This part we are just coming to is called Kensington Gardens; though why "gardens" I don't know.'

I rather longed to say, 'Well, *I* know'; but there were so many things about me which I did *not* know, in spite of his assumptions, that I thought it better to hold my tongue.

The road plunged at once into a beautiful wood spreading out on either side, but obviously much further on the north side, where even the oaks and sweet chestnuts were of a good growth; while the quicker-growing trees (amongst which I thought the planes and sycamores too numerous) were very big and fine-grown.

It was exceedingly pleasant in the dappled shadow, for the day was growing as hot as need be, and the coolness and shade soothed my excited mind into a condition of dreamy pleasure, so that I felt as if I should like to go on for ever through that balmy freshness. My companion seemed to share in my feelings, and let the horse go slower and slower as he sat inhaling the green forest scents, chief amongst which was the smell of the trodden bracken near the wayside.

Romantic as this Kensington wood was, however, it was not lonely. We came on many groups both coming and going, or wandering in the edges of the wood. Amongst these were many children from six to eight years old up to sixteen or seventeen. They seemed to me to be especially fine specimens of their race, and were clearly enjoying themselves to the utmost; some of them were hanging about little tents pitched on the greensward, and by some of these fires were burning, with pots hanging over them gipsey fashion. Dick explained to me that there were scattered houses in the forest, and indeed we caught a glimpse of one or two. He said they were mostly quite small, such as used to be called cottages when there were slaves in the land, but they were pleasant enough and fitting for the wood.

'They must be pretty well stocked with children,' said I, pointing to the many youngsters about the way.

'Oh,' said he, 'these children do not all come from the near houses, the woodland houses, but from the countryside generally. They often make up parties, and come to play in the woods for weeks together in summer-time, living in tents, as you see. We rather encourage them to it; they learn to do things for themselves, and get to notice the wild creatures; and, you see, the less they stew inside houses the better for them. Indeed, I must tell you that many grown people will go to live in the forests through the summer; though they for the most part go to the bigger ones, like Windsor, or the Forest of Dean, or the northern wastes. Apart from the other pleasures of it, it gives them a little rough work, which I am sorry to say is getting somewhat scarce for these last fifty years.'

He broke off, and then said, 'I tell you all this, because I see that if I talk I must be answering questions, which you are thinking, even if you are not speaking them out; but my kinsman will tell you more about it.'

I saw that I was likely to get out of my depth again, and so merely for the sake of tiding over an awkwardness and to say something, I said:

'Well, the youngsters here will be all the fresher for school when the summer gets over and they have to go back again.'

'School?' he said; 'yes, what do you mean by that word? I don't see how it can have anything to do with children. We talk, indeed, of a school of herring, and a school of painting, and in the former sense we might talk of a school of children – but otherwise,' said he, laughing, 'I must own myself beaten.'

Hang it! thought I, I can't open my mouth without digging up some new complexity. I wouldn't try to set my friend right in his etymology; and I thought I had best say nothing about the boy-farms which I had been used to call schools, as I saw pretty clearly that they had disappeared; and so I said after a little fumbling, 'I was using the word in the sense of a system of education.'

'Education?' said he meditatively, 'I know enough Latin to know that the word must come from *educere*, to lead out; and I have heard it used; but I have never met anybody who could give me a clear explanation of what it means.'

You may imagine how my new friends fell in my esteem when I heard this frank avowal; and I said, rather contemptuously, 'Well, education means a system of teaching young people.'

'Why not old people also?' said he with a twinkle in his eye. 'But,' he went on, 'I can assure you our children learn, whether they go through a "system of teaching" or not. Why, you will not find one of these children about here, boy or girl, who cannot swim, and every one of them has been used to tumbling about the little forest ponies – there's one of them now! They all of them know how to cook; the bigger lads can mow; many can thatch and do odd jobs at carpentering; or they know how to keep shop. I can tell you they know plenty of things.'

'Yes, but their mental education, the teaching of their minds,' said I, kindly translating my phrase.

'Guest,' said he, 'perhaps you have not learned to do these things I have been speaking about; and if that's the case, don't run away with the idea that it doesn't take some skill to do them, and doesn't give plenty of work for one's mind: you would change your opinion if you saw a Dorsetshire lad thatching, for instance. But, however, I understand you to be speaking of book-learning; and as to that, it is a simple affair. Most children, seeing books lying about, manage to read by the time they are four years old; though I am told it has not always been so. As to writing, we do not encourage them to scrawl too early (though scrawl a little they will), because it gets them into a habit of ugly writing; and what's the use of a lot of ugly writing being done, when rough printing can be done so easily. You understand that handsome writing we like, and many people will write their books out when they make them, or get them written; I mean books of which only a few copies are needed – poems, and such like, you know. However, I am wandering from my lambs; but you must excuse me, for I am interested in this matter of writing, being myself a fair writer.'

'Well,' said I, 'about the children; when they know how to read and write, don't they learn something else – languages, for instance?'

'Of course,' he said; 'sometimes even before they can read, they can talk French, which is the nearest language talked on the other side of the water; and they soon get to know German also, which is talked by a huge number of communes and colleges on the mainland. These are the principal languages we speak in these islands, along with English or Welsh, or Irish, which is another form of Welsh; and children pick them up very quickly, because their elders all know them; and besides our guests from over-sea often bring their children with them, and the little ones get together, and rub their speech into one another.'

'And the older languages?' said I.

'Oh yes,' said he, 'they mostly learn Latin and Greek along with the modern ones, when they do anything more than merely pick up the latter.'

'And history?' said I; 'how do you teach history?'

'Well,' said he, 'when a person can read, of course he reads what he likes to; and he can easily get some one to tell him what are the best books to read on such or such a subject, or to explain what he doesn't understand in the books when he is reading them.'

'Well,' said I, 'what else do they learn? I suppose they don't all learn history?'

'No, no,' said he; 'some don't care about it; in fact, I don't think many do. I have heard my great-grandfather say that it is mostly in periods of turmoil and strife and confusion that people care much about history; and you know,' said my friend, with an amiable smile, 'we are not like that now. No; many people study facts about the make of things and the matters of cause and effect, so that knowledge increases on us, if that be good; and some, as you heard about friend Bob yonder, will spend time over mathematics. 'Tis no use forcing people's tastes.'

Said I: 'But you don't mean that children learn all these things?'

Said he: 'That depends on what you mean by children: and also you must remember how much they differ. As a rule, they don't do much reading except for a few story-books, till they are about fifteen years old; we don't encourage early bookishness: though you will find some children who *will* take to books very early; which perhaps is not good for them, but it's no use thwarting them; and very often it doesn't last long with them, and they find their level before they are twenty years old. You see, children are mostly given to imitating their elders, and when they see most people about them engaged in genuinely amusing work, like house-building and street-paving, and gardening, and the like, that is what they want to be doing; so I don't think we need fear having too many book-learned men.'

What could I say? I sat and held my peace, for fear of fresh entanglements. Besides, I was using my eyes with all my might, wondering as the old horse jogged on, when I should come into London proper, and what it would be like now.

But my companion couldn't let his subject quite drop, and went on meditatively:

'After all, I don't know that it does them much harm, even if they do grow up book-students. Such people as that, 'tis a great pleasure seeing them so happy over work which is not much sought for. And besides, these students are generally such pleasant people; so kind and sweet-tempered; so humble, and at the same time so anxious to teach everybody all that they know. Really, I like those that I have met prodigiously.'

This seemed to me such *very* queer talk that I was on the point of asking him another question; when just as we came to the top of a rising ground, down a long glade of the wood on my right I caught sight of a stately building whose outline was familiar to me, and I cried out, 'Westminster Abbey!'

'Yes,' said Dick, 'Westminster Abbey – what there is left of it.'

'Why, what have you done with it?' quoth I in terror.

'What have *we* done with it?' said he; 'nothing much, save clean it. But you know the whole outside was spoiled centuries ago: as to the inside, that remains in its beauty after the great clearance, which took place over a hundred years ago, of the beastly monuments to fools and knaves, which once blocked it up, as great-grandfather says.'

We went on a little further, and I looked to the right again, and said, in rather a doubtful tone of voice, 'Why, there are the Houses of Parliament! Do you still use them?'[16]

He burst out laughing, and was some time before he could control himself; then he clapped me on the back and said:

'I take you, neighbour; you may well wonder at our keeping them standing, and I know something about that, and my old kinsman has given me books to read about the strange game that they played there. Use them! Well, yes, they are used for a sort of subsidiary market, and a storage place for manure, and they are handy for that, being on the water-side. I believe it was intended to pull them down quite at the beginning of our days; but there was, I am told, a queer antiquarian society, which had done some service in past times, and which straightway set up its pipe against their destruction, as it has done with many other buildings, which most people looked upon as worthless, and public nuisances;[17] and it was so energetic, and had such good reasons to give, that it generally gained its point; and I must say that when all is said I am glad of it: because you know at the worst these silly old buildings serve as a kind of foil to the beautiful ones which we build now. You will see several others in these parts; the place my great-grandfather lives in, for instance, and a big building called St Paul's. And you see, in this matter we need not grudge a few poorish buildings standing, because we can always build elsewhere; nor need we be anxious as to the breeding of pleasant work in such matters, for there is always room for more and more work in a new building, even without making it pretentious. For instance, elbow-room *within* doors is to me so delightful that if I were driven to it I would almost sacrifice out-door space to it. Then, of course, there is the ornament, which, as we must all allow, may easily be overdone in mere living houses, but can hardly be in mote-halls and markets, and so forth. I must tell you, though, that my great-grandfather sometimes tells me I am a little cracked on this subject of fine building; and indeed I *do* think that the energies of mankind are chiefly of use to them for such work; for in that direction I can see no end to the work, while in many others a limit does seem possible.'

Chapter VI
A LITTLE SHOPPING

As he spoke, we came suddenly out of the woodland into a short street of handsomely built houses, which my companion named to me at once as Piccadilly: the lower part of these I should have called shops, if it had not been that, as far as I could see, the people were ignorant of the arts of buying and selling. Wares were displayed in their finely designed fronts, as if to tempt people in, and people stood and looked at them, or went in and came out with parcels under their arms, just like the real thing. On each side of the street ran an elegant arcade to protect foot-passengers, as in some of the old Italian cities. About half way down, a huge building of the kind I was now prepared to expect told me that this also was a centre of some kind, and had its special public buildings.

Said Dick: 'Here you see, is another market on a different plan from most others: the upper stories of these houses are used for guest houses; for people from all about the country are apt to drift up hither from time to time, as folk are very thick upon the ground, which you will see evidence of presently, and there are people who are fond of crowds, though I can't say that I am.'

I couldn't help smiling to see how long a tradition would last. Here was the ghost of London still asserting itself as a centre, – an intellectual centre, for aught I knew. However, I said nothing, except that I asked him to drive very slowly, as the things in the booths looked exceedingly pretty.

'Yes,' said he, 'this is a very good market for pretty things, and is mostly kept for the handsomer goods, as the Houses-of-Parliament market, where they set out cabbages and turnips and such like things, along with beer and the rougher kind of wine, is so near.'

Then he looked at me curiously, and said, 'Perhaps you would like to do a little shopping, as 'tis called?'

I looked at what I could see of my rough blue duds, which I had plenty of opportunity of contrasting with the gay attire of the citizens we had come across; and I thought that if, as seemed likely, I should presently be shown about as a curiosity for the amusement of this most unbusinesslike people, I should like to look a little less like a discharged ship's purser. But in spite of all that had happened, my hand went down into my pocket again, where to my dismay it met nothing metallic except two rusty old keys, and I remembered that amidst our talk in the guest hall at Hammersmith I had taken the cash out of my pocket to show to the pretty Annie, and had left it lying there. My face fell fifty per cent, and Dick, beholding me, said rather sharply:

'Hilloa, Guest! what's the matter now? Is it a wasp?'

'No,' said I, 'but I've left it behind.'

'Well,' said he, 'whatever you have left behind, you can get in this market again, so don't trouble yourself about it.'

I had come to my senses by this time, and remembering the astounding customs of this country, had no mind for another lecture on social economy and the Edwardian coinage; so I said only:

'My clothes— Couldn't I? You see— What do you think could be done about them?'

He didn't seem in the least inclined to laugh, but said quite gravely:

'Oh don't get new clothes yet. You see, my great-grandfather is an antiquarian, and he will want to see you just as you are. And, you know, I mustn't preach to you, but surely it wouldn't be right for you to take away people's pleasure of studying your attire, by just going and making yourself like everybody else. You feel that, don't you?' said he, earnestly.

I did *not* feel it my duty to set myself up for a scarecrow amidst this beauty-loving people, but I saw I had got across some ineradicable prejudice, and that it wouldn't do to quarrel with my new friend. So I merely said, 'Oh certainly, certainly.'

'Well,' said he, pleasantly, 'you may as well see what the inside of these booths is like: think of something you want.'

Said I: 'Could I get some tobacco and a pipe?'

'Of course,' said he; 'what was I thinking of, not asking you before? Well, Bob is always telling me that we non-smokers are a selfish lot, and I'm afraid he is right. But come along; here is a place just handy.'

Therewith he drew rein and jumped down, and I followed. A very handsome woman, splendidly clad in figured silk, was slowly passing by, looking into the windows as she went. To her quoth Dick: 'Maiden, would you kindly hold our horse while we go in for a little?' She nodded to us with a kind smile, and fell to patting the horse with her pretty hand.

'What a beautiful creature!' said I to Dick as we entered.

'What, old Greylocks?' said he, with a sly grin.

'No, no,' said I; 'Goldylocks, – the lady.'

'Well, so she is,' said he. ''Tis a good job there are so many of them that every Jack may have his Jill: else I fear that we should get fighting for them. Indeed,' said he, becoming very grave, 'I don't say that it does not happen even now, sometimes. For you know love is not a very reasonable thing, and perversity and self-will are commoner than some of our moralists think.' He added, in a still more sombre tone: 'Yes, only a month ago there was a mishap down by us, that in the end cost the lives of two men and a woman, and, as it were, put out the sunlight for us for a while. Don't ask me about it just now; I may tell you about it later on.'

By this time we were within the shop or booth, which had a counter, and shelves on the walls, all very neat, though without any pretence of showiness, but otherwise not very different to what I had been used to. Within were a couple of children – a brown-skinned boy of about twelve, who sat reading a book, and a pretty little girl of about a year older, who was sitting also reading behind the counter; they were obviously brother and sister.

'Good-morning, little neighbours,' said Dick. 'My friend here wants tobacco and a pipe; can you help him?'

'Oh yes, certainly,' said the girl with a sort of demure alertness which was somewhat amusing. The boy looked up, and fell to staring at my outlandish attire, but presently reddened and turned his head, as if he knew that he was not behaving prettily.

'Dear neighbour,' said the girl, with the most solemn countenance of a child playing at keeping shop, 'what tobacco is it you would like?'

'Latakia,' quoth I, feeling as if I were assisting at a child's game, and wondering whether I should get anything but make-believe.

But the girl took a dainty little basket from a shelf beside her, went to a jar, and took out a lot of tobacco and put the filled basket down on the counter before me, where I could both smell and see that it was excellent Latakia.

'But you haven't weighed it,' said I, 'and – and how much am I to take?'

'Why,' she said, 'I advise you to cram your bag, because you may be going where you can't get Latakia. Where is your bag?'

I fumbled about, and at last pulled out my piece of cotton print which does duty with me for a tobacco pouch. But the girl looked at it with some disdain, and said:

'Dear neighbour, I can give you something much better than that cotton rag.' And she tripped up the shop and came back presently, and as she passed the boy whispered something in his ear, and he nodded and got up and went out. The girl held up in her finger and thumb a red morocco bag, gaily embroidered, and said, 'There, I have chosen one for you, and you are to have it: it is pretty, and will hold a lot.'

Therewith she fell to cramming it with the tobacco, and laid it down by me and said, 'Now for the pipe: that also you must let me choose for you; there are three pretty ones just come in.'

She disappeared again, and came back with a big-bowled pipe in her hand, carved out of some hard wood very elaborately, and mounted in gold sprinkled with little gems. It was, in short, as pretty and gay a toy as I had ever seen; something like the best kind of Japanese work, but better.

'Dear me!' said I, when I set eyes on it, 'this is altogether too grand for me, or for anybody but the Emperor of the World. Besides, I shall lose it: I always lose my pipes.'

The child seemed rather dashed, and said, 'Don't you like it, neighbour?'

'Oh yes,' I said, 'of course I like it.'

'Well, then, take it,' said she, 'and don't trouble about losing it. What will it matter if you do? Somebody is sure to find it, and he will use it, and you can get another.'

I took it out of her hand to look at it, and while I did so, forgot my caution, and said, 'But however am I to pay for such a thing as this?'

Dick laid his hand on my shoulder as I spoke, and turning I met his eyes with a comical expression in them, which warned me against another exhibition of extinct commercial morality; so I reddened and held my tongue, while the girl simply looked at me with the deepest gravity, as if I were a foreigner blundering in my speech, for she clearly didn't understand me a bit.

'Thank you so very much,' I said at last, effusively, as I put the pipe in my pocket, not without a qualm of doubt as to whether I shouldn't find myself before a magistrate presently.

'Oh, you are so very welcome,' said the little lass, with an affectation of grown-up manners at their best which was very quaint. 'It is such a pleasure to serve dear old gentlemen like you; specially when one can see at once that you have come from far over-sea.'

'Yes, my dear,' quoth I, 'I have been a great traveller.'

As I told this lie from pure politeness, in came the lad again, with a tray in his hands, on which I saw a long flask and two beautiful glasses. 'Neighbours,' said the girl (who did all the talking, her brother being very shy, clearly), 'please to drink a glass to us before you go, since we do not have guests like this every day.'

Therewith the boy put the tray on the counter and solemnly poured out a straw-coloured wine into the long bowls. Nothing loth, I drank, for I was thirsty with the hot day; and thinks I, I am yet in the world, and the grapes of the Rhine have not yet lost their flavour; for if ever I drank good Steinberg, I drank it that morning; and I made a mental note to ask Dick how they managed to make fine wine when there were no longer labourers compelled to drink rot-gut instead of the fine wine which they themselves made.

'Don't you drink a glass to us, dear little neighbours?' said I.

'I don't drink wine,' said the lass; 'I like lemonade better: but I wish your health!'

'And I like ginger-beer better,' said the little lad.

Well, well, thought I, neither have children's tastes changed much. And therewith we gave them good-day and went out of the booth.

To my disappointment, like a change in a dream, a tall old man was holding our horse instead of the beautiful woman. He explained to us that the maiden could not wait, and that he had taken her place; and he winked at us and laughed when he saw how our faces fell, so that we had nothing for it but to laugh also.

'Where are you going?' said he to Dick.

'To Bloomsbury,' said Dick.

'If you two don't want to be alone, I'll come with you,' said the old man.

'All right,' said Dick, 'tell me when you want to get down and I'll stop for you. Let's get on.'

So we got under way again; and I asked if children generally waited on people in the markets. 'Often enough,' said he, 'when it isn't a matter of dealing with heavy weights, but by no means always. The children like to amuse themselves with it, and it is good for them, because they handle a lot of diverse wares and get to learn about them, how they are made, and where they come from, and so on. Besides, it is such very easy work that anybody can do it. It is said that in the early days of our epoch there were a good many people who were hereditarily afflicted with a disease called Idleness, because they were the direct descendants of those who in the bad times used to force other people to work for them – the people, you know, who are called slave-holders or employers of labour in the history books. Well, these Idleness-stricken people used to serve booths *all* their time, because they were fit for so little. Indeed, I believe that at one time they were actually *compelled* to do some work, because they, especially the women, got so ugly and produced such ugly children if their disease was not treated sharply, that the neighbours couldn't stand it. However, I am happy to say that all that is gone by now; the disease is either extinct, or exists in such a mild form that a short course of aperient medicine carries it off. It is sometimes called the Blue-devils now, or the Mulleygrubs.[18] Queer names, ain't they?'

'Yes,' said I, pondering much. But the old man broke in:

'Yes, all that is true, neighbour; and I have seen some of those poor women grown old. But my father used to know some of them when they were young; and he said that they were as little like young women as might be: they had hands like bunches of skewers, and wretched little arms like sticks; and waists like hour glasses, and thin lips and peaked noses and pale cheeks; and they were always pretending to be offended at anything you said or did to them. No wonder they bore ugly children, for no one except men like them could be in love with them – poor things!'

He stopped, and seemed to be musing on his past life, and then said:

'And do you know, neighbours, that once on a time people were still anxious about that disease of Idleness: at one time we gave ourselves a great deal of trouble in trying to cure people of it. Have you not read any of the medical books on the subject?'

'No,' said I; for the old man was speaking to me.

'Well,' said he, 'it was thought at the time that it was the survival of the old mediaeval disease of leprosy: it seems it was very catching, for many of the people afflicted by it were much secluded, and were waited upon by a special class of diseased persons queerly dressed up, so that they might be known. They wore amongst other garments breeches made of worsted velvet, that stuff which used to be called plush some years ago.'

All this seemed very interesting to me, and I should like to have made the old man talk more. But Dick got rather restive under so much ancient history: besides, I suspect he wanted to keep me as fresh as he could for his great-grandfather. So he burst out laughing at last, and said: 'Excuse me, neighbours, but I can't help it. Fancy people not liking to work! – it's too ridiculous. Why, even you like to work, old fellow – sometimes,' said he, affectionately patting the old horse with the whip. 'What a queer disease! it may well be called Mulleygrubs!'

And he laughed out again most boisterously; rather too much so, I thought, for his usual good manners; and I laughed with him for company's sake, but from the teeth outward only; for *I* saw nothing funny in people not liking to work, as you may well imagine.

Chapter VII
TRAFALGAR SQUARE

And now again I was busy looking about me, for we were quite clear of Piccadilly Market, and were in a region of elegantly-built much ornamented houses, which I should have called villas if they had been ugly and pretentious, which was very far from being the case. Each house stood in a garden carefully cultivated, and running over with flowers. The blackbirds were singing their best amidst the garden trees, which, except for a bay here and there, and occasional groups of limes, seemed to be all fruit-trees: there were a great many cherry-trees now all laden with fruit, and several times as we passed by a garden we were offered baskets of fine fruit by children and young girls. Amidst all these gardens and houses it was of course impossible to trace the sites of the old streets, but it seemed to me that the main roadways were the same as of old.

We came presently into a large open space, sloping somewhat toward the south, the sunny site of which had been taken advantage of for planting an orchard, mainly, as I could see, of apricot-trees, in the midst of which was a pretty gay little structure of wood, painted and gilded, that looked like a refreshment stall. From the southern side of the said orchard ran a long road, chequered over with the shadow of tall old pear-trees, at the end of which showed the high tower of the Parliament House, or Dung Market.

A strange sensation came over me; I shut my eyes to keep out the sight of the sun glittering on this fair abode of gardens, and for a moment there passed before them a phantasmagoria of another day. A great space surrounded by tall ugly houses, with an ugly church at the corner and a nondescript ugly cupolaed building at my back; the roadway thronged with a sweltering and excited crowd, dominated by omnibuses crowded with spectators. In the midst a paved be-fountained square, populated only by a few men dressed in blue, and a good many singularly ugly bronze images (one on top of a tall column). The said square guarded up to the edge of the roadway by a four-fold line of big men clad in blue, and across the southern roadway the helmets of a band of horse-soldiers, dead white in the greyness of the chilly November afternoon—

I opened my eyes to the sunlight again and looked round me, and cried out among the whispering trees and odorous blossoms, 'Trafalgar Square!'

'Yes,' said Dick, who had drawn rein again, 'so it is. I don't wonder at your finding the name ridiculous: but after all, it was nobody's business to alter it, since the name of a dead folly doesn't bite. Yet sometimes I think we might have given it a name which would have commemorated the great battle which was fought on the spot itself in 1952, – *that* was important enough, if the historians don't lie.'

'Which they generally do, or at least did,' said the old man. 'For instance, what can you make of this, neighbours? I have read a muddled account in a book – Oh a stupid book! – called James' Social Democratic History, of a fight which took place here in or about the year 1887 (I am bad at dates). Some people, says this story, were going to hold a ward-mote here, or some such thing, and the Government of London, or the Council, or the Commission, or what not other barbarous half-hatched body of fools, fell upon these citizens (as they were then called) with the armed hand. That seems too ridiculous to be true; but according to this version of the story, nothing much came of it, which certainly *is* too ridiculous to be true.'[19]

'Well,' quoth I, 'but after all your Mr James is right so far and it *is* true; except that there was no fighting, merely unarmed and peaceable people attacked by ruffians armed with bludgeons.'

'And they put up with that?' said Dick, with the first unpleasant expression I had seen on his good-tempered face.

Said I reddening: 'We *had* to put up with it; we couldn't help it.'

The old man looked at me keenly, and said: 'You seem to know a great deal about it, neighbour! And is it really true that nothing came of it?'

'This came of it,' said I, 'that a good many people were sent to prison because of it.'

'What, of the bludgeoners?' said the old man. 'Poor devils!'

'No, no,' said I, 'of the bludgeoned.'

Said the old man rather severely: 'Friend, I expect that you have been reading some rotten collection of lies, and have been taken in by it too easily.'

'I assure you,' said I, 'what I have been saying is true.'

'Well, well, I am sure you think so, neighbour,' said the old man, 'but I don't see why you should be so cocksure.'

As I couldn't explain why, I held my tongue. Meanwhile Dick, who had been sitting with knit brows, cogitating, spoke at last, and said gently and rather sadly:

'How strange to think that there have been men like ourselves, and living in this beautiful and happy country, who I suppose had feelings and affections like ourselves, who could yet do such dreadful things.'

'Yes,' said I, in a didactic tone; 'yet after all, even those days were a great improvement on the days that had gone before them. Have you not read of the Mediaeval period, and the ferocity of its criminal laws; and how in those days men fairly seemed to have enjoyed tormenting their fellow-men? – nay, for the matter of that, they made their God a tormentor and a jailer rather than anything else.'

'Yes,' said Dick, 'there are good books on that period also, some of which I have read. But as to the great improvement of the nineteenth century, I don't see it. After all, the Mediaeval folk acted after their conscience, as your remark about their God (which is true) shows, and they were ready to bear what they inflicted on others; whereas the nineteenth-century ones were hypocrites and pretended to be humane, and yet went on tormenting those whom they dared to treat so by shutting them up in prison, for no reason at all, except that they were what they themselves, the prison-masters, had forced them to be. Oh, it's horrible to think of!'

'But perhaps,' said I, 'they did not know what the prisons were like.'

Dick seemed roused, and even angry. 'More shame for them,' said he, 'when you and I know it all these years afterwards. Look you, neighbour, they couldn't fail to know what a disgrace a prison is to the Commonwealth at the best, and that their prisons were a good step on towards being at the worst.'

Quoth I: 'But have you no prisons at all now?'

As soon as the words were out of my mouth, I felt that I had made a mistake, for Dick flushed red and frowned, and the old man looked surprised and pained; and presently Dick said angrily, yet as if restraining himself somewhat:

'Man alive! how can you ask such a question? Have I not told you that we know what a prison means by the undoubted evidence of really trustworthy books, helped out by our own imaginations? And haven't you specially called me to notice that the people about the roads and streets look happy? and how could they look happy if they knew that their neighbours were shut up in prison, while they bore such things quietly? And if there were people in prison, you couldn't hide it from folk, like you may an occasional man-slaying; because that isn't done of set purpose, with a lot of people backing up the slayer in cold blood, as this prison business is. Prisons, indeed! Oh no, no, no!'

He stopped, and began to cool down, and said in a kind voice: 'But forgive me! I needn't be so hot about it, since there are *not* any prisons: I'm afraid you will think the worse of me for losing my temper. Of course, you, coming from the outlands, cannot be expected to know about these things. And now I'm afraid I have made you feel uncomfortable.'

In a way he had; but he was so generous in his heat, that I liked him the better for it, and I said: 'No, really 'tis all my fault for being so stupid. Let me change the subject, and ask you what the stately building is on our left just showing at the end of that grove of plane trees?'

'Ah,' he said, 'that is an old building built before the middle of the twentieth century, and as you see, in a queer fantastic style not over beautiful; but there are some fine things inside it, too, mostly pictures, some very old. It is called the National Gallery; I have sometimes puzzled as to what the name means: anyhow, nowadays wherever there is a place where pictures are kept as curiosities permanently it is called a National Gallery, perhaps after this one. Of course there are a good many of them up and down the country.'

I didn't try to enlighten him, feeling the task too heavy; but I pulled out my magnificent pipe and fell a-smoking, and the old horse jogged on again. As we went, I said:

'This pipe is a very elaborate toy, and you seem so reasonable in this country, and your architecture is so good, that I rather wonder at your turning out such trivialities.'

It struck me as I spoke that this was rather ungrateful of me, after having received such a fine present; but Dick didn't seem to notice my bad manners, but said:

'Well, I don't know; it *is* a pretty thing, and since nobody need make such things unless they like, I don't see why they shouldn't make them, *if* they like. Of course, if carvers were scarce they would all be busy on the architecture, as you call it, and then these "toys" (a good word) would not be made; but since there are plenty of people who can carve – in fact, almost everybody, and as work is somewhat scarce, or we are afraid it may be, folk do not discourage this kind of petty work.'

He mused a little, and seemed somewhat perturbed; but presently his face cleared, and he said: 'After all, you must admit that the pipe is a very pretty thing, with the little people under the trees all cut so clean and sweet; – too elaborate for a pipe, perhaps, but – well, it is very pretty.'

'Too valuable for its use, perhaps,' said I.

'What's that?' said he; 'I don't understand.'

I was just going in a helpless way to try to make him understand, when we came by the gates of a big rambling building, in which work of some sort seemed going on. 'What building is that?' said I, eagerly; for it was a pleasure amidst all these strange things to see something a little like what I was used to: 'it seems to be a factory.'

'Yes,' he said, 'I think I know what you mean, and that's what it is; but we don't call them factories now, but Banded-workshops; that is, places where people collect who want to work together.'

'I suppose,' said I, 'power of some sort is used there?'

'No, no,' said he. 'Why should people collect together to use power, when they can have it at the places where they live, or hard by, any two or three of them; or any one, for the matter of that? No; folk collect in these Banded-workshops to do hand-work in which working together is necessary or convenient; such work is often very pleasant. In there, for instance, they make pottery and glass, – there, you can see the tops of the furnaces. Well, of course it's handy to have fair-sized ovens and kilns and glass-pots, and a good lot of things to use them for: though of course there are a good many such places, as it would be ridiculous if a man had a liking for pot-making or glass-blowing that he should have to live in one place or be obliged to forgo the work he liked.'

'I see no smoke coming from the furnaces,' said I.

'Smoke?' said Dick; 'why should you see smoke?'

I held my tongue, and he went on: 'It's a nice place inside, though as plain as you see outside. As to the crafts, throwing the clay must be jolly work: the glass-blowing is rather a sweltering job; but some folk like it very much indeed; and I don't wonder: there is such a sense of power, when you have got deft in it, in dealing with the hot metal. It makes a lot of pleasant work,' said he, smiling, 'for however much care you take of such goods, break they will, one day or another, so there is always plenty to do.'

I held my tongue and pondered.

We came just here on a gang of men road-mending, which delayed us a little; but I was not sorry for it; for all I had seen hitherto seemed a mere part of a summer holiday; and I wanted to see how this folk would set to on a piece of real necessary work. They had been resting, and had only just begun work again as we came up; so that the rattle of the picks was what woke me from my musing. There were about a dozen of them, strong young men, looking much like a boating party at Oxford would have looked in the days I remembered, and not troubled with their work: their outer raiment lay on the road-side in an orderly pile under the guardianship of a six-year-old boy, who had his arm thrown over the neck of a big mastiff, who was as happily lazy as if the summer day had been made for him alone. As I eyed the pile of clothes, I could see the gleam of gold and silk embroidery on it, and judged that some of these workmen had tastes akin to those of the Golden Dustman of Hammersmith. Beside them lay a good big basket that had hints about it of cold pie and wine: a half-dozen of young women stood by watching the work or the workers, both of which were worth watching, for the latter smote great strokes and were very deft in their labour, and as handsome clean-built fellows as you might find a dozen of in a summer day. They were laughing and talking merrily with each other and the women, but presently their foreman looked up and saw our way stopped. So he stayed his pick and sang out, 'Spell ho, mates! here are neighbours want to get past.' Whereon the others stopped also, and drawing around us, helped the old horse by easing our wheels over the half undone road, and then, like men with a pleasant task on hand, hurried back to their work, only stopping to give us a smiling good-day; so that the sound of the picks broke out again before Greylocks had taken to his jog-trot. Dick looked back over his shoulder at them and said:

'They are in luck to-day: it's right down good sport trying how much pick-work one can get into an hour; and I can see those neighbours know their business well. It is not a mere matter of strength getting on quickly with such work; is it, Guest?'

'I should think not,' said I, 'but to tell you the truth, I have never tried my hand at it.'

'Really?' said he gravely, 'that seems a pity; it is good work for hardening the muscles, and I like it; though I admit it is pleasanter the second week than the first. Not that I am a good hand at it: the fellows used to chaff me at one job where I was working, I remember, and sing out to me, "Well rowed, stroke!" "Put your back into it, bow!"'

'Not much of a joke,' quoth I.

'Well,' said Dick, 'everything seems like a joke when we have a pleasant spell of work on, and good fellows merry about us; we feel so happy, you know.' Again I pondered silently.[20]

Chapter VIII
AN OLD FRIEND

We now turned into a pleasant lane where the branches of great plane-trees nearly met overhead, but behind them lay low houses standing rather close together.

'This is Long Acre,' quoth Dick; 'so there must once have been a corn-field here. How curious it is that places change so, and yet keep their old names! Just look how thick the houses stand! and they are still going on building, look you!'

'Yes,' said the old man, 'but I think the corn-fields must have been built over before the middle of the nineteenth century. I have heard that about here was one of the thickest parts of the town. But I must get down here, neighbours; I have got to call on a friend who lives in the gardens behind this Long Acre. Good-bye and good luck, Guest!'

And he jumped down and strode away vigorously, like a young man.

'How old should you say that neighbour will be?' said I to Dick as we lost sight of him; for I saw that he was old, and yet he looked dry and sturdy like a piece of old oak; a type of old man I was not used to seeing.

'Oh, about ninety, I should say,' said Dick.

'How long-lived your people must be!' said I.

'Yes,' said Dick, 'certainly we have beaten the three-score-and-ten of the old Jewish proverb-book. But then you see that was written of Syria, a hot dry country, where people live faster than in our temperate climate. However, I don't think it matters much, so long as a man is healthy and happy while he *is* alive. But now, Guest, we are so near to my old kinsman's dwelling-place that I think you had better keep all future questions for him.'

I nodded a yes; and therewith we turned to the left, and went down a gentle slope through some beautiful rose-gardens, laid out on what I took to be the site of Endell Street. We passed on, and Dick drew rein an instant as we came across a long straightish road with houses scantily scattered up and down it. He waved his hand right and left, and said, 'Holborn that side, Oxford Road that. This was once a very important part of the crowded city outside the ancient walls of the Roman and Mediaeval burg: many of the feudal nobles of the Middle Ages, we are told, had big houses on either side of Holborn. I daresay you remember that the Bishop of Ely's house is mentioned in Shakespeare's play of King Richard III; and there are some remains of that still left. However, this road is not of the same importance, now that the ancient city is gone, walls and all.'

He drove on again, while I smiled faintly to think how the nineteenth century, of which such big words have been said, counted for nothing in the memory of this man, who read Shakespeare and had not forgotten the Middle Ages.

We crossed the road into a short narrow lane between the gardens, and came out again into a wide road, on one side of which was a great and long building, turning its gables away from the highway, which I saw at once was another public group. Opposite to it was a wide space of greenery, without any wall or fence of any kind. I looked through the trees and saw beyond them a pillared portico quite familiar to me – no less old a friend, in fact, than the British Museum. It rather took my breath away, amidst all the strange things I had seen; but I held my tongue and let Dick speak. Said he:

'Yonder is the British Museum, where my great-grandfather mostly lives; so I won't say much about it. The building on the left is the Museum Market, and I think we had better turn in there for a minute or two; for Greylocks will be wanting his rest and his oats; and I suppose you will stay with my kinsman the greater part of the day; and to say the truth, there may be some one there whom I particularly want to see, and perhaps have a long talk with.'

He blushed and sighed, not altogether with pleasure, I thought; so of course I said nothing, and he turned the horse under an archway which brought us into a very large paved quadrangle, with a big sycamore-tree in each corner and a plashing fountain in the midst. Near the fountain were a few market stalls, with awnings over them of gay striped linen cloth, about which some people, mostly women and children, were moving quietly, looking at the goods exposed there. The ground floor of the building round the quadrangle was occupied by a wide arcade or cloister, whose fanciful but strong architecture I could not enough admire. Here also a few people were sauntering or sitting reading on the benches.

Dick said to me apologetically: 'Here as elsewhere there is little doing to-day; on a Friday you would see it thronged, and gay with people, and in the afternoon there is generally music about the fountain. However, I daresay we shall have a pretty good gathering at our mid-day meal.'

We drove through the quadrangle and by an archway, into a large handsome stable on the other side, where we speedily stalled the old nag and made him happy with horse-meat, and then turned and walked back again through the market, Dick looking rather thoughtful, as it seemed to me.

I noticed that people couldn't help looking at me rather hard; and considering my clothes and theirs, I didn't wonder; but whenever they caught my eye they made me a very friendly sign of greeting.

We walked straight into the forecourt of the Museum, where, except that the railings were gone, and the whispering boughs of the trees were all about, nothing seemed changed; the very pigeons were wheeling about the building and clinging to the ornaments of the pediment as I had seen them of old.

Dick seemed grown a little absent, but he could not forbear giving me an architectural note, and said:

'It is rather an ugly old building, isn't it? Many people have wanted to pull it down and rebuild it: and perhaps if work does really get scarce we may yet do so. But, as my great-grandfather will tell you, it would not be quite a straightforward job; for there are wonderful collections in there of all kinds of antiquities, besides an enormous library with many exceedingly beautiful books in it, and many most useful ones as genuine records, texts of ancient works and the like; and the worry and anxiety, and even risk, there would be in moving all this has saved the buildings themselves. Besides, as we said before, it is not a bad thing to have some record of what our forefathers thought a handsome building. For there is plenty of labour and material in it.'

'I see there is,' said I, 'and I quite agree with you. But now hadn't we better make haste to see your great-grandfather?'

In fact, I could not help seeing that he was rather dallying with the time. He said, 'Yes, we will go into the house in a minute. My kinsman is too old to do much work in the Museum, where he was a custodian of the books for many years; but he still lives here a good deal; indeed I think,' said he, smiling, 'that he looks upon himself as a part of the books, or the books a part of him, I don't know which.'

He hesitated a little longer, then flushing up, took my hand, and saying, 'Come along, then!' led me toward the door of one of the old official dwellings.

Chapter IX
CONCERNING LOVE

'Your kinsman doesn't much care for beautiful buildings, then,' said I, as we entered the rather dreary classical house; which indeed was as bare as need be, except for some big pots of the June flowers which stood about here and there: though it was very clean and nicely white-washed.

'Oh, I don't know,' said Dick, rather absently. 'He is getting old, certainly, for he is over a hundred and five, and no doubt he doesn't care about moving. But of course he could live in a prettier house if he liked: he is not obliged to live in one place any more than any one else. This way, Guest.'

And he led the way upstairs, and opening a door we went into a fair-sized room of the old type, as plain as the rest of the house, with a few necessary pieces of furniture, and those very simple and even rude, but solid and with a good deal of carving about them, well designed but rather crudely executed. At the furthest corner of the room, at a desk near the window, sat a little old man in a roomy oak chair, well be-cushioned. He was dressed in a sort of Norfolk-jacket of blue serge worn threadbare, with breeches of the same, and grey worsted stockings. He jumped up from his chair, and cried out in a voice of considerable volume for such an old man, 'Welcome, Dick, my lad; Clara is here, and will be more than glad to see you; so keep your heart up.'

'Clara here?' quoth Dick; 'if I had known, I would not have brought— At least, I mean I would—'

He was stuttering and confused, clearly because he was anxious to say nothing to make me feel one too many. But the old man, who had not seen me at first, helped him out by coming forward and saying to me in a kind tone:

'Pray pardon me, for I did not notice that Dick, who is big enough to hide anybody, you know, had brought a friend with him. A most hearty welcome to you! All the more, as I almost hope that you are going to amuse an old man by giving him news from over-sea, for I can see that you are come from over the water and far-off countries.'

He looked at me thoughtfully, almost anxiously, as he said in a changed voice, 'Might I ask you where you come from, as you are so clearly a stranger?'

I said in an absent way: 'I used to live in England, and now I am come back again; and I slept last night at the Hammersmith Guest House.'

He bowed gravely, but seemed, I thought, a little disappointed with my answer. As for me, I was now looking at him harder than good manners allowed of, perhaps; for in truth his face, dried-apple-like as it was, seemed strangely familiar to me; as if I had seen it before – in a looking-glass it might be, said I to myself.

'Well,' said the old man, 'wherever you come from, you are come among friends. And I see my kinsman Richard Hammond has an air about him as if he had brought you here for me to do something for you. Is that so, Dick?'

Dick, who was getting still more absent-minded and kept looking uneasily at the door, managed to say, 'Well, yes, kinsman: our guest finds things much altered, and cannot understand it; nor can I; so I thought I would bring him to you, since you know more of all that has happened within the last two hundred years than anybody else does. – What's that?'

And he turned toward the door again. We heard footsteps outside; the door opened, and in came a very beautiful young woman, who stopped short on seeing Dick, and flushed as red as a rose, but faced him nevertheless. Dick looked at her hard, and half-reached out his hand toward her, and his whole face quivered with emotion.

The old man did not leave them long in this shy discomfort, but said, smiling with an old man's mirth: 'Dick, my lad, and you, my dear Clara, I rather think that we two oldsters are in your way; for I think you will have plenty to say to each other. You had better go into Nelson's room up above; I know he has gone out; and he has just been covering the walls all over with mediaeval books, so it will be pretty enough for you two and your renewed pleasure.'

The girl reached out her hand to Dick, and taking his led him out of the room, looking straight before her; but it was easy to see that her blushes came from happiness, not anger; as, indeed, love is far more self-conscious than wrath.

When the door had shut on them the old man turned to me, still smiling, and said:

'Frankly, my dear guest, you will do me a great service if you are come to set my old tongue wagging. My love of talk still abides with me, or rather grows on me; and though it is pleasant enough to see these youngsters moving about and playing together so seriously, as if the whole world depended on their kisses (as indeed it does somewhat), yet I don't think my tales of the past interest them much. The last harvest, the last baby, the last knot of carving in the market-place, is history enough for them. It was different, I think, when I was a lad, when we were not so assured of peace and continuous plenty as we are now— Well, well! Without putting you to the question, let me ask you this: Am I to consider you as an enquirer who knows a little of our modern ways of life, or as one who comes from some place where the very foundations of life are different from ours, – do you know anything or nothing about us?'

He looked at me keenly and with growing wonder in his eyes as he spoke; and I answered in a low voice:

'I know only so much of your modern life as I could gather from using my eyes on the way here from Hammersmith, and from asking some questions of Richard Hammond, most of which he could hardly understand.'

The old man smiled at this. 'Then,' said he, 'I am to speak to you as—'

'As if I were a being from another planet,' said I.

The old man, whose name, by the bye, like his kinsman's, was Hammond, smiled and nodded, and wheeling his seat round to me, bade me sit in a heavy oak chair, and said, as he saw my eyes fix on its curious carving:

'Yes, I am much tied to the past, *my* past, you understand. These very pieces of furniture belong to a time before my early days; it was my father who got them made; if they had been done within the last fifty years they would have been much cleverer in execution; but I don't think I should have liked them the better. We were almost beginning again in those days: and they were brisk, hot-headed times. But you hear how garrulous I am: ask me questions, ask me questions about anything, dear guest; since I *must* talk, make my talk profitable to you.'

I was silent for a minute, and then I said, somewhat nervously: 'Excuse me if I am rude; but I am so much interested in Richard, since he has been so kind to me, a perfect stranger, that I should like to ask a question about him.'

'Well,' said old Hammond, 'if he were not "kind", as you call it, to a perfect stranger he would be thought a strange person, and people would be apt to shun him. But ask on, ask on! don't be shy of asking.'

Said I: 'That beautiful girl, is he going to be married to her?'

'Well,' said he, 'yes, he is. He has been married to her once already, and now I should say it is pretty clear that he will be married to her again.'

'Indeed,' quoth I, wondering what that meant.

'Here is the whole tale,' said old Hammond; 'a short one enough; and now I hope a happy one: they lived together two years the first time; were both very young; and then she got it into her head that she was in love with somebody else. So she left poor Dick; I say *poor* Dick, because he had not found any one else. But it did not last long, only about a year. Then she came to me, as she was in the habit of bringing her troubles to the old carle, and asked me how Dick was, and whether he was happy, and all the rest of it. So I saw how the land lay, and said that he was very unhappy, and not at all well; which last at any rate was a lie. There, you can guess the rest. Clara came to have a long talk with me to-day, but Dick will serve her turn much better. Indeed, if he hadn't chanced in upon me to-day I should have had to have sent for him to-morrow.'

'Dear me,' said I. 'Have they any children?'

'Yes,' said he, 'two; they are staying with one of my daughters at present, where, indeed, Clara has mostly been. I wouldn't lose sight of her, as I felt sure they would come together again: and Dick, who is the best of good fellows, really took the matter to heart. You see, he had no other love to run to, as she had. So I managed it all; as I have done with such-like matters before.'

'Ah,' said I, 'no doubt you wanted to keep them out of the Divorce Court: but I suppose it often has to settle such matters.'

'Then you suppose nonsense,' said he. 'I know that there used to be such lunatic affairs as divorce courts. But just consider; all the cases that came into them were matters of property quarrels: and I think, dear guest,' said he, smiling, 'that though you do come from another planet, you can see from the mere outside look of our world that quarrels about private property could not go on amongst us in our days.'

Indeed, my drive from Hammersmith to Bloomsbury, and all the quiet happy life I had seen so many hints of, even apart from my shopping, would have been enough to tell me that 'the sacred rights of property', as we used to think of them, were now no more. So I sat silent while the old man took up the thread of the discourse again, and said:

'Well, then, property quarrels being no longer possible, what remains in these matters that a court of law could deal with? Fancy a court for enforcing a contract of passion or sentiment! If such a thing were needed as a *reductio ad absurdum* of the enforcement of contract, such a folly would do that for us.'

He was silent again a little, and then said: 'You must understand once for all that we have changed these matters; or rather, that our way of looking at them has changed, as we have changed within the last two hundred years. We do not deceive ourselves, indeed, or believe that we can get rid of all the trouble that besets the dealings between the sexes. We know that we must face the unhappiness that comes of man and woman confusing the relations between natural passion, and sentiment, and the friendship which, when things go well, softens the awakening from passing illusions: but we are not so mad as to pile up degradation on that unhappiness by engaging in sordid squabbles about livelihood and position, and the power of tyrannizing over the children who have been the result of love or lust.'

Again he paused awhile, and again went on: 'Calf love, mistaken for a heroism that shall be life-long, yet early waning into disappointment; the inexplicable desire that comes on a man of riper years to be the all-in-all to some one woman, whose ordinary human kindness and human beauty he has idealized into superhuman perfection, and made the one object of his desire; or lastly the reasonable longing of a strong and thoughtful man to become the most intimate friend of some beautiful and wise woman, the very type of the beauty and glory of the world which we love so well, – as we exult in all the pleasure and exaltation of spirit which goes with these things, so we set ourselves to bear the sorrow which not unseldom goes with them also; remembering those lines of the ancient poet (I quote roughly from memory one of the many translations of the nineteenth century):

For this the Gods have fashioned man's grief and evil day
That still for man hereafter might be the tale and the lay.[21]

Well, well, 'tis little likely anyhow that all tales shall be lacking,
or all sorrow cured.'

He was silent for some time, and I would not interrupt him. At
last he began again: 'But you must know that we of these generations
are strong and healthy of body, and live easily; we pass our lives in
reasonable strife with nature, exercising not one side of ourselves
only, but all sides, taking the keenest pleasure in all the life of the
world. So it is a point of honour with us not to be self-centred; not to
suppose that the world must cease because one man is sorry; therefore
we should think it foolish, or if you will, criminal, to exaggerate
these matters of sentiment and sensibility: we are no more inclined
to eke out our sentimental sorrows than to cherish our bodily pains;
and we recognize that there are other pleasures besides love-making.
You must remember, also, that we are long-lived, and that therefore
beauty both in man and woman is not so fleeting as it was in the
days when we were burdened so heavily by self-inflicted diseases. So
we shake off these griefs in a way which perhaps the sentimentalists
of other times would think contemptible and unheroic, but which we
think necessary and manlike. As on the other hand, therefore, we
have ceased to be commercial in our love-matters, so also we have
ceased to be *artificially* foolish. The folly which comes by nature, the
unwisdom of the immature man, or the older man caught in a trap,
we must put up with that, nor are we much ashamed of it; but to be
conventionally sensitive or sentimental – my friend, I am old and
perhaps disappointed, but at least I think we have cast off *some* of the
follies of the older world.'

He paused, as if for some words of mine; but I held my peace:
then he went on: 'At least, if we suffer from the tyranny and fickleness
of nature or our own want of experience, we neither grimace about
it, nor lie. If there must be sundering betwixt those who meant never
to sunder, so it must be: but there need be no pretext and unity when
the reality of it is gone: nor do we drive those who well know that
they are incapable of it to profess an undying sentiment which they
cannot really feel: thus it is that as that monstrosity of venal lust is

no longer possible, so also it is no longer needed. Don't misunderstand me. You did not seem shocked when I told you that there were no law-courts to enforce contracts of sentiment or passion; but so curiously are men made, that perhaps you will be shocked when I tell you that there is no code of public opinion which takes the place of such courts, and which might be as tyrannical and unreasonable as they were. I do not say that people don't judge their neighbours' conduct, sometimes, doubtless, unfairly. But I do say that there is no unvarying conventional set of rules by which people are judged; no bed of Procrustes[22] to stretch or cramp their minds and lives; no hypocritical excommunication which people are *forced* to pronounce, either by unconsidered habit, or by the unexpressed threat of the lesser interdict if they are lax in their hypocrisy. Are you shocked now?'

'N-o – no,' said I, with some hesitation. 'It is all so different.'

'At any rate,' said he, 'one thing I think I can answer for: whatever sentiment there is, it is real – and general; it is not confined to people very specially refined. I am also pretty sure, as I hinted to you just now, that there is not by a great way as much suffering involved in these matters either to men or to women as there used to be. But excuse me for being so prolix on this question! You know you asked to be treated like a being from another planet.'

'Indeed I thank you very much,' said I. 'Now may I ask you about the position of women in your society?'

He laughed very heartily for a man of his years, and said: 'It is not without reason that I have got a reputation as a careful student of history. I believe I really do understand "the Emancipation of Women movement" of the nineteenth century. I doubt if any other man now alive does.'

'Well?' said I, a little bit nettled by his merriment.

'Well,' said he, 'of course you will see that all that is a dead controversy now. The men have no longer any opportunity of tyrannizing over the women, or the women over the men; both of which things took place in those old times. The women do what they can do best, and what they like best, and the men are neither jealous of it or injured by it. This is such a commonplace that I am almost ashamed to state it.'

I said, 'Oh; and legislation? do they take any part in that?'

Hammond smiled and said: 'I think you may wait for an answer to that question till we get on to the subject of legislation. There may be novelties to you in that subject also.'

'Very well,' I said; 'but about this woman question? I saw at the Guest House that the women were waiting on the men: that seems a little like reaction, doesn't it?'

'Does it?' said the old man; 'perhaps you think housekeeping an unimportant occupation, not deserving of respect. I believe that was the opinion of the "advanced" women of the nineteenth century, and their male backers. If it is yours, I recommend to your notice an old Norwegian folk-lore tale called How the Man minded the House,[23] or some such title, the result of which minding was that, after various tribulations, the man and the family cow balanced each other at the end of a rope, the man hanging half-way up the chimney, the cow dangling from the roof, which, after the fashion of the country, was of turf and sloping down low to the ground. Hard on the cow, *I* think. Of course no such mishap could happen to such a superior person as yourself,' he added, chuckling.

I sat somewhat uneasy under this dry gibe. Indeed, his manner of treating this latter part of the question seemed to me a little disrespectful.

'Come, now, my friend,' quoth he, 'don't you know that it is a great pleasure to a clever woman to manage a house skilfully, and to do it so that all the house-mates about her look pleased, and are grateful to her? And then, you know, everybody likes to be ordered about by a pretty woman: why, it is one of the pleasantest forms of flirtation. You are not so old that you cannot remember that. Why, I remember it well.'

And the old fellow chuckled again, and at last fairly burst out laughing.

'Excuse me,' said he, after a while; 'I am not laughing at anything you could be thinking of, but at that silly nineteenth-century fashion, current amongst rich so-called cultivated people, of ignoring all the steps by which their daily dinner was reached, as matters too low for their lofty intelligence. Useless idiots! Come, now, I am a "literary man", as we queer animals used to be called, yet I am a pretty good cook myself.'[24]

'So am I,' said I.

'Well, then,' said he, 'I really think you can understand me better than you would seem to do, judging by your words and your silence.'

Said I: 'Perhaps that is so; but people putting in practice commonly this sense of interest in the ordinary occupations of life rather startles me. I will ask you a question or two presently about that. But I want to return to the position of women amongst you. You have studied the "emancipation of women" business of the nineteenth century: don't you remember that some of the "superior" women wanted to emancipate the more intelligent part of their sex from the bearing of children?'

The old man grew quite serious again. Said he: 'I *do* remember about that strange piece of baseless folly, the result, like all other follies of the period, of the hideous class tyranny which then obtained. What do we think of it now? you would say. My friend, that is a question easy to answer. How could it possibly be but that maternity should be highly honoured amongst us? Surely it is a matter of course that the natural and necessary pains which the mother must go through form a bond of union between man and woman, an extra stimulus to love and affection between them, and that this is universally recognized. For the rest, remember that all the *artificial* burdens of motherhood are now done away with. A mother has no longer any mere sordid anxieties for the future of her children. They may indeed turn out better or worse; they may disappoint her highest hopes; such anxieties as these are a part of the mingled pleasure and pain which goes to make up the life of mankind. But at least she is spared the fear (it was most commonly the certainty) that artificial disabilities would make her children something less than men and women: she knows that they will live and act according to the measure of their own faculties. In times past, it is clear that the "Society" of the day helped its Judaic god, and the "Man of Science" of the time, in visiting the sins of the father upon the children. How to reverse this process, how to take the sting out of heredity, has for long been one of the most constant cares of the thoughtful men amongst us. So that, you see, the ordinarily healthy woman (and almost all our women are both healthy and at least comely), respected as a child-bearer and rearer of children, desired as a woman, loved as a companion, unanxious for the future of her children, has far more instinct for maternity than the poor drudge and mother of drudges of past days could ever have had; or than her sister of the upper classes, brought up in affected ignorance of natural facts, reared in an atmosphere of mingled prudery and prurience.'

'You speak warmly,' I said, 'but I can see that you are right.'

'Yes,' he said, 'and I will point out to you a token of all the benefits which we have gained by our freedom. What did you think of the looks of the people whom you have come across to-day?'

Said I: 'I could hardly have believed that there could be so many good looking people in any civilized country.'

He crowed a little, like the old bird he was. 'What! are we still civilized?' said he. 'Well, as to our looks, the English and Jutish blood, which on the whole is predominant here, used not to produce much beauty. But I think we have improved it. I know a man who has a large collection of portraits printed from photographs of the nineteenth century, and going over those and comparing them with the everyday faces in these times, puts the improvement in our good looks beyond a doubt. Now, there are some people who think it not too fantastic to connect this increase of beauty directly with our freedom and good sense in the matters we have been speaking of: they believe that a child born from the natural and healthy love between a man and a woman, even if that be transient, is likely to turn out better in all ways, and especially in bodily beauty, than the birth of the respectable commercial marriage bed,[25] or of the dull despair of the drudge of that system. They say, Pleasure begets pleasure. What do you think?'

'I am much of that mind,' said I.

Chapter X
QUESTIONS AND ANSWERS

'Well,' said the old man, shifting in his chair, 'you must get on with your questions, guest; I have been some time answering this first one.'

Said I: 'I want an extra word or two about your ideas of education; although I gathered from Dick that you let your children run wild and didn't teach them anything; and in short, that you have so refined your education, that now you have none.'

'Then you gathered left-handed,' quoth he. 'But of course I understand your point of view about education, which is that of times past, when "the struggle for life," as men used to phrase it (*i.e.*, the struggle for a slave's rations on one side, and for a bouncing share of the slave-holders' privilege on the other), pinched "education" for most people into a niggardly dole of not very accurate information; something to be swallowed by the beginner in the art of living whether he liked it or not, and was hungry for it or not: and which had been chewed and digested over and over again by people who didn't care about it in order to serve it out to other people who didn't care about it.'

I stopped the old man's rising wrath by a laugh, and said: 'Well, *you* were not taught that way, at any rate, so you may let your anger run off you a little.'

'True, true,' said, he, smiling. 'I thank you for correcting my ill-temper: I always fancy myself as living in any period of which we may be speaking. But, however, to put it in a cooler way: you expected to see children thrust into schools when they had reached an age conventionally supposed to be the due age, whatever their varying faculties and dispositions might be, and when there, with like disregard to facts, to be subjected to a certain conventional course of "learning". My friend, can't you see that such a proceeding means ignoring the fact of *growth*, bodily and mental? No one could come out of such a mill uninjured; and those only would avoid being crushed by it who would have the spirit of rebellion strong in them. Fortunately most children have had that at all times, or I do not know that we should ever have reached our present position. Now you see what it all comes to. In the old times all this was the result of *poverty*. In the nineteenth century, society was so miserably poor, owing to the systematized robbery on which it was founded, that real education was impossible for anybody. The whole theory of their so-called education was that it was necessary to shove a little information into a child, even if it were by means of torture, and accompanied by twaddle which it was well known was of no use, or else he would lack information lifelong: the hurry of poverty forbade anything else. All that is past; we are no longer hurried, and the information lies ready to each one's hand when his own inclinations impel him to seek it. In this as in other matters we have become wealthy: we can afford to give ourselves time to grow.'

'Yes,' said I, 'but suppose the child, youth, man, never wants the information, never grows in the direction you might hope him to do: suppose, for instance, he objects to learning arithmetic or mathematics; you can't force him when he *is* grown; can't you force him while he is growing, and oughtn't you to do so?'

'Well,' said he, 'were you forced to learn arithmetic and mathematics?'

'A little,' said I.

'And how old are you now?'

'Say fifty-six,' said I.

'And how much arithmetic and mathematics do you know now?' quoth the old man, smiling rather mockingly.

Said I: 'None whatever, I am sorry to say.'

Hammond laughed quietly, but made no other comment on my admission, and I dropped the subject of education, perceiving him to be hopeless on that side.

I thought a little, and said: 'You were speaking just now of households: that sounded to me a little like the customs of past times; I should have thought you would have lived more in public.'

'Phalangsteries, eh?' said he. 'Well, we live as we like, and we like to live as a rule with certain house-mates that we have got used to. Remember, again, that poverty is extinct, and that the Fourierist phalangsteries[26] and all their kind, as was but natural at the time, implied nothing but a refuge from mere destitution. Such a way of life as that could only have been conceived of by people surrounded by the worst form of poverty. But you must understand therewith, that though separate households are the rule amongst us, and though they differ in their habits more or less, yet no door is shut to any good-tempered person who is content to live as the other house-mates do: only of course it would be unreasonable for one man to drop into a household and bid the folk of it to alter their habits to please him, since he can go elsewhere and live as he pleases. However, I need not say much about all this, as you are going up the river with Dick, and will find out for yourself by experience how these matters are managed.'

After a pause, I said: 'Your big towns, now; how about them? London, which – which I have read about as the modern Babylon of civilization, seems to have disappeared.'

'Well, well,' said old Hammond, 'perhaps after all it is more like ancient Babylon now than the "modern Babylon" of the nineteenth century was. But let that pass. After all there is a good deal of population in places between here and Hammersmith; nor have you seen the most populous part of the town yet.'

'Tell me, then,' said I, 'how is it towards the east?'[27]

Said he: 'Time was when if you mounted a good horse and rode straight away from my door here at a round trot for an hour and a half, you would still be in the thick of London, and the greater part of that would be "slums", as they were called; that is to say, places of torture for innocent men and women; or worse, stews for rearing and breeding men and women in such degradation that that torture should seem to them mere ordinary and natural life.'

'I know, I know,' I said, rather impatiently. 'That was what was; tell me something of what is. Is any of that left?'

'Not an inch,' said he; 'but some memory of it abides with us, and I am glad of it. Once a year, on May-day, we hold a solemn feast in those easterly communes of London to commemorate The Clearing of Misery, as it is called. On that day we have music and dancing, and merry games and happy feasting on the site of some of the worst of the old slums, the traditional memory of which we have kept. On that occasion the custom is for the prettiest girls to sing some of the old revolutionary songs, and those which were the groans of the discontent, once so hopeless, on the very spots where those terrible crimes of class-murder were committed day by day for so many years. To a man like me, who has studied the past so diligently, it is a curious and touching sight to see some beautiful girl, daintily clad, and crowned with flowers from the neighbouring meadows, standing amongst the happy people, on some mound where of old time stood the wretched apology for a house, a den in which men and women lived packed amongst the filth like pilchards in a cask; lived in such a way that they could only have endured it, as I said just now, by being degraded out of humanity – to hear the terrible words of threatening and lamentation coming from her sweet and beautiful lips, and she unconscious of their real meaning: to hear her, for instance, singing Hood's Song of the Shirt,[28] and to think that all the time she does not understand what it is all about – a tragedy grown inconceivable to her and her listeners. Think of that, if you can, and of how glorious life is grown!'

'Indeed,' said I, 'it is difficult for me to think of it.'

And I sat watching how his eyes glittered, and how the fresh life seemed to glow in his face, and I wondered how at his age he should think of the happiness of the world, or indeed anything but his coming dinner.

'Tell me in detail,' said I, 'what lies east of Bloomsbury now?'

Said he: 'There are but few houses between this and the outer part of the old city; but in the city we have a thickly-dwelling population. Our forefathers, in the first clearing of the slums were not in a hurry to pull down the houses in what was called at the end of the nineteenth century the business quarter of the town, and what later got to be known as the Swindling Kens.[29] You see, these houses, though they stood hideously thick on the ground, were roomy and fairly solid in building, and clean, because they were not used for living in, but as mere gambling booths; so the poor people from the cleared slums took them for lodgings and dwelt there, till the folk of those days had time to think of something better for them; so the buildings were pulled down so gradually that people got used to living thicker on the ground there than in most places; therefore it remains the most populous part of London, or perhaps of all these islands. But it is very pleasant there, partly because of the splendour of the architecture, which goes further than what you will see else-where. However, this crowding, if it may be called so, does not go further than a street called Aldgate, a name which perhaps you may have heard of. Beyond that the houses are scattered wide about the meadows there, which are very beautiful, especially when you get on to the lovely river Lea (where old Isaak Walton used to fish,[30] you know) about the places called Stratford and Old Ford, names which of course you will not have heard of, though the Romans were busy there once upon a time.'

Not heard of them! thought I to myself. How strange! that I who had seen the very last remnant of the pleasantness of the meadows by the Lea destroyed, should have heard them spoken of with pleasantness come back to them in full measure.

Hammond went on: 'When you get down to the Thames side you come on the Docks, which are works of the nineteenth century, and are still in use, although not so thronged as they once were, since we discourage centralization all we can, and we have long ago dropped the pretension to be the market of the world. About these Docks are a good few houses, which, however, are not inhabited by many people permanently; I mean, those who use them come and go a good deal, the place being too low and marshy for pleasant dwelling. Past the Docks eastward and landward it is all flat pasture, once marsh, except for a few gardens, and there are very few permanent dwellings there: scarcely anything but a few sheds, and cots for the men who come to look after the great herds of cattle pasturing there. But however, what with the beasts and the men, and the scattered red-tiled roofs and the big hayricks, it does not make a bad holiday to get a quiet pony and ride about there on a sunny afternoon of autumn, and look over the river and the craft passing up and down, and on to Shooters' Hill and the Kentish uplands, and then turn round to the wide green sea of the Essex marshland, with the great domed line of the sky, and the sun shining down in one flood of peaceful light over the long distance. There is a place called Canning's Town, and further out, Silvertown, where the pleasant meadows are at their pleasantest: doubtless they were once slums, and wretched enough.'

The names grated on my ear, but I could not explain why to him. So I said: 'And south of the river, what is it like?'

He said: 'You would find it much the same as the land about Hammersmith. North, again, the land runs up high, and there is an agreeable and well-built town called Hampstead, which fitly ends London on that side. It looks down on the north-western end of the forest you passed through.'

I smiled. 'So much for what was once London,' said I. 'Now tell me about the other towns of the country.'

He said: 'As to the big murky places which were once, as we know, the centres of manufacture, they have, like the brick and mortar desert of London, disappeared; only, since they were centres of nothing but "manufacture", and served no purpose but that of the gambling market, they have left less signs of their existence than London. Of course, the great change in the use of mechanical force made this an easy matter, and some approach to their break-up as centres would probably have taken place, even if we had not changed our habits so much: but they being such as they were, no sacrifice would have seemed too great a price to pay for getting rid of the "manufacturing districts", as they used to be called. For the rest, whatever coal or mineral we need is brought to grass and sent whither it is needed with as little as possible of dirt, confusion, and the distressing of quiet people's lives. One is tempted to believe from what one has read of the condition of those districts in the nineteenth century, that those who had them under their power worried, befouled, and degraded men out of malice prepense: but it was not so; like the miseducation of which we were talking just now, it came of their dreadful poverty. They were obliged to put up with everything, and even pretend that they liked it; whereas we can now deal with things reasonably, and refuse to be saddled with what we do not want.'

I confess I was not sorry to cut short with a question his glorifications of the age he lived in. Said I: 'How about the smaller towns? I suppose you have swept those away entirely?'

'No, no,' said he, 'it hasn't gone that way. On the contrary, there has been but little clearance, though much rebuilding, in the smaller towns. Their suburbs, indeed, when they had any, have melted away into the general country, and space and elbow-room has been got in their centres: but there are the towns still with their streets and squares and market-places; so that it is by means of these smaller towns that we of to-day can get some kind of idea of what the towns of the older world were like; – I mean to say at their best.'

'Take Oxford, for instance,' said I.

'Yes,' said he, 'I suppose Oxford was beautiful even in the nineteenth century. At present it has the great interest of still preserving a great mass of precommercial building, and is a very beautiful place, yet there are many towns which have become scarcely less beautiful.'

Said I: 'In passing, may I ask if it is still a place of learning?'

'Still?' said he, smiling. 'Well, it has reverted to some of its best traditions; so you may imagine how far it is from its nineteenth-century position. It is real learning, knowledge cultivated for its own sake – the Art of Knowledge, in short – which is followed there, not the Commercial learning of the past. Though perhaps you do not know that in the nineteenth century Oxford and its less interesting sister Cambridge became definitely commercial. They (and especially Oxford) were the breeding places of a peculiar class of parasites, who called themselves cultivated people; they were indeed cynical enough, as the so-called educated classes of the day generally were; but they affected an exaggeration of cynicism in order that they might be thought knowing and worldly-wise. The rich middle classes (they had no relation with the working classes) treated them with the kind of contemptuous toleration with which a mediaeval baron treated his jester; though it must be said that they were by no means so pleasant as the old jesters were, being, in fact, *the* bores of society. They were laughed at, despised – and paid. Which last was what they aimed at.'

Dear me! thought I, how apt history is to reverse contemporary judgments. Surely only the worst of them were as bad as that. But I must admit that they were mostly prigs, and that they *were* commercial. I said aloud, though more to myself than to Hammond, 'Well, how could they be better than the age that made them?'

'True,' he said, 'but their pretensions were higher.'

'Were they?' said I, smiling.

'You drive me from corner to corner,' said he, smiling in turn. 'Let me say at least that they were a poor sequence to the aspirations of Oxford of "the barbarous Middle Ages".'

'Yes, that will do,' said I.

'Also,' said Hammond, 'what I have been saying of them is true in the main. But ask on!'

I said: 'We have heard about London and the manufacturing districts and the ordinary towns: how about the villages?'

Said Hammond: 'You must know that toward the end of the nineteenth century the villages were almost destroyed, unless where they became mere adjuncts to the manufacturing districts, or formed a sort of minor manufacturing district themselves. Houses were allowed to fall into decay and actual ruin; trees were cut down for the sake of the few shillings which the poor sticks would fetch; the building became inexpressibly mean and hideous. Labour was scarce; but wages fell nevertheless. All the small country arts of life which once added to the little pleasures of country people were lost. The country produce which passed through the hands of the husbandman never got so far as their mouths. Incredible shabbiness and niggardly pinching reigned over the fields and acres which, in spite of the rude and careless husbandry of the times, were so kind and bountiful. Had you any inkling of all this?'

'I have heard that it was so,' said I; 'but what followed?'

'The change,' said Hammond, 'which in these matters took place very early in our epoch, was most strangely rapid. People flocked into the country villages, and, so to say, flung themselves upon the freed land like a wild beast upon his prey; and in a very little time the villages of England were more populous than they had been since the fourteenth century, and were still growing fast. Of course, this invasion of the country was awkward to deal with, and would have created much misery, if the folk had still been under the bondage of class monopoly. But as it was, things soon righted themselves. People found out what they were fit for, and gave up attempting to push themselves into occupations in which they must needs fail. The town invaded the country; but the invaders, like the warlike invaders of early days, yielded to the influence of their surroundings, and became country people; and in their turn, as they became more numerous than the townsmen, influenced them also; so that the difference between town and country grew less and less; and it was indeed this world of the country vivified by the thought and briskness of town-bred folk which has produced that happy and leisurely but eager life of which you have had a first taste. Again I say, many blunders were made, but we have had time to set them right. Much was left for the men of my earlier life to deal with. The crude ideas of the first half of the twentieth century, when men were still oppressed by the fear of poverty, and did not look enough to the present pleasure of ordinary daily life, spoilt a great deal of what the commercial age had left us of external beauty: and I admit that it was but slowly that men recovered from the injuries they had inflicted on themselves even after they became free. But slowly as the recovery came, it *did* come; and the more you see of us, the clearer it will be to you that we are happy. That we live amidst beauty without any fear of becoming effeminate; that we have plenty to do, and on the whole enjoy doing it. What more can we ask of life?'

He paused, as if he were seeking for words with which to express his thought. Then he said:

'This is how we stand. England was once a country of clearings amongst the woods and wastes, with a few towns interspersed, which were fortresses for the feudal army, markets for the folk, gathering places for the craftsmen. It then became a country of huge and foul workshops and fouler gambling-dens, surrounded by an ill-kept, poverty-stricken farm, pillaged by the masters of the workshops. It is now a garden,[31] where nothing is wasted and nothing is spoilt, with the necessary dwellings, sheds, and workshops scattered up and down the country, all trim and neat and pretty. For, indeed, we should be too much ashamed of ourselves if we allowed the making of goods, even on the large scale, to carry with it the appearance, even, of desolation and misery. Why, my friend, those housewives we were talking of just now would teach us better than that.'

Said I: 'This side of your change is certainly for the better. But though I shall soon see some of these villages, tell me in a word or two what they are like, just to prepare me.'

'Perhaps,' said he, 'you have seen a tolerable picture of these villages as they were before the end of the nineteenth century. Such things exist.'

'I have seen several of such pictures,' said I.

'Well,' said Hammond, 'our villages are something like the best of such places, with the church or mote-house of the neighbours for their chief building. Only note that there are no tokens of poverty about them: no tumble-down picturesque: which, to tell you the truth, the artist usually availed himself of to veil his incapacity for drawing architecture.[32] Such things do not please us, even when they indicate no misery. Like the mediaevals, we like everything trim and clean, and orderly and bright; as people always do when they have any sense of architectural power; because then they know that they can have what they want, and they won't stand any nonsense from Nature in their dealings with her.'

'Besides the villages, are there any scattered country houses?' said I.

'Yes, plenty,' said Hammond; 'in fact, except in the wastes and forests and amongst the sand-hills (like Hindhead in Surrey) it is not easy to be out of sight of a house; and where the houses are thinly scattered they run large, and are more like the old colleges than ordinary houses as they used to be. That is done for the sake of society, for a good many people can dwell in such houses, as the country dwellers are not necessarily husbandmen; though they almost all help in such work at times. The life that goes on in these big dwellings in the country is very pleasant, especially as some of the most studious men of our time live in them, and altogether there is a great variety of mind and mood to be found in them which brightens and quickens the society there.'

'I am rather surprised,' said I, 'by all this, for it seems to me that after all the country must be tolerably populous.'

'Certainly,' said he; 'the population is pretty much the same as it was at the end of the nineteenth century; we have spread it, that is all. Of course, also, we have helped to populate other countries – where we were wanted and were called for.'

Said I: 'One thing, it seems to me, does not go with your word of "garden" for the country. You have spoken of wastes and forests, and I myself have seen the beginning of your Middlesex and Essex forest. Why do you keep such things in a garden? and isn't it very wasteful to do so?'

'My friend,' he said, 'we like these pieces of wild nature, and can afford them, so we have them; let alone that as to the forests, we need a great deal of timber, and suppose that our sons and sons' sons will do the like. As to the land being a garden, I have heard that they used to have shrubberies and rockeries in gardens once; and though I might not like the artificial ones, I assure you that some of the natural rockeries of our garden are worth seeing. Go north this summer and look at the Cumberland and Westmoreland ones, – where, by the way, you will see some sheep feeding, so that they are not so wasteful as you think; not so wasteful as forcing-grounds for fruit out of season, *I* think. Go and have a look at the sheep-walks high up the slopes between Ingleborough and Pen-y-gwent, and tell me if you think we *waste* the land there by not covering it with factories for making things that nobody wants, which was the chief business of the nineteenth century.'

'I will try to go there,' said I.

'It won't take much trying,' said he.

Chapter XI
CONCERNING GOVERNMENT

'Now,' said I, 'I have come to the point of asking questions which I suppose will be dry for you to answer and difficult for you to explain; but I have foreseen for some time past that I must ask them, will I nill I. What kind of a government have you? Has republicanism finally triumphed? or have you come to a mere dictatorship, which some persons in the nineteenth century used to prophesy as the ultimate outcome of democracy? Indeed, this last question does not seem so very unreasonable, since you have turned your Parliament House into a dung-market. Or where do you house your present Parliament?'

The old man answered my smile with a hearty laugh, and said: 'Well, well, dung is not the worst kind of corruption; fertility may come of that, whereas mere dearth came from the other kind, of which those walls once held the great supporters. Now, dear guest, let me tell you that our present parliament would be hard to house in one place, because the whole people is our parliament.'

'I don't understand,' said I.

'No, I suppose not,' said he. 'I must now shock you by telling you that we have no longer anything which you, a native of another planet, would call a government.'

'I am not so much shocked as you might think,' said I, 'as I know something about governments. But tell me, how do you manage, and how have you come to this state of things?'

Said he: 'It is true that we have to make some arrangements about our affairs, concerning which you can ask presently; and it is also true that everybody does not always agree with the details of these arrangements; but, further, it is true that a man no more needs an elaborate system of government, with its army, navy, and police, to force him to give way to the will of the majority of his *equals*, than he wants a similar machinery to make him understand that his head and a stone wall cannot occupy the same space at the same moment. Do you want further explanation?'

'Well, yes, I do,' quoth I.

Old Hammond settled himself in his chair with a look of enjoyment which rather alarmed me, and made me dread a scientific disquisition: so I sighed and abided. He said:

'I suppose you know pretty well what the process of government was in the bad old times?'

'I am supposed to know,' said I.

HAMMOND What was the government of those days? Was it really the Parliament or any part of it?

I: No.

H: Was not the Parliament on the one side of a kind of watch-committee sitting to see that the interests of the Upper Classes took no hurt; and on the other side a sort of blind to delude the people into supposing that they had some share in the management of their own affairs?

I: History seems to show us this.

H: To what extent did the people manage their own affairs?

I: I judge from what I have heard that sometimes they forced the Parliament to make a law to legalize some alteration which had already taken place.

H: Anything else?

I: I think not. As I am informed, if the people made any attempt to deal with the *cause* of their grievances, the law stepped in and said, this is sedition, revolt, or what not, and slew or tortured the ringleaders of such attempts.

H: If Parliament was not the government then, nor the people either, what was the government?

I: Can you tell me?

H: I think we shall not be far wrong if we say that government was the law-courts, backed up by the executive, which handled the brute force that the deluded people allowed them to use for their own purposes; I mean the army, navy, and police.

I: Reasonable men must needs think you are right.

H: Now as to those law-courts. Were they places of fair dealing according to the ideas of the day? Had a poor man a good chance of defending his property and person in them?

I: It is a commonplace that even rich men looked upon a law-suit as a dire misfortune even if they gained the case; and as for a poor one – why, it was considered a miracle of justice and beneficence if a poor man who had once got into the clutches of the law escaped prison or utter ruin.

H: It seems, then, my son, that the government by law-courts and police, which was the real government of the nineteenth century, was not a great success even to the people of that day, living under a class system which proclaimed inequality and poverty as the law of God and the bond which held the world together.

I: So it seems, indeed.

H: And now that all this is changed, and the 'rights of property', which mean the clenching the fist on a piece of goods and crying out to the neighbours, You shan't have this! – now that all this has disappeared so utterly that it is no longer possible even to jest upon its absurdity, is such a government possible?

I: It is impossible.

H: Yes, happily. But for what other purpose than the protection of the rich from the poor, the strong from the weak, did this government exist?

I: I have heard that it was said that their office was to defend their own citizens against attack from other countries.

H: It was said; but was anyone expected to believe this? For instance did the English government defend the English citizen against the French?

I: So it was said.

H: Then if the French had invaded England and conquered it, they would not have allowed the English workman to live well?

I (laughing):   As far as I can make out, the English masters of the English workmen saw to that: they took from their workmen as much of their livelihood as they dared, because they wanted it for themselves.

H: But if the French had conquered, would they not have taken more still from the English workmen?

I: I do not think so; for in that case the English workmen would have died of starvation; and then the French conquest would have ruined the French, just as if the English horses and cattle had died of under-feeding. So that after all, the English *workmen* would have been no worse off for the conquest: their French masters could have got no more from them than their English masters did.

H: This is true; and we may admit that the pretensions of the government to defend the poor (*i.e.*, the useful) people against other countries came to nothing. But that is but natural; for we have seen already that it was the function of government to protect the rich against the poor. But did not the government defend its rich men against other nations?

I: I do not remember to have heard that the rich needed defence; because it is said that even when two nations were at war, the rich men of each nation gambled with each other pretty much as usual, and even sold each other weapons wherewith to kill their own countrymen.

H: In short, it comes to this, that whereas the so-called government of protection of property by means of the law-courts meant destruction of wealth, this defence of the citizens of one country against those of another country by means of war or the threat of war meant pretty much the same thing.

I: I cannot deny it.

H: Therefore the government really existed for the destruction of wealth?

I: So it seems. And yet—

H: Yet what?

I: There were many rich people in those times.

H: You see the consequences of that fact?

I: I think I do. But tell me out what they were.

H: If the government habitually destroyed wealth, the country must have been poor?

I: Yes, certainly.

H: Yet amidst this poverty the persons for the sake of whom the government existed insisted on being rich whatever might happen?

I: So it was.

H: What *must* happen if in a poor country some people insist on being rich at the expense of the others?

I: Unutterable poverty for the others. All this misery then, was caused by the destructive government of which we have been speaking?

H: Nay, it would be incorrect to say so. The government itself was but the necessary result of the careless, aimless tyranny of the times; it was but the machinery of tyranny. Now tyranny has come to an end, and we no longer need such machinery; we could not possibly use it since we are free. Therefore in your sense of the word we have no government. Do you understand this now?

I: Yes, I do. But I will ask you some more questions as to how you as free men manage your affairs.

H: With all my heart. Ask away.

Chapter XII

CONCERNING THE ARRANGEMENT OF LIFE

'Well,' I said, 'about those "arrangements" which you spoke of as taking the place of government, could you give me any account of them?'

'Neighbour,' he said, 'although we have simplified our lives a great deal from what they were, and have got rid of many conventionalities and many sham wants, which used to give our forefathers much trouble, yet our life is too complex for me to tell you in detail by means of words how it is arranged; you must find that out by living amongst us. It is true that I can better tell you what we don't do, than what we do do.'

'Well?' said I.

'This is the way to put it,' said he: 'We have been living for a hundred and fifty years, at least, more or less in our present manner, and a tradition or habit of life has been growing on us; and that habit has become a habit of acting on the whole for the best. It is easy for us to live without robbing each other. It would be possible for us to contend with and rob each other, but it would be harder for us than refraining from strife and robbery. That is in short the foundation of our life and our happiness.'

'Whereas in the old days,' said I, 'it was very hard to live without strife and robbery. That's what you mean, isn't it, by giving me the negative side of your good conditions?'

'Yes,' he said, 'it was so hard, that those who habitually acted fairly to their neighbours were celebrated as saints and heroes, and were looked up to with the greatest reverence.'

'While they were alive?' said I.

'No,' said he, 'after they were dead.'

'But as to these days,' I said; 'you don't mean to tell me that no one ever transgresses this habit of good fellowship?'

'Certainly not,' said Hammond, 'but when the transgressions occur, everybody, transgressors and all, know them for what they are; the errors of friends, not the habitual actions of persons driven into enmity against society.'

'I see,' said I: 'you mean that you have no "criminal" classes.'

'How could we have them,' said he, 'since there is no rich class to breed enemies against the state by means of the injustice of the state?'

Said I: 'I thought that I understood from something that fell from you a little while ago that you had abolished civil law. Is that so, literally?'

'It abolished itself, my friend,' said he. 'As I said before, the civil law courts were upheld for the defence of private property, for nobody ever pretended that it was possible to make people act fairly to each other by means of brute force. Well, private property being abolished, all the laws and all the legal "crimes" which it had manufactured of course came to an end. Thou shalt not steal, had to be translated into, Thou shalt work in order to live happily. Is there any need to enforce that commandment by violence?'

'Well,' said I, 'that is understood, and I agree with it; but how about the crimes of violence? would not their occurrence (and you admit that they occur) make criminal law necessary?'

Said he: 'In your sense of the word, we have no criminal law either. Let us look at the matter closer, and see whence crimes of violence spring. By far the greater part of these in past days were the result of the laws of private property, which forbade the satisfaction of their natural desires to all but a privileged few, and of the general visible coercion which came of those laws. All *that* cause of violent crime is gone. Again, many violent acts came from the artificial perversion of the sexual passions, which cause over-weening jealousy and the like miseries. Now, when you look carefully into these, you will find that what lay at the bottom of them was mostly the idea (a law-made idea) of the woman being the property of the man, whether he were husband, father, brother, or what not. That idea has of course vanished with private property, as well as certain follies about the "ruin" of women for following their natural desires in an illegal way, which of course was a convention caused by the laws of private property.

'Another cognate cause of crimes of violence was the family tyranny, which was the subject of so many novels and stories of the past, and which once more was the result of private property. Of course that is all ended, since families are held together by no bond of coercion, legal or social, but by mutual liking and affection, and everybody is free to come or go as he or she pleased. Furthermore, our standards of honour and public estimation are very different from the old ones; success in besting our neighbours is a road to renown now closed, let us hope for ever. Each man is free to exercise his special faculty to the utmost, and every one encourages him in so doing. So that we have got rid of the scowling envy, coupled by the poets with hatred, and surely with good reason; heaps of unhappiness and ill-blood were caused by it, which with irritable and passionate men – *i.e.*, energetic and active men – often led to violence.'

I laughed, and said: 'So that you now withdraw your admission, and say that there is no violence amongst you?'

'No,' said he, 'I withdraw nothing: as I told you, such things will happen. Hot blood will err sometimes. A man may strike another, and the stricken strike back again, and the result be a homicide, to put it at the worst. But what then? Shall we the neighbours make it worse still? Shall we think so poorly of each other as to suppose that the slain man calls on us to revenge him, when we *know* that if he had been maimed, he would, when in cold blood and able to weigh all the circumstances, have forgiven his maimer? Or will the death of the slayer bring the slain man to life again and cure the unhappiness his loss has caused?'

'Yes,' I said, 'but consider, must not the safety of society be safeguarded by some punishment?'

'There, neighbour!' said the old man, with some exultation. 'You have hit the mark. The *punishment* of which men used to talk so wisely and act so foolishly, what was it but the expression of their fear? And they had need to fear, since they – *i.e.,* the rulers of society – were dwelling like an armed band in a hostile country. But we who live amongst our friends need neither fear nor punish. Surely if we, in dread of an occasional rare homicide, an occasional rough blow, were solemnly and legally to commit homicide and violence, we could only be a society of ferocious cowards. Don't you think so, neighbour?'

'Yes, I do, when I come to think of it from that side,' said I.

'Yet you must understand,' said the old man, 'that when any violence is committed, we expect the transgressor to make any atonement possible to him, and he himself expects it. But again, think if the destruction or serious injury of a man momentarily overcome by wrath or folly can be any atonement to the commonwealth? Surely it can only be an additional injury to it.'

Said I: 'But suppose the man has a habit of violence – kills a man a year, for instance?'

'Such a thing is unknown,' said he. 'In a society where there is no punishment to evade, no law to triumph over, remorse will certainly follow transgression.'

'And lesser outbreaks of violence,' said I, 'how do you deal with them? for hitherto we have been talking of great tragedies, I suppose?'

Said Hammond: 'If the ill-doer is not sick or mad (in which case he must be restrained till his sickness or madness is cured) it is clear that grief and humiliation must follow the ill-deed; and society in general will make that pretty clear to the ill-doer if he should chance to be dull to it; and again, some kind of atonement will follow, – at the least, an open acknowledgment of the grief and humiliation. Is it so hard to say, I ask your pardon, neighbour? – Well, sometimes it is hard – and let it be.'

'You think that enough?' said I.

'Yes,' said he, 'and moreover it is all that we *can* do. If in addition we torture the man, we turn his grief into anger, and the humiliation he would otherwise feel for *his* wrong-doing is swallowed up by a hope of revenge for *our* wrong-doing to him. He has paid the legal penalty, and can "go and sin again" with comfort. Shall we commit such a folly, then? Remember Jesus had got the legal penalty remitted before he said "Go and sin no more". Let alone that in a society of equals you will not find any one to play the part of torturer or jailer, though many to act as nurse or doctor.'

'So,' said I, 'you consider crime a mere spasmodic disease, which requires no body of criminal law to deal with it?'

'Pretty much so,' said he; 'and since, as I told you, we are a healthy people generally, so we are not likely to be much troubled with *this* disease.'

'Well, you have no civil law, and no criminal law. But have you no laws of the market, so to say – no regulation for the exchange of wares? for you must exchange, even if you have no property.'

Said he: 'We have no obvious individual exchange, as you saw this morning when you went a-shopping; but of course there are regulations of the markets, varying according to the circumstances and guided by general custom. But as these are matters of general assent, which nobody dreams of objecting to, so also we have made no provision for enforcing them; therefore I don't call them laws. In law, whether it be criminal or civil, execution always follows judgment, and some one must suffer. When you see the judge on his bench, you see through him, as clearly as if he were made of glass, the policeman to imprison, and the soldier to slay some actual living person. Such follies would make an agreeable market, wouldn't they?'

'Certainly,' said I, 'that means turning the market into a mere battlefield, in which many people must suffer as much as in the battlefield of bullet and bayonet. And from what I have seen I should suppose that your marketing, great and little, is carried on in a way that makes it a pleasant occupation.'

'You are right, neighbour,' said he. 'Although there are so many, indeed by far the greater number amongst us, who would be unhappy if they were not engaged in actually making things, and things which turn out beautiful under their hands, – there are many, like the housekeepers I was speaking of, whose delight is in administration and organization, to use long-tailed words; I mean people who like keeping things together, avoiding waste, seeing that nothing sticks fast uselessly. Such people are thoroughly happy in their business, all the more as they are dealing with actual facts, and not merely passing counters round to see what share they shall have in the privileged taxation of useful people, which was the business of the commercial folk in the past days. Well, what are you going to ask me next?'

Chapter XIII
CONCERNING POLITICS

Said I: 'How do you manage with politics?'

Said Hammond, smiling: 'I am glad that it is of *me* that you ask the question: I do believe that anybody else would make you explain yourself, or try to do so, till you were sickened of asking questions. Indeed, I believe I am the only man in England who would know what you mean; and since I know, I will answer your question briefly by saying that we are very well off as to politics, – because we have none. If ever you make a book out of this conversation, put this in a chapter by itself, after the model of old Horrebow's Snakes in Iceland.'[33]

'I will,' said I.

Chapter XIV
HOW MATTERS ARE MANAGED

Said I: 'How about your relations with foreign nations?'

'I will not affect not to know what you mean,' said he, 'but I will tell you at once that the whole system of rival and contending nations which played so great a part in the "government" of the world of civilization has disappeared along with the inequality betwixt man and man in society.'

'Does not that make the world duller?' said I.

'Why?' said the old man.

'The obliteration of national variety,' said I.

'Nonsense,' he said, somewhat snappishly. 'Cross the water and see. You will find plenty of variety: the landscape, the building, the diet, the amusements, all various. The men and women varying in looks as well as in habits of thought: the costume far more various than in the commercial period. How should it add to the variety or dispel the dulness, to coerce certain families or tribes, often heterogeneous and jarring with one another, into certain artificial and mechanical groups, and call them nations, and stimulate their patriotism – *i.e.*, their foolish and envious prejudices?'

'Well – I don't know how,' said I.

'That's right,' said Hammond cheerily; 'you can easily understand that now we are freed from this folly it is obvious to us that by means of this very diversity the different strains of blood in the world can be serviceable and pleasant to each other, without in the least wanting to rob each other; we are all bent on the same enterprise, making the most of our lives. And I must tell you whatever quarrels or misunderstandings arise, they very seldom take place between people of different race; and consequently since there is less unreason in them, they are the more readily appeased.'

'Good,' said I, 'but as to those matters of politics; as to general differences of opinion in one and the same community. Do you assert that there are none?'[34]

'No, not at all,' said he, somewhat snappishly: 'but I do say that differences of opinion about real solid things need not, and with us do not, crystallize people into parties permanently hostile to one another, with different theories as to the build of the universe and the progress of time. Isn't that what politics used to mean?'

'H'm, well,' said I, 'I am not so sure of that.'

Said he: 'I take you, neighbour; they only *pretended* to this serious difference of opinion; for if it had existed they could not have dealt together in the ordinary business of life; couldn't have eaten together, bought and sold together, gambled together, cheated other people together, but must have fought whenever they met: which would not have suited them at all. The game of the masters of politics was to cajole or force the public to pay the expense of a luxurious life and exciting amusement for a few cliques of ambitious persons: and the *pretence* of serious difference of opinion, belied by every action of their lives, was quite good enough for that. What has all that got to do with us?'

Said I: 'Why, nothing, I should hope. But I fear – In short, I have been told that political strife was a necessary result of human nature.'

'Human nature!' cried the old boy, impetuously: 'what human nature? The human nature of paupers, of slaves, of slave-holders, or the human nature of wealthy freemen? Which? Come, tell me that!'

'Well,' said I, 'I suppose there would be a difference according to circumstances in people's action about these matters.'

'I should think so, indeed,' said he. 'At all events, experience shows that it is so. Amongst us, our differences concern matters of business, and passing events as to them, and could not divide men permanently. As a rule, the immediate outcome shows which opinion on a given subject is the right one; it is a matter of fact, not of speculation. For instance, it is clearly not easy to knock up a political party on the question as to whether haymaking in such and such a countryside shall begin this week or next, when all men agree that it must at latest begin the week after next, and when any man can go down into the fields himself and see whether the seeds are ripe enough for the cutting.'

Said I: 'And you settle these differences, great and small, by the will of the majority, I suppose?'

'Certainly,' said he; 'how else could we settle them? You see in matters which are merely personal which do not affect the welfare of the community – how a man shall dress, what he shall eat and drink, what he shall write and read, and so forth – there can be no difference of opinion, and everybody does as he pleases. But when the matter is of common interest to the whole community, and the doing or not doing something affects everybody, the majority must have their way; unless the minority were to take up arms and show by force that they were the effective or real majority; which, however, in a society of men who are free and equal is little likely to happen; because in such a community the apparent majority *is* the real majority, and the others, as I have hinted before, know that too well to obstruct from mere pigheadedness; especially as they have had plenty of opportunity of putting forward their side of the question.'

'How is that managed?' said I.

'Well,' said he, 'let us take one of our units of management, a commune, or a ward, or a parish (for we have all three names, indicating little real distinction between them now, though time was there was a good deal). In such a district as you would call it, some neighbours think that something ought to be done or undone: a new town-hall built; a clearance of inconvenient houses; or say a stone bridge substituted for some ugly old iron one, – there you have undoing and doing in one. Well, at the next ordinary meeting of the neighbours, or Mote, as we call it, according to the ancient tongue of the times before bureaucracy, a neighbour proposes the change, and of course, if everybody agrees, there is an end of discussion, except about details. Equally, if no one backs the proposer – "seconds him", it used to be called – the matter drops for the time being; a thing not likely to happen amongst reasonable men, however, as the proposer is sure to have talked it over with others before the Mote. But supposing the affair proposed and seconded, if a few of the neighbours disagree to it, if they think that the beastly iron bridge will serve a little longer and they don't want to be bothered with building a new one just then, they don't count heads that time, but put off the formal discussion to the next Mote; and meantime arguments *pro* and *con* are flying about, and some get printed, so that everybody knows what is going on; and when the Mote comes together again there is a regular discussion and at last a vote by show of hands. If the division is a close one, the question is again put off for further discussion; if the division is a wide one, the minority are asked if they will yield to the more general opinion, which they often, nay, most commonly do. If they refuse, the question is debated a third time, when, if the minority has not perceptibly grown, they always give way; though I believe there is some half-forgotten rule by which they might still carry it on further; but I say, what always happens is that they are convinced, not perhaps that their view is the wrong one, but they cannot persuade or force the community to adopt it.'

'Very good,' said I, 'but what happens if the divisions are still narrow?'

Said he: 'As a matter of principle and according to the rule of such cases, the question must then lapse, and the majority, if so narrow, has to submit to sitting down under the *status quo*. But I must tell you that in point of fact the minority very seldom enforces this rule, but generally yields in a friendly manner.'

'But do you know,' said I, 'that there is something in all this very like democracy;[35] and I thought that democracy was considered to be in a moribund condition many, many years ago.'

The old boy's eyes twinkled. 'I grant you that our methods have that drawback. But what is to be done? We can't get *any one* amongst us to complain of his not always having his own way in the teeth of the community, when it is clear that *everybody* cannot have that indulgence. What *is* to be done?'

'Well,' said I, 'I don't know.'

Said he: 'The only alternatives to our method that I can conceive of are these: First, that we should choose out, or breed, a class of superior persons capable of judging on all matters without consulting the neighbours; that, in short, we should get for ourselves what used to be called an aristocracy of intellect; or, secondly, that for the purpose of safeguarding the freedom of the individual will, we should revert to a system of private property again, and have slaves and slave-holders once more. What do you think of those two expedients?'

'Well,' said I, 'there is a third possibility – to wit, that every man should be quite independent of every other, and that thus the tyranny of society should be abolished.'[36]

He looked hard at me for a second or two, and then burst out laughing very heartily; and I confess that I joined him. When he recovered himself he nodded at me, and said: 'Yes, yes, I quite agree with you – and so we all do.'

'Yes,' I said, 'and besides, it does not press hardly on the minority:

for, take this matter of the bridge, no man is obliged to work on it if he doesn't agree to its building. At least, I suppose not.'

He smiled, and said: 'Shrewdly put; and yet from the point of view of the native of another planet. If the man of the minority does find his feelings hurt, doubtless he may relieve them by refusing to help in building the bridge. But, dear neighbour, that is not a very effective salve for the wound caused by the "tyranny of a majority" in our society; because all work that is done is either beneficial or hurtful to every member of society. The man is benefited by the bridge-building if it turns out a good thing, and hurt by it if it turns out a bad one, whether he puts a hand to it or not; and meanwhile he is benefiting the bridge-builders by his work, whatever that may be. In fact, I see no help for him except the pleasure of saying "I told you so" if the bridge-building turns out to be a mistake and hurts him; if it benefits him he must suffer in silence. A terrible tyranny our Communism, is it not? Folk used often to be warned against this very unhappiness in times past, when for every well-fed, contented person you saw a thousand miserable starvelings. Whereas for us, we grow fat and well-liking on the tyranny; a tyranny, to say the truth, not to be made visible by any microscope I know. Don't be afraid, my friend; we are not going to seek for troubles by calling our peace and plenty and happiness by ill names whose very meaning we have forgotten!'

He sat musing for a little, and then started and said: 'Are there any more questions, dear guest? This morning is waning fast amidst my garrulity.'

Chapter XV

ON THE LACK OF INCENTIVE TO LABOUR IN A COMMUNIST SOCIETY

'Yes,' said I. 'I was expecting Dick and Clara to make their appearance any moment: but is there time to ask just one or two questions before they come?'

'Try it, dear neighbour – try it,' said old Hammond. 'For the more you ask me the better I am pleased; and at any rate if they do come and find me in the middle of an answer, they must sit quiet and pretend to listen till I come to an end. It won't hurt them; they will find it quite amusing enough to sit side by side, conscious of their proximity to each other.'

I smiled, as I was bound to, and said: 'Good; I will go on talking without noticing them when they come in. Now, this is what I want to ask you about – to wit, how you get people to work when there is no reward of labour, and especially how you get them to work strenuously?'

'No reward of labour?' said Hammond, gravely. 'The reward of labour is *life*. Is that not enough?'

'But no reward for especially good work,' quoth I.

'Plenty of reward,' said he – 'the reward of creation. The wages which God gets, as people might have said time agone. If you are going to ask to be paid for the pleasure of creation, which is what excellence in work means, the next thing we shall hear of will be a bill sent in for the begetting of children.'

'Well, but,' said I, 'the man of the nineteenth century would say there is a natural desire towards the procreation of children, and a natural desire not to work.'

'Yes, yes,' said he, 'I know the ancient platitude, – wholly untrue; indeed, to us quite meaningless. Fourier, whom all men laughed at, understood the matter better.'[37]

'Why is it meaningless to you?' said I.

He said: 'Because it implies that all work is suffering, and we are so far from thinking that, that, as you may have noticed, whereas we are not short of wealth, there is a kind of fear growing up amongst us that we shall one day be short of work. It is a pleasure which we are afraid of losing, not a pain.'

'Yes,' said I, 'I have noticed that, and I was going to ask you about that also. But in the meantime, what do you positively mean to assert about the pleasurableness of work amongst you?'

'This, that *all* work is now pleasurable; either because of the hope of gain in honour and wealth with which the work is done, which causes pleasurable excitement, even when the actual work is not pleasant; or else because it has grown into a pleasurable *habit*, as in the case with what you may call mechanical work; and lastly (and most of our work is of this kind) because there is conscious sensuous pleasure in the work itself; it is done, that is, by artists.'

'I see,' said I. 'Can you now tell me how you have come to this happy condition? For, to speak plainly, this change from the conditions of the older world seems to me far greater and more important than all the other changes you have told me about as to crime, politics, property, marriage.'

'You are right there,' said he. 'Indeed, you may say rather that it is this change which makes all the others possible. What is the object of Revolution? Surely to make people happy. Revolution having brought its foredoomed change about, how can you prevent the counter-revolution from setting in except by making people happy? What! shall we expect peace and stability from unhappiness? The gathering of grapes from thorns and figs from thistles is a reasonable expectation compared with that! And happiness without happy daily work is impossible.'

'Most obviously true,' said I: for I thought the old boy was preaching a little. 'But answer my question, as to how you gained this happiness.'

'Briefly,' said he, 'by the absence of artificial coercion, and the freedom for every man to do what he can do best, joined to the knowledge of what productions of labour we really want. I must admit that this knowledge we reached slowly and painfully.'

'Go on,' said I, 'give me more detail; explain more fully. For this subject interests me intensely.'

'Yes, I will,' said he; 'but in order to do so I must weary you by talking a little about the past. Contrast is necessary for this explanation. Do you mind?'

'No, no,' said I.

Said he, settling himself in his chair again for a long talk: 'It is clear from all that we hear and read, that in the last age of civilization men had got into a vicious circle in the matter of production of wares. They had reached a wonderful facility of production, and in order to make the most of that facility they had gradually created (or allowed to grow, rather) a most elaborate system of buying and selling, which has been called the World-Market; and that World-

Market, once set a-going, forced them to go on making more and more of these wares, whether they needed them or not. So that while (of course) they could not free themselves from the toil of making real necessaries, they created in a never-ending series sham or artificial necessaries, which became, under the iron rule of the aforesaid World-Market, of equal importance to them with the real necessaries which supported life. By all this they burdened themselves with a prodigious mass of work merely for the sake of keeping their wretched system going.'

'Yes – and then?' said I.

'Why, then, since they had forced themselves to stagger along under this horrible burden of unnecessary production, it became impossible for them to look upon labour and its results from any other point of view than one – to wit, the ceaseless endeavour to expend the least possible amount of labour on any article made, and yet at the same time to make as many articles as possible. To this "cheapening of production", as it was called, everything was sacrificed: the happiness of the workman at his work, nay, his most elementary comfort and bare health, his food, his clothes, his dwelling, his leisure, his amusement, his education – his life, in short – did not weigh a grain of sand in the balance against this dire necessity of "cheap production" of things, a great part of which were not worth producing at all. Nay, we are told, and we must believe it, so overwhelming is the evidence, though many of our people scarcely *can* believe it, that even rich and powerful men, the masters of the poor devils aforesaid, submitted to live amidst sights and sounds and smells which it is in the very nature of man to abhor and flee from, in order that their riches might bolster up this supreme folly. The whole community, in fact, was cast into the jaws of this ravening monster, "the cheap production" forced upon it by the World-Market.'

'Dear me!' said I. 'But what happened? Did not their cleverness and facility in production master this chaos of misery at last? Couldn't they catch up with the World-Market, and then set to work to devise means for relieving themselves from this fearful task of extra labour?'

He smiled bitterly. 'Did they even try to?' said he. 'I am not sure.

You know that according to the old saw the beetle gets used to living in dung; and these people, whether they found the dung sweet or not, certainly lived in it.'

His estimate of the life of the nineteenth century made me catch my breath a little; and I said feebly, 'But the labour-saving machines?'

'Heyday!' quoth he. 'What's that you are saying? the labour-saving machines? Yes, they were made to "save labour" (or, to speak more plainly, the lives of men) on the piece of work in order that it might be expended – I will say wasted – on another, probably useless, piece of work. Friend, all their devices for cheapening labour simply resulted in increasing the burden of labour. The appetite of the World-Market grew with what it fed on: the countries within the ring of "civilization" (that is, organized misery) were glutted with the abortions of the market, and force and fraud were used unsparingly to "open up" countries *outside* that pale. This process of "opening up" is a strange one to those who have read the professions of the men of that period and do not understand their practice; and perhaps shows us at its worst the great vice of the nineteenth century, the use of hypocrisy and cant to evade the responsibility of vicarious ferocity. When the civilized World-Market coveted a country not yet in its clutches, some transparent pretext was found – the suppression of a slavery different from, and not so cruel as that of commerce; the pushing of a religion no longer believed in by its promoters; the "rescue" of some desperado or homicidal madman whose misdeeds had got him into trouble amongst the natives of the "barbarous" country – any stick, in short, which would beat the dog at all. Then some bold, unprincipled, ignorant adventurer was found (no difficult task in the days of competition), and he was bribed to "create a market" by breaking up whatever traditional society there might be in the doomed country, and by destroying whatever leisure or pleasure he found there. He forced wares on the natives which they did not want, and took their natural products in "exchange", as this form of robbery was called, and thereby he "created new wants", to supply which (that is, to be allowed to live by their new masters) the hapless, helpless people had to sell themselves into the slavery of hopeless toil so that they might have something wherewith to purchase the nullities of "civilization". Ah,' said the old man, pointing to the Museum, 'I have read books and papers in there, telling strange stories indeed of the dealings of civilization (or organized misery) with "non-civilization"; from the time when the British Government deliberately sent blankets infected with small-pox as choice gifts to inconvenient tribes of Red-skins, to the time when Africa was infested by a man named Stanley,[38] who—'

'Excuse me,' said I, 'but as you know, time presses; and I want to keep our question on the straightest line possible; and I want at once to ask this about these wares made for the World-Market – how about their quality; these people who were so clever about making goods, I suppose they made them well?'

'Quality!' said the old man crustily, for he was rather peevish at being cut short in his story; 'how could they possibly attend to such trifles as the quality of the wares they sold? The best of them were of a lowish average, the worst were transparent makeshifts for the things asked for, which nobody would have put up with if they could have got anything else. It was a current jest of the time that the wares were made to sell and not to use; a jest which you, as coming from another planet, may understand, but which our folk could not.'

Said I: 'What! did they make nothing well?'

'Why, yes,' said he, 'there was one class of goods which they did make thoroughly well, and that was the class of machines which were used for making things. These were usually quite perfect pieces of workmanship, admirably adapted to the end in view. So that it may be fairly said that the great achievement of the nineteenth century was the making of machines which were wonders of invention, skill, and patience, and which were used for the production of measureless quantities of worthless makeshifts. In truth, the owners of the machines did not consider anything which they made as wares, but simply as means for the enrichment of themselves. Of course, the only admitted test of utility in wares was the finding of buyers for them – wise men or fools, as it might chance.'

'And people put up with this?' said I.

'For a time,' said he.

'And then?'

'And then the overturn,' said the old man, smiling, 'and the nineteenth century saw itself as a man who has lost his clothes whilst bathing, and has to walk naked through the town.'

'You are very bitter about that unlucky nineteenth century,' said I.

'Naturally,' said he, 'since I know so much about it.'

He was silent a little, and then said: 'There are traditions – nay, real histories – in our family about it: my grandfather was one of its victims. If you know something about it, you will understand what he suffered when I tell you that he was in those days a genuine artist, a man of genius, and a revolutionist.'

'I think I do understand,' said I: 'but now, as it seems, you have reversed all this?'

'Pretty much so,' said he. 'The wares which we make are made because they are needed: men make for their neighbours' use as if they were making for themselves, not for a vague market of which they know nothing, and over which they have no control: as there is no buying and selling, it would be merely insanity to make goods on the chance of their being wanted; for there is no longer any one who can be *compelled* to buy them. So that whatever is made is good, and thoroughly fit for its purpose. Nothing *can* be made except for genuine use; therefore no inferior goods are made. Moreover, as aforesaid, we have now found out what we want, so we make no more than we want; and as we are not driven to make a vast quantity of useless things, we have time and resources enough to consider our pleasure in making them. All work which would be irksome to do by hand is done by immensely improved machinery; and in all work which it is a pleasure to do by hand machinery is done without. There is no difficulty in finding work which suits the special turn of mind of everybody; so that no man is sacrificed to the wants of an-other. From time to time, when we have found out that some piece of work was too disagreeable or troublesome, we have given it up and done altogether without the thing produced by it. Now, surely you can see that under these circumstances all the work that we do is an exercise of the mind and body more or less pleasant to be done: so that instead of avoiding work everybody seeks it: and, since people have got defter in doing the work generation after generation, it has become so easy to do, that it seems as if there were less done, though probably more is produced. I suppose this explains that fear, which I hinted at just now, of a possible scarcity in work, which perhaps you have already noticed, and which is a feeling on the increase, and has been for a score of years.'

'But do you think,' said I, 'that there is any fear of a work-famine?'

'No, I do not,' said he, 'and I will tell why; it is each man's business to make his own work pleasanter and pleasanter, which of course tends towards raising the standard of excellence, as no man enjoys turning out work which is not a credit to him, and also to greater deliberation in turning it out; and there is such a vast number of things which can be treated as works of art, that this alone gives employment to a host of deft people. Again, if art be inexhaustible, so is science also; and though it is no longer the only innocent occupation which is thought worth an intelligent man spending his time upon, as it once was, yet there are, and I suppose will be, many people who are excited by its conquest of difficulties, and care for it more than anything else. Again, as more and more of pleasure is imported into work, I think we shall take up kinds of work which produce desirable wares, but which we gave up because we could not carry them on pleasantly. Moreover, I think that it is only in parts of Europe which are more advanced than the rest of the world that you will hear this talk of the fear of a work-famine. Those lands which were once the colonies of Great Britain, for instance, and especially America – that part of it, above all, which was once the United States – are now and will be for a long while a great resource to us. For these lands, and, I say, especially the northern parts of America, suffered so terribly from the full force of the last days of civilization, and became such horrible places to live in, that they are now very backward in all that makes life pleasant. Indeed, one may say that for nearly a hundred years the people of the northern parts of America have been engaged in gradually making a dwelling-place out of a stinking dust-heap; and there is still a great deal to do, especially as the country is so big.'

'Well,' said I, 'I am exceedingly glad to think that you have such a prospect of happiness before you. But I should like to ask a few more questions, and then I have done for today.'

Chapter XVI

DINNER IN THE HALL OF THE BLOOMSBURY MARKET

As I spoke, I heard footsteps near the door; the latch yielded, and in came our two lovers, looking so handsome that one had no feeling of shame in looking on at their little-concealed love-making; for indeed it seemed as if all the world must be in love with them. As for old Hammond, he looked on them like an artist who has just painted a picture nearly as well as he thought he could when he began it, and was perfectly happy. He said:

'Sit down, sit down, young folk, and don't make a noise. Our guest here has still some questions to ask me.'

'Well, I should suppose so,' said Dick; 'you have only been three hours and a half together; and it isn't to be hoped that the history of two centuries could be told in three hours and a half: let alone that, for all I know, you may have been wandering into the realms of geography and craftsmanship.'

'As to noise, my dear kinsman,' said Clara, 'you will very soon be disturbed by the noise of the dinner-bell, which I should think will be very pleasant music to our guest, who breakfasted early, it seems, and probably had a tiring day yesterday.'

I said: 'Well, since you have spoken the word, I begin to feel that it is so; but I have been feeding myself with wonder this long time past: really, it's quite true,' quoth I, as I saw her smile, oh so prettily!

But just then from some tower high up in the air came the sound of silvery chimes playing a sweet clear tune, that sounded to my unaccustomed ears like the song of the first blackbird in the spring, and called a rush of memories to my mind, some of bad times, some of good, but all sweetened now into mere pleasure.

'No more questions now before dinner,' said Clara; and she took my hand as an affectionate child would, and led me out of the room and down stairs into the forecourt of the Museum, leaving the two Hammonds to follow as they pleased.

We went into the market-place which I had been in before, a thinnish stream of elegantly* dressed people going in along with us.

* 'Elegant,' I mean, as a Persian pattern is elegant; not like a rich 'elegant' lady out for a morning call. I should rather call that *genteel*.

We turned into the cloister and came to a richly moulded and carved doorway, where a very pretty dark-haired young girl gave us each a beautiful bunch of summer flowers, and we entered a hall much bigger than that of the Hammersmith Guest House, more elaborate in its architecture and perhaps more beautiful. I found it difficult to keep my eyes off the wall-pictures (for I thought it bad manners to stare at Clara all the time, though she was quite worth it). I saw at a glance that their subjects were taken from queer old-world myths and imaginations which in yesterday's world only about half a dozen people in the country knew anything about; and when the two Hammonds sat down opposite to us, I said to the old man, pointing to the frieze:

'How strange to see such subjects here!'

'Why?' said he. 'I don't see why you should be surprised; everybody knows the tales; and they are graceful and pleasant subjects, not too tragic for a place where people mostly eat and drink and amuse themselves, and yet full of incident.'

I smiled, and said: 'Well, I scarcely expected to find record of the Seven Swans and the King of the Golden Mountain and Faithful Henry, and such curious pleasant imaginations as Jacob Grimm got together from the childhood of the world, barely lingering even in his time: I should have thought you would have forgotten such childishness by this time.'

The old man smiled, and said nothing; but Dick turned rather red, and broke out:

'What *do* you mean, guest? I think them very beautiful, I mean not only the pictures, but the stories; and when we were children we used to imagine them going on in every wood-end, by the bight of every stream: every house in the fields was the Fairyland King's House to us. Don't you remember, Clara?'

'Yes,' she said; and it seemed to me as if a slight cloud came over her fair face. I was going to speak to her on the subject, when the pretty waitresses came to us smiling, and chattering sweetly like reed warblers by the river-side, and fell to giving us our dinner. As to this, as at our breakfast, everything was cooked and served with a daintiness which showed that those who had prepared it were interested in it; but there was no excess either of quantity or of gourmandize; everything was simple, though so excellent of its kind; and it was made clear to us that this was no feast, only an ordinary meal. The glass, crockery, and plate were very beautiful to my eyes, used to the study of mediaeval art; but a nineteenth-century club-haunter would, I daresay, have found them rough and lacking in finish; the crockery being lead-glazed pot-ware, though beautifully ornamented; the only porcelain being here and there a piece of old oriental ware. The glass, again, though elegant and quaint, and very varied in form, was somewhat bubbled and hornier in texture than the commercial articles of the nineteenth century. The furniture and general fittings of the hall were much of a piece with the table-gear, beautiful in form and highly ornamented, but without the commercial 'finish' of the joiners and cabinet-makers of our time. Withal, there was a total absence of what the nineteenth century calls 'comfort' – that is, stuffy inconvenience; so that, even apart from the delightful excitement of the day, I had never eaten my dinner so pleasantly before.

When we had done eating, and were sitting a little while, with a bottle of very good Bordeaux wine before us, Clara came back to the question of the subject-matter of the pictures, as though it had troubled her.

She looked up at them, and said: 'How is it that though we are so interested with our life for the most part, yet when people take to writing poems or painting pictures they seldom deal with our modern life, or if they do, take good care to make their poems or pictures unlike that life? Are we not good enough to paint ourselves? How is it that we find the dreadful times of the past so interesting to us – in pictures and poetry?'

Old Hammond smiled. 'It always was so, and I suppose always will be,' said he, 'however it may be explained. It is true that in the nineteenth century, when there was so little art and so much talk about it, there was a theory that art and imaginative literature ought to deal with contemporary life; but they never did so; for, if there was any pretence of it, the author always took care (as Clara hinted just now) to disguise, or exaggerate, or idealize, and in some way or another make it strange; so that, for all the verisimilitude there was, he might just as well have dealt with the times of the Pharaohs.'

'Well,' said Dick, 'surely it is but natural to like these things strange; just as when we were children, as I said just now, we used to pretend to be so-and-so in such-and-such a place. That's what these pictures and poems do; and why shouldn't they?'

'Thou hast hit it, Dick,' quoth old Hammond; 'it is the child-like part of us that produces work of imagination. When we are children time passes so slow with us that we seem to have time for everything.'

He sighed, and then smiled and said: 'At least let us rejoice that we have got back our childhood again. I drink to the days that are!'

'Second childhood,' said I in a low voice, and then blushed at my double rudeness, and hoped that he hadn't heard. But he had, and turned to me smiling, and said: 'Yes, why not? And for my part, I hope it may last long; and that the world's next period of wise and unhappy manhood, if that should happen, will speedily lead us to a third childhood: if indeed this age be not our third. Meantime, my friend, you must know that we are too happy, both individually and collectively, to trouble ourselves about what is to come hereafter.'

'Well, for my part,' said Clara, 'I wish we were interesting enough to be written or painted about.'

Dick answered her with some lover's speech, impossible to be written down, and then we sat quiet a little.

Chapter XVII
HOW THE CHANGE CAME

Dick broke the silence at last saying: 'Guest, forgive us for a little after-dinner dulness. What would you like to do? Shall we have out Greylocks and trot back to Hammersmith? or will you come with us and hear some Welsh folk sing in a hall close by here? or would you like presently to come with me into the City and see some really fine building? or – what shall it be?'

'Well,' said I, 'as I am a stranger, I must let you choose for me.'

In point of fact, I did not by any means want to be 'amused' just then; and also I rather felt as if the old man, with his knowledge of past times, and even a kind of inverted sympathy for them caused by his active hatred of them was as it were a blanket for me against the cold of this very new world, where I was, so to say, stripped bare of every habitual thought and way of acting; and I did not want to leave him too soon. He came to my rescue at once, and said –

'Wait a bit, Dick; there is someone else to be consulted besides you and the guest here, and that is I. I am not going to lose the pleasure of his company just now, especially as I know he has something else to ask me. So go to your Welshmen, by all means; but first of all bring us another bottle of wine to this nook, and then be off as soon as you like; and come again and fetch our friend to go westward, but not too soon.'

Dick nodded smilingly, and the old man and I were soon alone in the great hall, the afternoon sun gleaming on the red wine in our tall quaint-shaped glasses. Then said Hammond:

'Does anything especially puzzle you about our way of living, now you have heard a good deal and seen a little of it?'

Said I: 'I think what puzzles me most is how it all came about.'

'It well may,' said he, 'so great as the change is. It would be difficult indeed to tell you the whole story, perhaps impossible: knowledge, discontent, treachery, disappointment, ruin, misery, despair – those who worked for the change because they could see further than other people went through all these phases of suffering; and doubtless all the time the most of men looked on, not knowing what was doing, thinking it all a matter of course, like the rising and setting of the sun – and indeed it was so.'

'Tell me one thing, if you can,' said I. 'Did the change, the "revolution" it used to be called, come peacefully?'

'Peacefully?' said he; 'what peace was there amongst those poor confused wretches of the nineteenth century? It was war from beginning to end: bitter war, till hope and pleasure put an end to it.'

'Do you mean actual fighting with weapons,' said I, 'or the strikes and lock-outs and starvation of which we have heard?'

'Both, both,' he said. 'As a matter of fact, the history of the terrible period of transition from commercial slavery to freedom may thus be summarized. When the hope of realizing a communal condition of life for all men arose, quite late in the nineteenth century, the power of the middle classes, the then tyrants of society, was so enormous and crushing, that to almost all men, even those who had, you may say despite themselves, despite their reason and judgement, conceived such hopes, it seemed a dream. So much was this the case that some of those more enlightened men who were then called Socialists, although they well knew, and even stated in public, that the only reasonable condition of Society was that of pure Communism (such as you now see around you), yet shrunk from what seemed to them the barren task of preaching the realization of a happy dream. Looking back now, we can see that the great motive-power of the change was a longing for freedom and equality, akin if you please to the unreasonable passion of the lover; a sickness of heart that rejected with loathing the aimless solitary life of the well-to-do educated man of that time: phrases, my dear friend, which have lost their meaning to us of the present day; so far removed we are from the dreadful facts which they represent.

'Well, these men, though conscious of this feeling, had no faith in it, as a means of bringing about the change. Nor was that wonderful: for looking around them they saw the huge mass of the oppressed classes too much burdened with the misery of their lives, and too much overwhelmed by the selfishness of misery, to be able to form a conception of any escape from it except by the ordinary way prescribed by the system of slavery under which they lived; which was nothing more than a remote chance of climbing out of the oppressed into the oppressing class.

'Therefore, though they knew that the only reasonable aim for those who would better the world was a condition of equality; in their impatience and despair they managed to convince themselves that if they could by hook or by crook get the machinery of production and the management of property so altered that the "lower classes" (so the horrible word ran) might have their slavery somewhat ameliorated, they would be ready to fit into this machinery, and would use it for bettering their condition still more and still more, until at last the result would be a practical equality (they were very fond of using the word "practical"), because "the rich" would be forced to pay so much for keeping "the poor" in a tolerable condition that the condition of riches would become no longer valuable and would gradually die out. Do you follow me?'

'Partly,' said I. 'Go on.'

Said old Hammond: 'Well, since you follow me, you will see that as a theory this was not altogether unreasonable; but "practically", it turned out a failure.'

'How so?' said I.

'Well, don't you see,' said he, 'because it involved the making of a machinery by those who didn't know what they wanted the machines to do. So far as the masses of the oppressed class furthered this scheme of improvement, they did it to get themselves improved slave-rations – as many of them as could. And if those classes had really been incapable of being touched by that instinct which produced the passion for freedom and equality aforesaid, what would have happened, I think, would have been this: that a certain part of the working classes would have been so far improved in condition that they would have approached the condition of the middling rich men; but below them would have been a great class of most miserable slaves, whose slavery would have been far more hopeless than the older class-slavery had been.'

'What stood in the way of this?' said I.

'Why, of course,' said he, 'just that instinct for freedom aforesaid. It is true that the slave-class could not conceive the happiness of a free life. Yet they grew to understand (and very speedily too) that they were oppressed by their masters, and they assumed, you see how justly, that they could do without them, though perhaps they scarce knew how; so that it came to this, that though they could not look forward to the happiness or peace of the freeman, they did at least look forward to the war which a vague hope told them would bring that peace about.'

'Could you tell me rather more closely what actually took place?' said I; for I thought *him* rather vague here.

'Yes,' he said, 'I can. That machinery of life for the use of people who didn't know what they wanted of it, and which was known at the time as State Socialism,[39] was partly put in motion, though in a very piecemeal way. But it did not work smoothly; it was, of course, resisted at every turn by the capitalists; and no wonder, for it tended more and more to upset the commercial system I have told you of, without providing anything really effective in its place. The result was growing confusion, great suffering amongst the working classes, and, as a consequence, great discontent. For a long time matters went on like this. The power of the upper classes had lessened, as their command over wealth lessened, and they could not carry things wholly by the high hand as they had been used to in earlier days. So far the State Socialists were justified by the result. On the other hand, the working classes were ill-organized, and growing poorer in reality, in spite of the gains (also real in the long run) which they had forced from the masters. Thus matters hung in the balance, the masters could not reduce their slaves to complete subjection, though they put down some feeble and partial riots easily enough. The workers forced their masters to grant them ameliorations, real or imaginary, of their condition, but could not force freedom from them. At last came a great crash. To explain this you must understand that very great progress had been made amongst the workers, though as before said but little in the direction of improved livelihood.'

I played the innocent and said: 'In what direction could they improve if not in livelihood?'

Said he: 'In the power to bring about a state of things in which livelihood would be full, and easy to gain. They had at last learned how to combine after a long period of mistakes and disasters. The workmen had now a regular organization in the struggle against their masters, a struggle which for more than half a century had been accepted as an inevitable part of the conditions of the modern system of labour and production. This combination had now taken the form of a federation of all or almost all the recognized wage-paid employments, and it was by its means that those betterments of the condition of the workmen had been forced from the masters: and though they were not seldom mixed up with the rioting that happened, especially in the earlier days of their organization, it by no means formed an essential part of their tactics; indeed at the time I am now speaking of they had got to be so strong that most commonly the mere threat of a "strike" was enough to gain any minor point: because they had given up the foolish tactics of the ancient trades unions of calling out of work a part only of the workers of such and such an industry, and supporting them while out of work on the labour of those that remained in. By this time they had a biggish fund of money for the support of strikes, and could stop a certain industry altogether for a time if they so determined.'

Said I: 'Was there not a serious danger of such moneys being misused – of jobbery, in fact?'

Old Hammond wriggled uneasily on his seat, and said:

'Though all this happened so long ago, I still feel the pain of mere shame when I have to tell you that it was more than a danger: that such rascality often happened; indeed more than once the whole combination seemed dropping to pieces because of it: but at the time of which I am telling, things looked so threatening, and to the workmen at least the necessity of their dealing with the fast-gathering trouble which the labour-struggle had brought about, was so clear, that the conditions of the times had begot a deep seriousness amongst all reasonable people; a determination which put aside all non-essentials, and which to thinking men was ominous of the swiftly-approaching change; such an element was too dangerous for mere traitors and self-seekers, and one by one they were thrust out and mostly joined the declared reactionaries.'

'How about those ameliorations,' said I; 'what were they? or rather of what nature?'

Said he: 'Some of them, and these of the most practical importance to the men's livelihood, were yielded by the masters by direct compulsion on the part of the men; the new conditions of labour so gained were indeed only customary, enforced by no law: but, once established, the masters durst not attempt to withdraw them in face of the growing power of the combined workers. Some again were steps on the path of 'State Socialism'; the most important of which can be speedily summed up. At the end of the nineteenth century the cry arose for compelling the masters to employ their men a less number of hours in the day: this cry gathered volume quickly and the masters had to yield to it.[40] But it was, of course, clear that unless this meant a higher price for work per hour, it would be a mere nullity, and that the masters, unless forced, would reduce it to that. Therefore after a long struggle another law was passed fixing a minimum price for labour in the most important industries; which again had to be supplemented by a law fixing the maximum price on the chief wares then considered necessary for a workman's life.'

'You were getting perilously near to the late Roman poor-rates,' said I, smiling, 'and the doling out of bread to the proletariat.'

'So many said at the time,' said the old man drily; 'and it has long been a commonplace that that slough awaits State Socialism in the end, if it gets to the end, which as you know it did not with us. However, it went further than this minimum and maximum business, which by the by we can now see was necessary. The government now found it imperative on them to meet the outcry of the master class at the approaching destruction of commerce (as desirable, had they known it, as the extinction of the cholera, which has since happily taken place). And they were forced to meet it by a measure hostile to the masters, the establishment of government factories for the production of necessary wares, and markets for their sale. These measures taken altogether did do something: they were in fact of the nature of regulations made by the commander of a beleaguered city. But of course to the privileged classes it seemed as if the end of the world were come when such laws were enacted.

'Nor was that altogether without a warrant: the spread of communistic theories, and the partial practice of State Socialism had at first disturbed, and at last almost paralysed, the marvellous system of commerce under which the old world had lived so feverishly, and had produced for some few a life of gambler's pleasure, and for many, or most, a life of mere misery: over and over again came "bad times" as they were called, and indeed they were bad enough for the wage-slaves. The year 1952 was one of the worst of these times; the workmen suffered dreadfully: the partial, inefficient government factories, which were terribly jobbed, all but broke down, and a vast part of the population had for the time being to be fed on undisguised "charity" as it was called.

'The Combined Workers watched the situation with mingled hope and anxiety. They had already formulated their general demands; but now by a solemn and universal vote of the whole of their federated societies, they insisted on the first step being taken toward carrying out their demands: this step would have led directly to the handing over the management of the whole natural resources of the country, together with the machinery for using them, into the power of the Combined Workers, and the reduction of the privileged classes into the position of pensioners obviously dependent on the pleasure of the workers. The "Resolution", as it was called, which was widely published in the newspapers of the day, was in fact a declaration of war, and was so accepted by the master class. They began henceforward to prepare for a firm stand against the "brutal and ferocious communism of the day", as they phrased it. And as they were in many ways still very powerful, or seemed so to be, they still hoped by means of brute force to regain some of what they had lost, and perhaps in the end the whole of it. It was said amongst them on all hands that it had been a great mistake of the various governments not to have resisted sooner; and the liberals and radicals (the name as perhaps you may know of the more democratically inclined part of the ruling classes) were much blamed for having led the world to this pass by their mis-timed pedantry and foolish sentimentality: and one Gladstone, or Gladstein (probably, judging by this name, of Scandinavian descent), a notable politician of the nineteenth century, was especially singled out for reprobation in this respect. I need scarcely point out to you the absurdity of all this. But terrible tragedy lay hidden behind this grinning through a horse-collar of the reactionary party. "The insatiable greed of the lower classes must be repressed" – "The people must be taught a lesson" – these were the sacramental phrases current amongst the reactionists, and ominous enough they were.'

The old man stopped to look keenly at my attentive and wondering face, and then said:

'I know, dear guest, that I have been using words and phrases which few people amongst us could understand without long and laborious explanation; and not even then perhaps. But since you have not yet gone to sleep, and since I am speaking to you as to a being from another planet, I may venture to ask you if you have followed me thus far?'

'Oh yes,' said I, 'I quite understand: pray go on; a great deal of what you have been saying was commonplace with us – when – when—'

'Yes,' said he gravely, 'when you were dwelling in the other planet. Well, now for the crash aforesaid.[41]

'On some comparatively trifling occasion a great meeting was summoned by the workmen leaders to meet in Trafalgar Square (about the right to meet in which place there had for years and years been bickering). The civic *bourgeois* guard (called the police) attacked the said meeting with bludgeons, according to their custom; many people were hurt in the *mêlée*, of whom five in all died, either trampled to death on the spot, or from the effects of their cudgelling; the meeting was scattered, and some hundred of prisoners cast into gaol. A similar meeting had been treated in the same way a few days before at a place called Manchester, which has now disappeared. Thus the "lesson" began. The whole country was thrown into a ferment by this; meetings were held which attempted some rough organization for the holding of another meeting to retort on the authorities. A huge crowd assembled in Trafalgar Square and the neighbourhood (then a place of crowded streets), and was too big for the bludgeon-armed police to cope with; there was a good deal of dry-blow fighting; three or four of the people were killed, and half a score of policemen were crushed to death in the throng, and the rest got away as they could. This was a victory for the people as far as it went. The next day all London (remember what it was in those days) was in a state of turmoil. Many of the rich fled into the country; the executive got together soldiery, but did not dare to use them; and the police could not be massed in any one place, because riots or threats of riots were everywhere. But in Manchester, where the people were not so courageous or not so desperate as in London, several of the popular leaders were arrested. In London a convention of leaders was got together from the Federation of Combined Workmen, and sat under the old revolutionary name of the Committee of Public Safety; but as they had no drilled and armed body of men to direct, they attempted no aggressive measures, but only placarded the walls with somewhat vague appeals to the workmen not to allow themselves to be trampled upon. However, they called a meeting in Trafalgar Square for the day fortnight of the last mentioned skirmish.

'Meantime the town grew no quieter, and business came pretty much to an end. The newspapers – then, as always hitherto, almost entirely in the hands of the masters – clamoured to the Government for repressive measures; the rich citizens were enrolled as an extra body of police, and armed with bludgeons like them; many of these were strong, well-fed, full-blooded young men, and had plenty of stomach for fighting; but the Government did not dare to use them, and contented itself with getting full powers voted to it by the Parliament for suppressing any revolt, and bringing up more and more soldiers to London. Thus passed the week after the great meeting; almost as large a one was held on the Sunday, which went off peaceably on the whole, as no opposition to it was offered, and again the people cried "victory". But on the Monday the people woke up to find that they were hungry. During the last few days there had been groups of men parading the streets asking (or, if you please, demanding) money to buy food; and what for goodwill, what for fear, the richer people gave them a good deal. The authorities of the parishes also (I haven't time to explain that phrase at present) gave willy-nilly what provisions they could to wandering people; and the Government, by means of its feeble national workshops also fed a good number of half-starved folk. But in addition to this, several bakers' shops and other provision stores had been emptied without a great deal of disturbance. So far, so good. But on the Monday in question the Committee of Public Safety, on the one hand afraid of general unorganized pillage, and on the other emboldened by the wavering conduct of the authorities, sent a deputation provided with carts and all necessary gear to clear out two or three big provision stores in the centre of the town, leaving papers with the shop managers promising to pay the price of them: and also in the part of the town where they were strongest they took possession of several bakers' shops and set men at work in them for the benefit of the people; – all of which was done with little or no disturbance, the police assisting in keeping order at the sack of the stores, as they would have done at a big fire.

'But at this last stroke the reactionaries were so alarmed, that they were determined to force the executive into action. The newspapers next day all blazed into the fury of frightened people, and threatened the people, the Government, and everybody they could think of, unless "order were at once restored". A deputation of leading commercial people waited on the Government and told them that if they did not at once arrest the Committee of Public Safety, they themselves would gather, a body of men, arm them, and fall on "the incendiar-ies", as they called them.

'They, together with a number of the newspaper editors, had a long interview with the heads of the Government and two or three military men, the deftest in their art that the country could furnish. The deputation came away from that interview, says a contemporary eye-witness, smiling and satisfied, and said no more about raising an anti-popular army, but that afternoon left London with their families for their country seats or elsewhere.

'The next morning the Government proclaimed a state of siege in London, – a thing common enough amongst the absolutist govern-ments on the Continent, but unheard-of in England in those days. They appointed the youngest and cleverest of their generals to command the proclaimed district; a man who had won a certain sort of reputation in the disgraceful wars in which the country had been long engaged from time to time. The newspapers were in ecstasies, and all the most fervent of the reactionaries now came to the front; men who in ordinary times were forced to keep their opinions to themselves or their immediate circle, but who began to look forward to crushing once for all the Socialist, and even democratic tendencies, which, said they, had been treated with such foolish indulgence for the last sixty years.[42]

'But the clever general took no visible action; and yet only a few of the minor newspapers abused him; thoughtful men gathered from this that a plot was hatching. As for the Committee of Public Safety, whatever they thought of their position, they had now gone too far to draw back; and many of them, it seems, thought that the Government would not act. They went on quietly organizing their food supply, which was a miserable driblet when all is said; and also as a retort to the state of siege, they armed as many men as they could in the quarter where they were strongest, but did not attempt to drill or organize them, thinking, perhaps, that they could not at the best turn them into trained soldiers till they had some breathing space. The clever general, his soldiers, and the police did not meddle with all this in the least in the world; and things were quieter in London that week-end; though there were riots in many places of the provinces, which were quelled by the authorities without much trouble. The most serious of these were at Glasgow and Bristol.

'Well, the Sunday of the meeting came, and great crowds came to Trafalgar Square in procession, the greater part of the Committee amongst them, surrounded by their band of men armed somehow or other. The streets were quite peaceful and quiet, though there were many spectators to see the procession pass. Trafalgar Square had no body of police in it; the people took quiet possession of it, and the meeting began. The armed men stood round the principal platform, and there were a few others armed amidst the general crowd; but by far the greater part were unarmed.

'Most people thought the meeting would go off peaceably; but the members of the Committee had heard from various quarters that something would be attempted against them; but these rumours were vague, and they had no idea of what threatened. They soon found out.

'For before the streets about the Square were filled, a body of soldiers poured into it from the north-west corner and took up their places by the houses that stood on the west side. The people growled at the sight of the red-coats; the armed men of the Committee stood undecided, not knowing what to do; and indeed this new influx so jammed the crowd together that, unorganized as they were, they had little chance of working through it. They had scarcely grasped the fact of their enemies being there, when another column of soldiers, pouring out of the streets which led into the great southern road going down to the Parliament House (still existing, and called the Dung Market), and also from the embankment by the side of the Thames, marched up, pushing the crowd into a denser and denser mass, and formed along the south side of the Square. Then any of those who could see what was going on, knew at once that they were in a trap, and could only wonder what would be done with them.

'The closely-packed crowd would not or could not budge, except under the influence of the height of terror, which was soon to be supplied to them. A few of the armed men struggled to the front, or climbed up the base of the monument which then stood there, that they might face the wall of hidden fire before them; and to most men (there were many women amongst them) it seemed as if the end of the world had come, and to-day seemed strangely different from yesterday.[43] No sooner were the soldiers drawn up aforesaid than, says an eye-witness, "a glittering officer on horseback came prancing out from the ranks on the south, and read something from a paper which he held in his hand; which something, very few heard; but I was told afterwards that it was an order for us to disperse, and a warning that he had legal right to fire on the crowd else, and that he would do so. The crowd took it as a challenge of some sort, and a hoarse threatening roar went up from them; and after that there was comparative silence for a little, till the officer had got back into the ranks. I was near the edge of the crowd, towards the soldiers," says this eye-witness, "and I saw three little machines being wheeled out in front of the ranks, which I knew for mechanical guns. I cried out, 'Throw yourselves down! they are going to fire!' But no one scarcely could throw himself down, so tight as the crowd were packed. I heard a sharp order given, and wondered where I should be the next minute; and then— It was as if the earth had opened, and hell had come up bodily amidst us. It was no use trying to describe the scene that followed. Deep lanes were mowed amidst the thick crowd; the dead and dying covered the ground, and the shrieks and wails and cries of horror filled all the air, till it seemed as if there was nothing else in the world but murder and death. Those of our armed men who were still unhurt cheered wildly and opened a scattering fire on the soldiers. One or two soldiers fell; and I saw the officers going up and down the ranks urging the men to fire again; but they received the orders in sullen silence, and let the butts of their guns fall. Only one sergeant ran to a machine-gun and began to set it going; but a tall young man, an officer too, ran out of the ranks and dragged him back by the collar; and the soldiers stood there motionless whilst the horror-stricken crowd, nearly wholly unarmed (for most of the armed men had fallen in that first discharge), drifted out of the Square. I was told afterwards that the soldiers on the west side had fired also, and done their part of the slaughter. How I got out of the Square I scarcely know: I went, not feeling the ground under me, what with rage and terror and despair."

'So says our eye-witness. The number of the slain on the side of the people in that shooting during a minute was prodigious; but it was not easy to come at the truth about it; it was probably between one and two thousand. Of the soldiers, six were killed outright, and a dozen wounded.'

I listened, trembling with excitement. The old man's eyes glittered and his face flushed as he spoke, and told the tale of what I had often thought might happen. Yet I wondered that he should have got so elated about a mere massacre, and I said:

'How fearful! And I suppose that this massacre put an end to the whole revolution for that time?'

'No, no,' cried old Hammond; 'it began it!'

He filled his glass and mine, and stood up and cried out, 'Drink this glass to the memory of those who died there, for indeed it would be a long tale to tell how much we owe them.'

I drank, and he sat down again and went on.

'That massacre of Trafalgar Square began the civil war, though, like all such events, it gathered head slowly, and people scarcely knew what a crisis they were acting in.

'Terrible as the massacre was, and hideous and overpowering as the first terror had been, when the people had time to think about it, their feeling was one of anger rather than fear; although the military organization of the state of siege was now carried out without shrinking by the clever young general. For though the ruling classes when the news spread next morning felt one gasp of horror and even dread, yet the Government and their immediate backers felt that now the wine was drawn and must be drunk. However, even the most reactionary of the capitalist papers, with two exceptions, stunned by the tremendous news, simply gave an account of what had taken place, without making any comment upon it. The exceptions were one, a so-called "Liberal" paper (the Government of the day was of that complexion), which, after a preamble in which it declared its undeviating sympathy with the cause of labour, proceeded to point out that in times of revolutionary disturbance it behoved the Government to be just but firm, and that by far the most merciful way of dealing with the poor madmen who were attacking the very foundations of society (which had made them mad and poor) was to shoot them at once, so as to stop others from drifting into a position in which they would run a chance of being shot. In short, it praised the determined action of the Government as the *acmé* of human wisdom and mercy, and exulted in the inauguration of an epoch of reasonable democracy free from the tyrannical fads of Socialism.[44]

'The other exception was a paper thought to be one of the most violent opponents of democracy, and so it was; but the editor of it found his manhood, and spoke for himself and not for his paper. In a few simple, indignant words he asked people to consider what a society was worth which had to be defended by the massacre of unarmed citizens, and called on the Government to withdraw their state of siege and put the general and his officers who fired on the people on their trial for murder. He went further, and declared that whatever his opinion might be as to the doctrines of the Socialists, he for one should throw in his lot with the people, until the Government atoned for their atrocity by showing that they were prepared to listen to the demands of men who knew what they wanted, and whom the decrepitude of society forced into pushing their demands in some way or other.

'Of course, this editor was immediately arrested by the military power; but his bold words were already in the hands of the public, and produced a great effect: so great an effect that the Government, after some vacillation, withdrew the state of siege; though at the same time it strengthened the military organization and made it more stringent. Three of the Committee of Public Safety had been slain in Trafalgar Square: of the rest, the greater part went back to their old place of meeting, and there awaited the event calmly. They were arrested there on the Monday morning, and would have been shot at once by the general, who was a mere military machine, if the Government had not shrunk before the responsibility of killing men without any trial. There was at first a talk of trying them by a special commission of judges, as it was called – *i.e.*, before a set of men bound to find them guilty, and whose business it was to do so. But with the Government the cold fit had succeeded to the hot one; and the prisoners were brought before a jury at the assizes. There a fresh blow awaited the Government; for in spite of the judge's charge, which distinctly instructed the jury to find the prisoners guilty, they were acquitted, and the jury added to their verdict a presentment, in which they condemned the action of the soldiery, in the queer phraseology of the day, as "rash, unfortunate, and unnecessary". The Committee of Public Safety renewed its sittings, and from thenceforth was a popular rallying-point in opposition to the Parliament.

The Government now gave way on all sides, and made a show of yielding to the demands of the people, though there was a widespread plot for effecting a *coup d'état* set on foot between the leaders of the two so-called opposing parties in the parliamentary faction fight. The well-meaning part of the public was overjoyed, and thought that all danger of a civil war was over. The victory of the people was celebrated by huge meetings held in the parks and elsewhere, in memory of the victims of the great massacre.

'But the measures passed for the relief of the workers, though to the upper classes they seemed ruinously revolutionary, were not thorough enough to give the people food and a decent life, and they had to be supplemented by unwritten enactments without legality to back them. Although the Government and Parliament had the law-courts, the army, and "society" at their backs, the Committee of Public Safety began to be a force in the country, and really represented the producing classes. It began to improve immensely in the days which followed on the acquittal of its members. Its old members had little administrative capacity, though with the exception of a few self-seekers and traitors, they were honest, courageous men, and many of them were endowed with considerable talent of other kinds. But now that the times called for immediate action, came forward the men capable of setting it on foot; and a new network of workmen's associations grew up very speedily, whose avowed single object was the tiding over of the ship of the community into a simple condition of Communism; and as they practically undertook also the management of the ordinary labour-war, they soon became the mouthpiece and intermediary of the whole of the working classes; and the manufacturing profit-grinders now found themselves powerless before this combination; unless *their* committee, Parliament, plucked up courage to begin the civil war again, and to shoot right and left, they were bound to yield to the demands of the men whom they employed, and pay higher and higher wages for shorter and shorter day's work. Yet one ally they had, and that was the rapidly approaching breakdown of the whole system founded on the World-Market and its supply; which now became so clear to all people, that the middle classes shocked for the moment into condemnation of the Government for the great massacre, turned round nearly in a mass, and called on the Government to look to matters, and put an end to the tyranny of the Socialist leaders.

'Thus stimulated, the reactionist plot exploded probably before it was ripe; but this time the people and their leaders were forewarned, and, before the reactionaries could get under way, had taken the steps they thought necessary.

'The Liberal Government (clearly by collusion) was beaten by the Conservatives, though the latter were nominally much in the minority. The popular representatives in the House understood pretty well what this meant, and after an attempt to fight the matter out by divisions in the House of Commons, they made a protest, left the House, and came in a body to the Committee of Public Safety: and the civil war began again in good earnest.

'Yet its first act was not one of mere fighting. The new Tory Government determined to act, yet durst not re-enact the state of siege, but it sent a body of soldiers and police to arrest the Committee of Public Safety in the lump. They made no resistance, though they might have done so, as they had now a considerable body of men who were quite prepared for extremities. But they were determined to try first a weapon which they thought stronger than street fighting.

'The members of the Committee went off quietly to prison; but they had left their soul and their organization behind them. For they depended not on a carefully arranged centre with all kinds of checks and counter-checks about it, but on a huge mass of people in thorough sympathy with the movement, bound together by a great number of links of small centres with very simple instructions. These instructions were now carried out.

'The next morning, when the leaders of the reaction were chuckling at the effect which the report in the newspapers of their stroke would have upon the public – no newspapers appeared; and it was only towards noon that a few straggling sheets, about the size of the gazettes of the seventeenth century, worked by policemen, soldiers, managers, and press-writers, were dribbled through the streets. They were greedily seized on and read; but by this time the serious part of their news was stale, and people did not need to be told that the General Strike had begun. The railways did not run, the telegraph-wires were unserved; flesh, fish, and green stuff brought to market was allowed to lie there still packed and perishing; the thousands of middle-class families, who were utterly dependent for the next meal on the workers, made frantic efforts through their more energetic members to cater for the needs of the day, and amongst those of them who could throw off the fear of what was to follow, there was, I am told, a certain enjoyment of this unexpected picnic – a forecast of the days to come, in which all labour grew pleasant.

'So passed the first day, and towards evening the Government grew quite distracted. They had but one resource for putting down any popular movement – to wit, mere brute-force; but there was nothing for them against which to use their army and police: no armed bodies appeared in the streets; the offices of the Federated Workmen were now, in appearance, at least, turned into places for the relief of people thrown out of work, and under the circumstances, they durst not arrest the men engaged in such business, all the more, as even that night many quite respectable people applied at these offices for reiief, and swallowed down the charity of the revolutionists along with their supper. So the Government massed soldiers and police here and there – and sat still for that night, fully expecting on the morrow some manifesto from "the rebels", as they now began to be called, which would give them an opportunity of acting in some way or another. They were disappointed. The ordinary newspapers gave up the struggle that morning, and only one very violent reactionary paper (called the *Daily Telegraph*) attempted an appearance, and rated "the rebels" in good set terms for their folly and ingratitude in tearing out the bowels of their "common mother", the English Nation, for the benefit of a few greedy paid agitators, and the fools whom they were deluding. On the other hand, the Socialist papers (of which three only, representing somewhat different schools, were published in London) came out full to the throat of well-printed matter. They were greedily bought by the whole public, who, of course, like the Government, expected a manifesto in them. But they found no word of reference to the great subject. It seemed as if their editors had ransacked their drawers for articles which would have been in place forty years before, under the technical name of educational articles. Most of these were admirable and straightforward expositions of the doctrine and practice of Socialism, free from haste and spite and hard words, and came upon the public with a kind of May-day freshness amidst the worry and terror of the moment; and though the knowing well understood that the meaning of this move in the game was mere defiance, and a token of irreconcilable hostility to the then rulers of society, and though, also, they were meant for nothing else by "the rebels", yet they really had their effect as "educational articles". However, "education" of another kind was acting upon the public with irresistible power, and probably cleared their heads a little.

'As to the Government, they were absolutely terrified by this act of "boycotting" (the slang word then current for such acts of absten- tion). Their counsels became wild and vacillating to the last degree: one hour they were for giving way for the present till they could hatch another plot; the next they all but sent an order for the arrest in the lump of all the workmen's committees; the next they were on the point of ordering their brisk young general to take any excuse that offered for another massacre. But when they called to mind that the soldiery in that "Battle" of Trafalgar Square were so daunted by the slaughter which they had made, that they could not be got to fire a second volley, they shrank back again from the dreadful courage necessary for carrying out another massacre. Meantime the prisoners, brought the second time before the magistrates under a strong escort of soldiers, were the second time remanded.

'The strike went on this day also. The workmen's committees were extended, and gave relief to great numbers of people, for they had organized a considerable amount of production of food by men whom they could depend upon. Quite a number of well-to-do people were now compelled to seek relief of them. But another curious thing happened: a band of young men of the upper classes armed themselves, and coolly went marauding in the streets, taking what suited them of such eatables and portables that they came across in the shops which had ventured to open. This operation they carried out in Oxford Street, then a great street of shops of all kinds. The Government, being at that hour in one of their yielding moods, thought this a fine opportunity for showing their impartiality in the maintenance of "order", and sent to arrest these hungry rich youths;

who, however, surprised the police by a valiant resistance, so that all but three escaped. The Government did not gain the reputation for impartiality which they expected from this move; for they forgot that there were no evening papers; and the account of the skirmish spread wide indeed, but in a distorted form; for it was mostly told simply as an exploit of the starving people from the East-end; and everybody thought it was but natural for the Government to put them down when and where they could.

'That evening the rebel prisoners were visited in their cells by *very* polite and sympathetic persons, who pointed out to them what a suicidal course they were following, and how dangerous these extreme courses were for the popular cause. Says one of the prisoners: "It was great sport comparing notes when we came out anent the attempt of the Government to 'get at' us separately in prison, and how we answered the blandishments of the highly 'intelligent and refined' persons set on to pump us. One laughed; another told extravagant long-bow stories to the envoy; a third held a sulky silence; a fourth damned the polite spy and bade him hold his jaw – and that was all they got out of us."

'So passed the second day of the great strike. It was clear to all thinking people that the third day would bring on the crisis; for the present suspense and ill-concealed terror was unendurable. The ruling classes, and the middle-class non-politicians who had been their real strength and support, were as sheep lacking a shepherd; they literally did not know what to do.

'One thing they found they had to do: try to get the "rebels" to do something. So the next morning, the morning of the third day of the strike, when the members of the Committee of Public Safety appeared again before the magistrate, they found themselves treated with the greatest possible courtesy – in fact, rather as envoys and ambassadors than prisoners. In short, the magistrate had received his orders; and with no more to do than might come of a long stupid speech which might have been written by Dickens in mockery, he discharged the prisoners, who went back to their meeting place and at once began a due sitting. It was high time. For this third day the mass was fermenting indeed. There was, of course, a vast number of working people who were not organized in the least in the world:

men who had been used to act as their masters drove them, or rather as the system drove, of which their masters were a part. That system was now falling to pieces, and the old pressure of the master having been taken off these poor men, it seemed likely that nothing but the mere animal necessities and passions of men would have any hold on them, and that mere general overturn would be the result. Doubtless this would have happened if it had not been that the huge mass had been leavened by Socialist opinion in the first place, and in the second place by actual contact with declared Socialists, many or indeed most of whom were members of those bodies of workmen above said.

'If anything of this kind had happened some years before, when the masters of labour were still looked upon as the natural rulers of the people, and even the poorest and most ignorant men leaned upon them for support, while they submitted to their fleecing, the entire break-up of all society would have followed. But the long series of years during which the workmen had learned to despise their rulers, had done away with their dependence upon them, and they were now beginning to trust (somewhat dangerously, as events proved) in the non-legal leaders whom events had thrust forward; and though most of these were now become mere figure-heads, their names and reputations were useful in this crisis as a stop gap.

'The effect of the news, therefore, of the release of the Committee gave the Government some breathing time: for it was received with the greatest joy by the workers, and even the well-to-do saw in it a respite from the mere destruction which they had begun to dread, and the fear of which most of them attributed to the weakness of the Government. As far as the passing hour went, perhaps they were right in this.'

'How do you mean?' said I. 'What could the Government have done? I often used to think that they would be helpless in such a crisis.'

Said old Hammond: 'Of course I don't doubt that in the long run matters would have come about as they did. But if the Government could have treated their army as a real army, and used them strategically as a general would have done, looking on the people as a mere open enemy to be shot at and dispersed wherever they turned up, they would probably have gained the victory at the time.'

'But would the soldiers have acted against the people in this way?' said I.

Said he: 'I think from all I have heard that they would have done so if they had met bodies of men armed however badly, and however badly they had been organized. It seems also as if before the Trafalgar Square massacre they might as a whole have been depended upon to fire upon an unarmed crowd, though they were much honeycombed by Socialism. The reason for this was that they dreaded the use by apparently unarmed men of an explosive called dynamite, of which many loud boasts were made by the workers on the eve of these events; although it turned out to be of little use as a material for war in the way that was expected. Of course the officers of the soldiery fanned this fear to the utmost, so that the rank and file probably thought on that occasion that they were being led into a desperate battle with the men who were really armed, and whose weapon was the more dreadful, because it was concealed. After that massacre, however, it was at all times doubtful if the regular soldiers would fire upon an unarmed or half-armed crowd.'

Said I: 'The regular soldiers? Then there were other combatants against the people?'

'Yes,' said he, 'we shall come to that presently.'

'Certainly,' I said, 'you had better go on straight with your story. I see that time is wearing.'

Said Hammond: 'The Government lost no time in coming to terms with the Committee of Public Safety; for indeed they could think of nothing else than the danger of the moment. They sent a duly accredited envoy to treat with these men, who somehow had obtained dominion over people's minds, while the formal rulers had no hold except over their bodies. There is no need at present to go into the details of the truce (for such it was) between these high contracting parties, the Government of the empire of Great Britain and a handful of working men (as they were called in scorn in those days), amongst whom, indeed, were some capable and "square-headed" persons, though, as aforesaid, the abler men were not then the recognized leaders. The upshot of it was that all the definite claims of the people had to be granted. We can now see that most of these claims were of themselves not worth either demanding or resisting; but they were looked on at that time as most important, and they were at least tokens of revolt against the miserable system or life which was then beginning to tumble to pieces. One claim, however, was of the utmost immediate importance, and this the Government tried hard to evade; but as they were not dealing with fools, they had to yield at last. This was the claim of recognition and formal status for the Committee of Public Safety, and all the associations which it fostered under its wing. This it is clear meant two things: first, amnesty for "the rebels", great and small, who, without a distinct act of civil war, could no longer be attacked; and next, a continuance of the organized revolution. Only one point the Government could gain, and that was a name. The dreadful revolutionary title was dropped, and the body, with its branches, acted under the respectable name of the "Board of Conciliation and its local offices". Carrying this name, it became the leader of the people in the civil war which soon followed.'

'Oh,' said I, somewhat startled, 'so the civil war went on, in spite of all that had happened?'

'So it was,' said he. 'In fact, it was this very legal recognition which made the civil war possible in the ordinary sense of war; it took the struggle out of the element of mere massacres on one side, and endurance plus strikes on the other.'

'And can you tell me in what kind of way the war was carried on?' said I.

'Yes,' he said, 'we have records and to spare of all that; and the essence of them I can give you in a few words. As I told you, the rank and file of the army was not to be trusted by the reactionists; but the officers generally were prepared for anything, for they were mostly the very stupidest men in the country. Whatever the Government might do, a great part of the upper and middle classes were determined to set on foot a counter revolution; for the Communism which now loomed ahead seemed quite unendurable to them. Bands of young men, like the marauders in the great strike of whom I told you just now, armed themselves and drilled, and began on any opportunity or pretence to skirmish with the people in the streets. The Government neither helped them nor put them down, but stood by, hoping that something might come of it. These "Friends of

Order", as they were called, had some successes at first, and grew bolder; they got many officers of the regular army to help them, and by their means laid hold of munitions of war of all kinds. One part of their tactics consisted in their guarding and even garrisoning the big factories of the period: they held at one time, for instance, the whole of that place called Manchester which I spoke of just now. A sort of irregular war was carried on with varied success all over the country; and at last the Government, which at first pretended to ignore the struggle, or treat it as mere rioting, definitely declared for "the Friends of Order", and joined to their bands whatsoever of the regular army they could get together, and made a desperate effort to overwhelm "the rebels", as they were now once more called, and as indeed they called themselves.

'It was too late. All ideas of peace on a basis of compromise had disappeared on either side. The end, it was seen clearly, must be either absolute slavery for all but the privileged, or a system of life founded on equality and Communism. The sloth, the hopelessness, and, if I may say so, the cowardice of the last century, had given place to the eager, restless heroism of a declared revolutionary period. I will not say that the people of that time foresaw the life we are leading now, but there was a general instinct amongst them towards the essential part of that life, and many men saw clearly beyond the desperate struggle of the day into the peace which it was to bring about. The men of that day who were on the side of freedom were not unhappy, I think, though they were harassed by hopes and fears, and sometimes torn by doubts, and the conflict of duties hard to reconcile.'

'But how did the people, the revolutionists, carry on the war? What were the elements of success on their side?'

I put this question, because I wanted to bring the old man back to the definite history, and take him out of the musing mood so natural to an old man.

He answered: 'Well, they did not lack organizers; for the very conflict itself, in days when, as I told you, men of any strength of mind cast away all consideration for the ordinary business of life, developed the necessary talent amongst them. Indeed, from all I have read and heard, I much doubt whether, without this seemingly dreadful civil war, the due talent for administration would have been developed amongst the working men. Anyhow, it was there, and they soon got leaders far more than equal to the best men amongst the reactionaries. For the rest, they had no difficulty about the material of their army; for that revolutionary instinct so acted on the ordinary soldier in the ranks that the greater part, certainly the best part, of the soldiers joined the side of the people. But the main element of their success was this, that wherever the working people were not coerced, they worked, not for the reactionists, but for "the rebels". The reactionists could get no work done for them outside the districts where they were all-powerful: and even in those districts they were harassed by continual risings; and in all cases and every-where got nothing done without obstruction and black looks and sulkiness; so that not only were their armies quite worn out with the difficulties which they had to meet, but the non-combatants who were on their side were so worried and beset with hatred and a thousand little troubles and annoyances that life became almost unendurable to them on those terms. Not a few of them actually died of the worry; many committed suicide. Of course, a vast number of them joined actively in the cause of reaction, and found some solace to their misery in the eagerness of conflict. Lastly, many thousands gave way and submitted to "the rebels"; and as the num-bers of these latter increased, it at last became clear to all men that the cause which was once hopeless, was now triumphant, and that the hopeless cause was that of slavery and privilege.'

Chapter XVIII
THE BEGINNING OF THE NEW LIFE

'Well,' said I, 'so you got clear out of all your trouble. Were people satisfied with the new order of things when it came?'

'People?' he said. 'Well, surely all must have been glad of peace when it came; especially when they found, as they must have found, that after all, they – even the once rich – were not living very badly. As to those who had been poor, all through the war, which lasted about two years, their condition had been bettering, in spite of the struggle; and when peace came at last, in a very short time they made great strides towards a decent life. The great difficulty was that the once-poor had such a feeble conception of the real pleasure of life: so to say, they did not ask enough, did not know how to ask enough, from the new state of things. It was perhaps rather a good than an evil thing that the necessity for restoring the wealth destroyed during the war forced them into working at first almost as hard as they had been used to before the Revolution. For all historians are agreed that there never was a war in which there was so much destruction of wares, and instruments for making them as in this civil war.'

'I am rather surprised at that,' said I.

'Are you? I don't see why,' said Hammond.

'Why,' I said, 'because the party of order would surely look upon the wealth as their own property, no share of which, if they could help it, should go to their slaves, supposing they conquered. And on the other hand, it was just for the possession of that wealth that "the rebels" were fighting, and I should have thought, especially when they saw that they were winning, that they would have been careful to destroy as little as possible of what was so soon to be their own.'

'It was as I have told you, however,' said he. 'The party of order, when they recovered from their first cowardice of surprise – or, if you please, when they fairly saw that, whatever happened, they would be ruined, fought with great bitterness, and cared little what they did, so long as they injured the enemies who had destroyed the sweets of life for them. As to "the rebels", I have told you that the outbreak of actual war made them careless of trying to save the wretched scraps of wealth that they had. It was a common saying amongst them, Let the country be cleared of everything except valiant living men, rather than that we fall into slavery again!'

He sat silently thinking a little while, and then said:

'When the conflict was once really begun, it was seen how little of any value there was in the old world of slavery and inequality. Don't you see what it means? In the times which you are thinking of, and of which you seem to know so much, there was no hope; nothing but the dull jog of the mill-horse under compulsion of collar and whip; but in that fighting-time that followed, all was hope: "the rebels" at least felt themselves strong enough to build up the world again from its dry bones, – and they did it, too!' said the old man, his eyes glittering under his beetling brows. He went on: 'And their opponents at least and at last learned something about the reality of life, and its sorrows, which they – their class, I mean – had once known nothing of. In short, the two combatants, the workman and the gentleman, between them—'

'Between them,' said I, quickly, 'they destroyed commercialism!'

'Yes, yes, YES,' said he; 'that is it. Nor could it have been destroyed otherwise; except, perhaps, by the whole of society gradually falling into lower depths, till it should at last reach a condition as rude as barbarism, but lacking both the hope and the pleasures of barbarism. Surely the sharper, shorter remedy was the happiest?'

'Most surely,' said I.

'Yes,' said the old man, 'the world was being brought to its second birth; how could that take place without a tragedy? Moreover, think of it. The spirit of the new days, of our days, was to be delight in the life of the world; intense and overweening love of the very skin and surface of the earth on which man dwells, such as a lover has in the fair flesh of the woman he loves; this, I say, was to be the new spirit of the time. All other moods save this had been exhausted: the unceasing criticism, the boundless curiosity in the ways and thoughts of man, which was the mood of the ancient Greek, to whom these things were not so much a means, as an end, was gone past recovery; nor had there been really any shadow of it in the so-called science of the nineteenth century, which, as you must know, was in the main an appendage to the commercial system; nay, not seldom an append-age to the police of that system. In spite of appearances, it was limited and cowardly, because it did not really believe in itself. It was the outcome, as it was the sole relief, of the unhappiness of the period which made life so bitter even to the rich, and which, as you may see with your bodily eyes, the great change had swept away. More akin to our way of looking at life was the spirit of the Middle Ages to whom heaven and the life of the next world was such a reality, that it became to them a part of the life upon the earth; which accordingly they loved and adorned, in spite of the ascetic doctrines of their formal creed, which bade them contemn it.

'But that also, with its assured belief in heaven and hell as two countries in which to live, has gone, and now we do, both in word and in deed, believe in the continuous life of the world of men, and as it were, add every day of that common life to the little stock of days which our own mere individual experience wins for us: and consequently we are happy. Do you wonder at it? In times past, indeed, men were told to love their kind, to believe in the religion of humanity and so forth. But look you, just in the degree that a man had elevation of mind and refinement enough to be able to value this idea, was he repelled by the obvious aspect of the individuals composing the mass which he was to worship; and he could only evade that repulsion by making a conventional abstraction of mankind that had little actual or historical relation to the race; which to his eyes was divided into blind tyrants on the one hand and apathetic degraded slaves on the other. But now, where is the difficulty in accepting the religion of humanity, when the men and women who go to make up humanity are free, happy, and energetic at least, and most commonly beautiful of body also, and surrounded by beautiful things of their own fashioning, and a nature bettered and not worsened by contact with mankind? This is what this age of the world has reserved for us.'

'It seems true,' said I, 'or ought to be, if what my eyes have seen is a token of the general life you lead. Can you now tell me anything of your progress after the years of the struggle?'

Said he: 'I could easily tell you more than you have time to listen to; but I can at least hint at one of the chief difficulties which had to be met: and that was, that when men began to settle down after the war, and their labour had pretty much filled up the gap in wealth caused by the destruction of that war, a kind of disappointment seemed coming over us, and the prophecies of some of the reactionists of past times seemed as if they would come true, and a dull level of utilitarian comfort be the end for a while of our aspirations and success. The loss of the competitive spur to exertion had not, indeed, done anything to interfere with the necessary production of the community, but how if it should make men dull by giving them too much time for thought or idle musing? But, after all, this dull thundercloud only threatened us, and then passed over. Probably, from what

I have told you before, you will have a guess at the remedy for such a disaster; remembering always that many of the things which used to be produced – slave-wares for the poor and mere wealth-wasting wares for the rich – ceased to be made. That remedy was, in short, the production of what used to be called art, but which has no name amongst us now, because it has become a necessary part of the labour of every man who produces.'[45]

Said I: 'What! had men any time or opportunity for cultivating the fine arts amidst the desperate struggle for life and freedom that you have told me of?'

Said Hammond: 'You must not suppose that the new form of art was founded chiefly on the memory of the art of the past; although, strange to say, the civil war was much less destructive of art than of other things, and though what of art existed under the old forms, revived in a wonderful way during the latter part of the struggle, especially as regards music and poetry. The art or work-pleasure, as one ought to call it, of which I am now speaking, sprung up almost spontaneously, it seems, from a kind of instinct amongst people, no longer driven desperately to painful and terrible overwork, to do the best they could with the work in hand – to make it excellent of its kind; and when that had gone on for a little, a craving for beauty seemed to awaken in men's minds, and they began rudely and awkwardly to ornament the wares which they made; and when they had once set to work at that, it soon began to grow. All this was much helped by the abolition of the squalor which our immediate ancestors put up with so coolly; and by the leisurely, but not stupid, country-life which now grew (as I told you before) to be common amongst us.[46] Thus at last and by slow degrees we got pleasure into our work; then we became conscious of that pleasure, and cultivated it, and took care that we had our fill of it; and then all was gained, and we were happy. So may it be for ages and ages!'

The old man fell into a reverie, not altogether without melancholy I thought; but I would not break it. Suddenly he started, and said: 'Well, dear guest, here are come Dick and Clara to fetch you away, and there is an end of my talk; which I daresay you will not be sorry for; the long day is coming to an end, and you will have a pleasant ride back to Hammersmith.'

Chapter XIX
THE DRIVE BACK TO HAMMERSMITH

I said nothing, for I was not inclined for mere politeness to him after such very serious talk; but in fact I should like to have gone on talking with the older man, who could understand something at least of my wonted ways of looking at life, whereas, with the younger people, in spite of all their kindness, I really was a being from another planet. However, I made the best of it, and smiled as amiably as I could on the young couple; and Dick returned the smile by saying, 'Well, guest, I am glad to have you again, and to find that you and my kinsman have not quite talked yourselves into another world; I was half suspecting as I was listening to the Welshmen yonder that you would presently be vanishing away from us, and began to picture my kinsman sitting in the hall staring at nothing and finding that he had been talking a while past to nobody.'

I felt rather uncomfortable at this speech, for suddenly the picture of the sordid squabble, the dirty and miserable tragedy of the life I had left for a while, came before my eyes; and I had, as it were, a vision of all my longings for the rest and peace in the past, and I loathed the idea of going back to it again. But the old man chuckled and said:

'Don't be afraid, Dick. In any case, I have not been talking to thin air; nor, indeed to this new friend of ours only. Who knows but I may not have been talking to many people? For perhaps our guest may some day go back to the people he has come from, and may take a message from us which may bear fruit for them, and consequently for us.'

Dick looked puzzled, and said: 'Well, gaffer, I do not quite understand what you mean. All I can say is, that I hope he will not leave us: for don't you see, he is another kind of man to what we are used to, and somehow he makes us think of all kind of things; and already I feel as if I could understand Dickens the better for having talked with him.'

'Yes,' said Clara, 'and I think in a few months we shall make him look younger; and I should like to see what he was like with the wrinkles smoothed out of his face. Don't you think he will look younger after a little time with us?'

The old man shook his head, and looked earnestly at me, but did not answer, and for a moment or two we were silent. Then Clara broke out:

'Kinsman, I don't like this: something or another troubles me, and I feel as if something untoward were going to happen. You have been talking of past miseries to the guest, and have been living in past unhappy times, and it is in the air all round us, and makes us feel as if we were longing for something that we cannot have.'

The old man smiled on her kindly, and said: 'Well, my child, if that be so, go and live in the present, and you will soon shake it off.' Then he turned to me, and said: 'Do you remember anything like that, guest, in the country from which you come?'

The lovers had turned aside now, and were talking together softly, and not heeding us; so I said, but in a low voice: 'Yes, when I was a happy child on a sunny holiday, and had everything that I could think of.'

'So it is,' said he. 'You remember just now you twitted me with living in the second childhood of the world. You will find it a happy world to live in; you will be happy there – for a while.'

Again I did not like his scarcely veiled threat, and was beginning to trouble myself with trying to remember how I had got amongst this curious people, when the old man called out in a cheery voice: 'Now, my children, take your guest away, and make much of him; for it is your business to make him sleek of skin and peaceful of mind: he has by no means been as lucky as you have. Farewell, guest!' and he grasped my hand warmly.

'Good-bye,' said I, 'and thank you very much for all that you have told me. I will come and see you as soon as I come back to London. May I?'

'Yes,' he said, 'come by all means – if you can.'

'It won't be for some time yet,' quoth Dick, in his cheery voice; 'for when the hay is in up the river, I shall be for taking him a round through the country between hay and wheat harvest, to see how our friends live in the north country. Then in the wheat harvest we shall do a good stroke of work, I should hope, – in Wiltshire by preference;

for he will be getting a little hard with all the open-air living, and I shall be as tough as nails.'

'But you will take me along, won't you, Dick?' said Clara, laying her pretty hand on his shoulder.

'Will I not?' said Dick, somewhat boisterously. 'And we will manage to send you to bed pretty tired every night; and you will look so beautiful with your neck all brown, and your hands too, and you under your gown as white as privet, that you will get some of those strange discontented whims out of your head, my dear. However, our week's haymaking will do all that for you.'

The girl reddened very prettily, and not for shame but for pleasure; and the old man laughed, and said:

'Guest, I see that you will be as comfortable as need be; for you need not fear that those two will be too officious with you: they will be so busy with each other, that they will leave you a good deal to yourself, I am sure, and that is a real kindness to a guest, after all. Oh, you need not be afraid of being one too many, either: it is just what these birds in a nest like, to have a good convenient friend to turn to, so that they may relieve the ecstasies of love with the solid commonplace of friendship. Besides, Dick, and much more Clara, likes a little talking at times; and you know lovers do not talk unless they get into trouble, they only prattle. Good-bye, guest; may you be happy!'

Clara went up to old Hammond, threw her arms about his neck and kissed him heartily, and said: 'You are a dear old man, and may have your jest about me as much as you please; and it won't be long before we see you again; and you may be sure we shall make our guest happy; though, mind you, there is some truth in what you say.'

Then I shook hands again, and we went out of the hall and into the cloisters, and so in the street found Greylocks in the shafts waiting for us. He was well looked after; for a little lad of about seven years old had his hand on the rein and was solemnly looking up into his face; on his back, withal, was a girl of fourteen, holding a three-year-old sister on before her; while another girl, about a year older than the boy, hung on behind. The three were occupied partly with eating cherries, partly with patting and punching Greylocks, who took all their caresses in good part, but pricked up his ears when Dick made his appearance. The girls got off quietly, and going up to Clara, made much of her and snuggled up to her. And then we got into the carriage, Dick shook the reins, and we got under way at once, Greylocks trotting soberly between the lovely trees of the London streets, that were sending floods of fragrance into the cool evening air; for it was now getting toward sunset.

We could hardly go but fair and softly all the way, as there were a great many people abroad on that cool hour. Seeing so many people made me notice their looks the more; and I must say, my taste, cultivated in the sombre greyness, or rather brownness, of the nine-teenth century, was rather apt to condemn the gaiety and brightness of the raiment; and I even ventured to say as much to Clara. She seemed rather surprised, and even slightly indignant, and said: 'Well, well, what's the matter? They are not about any dirty work; they are only amusing themselves in the fine evening; there is nothing to foul their clothes. Come, doesn't it all look very pretty? It isn't gaudy, you know.'

Indeed that was true; for many of the people were clad in colours that were sober enough, though beautiful, and the harmony of the colours was perfect and most delightful.

I said, 'Yes, that is so; but how can everybody afford such costly garments? Look! there goes a middle-aged man in a sober grey dress; but I can see from here that it is made of very fine woollen stuff, and is covered with silk embroidery.'

Said Clara: 'He could wear shabby clothes if he pleased, – that is, if he didn't think he would hurt people's feelings by doing so.'

'But please tell me,' said I, 'how can they afford it?'

As soon as I had spoken I perceived that I had got back to my old blunder; for I saw Dick's shoulders shaking with laughter; but he wouldn't say a word, but handed me over to the tender mercies of Clara, who said:

'Why, I don't know what you mean. Of course we can afford it, or else we shouldn't do it. It would be easy enough for us to say, we will only spend our labour on making our clothes comfortable: but we don't choose to stop there. Why do you find fault with us? Does it seem to you as if we starved ourselves of food in order to make ourselves fine clothes? or do you think there is anything wrong in

liking to see the coverings of our bodies beautiful like our bodies
are? – just as a deer's or an otter's skin has been made beautiful from
the first? Come, what is wrong with you?'

I bowed before the storm, and mumbled out some excuse or other.
I must say, I might have known that people who were so fond of
architecture generally, would not be backward in ornamenting themselves; all the more as the shape of their raiment, apart from its
colour, was both beautiful and reasonable – veiling the form, without
either muffling or caricaturing it.

Clara was soon mollified; and as we drove along toward the wood
before mentioned, she said to Dick:

'I tell you what, Dick: now that kinsman Hammond the Elder has
seen our guest in his queer clothes, I think we ought to find him
something decent to put on for our journey tomorrow: especially
since, if we do not, we shall have to answer all sorts of questions as
to his clothes and where they came from. Besides,' she said slyly,
'when he is clad in handsome garments he will not be so quick to
blame us for our childishness in wasting our time in making ourselves
look pleasant to each other.'

'All right, Clara,' said Dick; 'he shall have everything that you –
that he wants to have. I will look something out for him before he
gets up to-morrow.'

Chapter XX
THE HAMMERSMITH GUEST HOUSE AGAIN

Amidst such talk, driving quietly through the balmy evening, we
came to Hammersmith, and were well received by our friends there.
Boffin, in a fresh suit of clothes, welcomed me back with stately
courtesy; the weaver wanted to button-hole me and get out of me
what old Hammond had said, but was very friendly and cheerful
when Dick warned him off; Annie shook hands with me, and hoped I
had had a pleasant day – so kindly, that I felt a slight pang as our
hands parted; for to say the truth, I liked her better than Clara, who
seemed to be always a little on the defensive, whereas Annie was as

frank as could be, and seemed to get honest pleasure from everything and everybody about her without the least effort.

We had quite a little feast that evening, partly in my honour, and partly, I suspect, though nothing was said about it, in honour of Dick and Clara coming together again. The wine was of the best; the hall was redolent of rich summer flowers; and after supper we not only had music (Annie, to my mind, surpassing all the others for sweetness and clearness of voice, as well as for feeling and meaning) but, at last we even got to telling stories, and sat there listening, with no other light but that of the summer moon streaming through the beautiful traceries of the windows, as if we had belonged to time long passed, when books were scarce and the art of reading somewhat rare. Indeed, I may say here, that, though, as you will have noted, my friends had mostly something to say about books, yet they were not great readers, considering the refinement of their manners and the great amount of leisure which they obviously had. In fact, when Dick, especially, mentioned a book, he did so with an air of a man who has accomplished an achievement; as much as to say, 'There, you see, I have actually read that!'

The evening passed all too quickly for me; since that day, for the first time in my life, I was having my fill of the pleasure of the eyes without any of that sense of incongruity, that dread of approaching ruin, which had always beset me hitherto when I had been amongst the beautiful works of art of the past, mingled with the lovely nature of the present; both of them, in fact, the result of the long centuries of tradition, which had compelled men to produce the art, and compelled nature to run into the mould of the ages. Here I could enjoy everything without an after-thought of the injustice and miser-able toil which made my leisure; the ignorance and dulness of life which went to make my keen appreciation of history; the tyranny and the struggle full of fear and mishap which went to make my romance. The only weight I had upon my heart was a vague fear as it drew toward bed-time concerning the place where I should wake on the morrow: but I choked that down, and went to bed happy, and in a very few moments was in a dreamless sleep.

Chapter XXI
GOING UP THE RIVER

When I did wake, to a beautiful sunny morning, I leapt out of bed with my over-night apprehension still clinging to me, which vanished delightfully however in a moment as I looked around my little sleeping chamber and saw the pale but pure-coloured figures painted on the plaster of the wall, with verses written underneath them which I knew somewhat over-well. I dressed speedily, in a suit of blue laid ready for me, so handsome that I quite blushed when I had got into it, feeling as I did so that excited pleasure of anticipation of a holiday, which, well remembered as it was, I had not felt since I was a boy, new come home for the summer holidays.

It seemed quite early in the morning, and I expected to have the hall to myself when I came into it out of the corridor wherein was my sleeping chamber; but I met Annie at once, who let fall her broom and gave me a kiss, quite meaningless I fear, except as betokening friendship, though she reddened as she did it, not from shyness, but from friendly pleasure, and then stood and picked up her broom again, and went on with her sweeping, nodding to me as if to bid me stand out of the way and look on; which, to say the truth, I thought amusing enough, as there were five other girls helping her, and their graceful figures engaged in the leisurely work were worth going a long way to see, and their merry talk and laughing as they swept in quite a scientific manner was worth going a long way to hear. But Annie presently threw me back a word or two as she went on to the other end of the hall: 'Guest,' she said, 'I am glad that you are up early, though we wouldn't disturb you; for our Thames is a lovely river at half-past six on a June morning: and as it would be a pity for you to lose it, I am told just to give you a cup of milk and a bit of bread outside there, and put you into the boat: for Dick and Clara are all ready now. Wait half a minute till I have swept down this row.'

So presently she let her broom drop again, and came and took me by the hand and led me out on to the terrace above the river, to a little table under the boughs, where my bread and milk took the form of as dainty a breakfast as any one could desire, and then sat by me as I ate. And in a minute or two Dick and Clara came to me, the latter looking most fresh and beautiful in a light silk embroidered gown, which to my unused eyes was extravagantly gay and bright; while Dick was also handsomely dressed in white flannel prettily embroidered. Clara raised her gown in her hands as she gave me the morning greeting, and said laughingly: 'Look, guest! you see we are at least as fine as any of the people you felt inclined to scold last night; you see we are not going to make the bright day and the flowers feel ashamed of themselves. Now scold me!'

Quoth I: 'No, indeed; the pair of you seem as if you were born out of the summer day itself; and I will scold you when I scold it.'

'Well, you know,' said Dick, 'this is a special day – all these days are, I mean. The hay-harvest is in some ways better than corn-harvest because of the beautiful weather; and really, unless you had worked in the hay-field in fine weather, you couldn't tell what pleasant work it is. The women look so pretty at it, too,' he said, shyly; 'so all things considered, I think we are right to adorn it in a simple manner.'

'Do the women work at it in silk dresses?' said I, smiling.

Dick was going to answer me soberly; but Clara put her hand over his mouth, and said, 'No, no, Dick; not too much information for him, or I shall think that you are your old kinsman again. Let him find out for himself: he will not have long to wait.'

'Yes,' quoth Annie, 'don't make your description of the picture too fine, or else he will be disappointed when the curtain is drawn. I don't want him to be disappointed. But now it's time for you to be gone, if you are to have the best of the tide, and also of the sunny morning. Good-bye, guest.'

She kissed me in her frank friendly way, and almost took away from me my desire for the expedition thereby; but I had to get over that, as it was clear that so delightful a woman would hardly be without a due lover of her own age. We went down the steps of the landing-stage, and got into a pretty boat, not too light to hold us and our belongings comfortably, and handsomely ornamented; and just as we got in, down came Boffin and the weaver to see us off. The former had now veiled his splendour in a due suit of working clothes, crowned with a fantail hat, which he took off, however, to wave us farewell with his grave old-Spanish-like courtesy. Then Dick pushed off into the stream, and bent vigorously to his sculls, and Hammersmith, with its noble trees and beautiful water-side houses, began to slip away from us.

As we went, I could not help putting beside his promised picture of the hay-field as it was then the picture of it as I remembered it, and especially the images of the women engaged in the work rose up before me: the row of gaunt figures, lean, flat-breasted, ugly, without a grace of form or face about them; dressed in wretched skimpy print gowns, and hideous flapping sun-bonnets, moving their rakes in a listless mechanical way. How often had that marred the loveliness of the June day to me; how often had I longed to see the hay-fields peopled with men and women worthy of the sweet abundance of midsummer, of its endless wealth of beautiful sights, and delicious sounds and scents. And now, the world had grown old and wiser, and I was to see my hope realized at last.

Chapter XXII
HAMPTON COURT. AND A PRAISER OF PAST TIMES

So on we went, Dick rowing in an easy tireless way, and Clara sitting by my side admiring his manly beauty and heartily good-natured face, and thinking, I fancy, of nothing else. As we went higher up the river, there was less difference between the Thames of that day and the Thames as I remembered it; for setting aside the hideous vulgarity of the cockney[47] villas of the well-to-do, stock-brokers and other such, which in older time marred the beauty of the bough-hung banks, even this beginning of the country Thames was always beautiful; and as we slipped between the lovely summer greenery, I almost felt my youth come back to me, and as if I were on one of those water excursions which I used to enjoy so much in days when I was too happy to think that there could be much amiss anywhere.

At last we came to a reach of the river where on the left hand a very pretty little village with some old houses in it came down to the edge of the water, over which was a ferry; and beyond these houses the elm-beset meadows ended in a fringe of tall willows, while on the right hand went the tow-path and a clear space before a row of trees, which rose up behind huge and ancient, the ornaments of a great park: but these drew back still further from the river at the end of the reach to make way for a little town of quaint and pretty houses, some new, some old dominated by the long walls and sharp gables of a great red-brick pile of building, partly of the latest Gothic, partly of the court-style of Dutch William, but so blended together by the bright sun and beautiful surroundings, including the bright blue river, which it looked down upon, that even amidst the beautiful buildings of that new happy time it had a strange charm about it. A great wave of fragrance, amidst which the lime-tree blossom was clearly to be distinguished, came down to us from its unseen gardens, as Clara sat up in her place, and said:

'Oh, Dick, dear, couldn't we stop at Hampton Court for to-day, and take the guest about the park a little, and show him those sweet old buildings? Somehow, I suppose because you have lived so near it, you have seldom taken me to Hampton Court.'

Dick rested on his oars a little, and said: 'Well, well, Clara, you are lazy to-day. I didn't feel like stopping short of Shepperton for the night; suppose we just go and have our dinner at the Court, and go on again about five o'clock?'

'Well,' she said, 'so be it; but I should like the guest to have spent an hour or two in the Park.'

'The Park!' said Dick; 'why, the whole Thames-side is a park this time of the year; and for my part, I had rather lie under an elm-tree on the borders of a wheat-field, with the bees humming about me and the corn-crake crying from furrow to furrow, than in any park in England. Besides—'

'Besides,' said she, 'you want to get on to your dearly-loved upper Thames, and show your prowess down the heavy swathes of the mowing grass.'

She looked at him fondly, and I could tell that she was seeing him in her mind's eye showing his splendid form at its best amidst the rhymed strokes of the scythes; and she looked down at her own pretty feet with a half sigh, as though she were contrasting her slight woman's beauty with his man's beauty; as women will when they are really in love, and are not spoiled with conventional sentiment.

As for Dick, he looked at her admiringly a while, and then said at last: 'Well, Clara, I do wish we were there! But, hilloa! we are getting back way.' And he set to work sculling again, and in two minutes we were all standing on the gravelly strand below the bridge, which, as you may imagine, was no longer the old hideous iron abortion, but a handsome piece of very solid oak framing.

We went into the Court and straight into the great hall, so well remembered, where there were tables spread for dinner, and every-thing arranged much as in Hammersmith Guest Hall. Dinner over, we sauntered through the ancient rooms, where the pictures and tapestry were still preserved, and nothing was much changed, except that the people whom we met there had an indefinable kind of look of being at home and at ease, which communicated itself to me, so that I felt that the beautiful old place was mine in the best sense of the word; and my pleasure of past days seemed to add itself to that of to-day, and filled my whole soul with content.

Dick (who, in spite of Clara's gibe, knew the place very well) told me that the beautiful old Tudor rooms, which I remembered had been the dwellings of the lesser fry of Court flunkies, were now much used by people coming and going; for, beautiful as architecture had now become and although the whole face of the country had quite recovered its beauty, there was still a sort of tradition of pleasure and beauty which clung to that group of buildings, and people thought going to Hampton Court a necessary summer outing, as they did in the days when London was so grimy and miserable. We went into some of the rooms looking into the old garden, and were well received by the people in them, who got speedily into talk with us, and looked with politely half-concealed wonder at my strange face. Besides these birds of passage, and a few regular dwellers in the place, we saw out in the meadows near the garden, down 'the Long Water', as it used to be called, many gay tents with men, women, and children round about them. As it seemed, this pleasure-loving people were fond of tent-life with all its inconveniences, which, indeed, they turned into pleasure also.

We left this old friend by the time appointed, and I made some feeble show of taking the sculls; but Dick repulsed me, not much to my grief, I must say, as I found I had quite enough to do between the enjoyment of the beautiful time and my own lazily blended thoughts.

As to Dick, it was quite right to let him pull, for he was as strong as a horse, and had the greatest delight in bodily exercise, whatever it was. We really had some difficulty in getting him to stop when it was getting rather more than dusk, and the moon was brightening just as we were off Runnymede. We landed there, and were looking about for a place whereon to pitch our tents (for we had brought two with us), when an old man came up to us, bade us good-evening, and asked if we were housed for that night; and finding that we were not, bade us home to his house. Nothing loth, we went with him, and Clara took his hand in a coaxing way which I noticed she used with old men; and as we went on our way, made some commonplace remark about the beauty of the day. The old man stopped short, and looked at her and said: 'You really like it, then?'

'Yes,' she said, looking very much astonished, 'don't you?'

'Well,' said he, 'perhaps I do. I did, at any rate, when I was younger; but now I think I should like it cooler.'

She said nothing, and went on, the night growing about as dark as it would be; till just at the rise of the hill we came to a hedge with a gate in it, which the old man unlatched and led us into a garden, at the end of which we could see a little house, one of whose little windows was already yellow with candlelight. We could see even under the doubtful light of the moon and the last of the western glow that the garden was stuffed full of flowers; and the fragrance it gave out in the gathering coolness was so wonderfully sweet, that it seemed the very heart of the delight of the June dusk; so that we three stopped instinctively, and Clara gave forth a little sweet 'Oh', like a bird beginning to sing.

'What's the matter?' said the old man, a little testily, and pulling at her hand. 'There's no dog; or have you trodden on a thorn and hurt your foot?'

'No, no, neighbour,' she said; 'but how sweet, how sweet it is!'

'Of course it is,' said he, 'but do you care so much for that?'

She laughed out musically, and we followed suit in our gruffer voices; and then she said: 'Of course I do, neighbour; don't you!'

'Well, I don't know,' quoth the old fellow: then he added, as if somewhat ashamed of himself; 'Besides, you know, when the waters are out and all Runnymede is flooded, it's none so pleasant.'

'*I* should like it,' quoth Dick. 'What a jolly sail one would get about here on the floods on a bright frosty January morning!'

'*Would* you like it?' said our host. 'Well, I won't argue with you, neighbour; it isn't worth while. Come in and have some supper.'

We went up a paved path between the roses, and straight into a very pretty room, panelled and carved, and as clean as a new pin; but the chief ornament of which was a young woman, light-haired and grey-eyed, but with her face and hands and bare feet tanned quite brown with the sun. Though she was very lightly clad, that was clearly from choice, not from poverty, though these were the first cottage-dwellers I had come across; for her gown was of silk, and on her wrists were bracelets that seemed to me of great value. She was lying on a sheep-skin near the window, but jumped up as soon as we entered, and when she saw the guests behind the old man, she clapped her hands and cried out with pleasure, and when she got us into the middle of the room, fairly danced round us in delight of our company.

'What!' said the old man, 'you are pleased, are you, Ellen?'

The girl danced up to him and threw her arms round him, and said: 'Yes I am, and so ought you to be, grandfather.'

'Well, well, I am,' said he, 'as much as I can be pleased. Guests, please be seated.'

This seemed rather strange to us; stranger, I suspect, to my friends than to me; but Dick took the opportunity of both the host and his grand-daughter being out of the room to say to me, softly: 'A grumbler: there are a few of them still. Once upon a time, I am told, they were quite a nuisance.'

The old man came in as he spoke and sat down beside us with a sigh, which, indeed, seemed fetched up as if he wanted us to take notice of it; but just then the girl came in with the victuals, and the carle missed his mark, what between our hunger generally and that I was pretty busy watching the grand-daughter moving about as beautiful as a picture.

Everything to eat and drink, though it was somewhat different to what we had had in London, was better than good, but the old man eyed rather sulkily the chief dish on the table, on which lay a leash of fine perch, and said:

'H'm, perch! I am sorry we can't do better for you, guests. The time was when we might have had a good piece of salmon up from London for you; but the times have grown mean and petty.'

'Yes, but you might have had it now,' said the girl, giggling, 'if you had known that they were coming.'

'It's our fault for not bringing it with us, neighbours,' said Dick, good-humouredly. 'But if the times have grown petty, at any rate the perch haven't; that fellow in the middle there must have weighed a good two pounds when he was showing his dark stripes and red fins to the minnows yonder. And as to the salmon, why, neighbour, my friend here, who comes from the outlands, was quite surprised yesterday morning when I told him we had plenty of salmon at Hammersmith. I am sure I have heard nothing of the times worsening.'

He looked a little uncomfortable. And the old man, turning to me, said very courteously:

'Well, sir, I am happy to see a man from over the water; but I really must appeal to you to say whether on the whole you are not better off in your country; where I suppose, from what our guest says, you are brisker and more alive, because you have not wholly got rid of competition. You see, I have read not a few books of the past days, and certainly *they* are much more alive than those which are written now; and good sound unlimited competition was the condition under which they were written, – if we didn't know that from the record of history, we should know it from the books themselves. There is a spirit of adventure in them, and signs of a capacity to extract good out of evil which our literature quite lacks now; and I cannot help thinking that our moralists and historians exaggerate hugely the unhappiness of the past days, in which such splendid works of imagination and intellect were produced.'

Clara listened to him with restless eyes, as if she were excited and pleased; Dick knitted his brow and looked still more uncomfortable, but said nothing. Indeed, the old man gradually, as he warmed to his subject, dropped his sneering manner, and both spoke and looked very seriously. But the girl broke out before I could deliver myself of the answer I was framing:

'Books, books! always books, grandfather! When will you understand that after all it is the world we live in which interests us; the world of which we are a part, and which we can never love too much? Look!' she said, throwing open the casement wider and showing us the white light sparkling between the black shadows of the moonlit garden, through which ran a little shiver of the summer night-wind, 'look! these are our books in these days! – and these,' she said, stepping lightly up to the two lovers and laying a hand on each of their shoulders; 'and the guest there, with his over-sea knowledge and experience; – yes, and even you, grandfather' (a smile ran over her face as she spoke), 'with all your grumbling and wishing yourself back again in the good old days, – in which, as far as I can make out, a harmless and lazy old man like you would either have pretty nearly starved, or have had to pay soldiers and people to take the folk's victuals and clothes and houses away from them by force. Yes, these are our books; and if we want more, can we not find work to do in the beautiful buildings that we raise up all over the country (and I know there was nothing like them in past times), wherein a man can put forth whatever is in him, and make his hands set forth his mind and his soul.'

She paused a little, and I for my part could not help staring at her, and thinking that if she were a book, the pictures in it were most lovely. The colour mantled in her delicate sunburnt cheeks; her grey eyes, light amidst the tan of her face, kindly looked on us all as she spoke. She paused, and said again:

'As for your books, they were well enough for times when intelligent people had but little else in which they could take pleasure, and when they must needs supplement the sordid miseries of their own lives with imaginations of the lives of other people. But I say flatly that in spite of all their cleverness and vigour, and capacity for story-telling, there is something loathsome about them. Some of them, indeed, do here and there show some feeling for those whom the history-books call "poor", and of the misery of whose lives we have some inkling; but presently they give it up, and towards the end of the story we must be contented to see the hero and heroine living happily in an island of bliss on other people's troubles; and that after a long series of sham troubles (or mostly sham) of their own making, illustrated by dreary introspective nonsense about their feelings and aspirations, and all the rest of it; while the world must even then have gone on its way, and dug and sewed and baked and built and carpentered round about these useless – animals.'

'There!' said the old man, reverting to his dry sulky manner again. 'There's eloquence! I suppose you like it?'

'Yes,' said I, very emphatically.

'Well,' said he, 'now the storm of eloquence has lulled for a little, suppose you answer my question? – that is, if you like, you know,' quoth he, with a sudden access of courtesy.

'What question?' said I. For I must confess that Ellen's strange and almost wild beauty had put it out of my head.

Said he: 'First of all (excuse my catechizing), is there competition in life, after the old kind, in the country whence you come?'

'Yes,' said I, 'it is the rule there.' And I wondered as I spoke what fresh complications I should get into as a result of this answer.

'Question two,' said the carle: 'Are you not on the whole much freer, more energetic – in a word, healthier and happier – for it?'

I smiled. 'You wouldn't talk so if you had any idea of our life. To me you seem here as if you were living in heaven compared with us of the country from which I came.'

'Heaven?' said he: 'you like heaven, do you?'

'Yes,' said I – snappishly, I am afraid; for I was beginning rather to resent his formula.

'Well, I am far from sure that I do,' quoth he. 'I think one may do more with one's life than sitting on a damp cloud and singing hymns.'

I was rather nettled by this inconsequence, and said: 'Well, neighbour, to be short, and without using metaphors, in the land whence I come, where the competition which produced those literary works which you admire so much is still the rule, most people are thoroughly unhappy; here, to me at least, most people seem thoroughly happy.'

'No offence, guest – no offence,' said he; 'but let me ask you; you like that, do you?'

His formula, put with such obstinate persistence, made us all laugh heartily; and even the old man joined in the laughter on the sly. However, he was by no means beaten, and said presently:

'From all I can hear, I should judge that a young woman so beautiful as my dear Ellen yonder would have been a lady, as they called it in the old time, and wouldn't have had to wear a few rags of silk as she does now, or to have browned herself in the sun as she has to do now. What do you say to that, eh?'

Here Clara, who had been pretty much silent hitherto, struck in, and said: 'Well, really, I don't think that you would have mended matters, or that they want mending. Don't you see that she is dressed deliciously for this beautiful weather? And as for the sun-burning of your hay-fields, why, I hope to pick up some of that for myself when we get a little higher up the river. Look if I don't need a little sun on my pasty white skin!'

And she stripped up the sleeve from her arm and laid it beside Ellen's who was now sitting next her. To say the truth, it was rather amusing to me to see Clara putting herself forward as a town-bred fine lady, for she was as well-knit and clean-skinned a girl as might be met with anywhere at the best. Dick stroked the beautiful arm rather shyly, and pulled down the sleeve again, while she blushed at his touch; and the old man said laughingly: 'Well, I suppose you *do* like that; don't you?'

Ellen kissed her new friend, and we all sat silent for a little, till she broke out into a sweet shrill song, and held us all entranced with the wonder of her clear voice; and the old grumbler sat looking at her lovingly. The other young people sang also in due time; and then Ellen showed us to our beds in small cottage chambers, fragrant and clean as the ideal of the old pastoral poets; and the pleasure of the evening quite extinguished my fear of the last night, that I should wake up in the old miserable world of worn-out pleasures, and hopes that were half fears.

Chapter XXIII

AN EARLY MORNING BY RUNNYMEDE

Though there were no rough noises to wake me, I could not lie long abed the next morning, where the world seemed so well awake, and, despite the old grumbler, so happy; so I got up, and found that, early

as it was, some one had been stirring, since all was trim and in its
place in the little parlour, and the table laid for the morning meal.
Nobody was afoot in the house as then, however, so I went out
a-doors, and after a turn or two round the superabundant garden,
I wandered down over the meadow to the river-side, where lay our
boat, looking quite familiar and friendly to me. I walked up-stream a
little, watching the light mist curling up from the river till the sun
gained power to draw it all away; saw the bleak speckling the water
under the willow boughs, whence the tiny flies they fed on were
falling in myriads; heard the great chub splashing here and there at
some belated moth or other, and felt almost back again in my
boyhood. Then I went back again to the boat, and loitered there a
minute or two, and then walked slowly up the meadow towards the
little house. I noted now that there were four more houses of about
the same size on the slope away from the river. The meadow in
which I was going was not up for hay; but a row of flake-hurdles ran
up the slope not far from me on each side, and in the field so parted
off from ours on the left they were making hay busily by now, in the
simple fashion of the days when I was a boy. My feet turned that
way instinctively, as I wanted to see how haymakers looked in these
new and better times, and also I rather expected to see Ellen there. I
came to the hurdles and stood looking over into the hay-field, and
was close to the end of the long line of haymakers who were
spreading the low ridges to dry off the night dew. The majority of
these were young women clad much like Ellen last night, though not
mostly in silk, but in light woollen most gaily embroidered; the men
being all clad in white flannel embroidered in bright colours. The
meadow looked like a gigantic tulip-bed because of them. All hands
were working deliberately but well and steadily, though they were
as noisy with merry talk as a grove of autumn starlings. Half a dozen
of them, men and women, came up to me and shook hands, gave me
the sele[48] of the morning, and asked a few questions as to whence
and whither, and wishing me good luck, went back to their work.
Ellen, to my disappointment, was not amongst them,[49] but presently
I saw a light figure come out of the hay-field higher up the slope,
and make for our house; and that was Ellen, holding a basket in her
hand. But before she had come to the garden gate, out came Dick

and Clara, who, after a minute's pause, came down to meet me, leaving Ellen in the garden; then we three went down to the boat, talking mere morning prattle. We stayed there a little, Dick arranging some of the matters in her, for we had only taken up to the house such things as we thought the dew might damage; and then we went toward the house again; but when we came near the garden, Dick stopped us by laying a hand on my arm and said:

'Just look a moment.'

I looked, and over the low hedge saw Ellen, shading her eyes against the sun as she looked toward the hay-field, a light wind stirring in her tawny hair, her eyes like light jewels amidst her sunburnt face, which looked as if the warmth of the sun were yet in it.

'Look, guest,' said Dick; 'doesn't it all look like one of those very stories out of Grimm that we were talking about up in Bloomsbury? Here are we two lovers wandering about the world, and we have come to a fairy garden, and there is the very fairy herself amidst of it: I wonder what she will do for us.'

Said Clara demurely, but not stiffly: 'Is she a good fairy, Dick?'

'Oh yes,' said he; 'and according to the card, she would do better, if it were not for the gnome or wood-spirit, our grumbling friend of last night.'

We laughed at this; and I said, 'I hope you see that you have left me out of the tale.'

'Well,' said he, 'that's true. You had better consider that you have got the cap of darkness, and are seeing everything, yourself invisible.'

That touched me on my weak side of not feeling sure of my position in this beautiful new country; so in order not to make matters worse, I held my tongue, and we all went into the garden and up to the house together. I noticed by the way that Clara must really rather have felt the contrast between herself as a town madam and this piece of the summer country that we all admired so, for she had rather dressed after Ellen that morning as to thinness and scantiness, and went barefoot also, except for light sandals.

The old man greeted us kindly in the parlour, and said: 'Well, guests, so you have been looking about to search into the nakedness of the land: I suppose your illusions of last night have given way a bit before the morning light? Do you still like it, eh?'

'Very much,' said I, doggedly; 'it is one of the prettiest places on the lower Thames.'

'Oho!' said he; 'so you know the Thames, do you?'

I reddened, for I saw Dick and Clara looking at me, and scarcely knew what to say. However, since I had said in our early intercourse with my Hammersmith friends that I had known Epping Forest, I thought a hasty generalization might be better in avoiding complications than a downright lie; so I said:

'I have been in this country before; and I have been on the Thames in those days.'

'Oh,' said the old man, eagerly, 'so you have been in this country before. Now really, don't you *find* it (apart from all theory, you know) much changed for the worse?'

'No, not at all,' said I; 'I find it much changed for the better.'

'Ah,' quoth he, 'I fear that you have been prejudiced by some theory or another. However, of course the time when you were here before must have been so near our own days that the deterioration might not be very great: as then we were, of course, still living under the same customs as we are now. I was thinking of earlier days than that.'

'In short,' said Clara, 'you have *theories* about the change which has taken place.'

'I have facts as well,' said he. 'Look here! from this hill you can see just four little houses, including this one. Well, I know for certain that in old times, even in the summer, when the leaves were thickest, you could see from the same place six quite big and fine houses; and higher up the water, garden joined garden right up to Windsor; and there were big houses in all the gardens. Ah! England was an important place in those days.'

I was getting nettled, and said: 'What you mean is that you de-cockneyized the place, and sent the damned flunkies packing, and that everybody can live comfortably and happily, and not a few damned thieves only, who were centres of vulgarity and corruption wherever they were, and who, as to this lovely river, destroyed its beauty morally, and had almost destroyed it physically, when they were thrown out of it.'

There was silence after this outburst, which for the life of me I could not help, remembering how I had suffered from cockneyism and its cause on those same waters of old time. But at last the old man said, quite coolly:

'My dear guest, I really don't know what you mean by either cockneys, or flunkies, or thieves, or damned; or how only a few people could live happily and comfortably in a wealthy country. All I can see is that you are angry, and I fear with me; so if you like we will change the subject.'

I thought this kind and hospitable in him, considering his obstinacy about his theory; and hastened to say that I did not mean to be angry, only emphatic. He bowed gravely, and I thought the storm was over, when suddenly Ellen broke in:

'Grandfather, our guest is reticent from courtesy; but really what he has in his mind to say to you ought to be said; so as I know pretty well what it is, I will say it for him: for as you know, I have been taught these things by people who—'

'Yes,' said the old man, 'by the sage of Bloomsbury, and others.'

'Oh,' said Dick, 'so you know my old kinsman Hammond?'

'Yes,' said she, 'and other people too, as my grandfather says, and they have taught me things: and this is the upshot of it. We live in a little house now, not because we have nothing grander to do than working in the fields, but because we please; for if we liked, we could go and live in a big house amongst pleasant companions.'

Grumbled the old man: 'Just so! As if I would live among those conceited fellows; all of them looking down upon me!'

She smiled on him kindly, but went on as if he had not spoken. 'In the past times, when those big houses of which grandfather speaks were so plenty, we *must* have lived in a cottage whether we had liked it or not; and the said cottage instead of having in it everything we want, would have been bare and empty. We should not have got enough to eat; our clothes would have been ugly to look at, dirty and frowsy. You, grandfather, have done no hard work for years now, but wander about and read your books and have nothing to worry you; and as for me, I work hard when I like it, because I like it, and think it does me good, and knits up my muscles, and makes me prettier to look at, and healthier and happier. But in those past days you, grandfather, would have had to work hard after you were old; and would have been always afraid of having to be shut up in a kind of prison along with other old men, half-starved and without amusement. And as for me, I am twenty years old. In those days my middle age would be beginning now, and in a few years I should be pinched, thin, and haggard, beset with troubles and miseries, so that no one could have guessed that I was once a beautiful girl.

'Is this what you have had in your mind, guest?' said she, the tears in her eyes at thought of the past miseries of people like herself.

'Yes,' said I, much moved; 'that and more. Often – in my country I have seen that wretched change you have spoken of, from the fresh handsome country lass to the poor draggle-tailed country woman.'

The old man sat silent for a little, but presently recovered himself and took comfort in his old phrase of 'Well, you like it so, do you?'

'Yes,' said Ellen, 'I love life better than death.'

'Oh, you do, do you?' said he. 'Well, for my part I like reading a good old book with plenty of fun in it, like Thackeray's *Vanity Fair*. Why don't you write books like that now? Ask that question of your Bloomsbury sage.'

Seeing Dick's cheeks reddening a little at this sally, and noting that silence followed, I thought I had better do something. So I said: 'I am only the guest, friends; but I know you want to show me your river at its best, so don't you think we had better be moving presently, as it is certainly going to be a hot day?'

Chapter XXIV
UP THE THAMES: THE SECOND DAY

They were not slow to take my hint; and indeed, as to the mere time of day, it was best for us to be off, as it was past seven o'clock, and the day promised to be very hot. So we got up and went down to our boat – Ellen thoughtful and abstracted; the old man very kind and courteous, as if to make up for his crabbedness of opinion. Clara was cheerful and natural, but a little subdued, I thought; and she at least was not sorry to be gone, and often looked shyly and timidly at Ellen and her strange wild beauty. So we got into the boat, Dick saying as he took his place, 'Well, it *is* a fine day!' and the old man answering. 'What! you like that, do you?' once more; and presently Dick was sending the bows swiftly through the slow weed-checked stream. I turned round as we got into mid-stream, and waving my hand to our hosts, saw Ellen leaning on the old man's shoulder, and caressing his healthy apple-red cheek, and quite a keen pang smote me as I thought how I should never see the beautiful girl again.[50] Presently I insisted on taking the sculls, and I rowed a good deal that day; which no doubt accounts for the fact that we got very late to the place which Dick had aimed at. Clara was particularly affectionate to Dick, as I noticed from the rowing thwart; but as for him, he was as frankly kind and merry as ever; and I was glad to see it, as a man of his temperament could not have taken her caresses cheerfully and without embarrassment if he had been at all entangled by the fairy of our last night's abode.

I need say little about the lovely reaches of the river here. I duly noted that absence of cockney villas which the old man had lamented; and I saw with pleasure that my old enemies the 'Gothic' cast-iron bridges had been replaced by handsome oak and stone ones. Also the banks of the forest that we passed through had lost their courtly gamekeeperish trimness, and were as wild and beautiful as need be, though the trees were clearly well seen to. I thought it best, in order to get the most direct information, to play the innocent about Eton and Windsor; but Dick volunteered his knowledge to me as we lay in Datchet lock about the first. Quoth he:

'Up yonder are some beautiful old buildings, which were built for a great college or teaching-place by one of the mediaeval kings – Edward VI, I think' (I smiled to myself at his rather natural blunder).[51] 'He meant poor people's sons to be taught there what knowledge was going in his days; but it was a matter of course that in the times of which you seem to know so much they spoilt whatever good there was in the founder's intentions. My old kinsman says that they treated them in a very simple way, and instead of teaching poor men's sons to know something, they taught rich men's sons to know nothing. It seems from what he says that it was a place for the "aristocracy" (if you know what the word means; I have been told its meaning) to get rid of the company of their male children for a great part of the year. I daresay old Hammond would give you plenty of information in detail about it.'

'What is it used for now?' said I.

'Well,' said he, 'the buildings were a good deal spoilt by the last few generations of aristocrats, who seem to have had a great hatred against beautiful old buildings, and indeed all records of past history; but it is still a delightful place. Of course, we cannot use it quite as the founder intended, since our ideas about teaching young people are so changed from the ideas of his time; so it is used now as a dwelling for people engaged in learning; and folk from round about come and get taught things that they want to learn; and there is a great library there of the best books. So that I don't think that the old dead king would be much hurt if he were to come to life and see what we are doing there.'

'Well,' said Clara, laughing, 'I think he would miss the boys.'

'Not always, my dear,' said Dick, 'for there are often plenty of boys there, who come to get taught; and also,' said he, smiling, 'to learn boating and swimming. I wish we could stop there: but perhaps we had better do that coming down the water.'

The lock-gates opened as he spoke, and out we went, and on. And as for Windsor, he said nothing till I lay on my oars (for I was sculling then) in Clewer reach, and looking up, said, 'What is all that building up there?'

Said he: 'There, I thought I would wait till you asked, yourself. That is Windsor Castle: that also I thought I would keep for you till we come down the water. It looks fine from here, doesn't it? But a great deal of it had been built or skinned in the time of the Degradation, and we wouldn't pull the buildings down, since they were there; just as with the buildings of the Dung Market. You know, of course, that it was the palace of our old mediaeval kings, and was used later on for the same purpose by the parliamentary commercial sham-kings, as my old kinsman calls them.'

'Yes,' said I, 'I know all that. What is it used for now?'

'A great many people live there,' said he, 'as, with all drawbacks, it is a pleasant place; there is also a well-arranged store of antiquities of various kinds that have seemed worth keeping – a museum, it would have been called in the times you understand so well.'

I drew my sculls through the water on that last word, and pulled as if I were fleeing from those times which I understood so well; and we were soon going up the once sorely becockneyed reaches of the river about Maidenhead, which now looked as pleasant and enjoyable as the up-river reaches.

The morning was now getting on, the morning of a jewel of a summer day; one of those days which, if they were commoner in these islands, would make our climate the best of all climates, without dispute. A light wind blew from the west; the little clouds that had arisen at about our breakfast time had seemed to get higher and higher in the heavens; and in spite of the burning sun we no more longed for rain than we feared it. Burning as the sun was, there was a fresh feeling in the air that almost set us a-longing for the rest of the hot afternoon, and the stretch of blossoming wheat seen from the shadow of the boughs. No one unburdened with very heavy anxieties could have felt otherwise than happy that morning: and it must be said that whatever anxieties might lie beneath the surface of things, we didn't seem to come across any of them.

We passed by several fields where haymaking was going on, but Dick, and especially Clara, were so jealous of our up-river festival that they would not allow me to have much to say to them. I could only notice that the people in the fields looked strong and handsome, both men and women, and that so far from there being any appearance of sordidness about their attire, they seemed to be dressed specially for the occasion – lightly, of course, but gaily and with plenty of adornment.

Both on this day as well as yesterday we had, as you may think, met and passed and been passed by many craft of one kind and another. The most part of these were being rowed like ourselves, or were sailing, in the sort of way that sailing is managed on the upper reaches of the river; but every now and then we came on barges, laden with hay or other country produce, or carrying bricks, lime, timber, and the like, and these were going on their way without any means of propulsion visible to me – just a man at the tiller, with often a friend or two laughing and talking with him. Dick, seeing on one occasion this day that I was looking rather hard on one of these, said: 'That is one of our force-barges; it is quite as easy to work vehicles by force by water as by land.'

I understood pretty well that these 'force vehicles' had taken the place of our old steam-power carrying;[52] but I took good care not to ask any questions about them, as I knew well enough both that I should never be able to understand how they were worked, and that in attempting to do so I should betray myself, or get into some complication impossible to explain; so I merely said, 'Yes, of course, I understand.'

We went ashore at Bisham, where the remains of the old Abbey and the Elizabethan house that had been added to them yet remained, none the worse for many years of careful and appreciative habitation. The folk of the place, however, were mostly in the fields that day, both men and women; so we met only two old men there, and a younger one who had stayed at home to get on with some literary work, which I imagine we considerably interrupted. Yet I also think that the hard-working man who received us was not very sorry for the interruption. Anyhow, he kept on pressing us to stay over and over again, till at last we did not get away till the cool of the evening.

However, that mattered little to us; the nights were light, for the moon was shining in her third quarter, and it was all one to Dick whether he sculled or sat quiet in the boat: so we went away a great pace. The evening sun shone bright on the remains of the old buildings at Medmenham; close beside which arose an irregular pile of building which Dick told us was a very pleasant house; and there were plenty of houses visible on the wide meadows opposite, under the hill; for, as it seems that the beauty of Hurley had compelled people to build and live there a good deal. The sun very low down showed us Henley little altered in outward aspect from what I remembered it. Actual daylight failed us as we passed through the lovely reaches of Wargrave and Shiplake; but the moon rose behind us presently. I should like to have seen with my eyes what success the new order of things had had in getting rid of the sprawling mess with which commercialism had littered the banks of the wide stream about Reading and Caversham: certainly everything smelt too deliciously in the early night for there to be any of the old careless sordidness of so-called manufacture; and in answer to my question as to what sort of a place Reading was, Dick answered:

'Oh, a nice town enough in its way; mostly rebuilt within the last hundred years; and there are a good many houses, as you can see by the lights just down under the hills yonder. In fact, it is one of the most populous places on the Thames round about here. Keep up your spirits, guest! we are close to our journey's end for the night. I ought to ask your pardon for not stopping at one of the houses here or higher up; but a friend, who is living in a very pleasant house in the Maple-Durham meads, particularly wanted me and Clara to come and see him on our way up the Thames; and I thought you wouldn't mind this bit of night travelling.'

He need not have adjured me to keep up my spirits, which were as high as possible; though the strangeness and excitement of the happy and quiet life which I saw everywhere around me was, it is true, a little wearing off, yet a deep content, as different as possible from languid acquiescence, was taking its place, and I was, as it were, really new-born.

We landed presently just where I remembered the river making an elbow to the north towards the ancient house of the Blunts;[53] with the wide meadows spreading on the right-hand side, and on the left the long line of beautiful old trees overhanging the water. As we got out of the boat, I said to Dick:

'Is it the old house we are going to?'

'No,' he said, 'though that is standing still in green old age, and is well inhabited. I see, by the way, that you know your Thames well. But my friend Walter Allen, who asked me to stop here, lives in a house, not very big, which has been built here lately, because these meadows are so much liked, especially in summer, that there was getting to be rather too much of tenting on the open field; so the parishes here about, who rather objected to that, built three houses between this and Caversham, and quite a large one at Basildon, a little higher up. Look, yonder are the lights of Walter Allen's house!'

So we walked over the grass of the meadows under a flood of moonlight, and soon came to the house, which was low and built round a quadrangle big enough to get plenty of sunshine in it. Walter Allen, Dick's friend, was leaning against the jamb of the doorway waiting for us, and took us into the hall without overplus of words. There were not many people in it, as some of the dwellers there were away at the haymaking in the neighbourhood, and some, as Walter told us, were wandering about the meadow enjoying the beautiful moonlit night. Dick's friend looked to be a man of about forty; tall, black-haired, very kind-looking and thoughtful; but rather to my surprise there was a shade of melancholy on his face, and he seemed a little abstracted and inattentive to our chat, in spite of obvious efforts to listen.

Dick looked on him from time to time, and seemed troubled; and at last he said: 'I say, old fellow, if there is anything the matter which we didn't know of when you wrote to me, don't you think you had better tell us about it at once? or else we shall think we have come here at an unlucky time, and are not quite wanted.'

Walter turned red, and seemed to have some difficulty in restraining his tears, but said at last: 'Of course everybody here is very glad to see you, Dick, and your friends; but it is true that we are not at our best, in spite of the fine weather and the glorious hay-crop. We have had a death here.'

Said Dick: 'Well, you should get over that, neighbour: such things must be.'

'Yes,' Walter said, 'but this was a death by violence and it seems likely to lead to at least one more; and somehow it makes us feel rather shy of one another; and to say the truth, that is one reason why there are so few of us present to-night.'

'Tell us the story, Walter,' said Dick; 'perhaps telling it will help you to shake off your sadness.'

Said Walter: 'Well, I will; and I will make it short enough, though I daresay it might be spun out into a long one, as used to be done with such subjects in the old novels. There is a very charming girl here whom we all like, and whom some of us do more than like; and she very naturally liked one of us better than anybody else. And another of us (I won't name him) got fairly bitten with love-madness, and used to go about making himself as unpleasant as he could – not of malice prepense, of course; so that the girl, who liked him well enough at first, though she didn't love him, began fairly to dislike him. Of course, those of us who knew him best – myself amongst others – advised him to go away, as he was making matters worse and worse for himself every day. Well, he wouldn't take our advice (that also, I suppose, was a matter of course), so we had to tell him that he *must* go, or the inevitable sending to Coventry would follow; for his individual trouble had so overmastered him that we felt that *we* must go if he did not.

'He took that better than we expected, when something or other – an interview with the girl, I think, and some hot words with the successful lover following close upon it – threw him quite off his balance; and he got hold of an axe and fell upon his rival when there was no one by; and in the struggle that followed the man attacked hit him an unlucky blow and killed him. And now the slayer in his turn is so upset that he is like to kill himself; and if he does, the girl will do as much, I fear. And all this we could no more help than the earthquake of the year before last.'

'It is very unhappy,' said Dick; 'but since the man is dead, and cannot be brought to life again, and since the slayer had no malice in him, I cannot for the life of me see why he shouldn't get over it before long. Besides, it was the right man that was killed and not the wrong. Why should a man brood over a mere accident for ever? And the girl?'

'As to her,' said Walter, 'the whole thing seems to have inspired her with terror rather than grief. What you say about the man is true, or it should be; but then, you see, the excitement and jealousy that was the prelude to this tragedy had made an evil and feverish element round about him, from which he does not seem to be able to escape. However, we have advised him to go away – in fact, to cross the seas; but he is in such a state that I do not think he *can* go unless some one *takes* him, and I think it will fall to my lot to do so; which is scarcely a cheerful outlook for me.'

'Oh, you will find a certain kind of interest in it,' said Dick. 'And of course he *must* soon look upon the affair from a reasonable point of view sooner or later.'

'Well, at any rate,' quoth Walter, 'now that I have eased my mind by making you uncomfortable, let us have an end of the subject for the present. Are you going to take your guest to Oxford?'

'Why, of course we must pass through it,' said Dick, smiling, 'as we are going into the upper waters: but I thought that we wouldn't stop there, or we shall be belated as to the haymaking up our way. So

Oxford and my learned lecture on it, all got at second-hand from my old kinsman, must wait till we come down the water a fortnight hence.'

I listened to this story with much surprise, and could not help wondering at first that the man who had slain the other had not been put in custody till it could be proved that he killed his rival in self-defence only. However, the more I thought of it, the plainer it grew to me that no amount of examination of witnesses, who had witnessed nothing but the ill-blood between the two rivals, would have done anything to clear up the case. I could not help thinking, also, that the remorse of this homicide gave point to what old Hammond had said to me about the way in which this strange people dealt with what I had been used to hear called crimes. Truly, the remorse was exaggerated; but it was quite clear that the slayer took the whole consequences of the act upon himself, and did not expect society to whitewash him by punishing him. I had no fear any longer that 'the sacredness of human life' was likely to suffer amongst my friends from the absence of gallows and prison.

Chapter XXV
THE THIRD DAY ON THE THAMES

As we went down to the boat next morning, Walter could not quite keep off the subject of last night, though he was more hopeful than he had been then, and seemed to think that if the unlucky homicide could not be got to go over-sea, he might at any rate go and live somewhere in the neighbourhood pretty much by himself; at any rate, that was what he himself had proposed. To Dick, and I must say to me also, this seemed a strange remedy; and Dick said as much. Quoth he:

'Friend Walter, don't set the man brooding on the tragedy by letting him live alone. That will only strengthen his idea that he has committed a crime, and you will have him killing himself in good earnest.'

Said Clara: 'I don't know. If I may say what I think of it, it is that he had better have his fill of gloom now, and, so to say, wake up presently to see how little need there has been for it; and then he will live happily afterwards. As for his killing himself, you need not be afraid of that; for, from all you can tell me, he is really very much in love with the woman; and to speak plainly, until his love is satisfied, he will not only stick to life as tightly as he can, but will also make the most of every event of his life – will, so to say, hug himself up in it; and I think that this is the real explanation of his taking the whole matter with such an excess of tragedy.'

Walter looked thoughtful, and said: 'Well, you may be right; and perhaps we should have treated it all more lightly: but you see, guest' (turning to me), 'such things happen so seldom, that when they do happen, we cannot help being much taken up with it. For the rest, we are all inclined to excuse our poor friend for making us so unhappy, on the ground that he does it out of an exaggerated respect for human life and its happiness. Well, I will say no more about it; only this: will you give me a cast up-stream, as I want to look after a lonely habitation for the poor fellow, since he will have it so, and I hear that there is one which would suit us very well on the downs beyond Streatley; so if you will put me ashore there I will walk up the hill and look to it.'

'Is the house in question empty?' said I.

'No,' said Walter, 'but the man who lives there will go out of it, of course, when he hears that we want it. You see, we think that the fresh air of the downs and the very emptiness of the landscape will do our friend good.'

'Yes,' said Clara, smiling, 'and he will not be so far from his beloved that they cannot easily meet if they have a mind to – as they certainly will.'

This talk had brought us down to the boat, and we were presently afloat on the beautiful broad stream, Dick driving the prow swiftly through the windless water of the early summer morning, for it was not yet six o'clock. We were at the lock in a very little time; and as we lay rising and rising on the in-coming water, I could not help wondering that my old friend the pound-lock, and that of the very simplest and most rural kind, should hold its place there; so I said:

'I have been wondering, as we passed lock after lock, that you people, so prosperous as you are, and especially since you are so anxious for pleasant work to do, have not invented something which would get rid of this clumsy business of going upstairs by means of these rude contrivances.'

Dick laughed. 'My dear friend,' said he, 'as long as water has the clumsy habit of running down hill, I fear we must humour it by going upstairs when we have our faces turned from the sea. And really I don't see why you should fall foul of Maple-Durham lock, which I think a very pretty place.'

There was no doubt about the latter assertion, I thought, as I looked up at the overhanging boughs of the great trees, with the sun coming glittering through the leaves, and listened to the song of the summer blackbirds as it mingled with the sound of the backwater near us. So not being able to say why I wanted the locks away – which, indeed, I didn't do at all – I held my peace. But Walter said:

'You see, guest, this is not an age of inventions. The last epoch did all that for us, and we are now content to use such of its inventions as we find handy, and leaving those alone which we don't want. I believe, as a matter of fact, that some time ago (I can't give you a date) some elaborate machinery was used for the locks, though people did not go so far as try to make the water run uphill. However, it was troublesome, I suppose, and the simple hatches, and the gates, with a big counterpoising beam, were found to answer every purpose, and were easily mended when wanted with material always to hand: so here they are, as you see.'

'Besides,' said Dick, 'this kind of lock is pretty, as you can see; and I can't help thinking that your machine-lock, winding up like a watch, would have been ugly and would have spoiled the look of the river: and that is surely reason enough for keeping such locks as these. Good-bye, old fellow!' said he to the lock, as he pushed us out through the now open gates by a vigorous stroke of the boat-hook. 'May you live long, and have your green old age renewed for ever!'

On we went; and the water had the familiar aspect to me of the days before Pangbourne had been thoroughly cockneyfied, as I have seen it. It (Pangbourne) was distinctly a village still – *i.e.*, a definite group of houses, and as pretty as might be. The beech-woods still covered the hill that rose above Basildon; but the flat fields beneath them were much more populous than I remembered them, as there were five large houses in sight, very carefully designed so as not to hurt the character of the country. Down on the green lip of the river, just where the water turns toward the Goring and Streatley reaches, were half a dozen girls playing about on the grass. They hailed us as we were about passing them, as they noted that we were travellers and we stopped a minute to talk with them. They had been bathing and were light clad and barefooted, and were bound for the meadows on the Berkshire side, where the haymaking had begun, and were passing the time merrily enough till the Berkshire folk came in their punt to fetch them. At first nothing would content them but we must go with them into the hay-field, and breakfast with them; but Dick put forward his theory of beginning the hay-harvest higher up the water, and not spoiling my pleasure therein by giving me a taste of it elsewhere, and they gave way, though unwillingly. In revenge they asked me a great many questions about the country I came from and the manners of life there, which I found rather puzzling to answer; and doubtless what answers I did give were puzzling enough to them. I noticed both with these pretty girls and with everybody else we met, that in default of serious news, such as we had heard at Maple-Durham, they were eager to discuss all the little details of life: the weather, the hay-crop, the last new house, the plenty or lack of such and such birds, and so on; and they talked of these things not in a fatuous and conventional way, but as taking, I say, real interest in them. Moreover, I found that the women knew as much about all these things as the men: could name a flower, and knew its qualities; could tell you the habitat of such and such birds and fish, and the like.

It is almost strange what a difference this intelligence made in my estimate of the country life of that day; for it used to be said in past times, and on the whole truly, that outside their daily work country people knew little of the country, and at least could tell you nothing about it; while here were these people as eager about all the goings on in the fields and woods and downs as if they had been Cockneys newly escaped from the tyranny of bricks and mortar.

I may mention as a detail worth noticing that not only did there seem to be a great many more birds about of the non-predatory kinds, but their enemies the birds of prey were also commoner. A kite hung over our heads as we passed Medmenham yesterday; magpies were quite common in the hedgerows; I saw several sparrow-hawks, and I think a merlin; and now just as we were passing the pretty bridge which had taken the place of Basildon railwaybridge, a couple of ravens croaked above our boat, as they sailed off to the higher ground of the downs. I concluded from all this that the days of the gamekeeper were over, and did not even need to ask Dick a question about it.

Chapter XXVI [54]
THE OBSTINATE REFUSERS

Before we parted from these girls we saw two sturdy young men and a woman putting off from the Berkshire shore, and then Dick bethought him of a little banter of the girls, and asked them how it was that there was nobody of the male kind to go with them across the water, and where their boats were gone to. Said one, the youngest of the party: 'Oh, they have got the big punt to lead stone from up the water.'

'Who do you mean by "they", dear child?' said Dick.

Said an older girl, laughing: 'You had better go and see them. Look there,' and she pointed north-west, 'don't you see building going on there?'

'Yes,' said Dick, 'and I am rather surprised at this time of the year; why are they not haymaking with you?'

The girls all laughed at this, and before their laugh was over, the Berkshire boat had run on to the grass and the girls stepped in lightly, still sniggering, while the newcomers gave us the sele of the day. But before they were under way again, the tall girl said: 'Excuse us for laughing, dear neighbours, but we have had some friendly bickering with the builders up yonder, and as we have no time to tell you the story, you had better go and ask them: they will be glad to see you – if you don't hinder their work.'

They all laughed again at that, and waved us a pretty farewell as

the punters set them over toward the other shore, and left us standing
on the bank beside the boat.

'Let us go and see them,' said Clara; 'that is, if you are not in a
hurry to get to Streatley, Walter?'

'Oh no,' said Walter, 'I shall be glad of the excuse to have a little
more of your company.'

So we left the boat moored there, and went on up the slow slope
of the hill; but I said to Dick on the way, being somewhat mystified:
'What was all that laughing about? what was the joke?'

'I can guess pretty well,' said Dick; 'some of them up there
have got a piece of work which interests them, and they won't go to
the haymaking, which doesn't matter at all, because there are plenty
of people to do such easy-hard work as that; only, since haymaking
is a regular festival, the neighbours find it amusing to jeer good-
humouredly at them.'

'I see,' said I, 'much as if in Dickens's time some young people
were so wrapped up in their work that they wouldn't keep Christ-
mas.'

'Just so,' said Dick, 'only these people need not be young either.'

'But what did you mean by easy-hard work?' said I.

Quoth Dick: 'Did I say that? I mean work that tries the muscles
and hardens them and sends you pleasantly weary to bed, but which
isn't trying in other ways: doesn't harass you, in short. Such work is
always pleasant if you don't overdo it. Only, mind you, good mowing
requires some little skill. I'm a pretty good mower.'

This talk brought us up to the house that was a-building, not a
large one, which stood at the end of a beautiful orchard surrounded
by an old stone wall. 'Oh yes, I see,' said Dick; 'I remember, a
beautiful place for a house; but a starveling of a nineteenth-century
house stood there: I am glad they are rebuilding: it's all stone, too,
though it need not have been in this part of the country: my word,
though, they are making a neat job of it: but I wouldn't have made it
all ashlar.'[55]

Walter and Clara were already talking to a tall man clad in his
mason's blouse, who looked about forty, but was, I daresay, older,
who had his mallet and chisel in hand; there were at work in the
shed and on the scaffold about half a dozen men and two women,

blouse-clad like the carles, while a very pretty woman who was not in the work but was dressed in an elegant suit of blue linen came sauntering up to us with her knitting in her hand. She welcomed us and said, smiling: 'So you are come up from the water to see the Obstinate Refusers: where are you going haymaking, neighbours?'

'Oh, right up above Oxford,' said Dick; 'it is rather a late country. But what share have you got with the Refusers, pretty neighbour?'

Said she, with a laugh: 'Oh, I am the lucky one who doesn't want to work; though sometimes I get it, for I serve as model to Mistress Philippa there when she wants one; she is our head carver; come and see her.'

She led us up to the door of the unfinished house, where a rather little woman was working with mallet and chisel on the wall near by. She seemed very intent on what she was doing, and did not turn round when we came up; but a taller woman, quite a girl she seemed, who was at work near by, had already knocked off, and was standing looking from Clara to Dick with delighted eyes. None of the others paid much heed to us.

The blue-clad girl laid her hand on the carver's shoulder and said: 'Now, Philippa, if you gobble up your work like that, you will soon have none to do; and what will become of you then?'

The carver turned round hurriedly and showed us the face of a woman of forty (or so she seemed), and said rather pettishly, but in a sweet voice:

'Don't talk nonsense, Kate, and don't interrupt me if you can help it.' She stopped short when she saw us, then went on with the kind smile of welcome which never failed us. 'Thank you for coming to see us, neighbours; but I am sure that you won't think me unkind if I go on with my work, especially when I tell you that I was ill and unable to do anything all through April and May; and this open air and the sun and the work together, and my feeling well again too, make a mere delight of every hour to me; and excuse me, I must go on.'

She fell to work accordingly on a carving in low relief of flowers and figures, but talked on amidst her mallet strokes: 'You see, we all think this the prettiest place for a house up and down these reaches; and the site has been so long encumbered with an unworthy one, that we masons were determined to pay off fate and destiny for once, and build the prettiest house we could compass here – and so – and so—'

Here she lapsed into mere carving, but the tall foreman came up and said: 'Yes, neighbours, that is it: so it is going to be all ashlar because we want to carve a kind of wreath of flowers and figures all round it; and we have been much hindered by one thing or other – Philippa's illness amongst others, – and though we could have managed our wreath without her—'

'Could you, though?' grumbled the last-named from the face of the wall.

'Well, at any rate, she is our best carver, and it would not have been kind to begin the carving without her. So you see,' said he, looking at Dick and me, 'we really couldn't go haymaking, could we, neighbours? But you see, we are getting on so fast now with this splendid weather, that I think we may well spare a week or ten days at wheat-harvest; and won't we go at *that* work then! Come down then to the acres that lie north and by west here at our backs and you shall see good harvesters, neighbours.'

'Hurrah, for a good brag!' called a voice from the scaffold above us: 'our foreman thinks that an easier job than putting one stone on another!'

There was a general laugh at this sally, in which the tall foreman joined; and with that we saw a lad bringing out a little table into the shadow of the stone-shed, which he set down there, and then going back, came out again with the inevitable big wickered flask and tall glasses, whereon the foreman led us up to due seats on blocks of stone, and said:

'Well, neighbours, drink to my brag coming true, or I shall think you don't believe me! Up there!' said he, hailing the scaffold, 'are you coming down for a glass?' Three of the workmen came running down the ladder as men with good 'building legs' will do; but the others didn't answer, except the joker (if he must so be called), who called out without turning round: 'Excuse me, neighbours, for not getting down. I must get on; my work is not superintending, like the gaffer's yonder; but, you fellows, send us up a glass to drink the haymaker's health.' Of course, Philippa would not turn away from her beloved work; but the other woman carver came; she turned out to be Philippa's daughter, but was a tall strong girl, black-haired and gipsey-like of face and curiously solemn of manner. The rest gathered round us and clinked glasses, and the men on the scaffold turned about and drank to our healths; but the busy little woman by the door would have none of it all, but only shrugged her shoulders when her daughter came up to her and touched her.

So we shook hands and turned our backs on the Obstinate Refusers, went down the slope to our boat, and before we had gone many steps heard the full tune of tinkling trowels mingle with the humming of the bees and the singing of the larks above the little plain of Basildon.[56]

Chapter XXVII
THE UPPER WATERS

We set Walter on the Berkshire side, amidst all the beauties of Streatley, and so went our ways into what once would have been the deeper country under the foot-hills of the White Horse;[57] and though the contrast between half-cockneyfied and wholly unsophisticated country existed no longer, a feeling of exultation rose within me (as it used to do) at sight of the familiar and still unchanged hills of the Berkshire range.

We stopped at Wallingford for our midday meal; of course, all signs of squalor and poverty had disappeared from the streets of the ancient town, and many ugly houses had been taken down and many pretty new ones built, but I thought it curious, that the town still looked like the place I remembered so well; for indeed it looked like that ought to have looked.

At dinner we fell in with an old, but very bright and intelligent man, who seemed in a country way to be another edition of old Hammond. He had an extraordinary detailed knowledge of the ancient history of the countryside from the time of Alfred to the days of the Parliamentary Wars, many events of which, as you may know, were enacted round about Wallingford. But, what was more interesting to us, he had detailed record of the period of the change to the present state of things, and told us a great deal about it, and especially of that exodus of the people from the town to the country, and the gradual recovery by the town-bred people on one side, and the country-bred people on the other, of those arts of life which they had each lost; which loss, as he told us, had at one time gone so far that not only was it impossible to find a carpenter or a smith in a village or small country town, but that people in such places had even forgotten how to bake bread, and that at Wallingford, for instance, the bread came down with the newspapers by an early train from London, worked in some way, the explanation of which I could not understand. He told us also that the townspeople who came into the country used to pick up the agricultural arts by carefully watching the way in which the machines worked, gathering an idea of handicraft from machinery; because at that time almost everything in and about the fields was done by elaborate machines used quite unintelligently by the labourers. On the other hand, the old men amongst the labourers managed to teach the younger ones gradually a little artisanship, such as the use of the saw and the plane, the work of the smithy, and so forth; for once more, by that time it was as much as – or rather, more than – a man could do to fix an ash pole to a rake by handiwork; so that it would take a machine worth a thousand pounds, a group of workmen, and half a day's travelling, to do five shillings' worth of work. He showed us, among other things, an account of a certain village council who were working hard at all this business; and the record of their intense earnestness in getting to the bottom of some matter which in time past would have been thought quite trivial, as, for example, the due proportions of alkali and oil for soap-making for the village wash, or the exact heat of the water into which a leg of mutton should be plunged for boiling – all this, joined to the utter absence of anything like party feeling, which even in a village assembly would certainly have made its appearance in an earlier epoch, was very amusing, and at the same time instructive.

This old man, whose name was Henry Morsom, took us, after our meal and a rest, into a biggish hall which contained a large collection of articles of manufacture and art from the last days of the machine period to that day; and he went over them with us, and explained them with great care. They also were very interesting, showing the transition from the makeshift work of the machines (which was at about its worst a little after the Civil War before told of) into the first years of the new handicraft period. Of course, there was much overlapping of the periods: and at the first the new handwork came in very slowly.

'You must remember,' said the old antiquary, 'that the handicraft was not the result of what used to be called material necessity: on the contrary, by that time the machines had been done so much improved that almost all necessary work might have been done by them: and indeed many people at that time, and before it, used to think that machinery would entirely supersede handicraft; which certainly, on the face of it, seemed more than likely. But there was another opinion, far less logical, prevalent amongst the rich people before the days of freedom, which did not die out at once after that epoch had begun. This opinion, which from all I can learn seemed as natural then, as it seems absurd now, was, that while the ordinary daily work of the world would be done entirely by automatic machinery, the energies of the more intelligent part of mankind would be set free to follow the higher forms of the arts, as well as science and the study of history. It was strange, was it not, that they should thus ignore that aspiration after complete equality which we now recognize as the bond of all happy human society?'

I did not answer, but thought the more. Dick looked thoughtful, and said:

'Strange, neighbour? Well, I don't know. I have often heard my old kinsman say the one aim of all people before our time was to avoid work, or at least they thought it was; so of course the work which their daily life *forced* them to do, seemed more like work than that which they *seemed* to choose for themselves.'

'True enough,' said Morsom. 'Anyhow, they soon began to find out their mistake, and that only slaves and slave-holders could live solely by setting machines going.'

Clara broke in here, flushing a little as she spoke: 'Was not their mistake once more bred of the life of slavery that they had been living? – a life which was always looking upon everything, except mankind, animate and inanimate – "nature", as people used to call it – as one thing, and mankind as another. It was natural to people thinking in this way, that they should try to make "nature" their slave, since they thought "nature" was something outside them.'

'Surely,' said Morsom; 'and they were puzzled as to what to do, till they found the feeling against a mechanical life, which had begun before the Great Change amongst people who had leisure to think of such things, was spreading insensibly; till at last under the guise of pleasure that was not supposed to be work, work that was pleasure began to push out the mechanical toil, which they had once hoped at the best to reduce to narrow limits indeed, but never to get rid of; and which, moreover, they found they could not limit as they had hoped to do.'

'When did this new revolution gather head?' said I.

'In the half-century that followed the Great Change,' said Morsom, 'it began to be noteworthy; machine after machine was quietly dropped under the excuse that the machines could not produce works of art, and that works of art were more and more called for. Look here,' he said, 'here are some of the works of that time – rough and unskilful in handiwork, but solid and showing some sense of pleasure in the making.'

'They are very curious,' said I, taking up a piece of pottery from amongst the specimens which the antiquary was showing us; 'not a bit like the work of either savages or barbarians, and yet with what would once have been called a hatred of civilization impressed upon them.'[58]

'Yes,' said Morsom, 'you must not look for delicacy there: in that period you could only have got that from a man who was practically a slave. But now, you see,' said he, leading me on a little, 'we have learned the trick of handicraft, and have added the utmost refinement of workmanship to the freedom of fancy and imagination.'

I looked, and wondered indeed at the deftness and abundance of beauty of the work of men who had at last learned to accept life itself as a pleasure, and the satisfaction of the common needs of mankind and the preparation for them, as work fit for the best of the race. I mused silently; but at last I said:

'What is to come after this?'

The old man laughed. 'I don't know,' said he; 'we will meet it when it comes.'

'Meanwhile,' quoth Dick, 'we have got to meet the rest of our day's journey; so out into the street and down to the strand! Will you come a turn with us, neighbour? Our friend is greedy of your stories.'

'I will go as far as Oxford with you,' said he; 'I want a book or two out of the Bodleian Library. I suppose you will sleep in the old city?'

'No,' said Dick, 'we are going higher up; the hay is waiting us there, you know.'

Morsom nodded, and we all went into the street together, and got into the boat a little above the town bridge. But just as Dick was getting the sculls into the rowlocks, the bows of another boat came thrusting through the low arch. Even at first sight it was a gay little craft indeed – bright green, and painted over with elegantly drawn flowers. As it cleared the arch, a figure as bright and gay-clad as the boat rose up in it; a slim girl dressed in light blue silk that fluttered in the draughty wind of the bridge. I thought I knew the figure, and sure enough, as she turned her head to us, and showed her beautiful face, I saw with joy that it was none other than the fairy godmother from the abundant garden on Runnymede – Ellen, to wit.

We all stopped to receive her. Dick rose in the boat and cried out a genial good morrow; I tried to be as genial as Dick, but failed; Clara waved a delicate hand to her; and Morsom nodded and looked on with interest. As to Ellen, the beautiful brown of her face was deepened by a flush, as she brought the gunwale of her boat alongside ours, and said:

'You see, neighbours, I had some doubt if you would all three come back past Runnymede, or if you did, whether you would stop there; and besides, I am not sure whether we – my father and I – shall not be away in a week or two, for he wants to see a brother of his in the north country, and I should not like him to go without me. So I thought I might never see you again, and that seemed uncomfortable to me, and – and so I came after you.'

'Well,' said Dick, 'I am sure we are all very glad of that; although you may be sure that as for Clara and me, we should have made a point of coming to see you, and of coming the second time, if we had found you away the first. But, dear neighbour, there you are alone in the boat, and you have been sculling pretty hard, I should think, and might find a little quiet sitting pleasant; so we had better part our company into two.'

'Yes,' said Ellen, 'I thought you would do that, so I have brought a rudder for my boat: will you help me to ship it, please?'

And she went aft in her boat and pushed along our side till she had brought the stern close to Dick's hand. He knelt down in our boat and she in hers, and the usual fumbling took place over hanging the rudder on its hooks; for, as you may imagine, no change had taken place in the arrangement of such an unimportant matter as the rudder of a pleasure-boat. As the two beautiful young faces bent over the rudder, they seemed to me to be very close together, and though it only lasted a moment, a sort of pang shot through me as I looked on. Clara sat in her place and she did not look round, but presently she said, with just the least stiffness in her tone:

'How shall we divide? Won't you go into Ellen's boat, Dick, since, without offence to our guest, you are the better sculler?'

Dick stood up and laid his hand on her shoulder, and said: 'No, no; let Guest try what he can do – he ought to be getting into training now. Besides, we are in no hurry: we are not going far above Oxford; and even if we are benighted, we shall have the moon, which will give us nothing worse of a night than a greyer day.'

'Besides,' said I, 'I may manage to do a little more with my sculling than merely keeping the boat from drifting down-stream.'

They all laughed at this, as if it had been a very good joke; and I thought that Ellen's laugh, even amongst the others, was one of the pleasantest sounds I had ever heard.

To be short, I got into the new-come boat, not a little elated, and taking the sculls, set to work to show off a little. For – must I say it? – I felt as if even that happy world were made the happier for my being so near this strange girl; although I must say that of all the persons I had seen in that world renewed, she was the most unfamiliar to me, the most unlike what I could have thought of. Clara, for instance, beautiful and bright as she was, was not unlike a *very* pleasant and unaffected young lady; and the other girls also seemed nothing more than specimens of very much improved types which I had known in other times. But this girl was not only beautiful with a beauty quite different from that of 'a young lady', but was in all ways so strangely interesting; so that I kept wondering what she would say or do next to surprise and please me. Not, indeed, that there was anything startling in what she actually said or did; but it was all done in a new way, and always with that indefinable interest and pleasure of life, which I had noticed more or less in everybody, but which in her was more marked and more charming than in any one else that I had seen.

We were soon under way and going at a fair pace through the beautiful reaches of the river, between Bensington and Dorchester. It was now about the middle of the afternoon, warm rather than hot, and quite windless; the clouds high up and light, pearly white, and gleaming, softened the sun's burning, but did not hide the pale blue in most places, though they seemed to give it height and consistency; the sky, in short, looked really like a vault, as poets have sometimes called it, and not like mere limitless air, but a vault so vast and full of light that it did not in any way oppress the spirits. It was the sort of afternoon that Tennyson must have been thinking about, when he said of the Lotos-Eaters' land that it was a land where it was always afternoon.[59]

Ellen leaned back in the stern and seemed to enjoy herself thoroughly. I could see that she was really looking at things and let nothing escape her, and as I watched her, an uncomfortable feeling that she had been a little touched by love of the deft, ready and handsome Dick, and that she had been constrained to follow us because of it, faded out of my mind; since if it had been so, she surely could not have been so excitedly pleased, even with the beautiful scenes we were passing through. For some time she did not say much, but at last, as we had passed under Shillingford Bridge (new built, but somewhat on its old lines), she bade me hold the boat while she had a good look at the landscape through the graceful arch. Then she turned about to me and said:

'I do not know whether to be sorry or glad that this is the first time that I have been in these reaches. It is true that it is a great pleasure to see all this for the first time; but if I had had a year or two of memory of it, how sweetly it would all have mingled with my life, waking or dreaming! I am so glad Dick has been pulling slowly, so as to linger out the time here. How do you feel about your first visit to these waters?'

I do not suppose she meant a trap for me, but anyhow I fell into it, and said: 'My first visit! It is not my first visit by many a time. I know these reaches well; indeed, I may say that I know every yard of the Thames from Hammersmith to Cricklade.'

I saw the complication that might follow, as her eyes fixed mine with a curious look in them, that I had seen before at Runnymede, when I had said something which made it difficult for others to understand my present position amongst these people. I reddened, and said, in order to cover my mistake: 'I wonder you have never been up so high as this, since you live on the Thames, and moreover row so well that it would be no great labour to you. Let alone,' quoth I, insinuatingly, 'that anybody would be glad to row you.'

She laughed, clearly not at my compliment (as I am sure she need not have done, since it was a very commonplace fact), but at something which was stirring in her mind; and she still looked at me kindly, but with the above-said keen look in her eyes, and then she said:

'Well, perhaps it is strange, though I have a good deal to do at home, what with looking after my father, and dealing with two or three young men who have taken a special liking to me, and all of whom I cannot please at once. But you, dear neighbour; it seems to me stranger that you should know the upper river, than that I should not know it; for, as I understand, you have only been in England a few days. But perhaps you mean that you have read about it in books, and seen pictures of it? – though that does not come to much, either.'

'Truly,' said I. 'Besides, I have not read any books about the Thames: it was one of the minor stupidities of our time that no one thought fit to write a decent book about what may fairly be called our only English river.'

The words were no sooner out of my mouth than I saw that I had made another mistake; and I felt really annoyed with myself, as I did not want to go into a long explanation just then, or begin another series of Odyssean lies. Somehow, Ellen seemed to see this, and she took no advantage of my slip; her piercing look changed into one of mere frank kindness, and she said:

'Well, anyhow I am glad that I am travelling these waters with you, since you know our river so well, and I know little of it past Pangbourne, for you can tell me all I want to know about it.' She paused a minute, and then said: 'Yet you must understand that the part I do know, I know as thoroughly as you do. I should be sorry for you to think that I am careless of a thing so beautiful and interesting as the Thames.'

She said this quite earnestly, and with an air of affectionate appeal to me which pleased me very much; but I could see that she was only keeping her doubts about me for another time.

Presently we came to Day's Lock, where Dick and his two sitters had waited for us. He would have me go ashore, as if to show me something which I had never seen before; and nothing loth I followed him, Ellen by my side, to the well-remembered Dykes, and the long church beyond them, which was still used for various purposes by the good folk of Dorchester: where, by the way, the village guesthouse still had the sign of the Fleur-de-luce which it used to bear in the days when hospitality had to be bought and sold. This time, however, I made no sign of all this being familiar to me: though as we sat for a while on the mound of the Dykes looking up at Sinodun and its clear-cut trench, and its sister *mamelon*[60] of Whittenham, I felt somewhat uncomfortable under Ellen's serious attentive look, which almost drew from me the cry, 'How little anything is changed here!'

We stopped again at Abingdon, which, like Wallingford, was in a way both old and new to me, since it had been lifted out of its nineteenth-century degradation, and otherwise was as little altered as might be.

Sunset was in the sky as we skirted Oxford by Oseney; we stopped a minute or two hard by the ancient castle to put Henry Morsom ashore. It was a matter of course that so far as they could be seen from the river, I missed none of the towers and spires of that once don-beridden city; but the meadows all round, which, when I had last passed through them, were getting daily more and more squalid, more and more impressed with the seal of the 'stir and intellectual life of the nineteenth century', were no longer intellectual, but had once again become as beautiful as they should be, and the little hill of Hinksey, with two or three very pretty stone houses new-grown on it (I use the word advisedly; for they seemed to belong to it) looked down happily on the full streams and waving-grass, grey now, but for the sunset, with its fast-ripening seeds.

The railway having disappeared, and therewith the various level bridges over the streams of Thames, we were soon through Medley Lock and in the wide water that washes Port Meadow, with its numerous population of geese nowise diminished; and I thought with interest how its name and use had survived from the older imperfect communal period, through the time of the confused struggle and tyranny of the rights of property, into the present rest and happiness of complete Communism.

I was taken ashore again at Godstow, to see the remains of the old nunnery, pretty nearly in the same condition as I had remembered them; and from the high bridge over the cut close by, I could see, even in the twilight, how beautiful the little village with its grey stone houses had become; for we had now come into the stone-country, in which every house must be either built, walls and roof, of grey stone or be a blot on the landscape.

We still rowed on after this, Ellen taking the sculls in my boat; we passed a weir a little higher up, and about three miles beyond it came by moonlight again to a little town, where we slept at a house thinly inhabited, as its folk were mostly tented in the hay-fields.

Chapter XXVIII

THE LITTLE RIVER

We started before six o'clock the next morning, as we were still twenty-five miles from our resting-place, and Dick wanted to be there before dusk. The journey was pleasant, though to those who do not know the upper Thames, there is little to say about it. Ellen and I were once more together in her boat, though Dick, for fairness' sake, was for having me in his, and letting the two women scull the green toy. Ellen, however, would not allow this, but claimed me as the interesting person of the company. 'After having come so far,' said she, 'I will not be put off with a companion who will be always thinking of somebody else than me: the guest is the only person who can amuse me properly. I mean that really,' said she, turning to me, 'and have not said it merely as a pretty saying.'

Clara blushed and looked very happy at all this; for I think up to this time she had been rather frightened of Ellen. As for me I felt young again, and strange hopes of my youth were mingling with the pleasure of the present; almost destroying it, and quickening it into something like pain.

As we passed through the short and winding reaches of the now quickly lessening stream, Ellen said: 'How pleasant this little river is to me, who am used to a great wide wash of water; it almost seems as if we shall have to stop at every reach-end. I expect before I get home this evening I shall have realized what a little country England is, since we can so soon get to the end of its biggest river.'

'It is not big,' said I, 'but it is pretty.'

'Yes,' she said, 'and don't you find it difficult to imagine the times when this little pretty country was treated by its folk as if it had been an ugly characterless waste, with no delicate beauty to be guarded, with no heed taken of the ever fresh pleasure of the recurring seasons, and changeful weather, and diverse quality of the soil, and so forth? How could people be so cruel to themselves?'

'And to each other,' said I. Then a sudden resolution took hold of me, and I said: 'Dear neighbour, I may as well tell you at once that I find it easier to imagine all that ugly past than you do, because I myself have been part of it. I see both that you have divined something of this in me; and also I think you will believe me when I tell you of it, so that I am going to hide nothing from you at all.'

She was silent a little, and then she said: 'My friend, you have guessed right about me; and to tell you the truth I have followed you up from Runnymede in order that I might ask you many questions, and because I saw that you were not one of us; and that interested and pleased me, and I wanted to make you as happy as you could be. To say the truth, there was a risk in it,' said she, blushing – 'I mean as to Dick and Clara; for I must tell you, since we are going to be such close friends, that even amongst us, where there are so many beautiful women, I have often troubled men's minds disastrously. That is one reason why I was living alone with my father in the cottage at Runnymede. But it did not answer on that score; for of course people came there, as the place is not a desert, and they seemed to find me all the more interesting for living alone like that, and fell to making stories of me to themselves – like I know you did, my friend. Well, let that pass. This evening, or tomorrow morning, I shall make a proposal to you to do something which would please me very much, and I think would not hurt you.'

I broke in eagerly, saying that I would do anything in the world for her; for indeed, in spite of my years and the too obvious signs of them (though that feeling of renewed youth was not a mere passing sensation, I think) – in spite of my years, I say, I felt altogether too happy in the company of this delightful girl, and was prepared to take her confidences for more than they meant perhaps.

She laughed now, but looked very kindly on me. 'Well,' she said, 'meantime for the present we will let it be; for I must look at this new country that we are passing through. See how the river has changed character again: it is broad now, and the reaches are long and very slow-running. And look, there is a ferry!'

I told her the name of it, as I slowed off to put the ferry-chain over our heads; and on we went passing by a bank clad with oak trees on our left hand, till the stream narrowed again and deepened, and we rowed on between walls of tall reeds, whose population of reed sparrows and warblers were delightfully restless, twittering and chuckling as the wash of the boats stirred the reeds from the water upwards in the still, hot morning.

She smiled with pleasure, and her lazy enjoyment of the new scene seemed to bring out her beauty doubly as she leaned back amidst the cushions, though she was far from languid; her idleness being the idleness of a person, strong and well-knit both in body and mind, deliberately resting.

'Look!' she said, springing up suddenly from her place without any obvious effort, and balancing herself with exquisite grace and ease; 'look at the beautiful old bridge ahead!'

'I need scarcely look at that,' said I, not turning my head away from her beauty. 'I know what it is; though' (with a smile) 'we used not to call it the Old Bridge time agone.'

She looked down upon me kindly, and said, 'How well we get on now you are no longer on your guard against me!'

And she stood looking thoughtfully at me still, till she had to sit down as we passed under the middle one of the row of little pointed arches of the oldest bridge across the Thames.

'Oh the beautiful fields!' she said; 'I had no idea of the charm of a very small river like this. The smallness of the scale of everything, the short reaches, and the speedy change of the banks, give one a feeling of going somewhere, of coming to something strange, a feeling of adventure which I have not felt in bigger waters.'

I looked up at her delightedly; for her voice, saying the very thing which I was thinking, was like a caress to me. She caught my eye and her cheeks reddened under their tan, and she said simply:

'I must tell you, my friend, that when my father leaves the Thames this summer he will take me away to a place near the Roman wall in Cumberland; so that this voyage of mine is farewell to the south; of course with my goodwill in a way; and yet I am sorry for it. I hadn't the heart to tell Dick yesterday that we were as good as gone from the Thames-side; but somehow to you I must needs tell it.'

She stopped and seemed very thoughtful for a while, and then said, smiling:

'I must say that I don't like moving about from one home to another; one gets so pleasantly used to all the detail of the life about one; it fits so harmoniously and happily into one's own life, that beginning again, even in a small way, is a kind of pain. But I daresay in the country which you come from, you would think this petty and unadventurous, and would think the worse of me for it.'

She smiled at me caressingly as she spoke, and I made haste to answer: 'Oh no, indeed; again you echo my very thoughts. But I hardly expected to hear you speak so. I gathered from all I have heard that there was a great deal of changing of abode amongst you in this country.'

'Well,' she said, 'of course people are free to move about; but except for pleasure-parties, especially in harvest and hay-time, like this of ours, I don't think they do so much. I admit that I also have other moods than that of stay-at-home, as I hinted just now, and I should like to go with you all through the west country – thinking of nothing,' concluded she, smiling.

'I should have plenty to think of,' said I.

Chapter XXIX
A RESTING-PLACE ON THE UPPER THAMES

Presently at a place where the river flowed round a headland of the meadows, we stopped a while for rest and victuals, and settled ourselves on a beautiful bank which almost reached the dignity of a hill-side: the wide meadows spread before us, and already the scythe was busy amidst the hay. One change I noticed amidst the quiet beauty of the fields – to wit, that they were planted with trees here and there, often fruit-trees, and that there was none of the niggardly begrudging of space to a handsome tree which I remembered too well; and though the willows were often polled (or shrowded, as they call it in that countryside), this was done with some regard to beauty: I mean that there was no polling of rows on rows so as to destroy the pleasantness of half a mile of country, but a thoughtful sequence in the cutting, that prevented a sudden bareness anywhere. To be short, the fields were everywhere treated as a garden made for the pleasure as well as the livelihood of all, as old Hammond told me was the case.

On this bank or bent of the hill, then, we had our mid-day meal; somewhat early for dinner, if that mattered, but we had been stirring early: the slender stream of the Thames winding below us between the garden of a country I have been telling of; a furlong from us was a beautiful little islet begrown with graceful trees; on the slopes westward of us was a wood of varied growth overhanging the narrow meadow on the south side of the river; while to the north was a wide stretch of mead rising very gradually from the river's edge. A delicate spire of an ancient building rose up from out of the trees in the middle distance, with a few grey houses clustered about it; while nearer to us, in fact not half a furlong from the water, was a quite modern stone house – a wide quadrangle of one story, the buildings that made it being quite low. There was no garden between it and the river, nothing but a row of pear-trees still quite young and slender; and though there did not seem to be much ornament about it, it had a sort of natural elegance, like that of the trees themselves.

As we sat looking down on all this in the sweet June day, rather happy than merry, Ellen, who sat next me, her hand clasped about one knee, leaned sideways to me, and said in a low voice which Dick and Clara might have noted if they had not been busy in happy wordless love-making: 'Friend, in your country were the houses of your field-labourers anything like that?'

I said: 'Well, at any rate the houses of our rich men were not; they were mere blots upon the face of the land.'

'I find that hard to understand,' she said. 'I can see why the workmen, who were so oppressed, should not have been able to live in beautiful houses; for it takes time and leisure, and minds not over-burdened with care, to make beautiful dwellings; and I quite understand that these poor people were not allowed to live in such a way as to have these (to us) necessary good things. But why the rich men, who had the time and the leisure and the materials for building, as it would be in this case, should not have housed themselves well, I do not understand as yet. I know what you are meaning to say to me,' she said, looking me full in the eyes and blushing, 'to wit that their houses and all belonging to them were generally ugly and base, unless they chanced to be ancient like yonder remnant of our fore-fathers' work' (pointing to the spire); 'that they were – let me see; what is the word?'

'Vulgar,' said I. 'We used to say,' said I, 'that the ugliness and vulgarity of the rich men's dwellings was a necessary reflection from the sordidness and bareness of life which they forced upon the poor people.'

She knit her brows as in thought; then turned a brightened face on me, as if she had caught the idea, and said: 'Yes, friend, I see what you mean. We have sometimes – those of us who look into these things – talked this very matter over; because, to say the truth, we have plenty of record of the so-called arts of the time before Equality of Life; and there are not wanting people who say that the state of that society was not the cause of all that ugliness; that they were ugly in their life because they liked to be, and could have had beautiful things about them if they had chosen; just as a man or a body of men now may, if they please, make things more or less beautiful— Stop! I know what you are going to say.'

'Do you?' said I, smiling, yet with a beating heart.

'Yes,' she said; 'you are answering me, teaching me, in some way or another, although you have not spoken the words aloud. You were going to say that in times of inequality it was an essential condition of the life of these rich men that they should not themselves make what they wanted for the adornment of their lives, but should force those to make them whom they forced to live pinched and sordid lives; and that as a necessary consequence the sordidness and pinching, the ugly barrenness of those ruined lives, were worked up into the adornment of the lives of the rich, and art died out amongst men? Was that what you would say, my friend?'

'Yes, yes,' I said, looking at her eagerly; for she had risen and was standing on the edge of the bent, the light wind stirring her dainty raiment, one hand laid on her bosom, the other arm stretched downward and clenched in her earnestness.

'It is true,' she said, 'it is true! We have proved it true!'

I think amidst my – something more than interest in her, and admiration for her, I was beginning to wonder how it would all end. I had a glimmering of fear of what might follow; of anxiety as to the remedy which this new age might offer for the missing of something one might set one's heart on. But now Dick rose to his feet and cried out in his hearty manner: 'Neighbour Ellen, are you quarrelling with the guest, or are you worrying him to tell you things which he cannot properly explain to our ignorance?'

'Neither, dear neighbour,' she said. 'I was so far from quarrelling with him that I think I have been making him good friends both with himself and me. Is it so, dear guest?' she said, looking down at me with a delightful smile of confidence in being understood.

'Indeed it is,' said I.

'Well, moreover,' she said, 'I must say for him that he has explained himself to me very well indeed, so that I quite understand him.'

'All right,' quoth Dick. 'When I first set eyes on you at Runnymede I knew that there was something wonderful in your keenness of wits. I don't say that as a mere pretty speech to please you,' said he quickly, 'but because it is true; and it made me want to see more of you. But, come, we ought to be going; for we are not half way, and we ought to be in well before sunset.'

And therewith he took Clara's hand, and led her down the bent. But Ellen stood thoughtfully looking down for a little, and as I took her hand to follow Dick, she turned round to me and said:

'You might tell me a great deal and make many things clear to me, if you would.'

'Yes,' said I, 'I am pretty well fit for that, – and for nothing else – an old man like me.'

She did not notice the bitterness which, whether I liked it or not, was in my voice as I spoke, but went on: 'It is not so much for myself; I should be quite content to dream about past times, and if I could not idealize them, yet at least idealize some of the people who lived in them. But I think sometimes people are too careless of the history of the past – too apt to leave it in the hands of old learned men like Hammond. Who knows? happy as we are, times may alter; we may be bitten with some impulse towards change, and many things may seem too wonderful for us to resist, too exciting not to catch at, if we do not know that they are but phases of what has been before; and withal ruinous, deceitful, and sordid.'

As we went slowly down toward the boats she said again: 'Not for myself alone, dear friend; I shall have children; perhaps before the end a good many; – I hope so. And though of course I cannot force any special kind of knowledge upon them, yet, my friend, I cannot help thinking that just as they might be like me in body, so I might impress upon them some part of my ways of thinking; that is, indeed, some of the essential part of myself; that part which was not mere moods, created by the matters and events round about me. What do you think?'

Of one thing I was sure, that her beauty and kindness and eagerness combined, forced me to think as she did, when she was not earnestly laying herself open to receive my thoughts. I said, what at the time was true, that I thought it most important; and presently stood entranced by the wonder of her grace as she stepped into the light boat, and held out her hand to me. And so on we went up the Thames still – or whither?

Chapter XXX
THE JOURNEY'S END

On we went. In spite of my new-born excitement about Ellen, and my gathering fear of where it would land me, I could not help taking abundant interest in the condition of the river and its banks; all the more as she never seemed weary of the changing picture, but looked at every yard of flowery bank and gurgling eddy with the same kind of affectionate interest which I myself once had so fully, as I used to think, and perhaps had not altogether lost even in this strangely changed society with all its wonders. Ellen seemed delighted with my pleasure at this, that, or the other piece of carefulness in dealing with the river: the nursing of pretty corners; the ingenuity in dealing with difficulties of water-engineering, so that the most obviously useful works looked beautiful and natural also. All this, I say, pleased me hugely, and she was pleased at my pleasure – but rather puzzled too.

'You seem astonished,' she said, just after we had passed a mill* which spanned all the stream save the waterway for traffic, but which was as beautiful in its way as a Gothic cathedral[61] – 'you seem astonished at this being so pleasant to look at.'

'Yes,' I said, 'in a way I am; though I don't see why it should not be.'

'Ah!' she said, looking at me admiringly, yet with a lurking smile in her face, 'you know all about the history of the past. Were they not always careful about this little stream which now adds so much pleasantness to the countryside? It would always be easy to manage this little river. Ah! I forgot, though,' she said, as her eye caught mine, 'in the days we are thinking of, pleasure was wholly neglected in such matters. But how did they manage the river in the days that you—' Lived in she was going to say; but correcting herself, said: 'in the days of which you have record?'

'They *mis*managed it,' quoth I. 'Up to the first half of the nineteenth century, when it was still more or less of a highway for the country people, some care was taken of the river and its banks; and though I don't suppose any one troubled himself about its aspect, yet it was trim and beautiful. But when the railways – of which no doubt you have heard – came into power, they would not allow the people of the country to use either the natural or artificial waterways, of which latter there were a great many. I suppose when we get higher up we shall see one of these: a very important one, which one of these railways entirely closed to the public, so that they might force people to send their goods by their private road, and so tax them as heavily as they could.'

Ellen laughed heartily. 'Well,' she said, 'that is not stated clearly enough in our history books, and it is worth knowing. But certainly

---

*I should have said that all along the Thames there were abundance of mills used for various purposes; none of which were in any degree unsightly, and many strikingly beautiful; and the gardens about them marvels of loveliness.

the people of those days must have been a curiously lazy set. We are not either fidgety or quarrelsome now, but if any one tried such a piece of folly on us, we should use the said waterways, whoever gainsaid us: surely that would be simple enough. However, I remember other cases of this stupidity: when I was on the Rhine two years ago, I remember they showed us ruins of old castles, which, according to what we heard, must have been made for pretty much the same purpose as the railways were. But I am interrupting your history of the river: pray go on.'

'It is both short and stupid enough,' said I. 'The river having lost its practical or commercial value – that is, being of no use to make money of—'

She nodded. 'I understand what that queer phrase means,' said she. 'Go on!'

'Well, it was utterly neglected, till at last it became a nuisance—'

'Yes,' quoth Ellen, 'I understand: like the railways and the robber knights. Yes?'

'So then they turned the makeshift business on to it, and handed it over to a body up in London, who from time to time, in order to show that they had something to do, did some damage here and there, – cut down trees, destroying the banks thereby; dredged the river (where it was not needed always), and threw the dredgings on the fields so as to spoil them; and so forth. But for the most part they practised "masterly inactivity", as it was then called – that is, they drew their salaries, and let things alone.'[62]

'Drew their salaries,' she said. 'I know that means that they were allowed to take an extra lot of other people's goods for doing nothing. And if that had been all, it really might have been worth while to let them do so, if you couldn't find any other way of keeping them quiet; but it seems to me that being so paid, they could not help doing something, and that something was bound to be mischief, – because,' said she, kindling with sudden anger, 'the whole business was founded on lies and false pretensions. I don't mean only these river-guardians, but all these master-people I have read of.'

'Yes,' said I, 'how happy you are to have got out of the parsimony of oppression!'

'Why do you sigh?' she said, kindly and somewhat anxiously. 'You seem to think that it will not last?'

'It will last for you,' quoth I..

'But why not for you?' said she. 'Surely it is for all the world; and if your country is somewhat backward, it will come into line before long. Or,' she said quickly, 'are you thinking that you must soon go back again? I will make my proposal which I told you of at once, and so perhaps put an end to your anxiety. I was going to propose that you should live with us where we are going. I feel quite old friends with you, and should be sorry to lose you.' Then she smiled on me, and said: 'Do you know, I begin to suspect you of wanting to nurse a sham sorrow, like the ridiculous characters in some of those queer old novels that I have come across now and then.'

I really had almost begun to suspect it myself, but I refused to admit so much; so I sighed no more, but fell to giving my delightful companion what little pieces of history I knew about the river and its borderlands; and the time passed pleasantly enough; and between the two of us (she was a better sculler than I was, and seemed quite tireless) we kept up fairly well with Dick, hot as the afternoon was, and swallowed up the way at a great rate. At last we passed under another ancient bridge; and through meadows bordered at first with huge elm-trees mingled with sweet chestnut of younger but very elegant growth; and the meadows widened out so much that it seemed as if the trees must now be on the bents only, or about the houses, except for the growth of willows on the immediate banks; so that the wide stretch of grass was little broken here. Dick got very much excited now, and often stood up in the boat to cry out to us that this was such and such a field, and so forth; and we caught fire at his enthusiasm for the hay-field and its harvest, and pulled our best.

At last as we were passing through a reach of the river where on the side of the towing-path was a highish bank with a thick whispering bed of reeds before it, and on the other side a higher bank, clothed with willows that dipped into the stream and crowned by ancient elm-trees, we saw bright figures coming along close to the bank, as if they were looking for something; as, indeed, they were, and we – that is, Dick and his company – were what they were looking for. Dick lay on his oars, and we followed his example. He gave a joyous shout to the people on the bank, which was echoed back from it in many voices, deep and sweetly shrill; for there were above a dozen persons, both men, women, and children. A tall handsome woman, with black wavy hair and deep-set grey eyes, came forward on the bank and waved her hand gracefully to us, and said:

'Dick, my friend, we have almost had to wait for you! What excuse have you to make for your slavish punctuality? Why didn't you take us by surprise, and come yesterday?'

'Oh,' said Dick, with an almost imperceptible jerk of his head toward our boat, 'we didn't want to come too quick up the water; there is so much to see for those who have not been up here before.'

'True, true,' said the stately lady, for stately is the word that must be used for her; 'and we want them to get to know the wet way from the east thoroughly well, since they must often use it now. But come ashore at once, Dick, and you, dear neighbours; there is a break in the reeds and a good landing-place just round the corner. We can carry up your things, or send some of the lads after them.'

'No, no,' said Dick; 'it is easier going by water, though it is but a step. Besides, I want to bring my friend here to the proper place. We will go on to the Ford; and you can talk to us from the bank as we paddle along.'

He pulled his sculls through the water, and on we went, turning a sharp angle and going north a little. Presently we saw before us a bank of elm-trees, which told us of a house amidst them, though I looked in vain for the grey walls that I expected to see there. As we went, the folk on the bank talked indeed, mingling their kind voices with the cuckoo's song, the sweet strong whistle of the blackbirds, and the ceaseless note of the corn-crake as he crept through the long grass of the mowing-field; whence came waves of fragrance from the flowering clover amidst of the ripe grass.

In a few minutes we had passed through a deep eddying pool into the sharp stream that ran from the ford, and beached our craft on a tiny strand of limestone-gravel, and stepped ashore into the arms of our up-river friends, our journey done.

I disentangled myself from the merry throng, and mounting on the cart-road that ran along the river some feet above the water, I looked round about me. The river came down through a wide meadow on my left, which was grey now with the ripened seeding grasses; the gleaming water was lost presently by a turn of the bank, but over the meadow I could see the mingled gables of a building where I knew the lock must be, and which now seemed to combine a mill with it. A low wooded ridge bounded the river-plain to the south and south-east, whence we had come, and a few low houses lay about its feet and up its slope. I turned a little to my right, and through the hawthorn sprays and long shoots of the wild roses could see the flat country spreading out far away under the sun of the calm evening, till something that might be called hills with a look of sheep-pastures about them bounded it with a soft blue line. Before me, the elm-boughs still hid most of what houses there might be in this river-side dwelling of men; but to the right of the cart-road a few grey buildings of the simplest kind showed here and there.

There I stood in a dreamy mood, and rubbed my eyes as if I were not wholly awake, and half expected to see the gay-clad company of beautiful men and women change to two or three spindle-legged back-bowed men and haggard, hollow-eyed, ill-favoured women, who once wore down the soil of this land with their heavy hopeless feet, from day to day, and season to season, and year to year. But no change came as yet, and my heart swelled with joy as I thought of all the beautiful grey villages, from the river to the plain and the plain to the uplands, which I could picture to myself so well, all peopled now with this happy and lovely folk, who had cast away riches and attained to wealth.

Chapter XXXI

AN OLD HOUSE AMONGST NEW FOLK

As I stood there Ellen detached herself from our happy friends who still stood on the little strand and came up to me. She took me by the hand, and said softly, 'Take me on to the house at once; we need not wait for the others: I had rather not.'

I had a mind to say that I did not know the way thither, and that the river-side dwellers should lead; but almost without my will my feet moved on along the road they knew. The raised way led us into a little field bounded by a backwater of the river on one side; on the right hand we could see a cluster of small houses and barns, new and old, and before us a grey stone barn and a wall partly overgrown with ivy, over which a few grey gables showed. The village road ended in the shallow of the aforesaid backwater. We crossed the road, and again almost without my will my hand raised the latch of a door in the wall, and we stood presently on a stone path which led up to the old house to which fate in the shape of Dick had so strangely brought me in this new world of men. My companion gave a sigh of pleased surprise and enjoyment; nor did I wonder, for the garden between the wall and the house was redolent of the June flowers, and the roses were rolling over one another with that delicious super-abundance of small well-tended gardens which at first sight takes away all thought from the beholder save that of beauty. The blackbirds were singing their loudest, the doves were cooing on the roof-ridge, the rooks in the high elm-trees beyond were garrulous among the young leaves, and the swifts wheeled whining about the gables. And the house itself was a fit guardian for all the beauty of this heart of summer.[63]

Once again Ellen echoed my thoughts as she said: 'Yes, friend, this is what I came out for to see; this many-gabled old house built by the simple country-folk of the long-past times, regardless of all the turmoil that was going on in cities and courts, is lovely still amidst all the beauty which these latter days have created; and I do not wonder at our friends tending it carefully and making much of it. It seems to me as if it had waited for these happy days, and held in it the gathered crumbs of happiness of the confused and turbulent past.'

She led me up close to the house, and laid her shapely sun browned hand and arm on the lichened wall as if to embrace it, and cried out, 'Oh me! Oh me! How I love the earth, and the seasons, and weather, and all things that deal with it, and all that grows out of it, – as this has done!'

I could not answer her, or say a word. Her exultation and pleasure was so keen and exquisite, and her beauty, so delicate, yet so inter-fused with energy, expressed it so fully, that any added word would have been commonplace and futile. I dreaded lest the others should come in suddenly and break the spell she had cast about me; but we stood there a while by the corner of the big gable of the house, and no one came. I heard the merry voices some way off presently, and knew that they were going along the river to the great meadow on the other side of the house and garden.

We drew back a little, and looked up at the house: the door and the windows were open to the fragrant sun-cured air: from the upper window-sills hung festoons of flowers in honour of the festival, as if the others shared in the love for the old house.

'Come in,' said Ellen. 'I hope nothing will spoil it inside; but I don't think it will. Come! we must go back presently to the others. They have gone on to the tents; for surely they must have tents pitched for the haymakers – the house would not hold a tithe of the folk, I am sure.'

She led me on to the door, murmuring little above her breath as she did so, 'The earth and the growth of it and the life of it! If I could but say or show how I love it!'

We went in, and found no soul in any room as we wandered from room to room, – from the rose-covered porch to the strange and quaint garrets amongst the great timbers of the roof, where of old time the tillers and herdsmen of the manor slept, but which a-nights seemed now, by the small size of the beds, and the litter of useless and disregarded matters – bunches of dying flowers, feathers of birds, shells of starlings' eggs, caddis worms in mugs, and the like – seemed to be inhabited for the time by children.

Everywhere there was but little furniture, and that only the most necessary, and of the simplest forms. The extravagant love of ornament which I had noted in this people elsewhere seemed here to have given place to the feeling that the house itself and its associations was the ornament of the country life amidst which it had been left stranded from old times, and that to re-ornament it would but take away its use as a piece of natural beauty.

We sat down at last in a room over the wall which Ellen had caressed, and which was still hung with old tapestry, originally of no artistic value, but now faded into pleasant grey tones which harmonized thoroughly well with the quiet of the place, and which would have been ill supplanted by brighter and more striking decoration.

I asked a few random questions of Ellen as we sat there, but scarcely listened to her answers, and presently became silent, and then scarce conscious of anything, but that I was there in that old room, the doves crooning from the roofs of the barn and dovecot beyond the window opposite to me.

My thought returned to me after what I think was but a minute or two, but which, as in a vivid dream, seemed as if it had lasted a long time, when I saw Ellen sitting, looking all the fuller of life and pleasure and desire from the contrast with the grey faded tapestry with its futile design, which was now only bearable because it had grown so faint and feeble.

She looked at me kindly, but as if she read me through and through. She said: 'You have begun again your never-ending contrast between the past and this present. Is it not so?'

'True,' said I. 'I was thinking of what you, with your capacity and intelligence, joined to your love of pleasure, and your impatience of unreasonable restraint – of what you would have been in that past. And even now, when all is won and has been for a long time, my heart is sickened with thinking of all the waste of life that has gone on for so many years!'

'So many centuries,' she said, 'so many ages!'

'True,' I said; 'too true,' and sat silent again.

She rose up and said: 'Come, I must not let you go off into a dream again so soon. If we must lose you, I want you to see all that you can see first before you go back again.'

'Lose me?' I said – 'go back again? Am I not to go up to the North with you? What do you mean?'

She smiled somewhat sadly, and said: 'Not yet; we will not talk of that yet. Only, what were you thinking of just now?'

I said falteringly: 'I was saying to myself, The past, the present? Should she not have said the contrast of the present with the future: of blind despair with hope?'

'I knew it,' she said. Then she caught my hand and said excitedly, 'Come, while there is yet time! Come!' And she led me out of the room; and as we were going downstairs and out of the house into the garden by a little side door which opened out of a curious lobby, she said in a calm voice, as if she wished me to forget her sudden nervousness: 'Come! we ought to join the others before they come here looking for us. And let me tell you, my friend, that I can see you are too apt to fall into mere dreamy musing: no doubt because you are not yet used to our life of repose amidst of energy; of work which is pleasure and pleasure which is work.'

She paused a little, and as we came out into the lovely garden again, she said: 'My friend, you were saying that you wondered what I should have been if I had lived in those past days of turmoil and oppression. Well, I think I have studied the history of them to know pretty well. I should have been one of the poor, for my father when he was working was a mere tiller of the soil. Well, I could not have borne that; therefore my beauty and cleverness and brightness' (she spoke with no blush or simper of false shame) 'would have been sold to rich men, and my life would have been wasted indeed; for I know enough of that to know that I should have had no choice, no power of will over my life; and that I should never have bought pleasure from the rich men, or even opportunity of action, whereby I might have won some true excitement. I should have been wrecked and wasted in one way or another, either by penury or by luxury. Is it not so?'

'Indeed it is,' said I.

She was going to say something else, when a little gate in the fence, which led into a small elm-shaded field, was opened, and Dick came with hasty cheerfulness up the garden path, and was presently standing between us, a hand laid on the shoulder of each. He said: 'Well, neighbours, I thought you two would like to see the old house quietly without a crowd in it. Isn't it a jewel of a house after its kind? Well, come along, for it is getting towards dinner-time. Perhaps you, guest, would like a swim before we sit down to what I fancy will be a pretty long feast?'

'Yes,' I said, 'I should like that.'

'Well, good-bye for the present, neighbour Ellen,' said Dick. 'Here comes Clara to take care of you, as I fancy she is more at home amongst our friends here.'

Clara came out of the fields as he spoke; and with one look at Ellen I turned and went with Dick, doubting, if I must say the truth, whether I should see her again.

Chapter XXXII
THE FEAST'S BEGINNING — THE END

Dick brought me at once into the little field which, as I had seen from the garden, was covered with gaily-coloured tents arranged in orderly lanes, about which were sitting and lying on the grass some fifty or sixty men, women, and children, all of them in the height of good temper and enjoyment – with their holiday mood on, so to say.

'You are thinking that we don't make a great show as to numbers,' said Dick; 'but you must remember that we shall have more to-morrow; because in this haymaking work there is room for a great many people who are not over-skilled in country matters: and there are many who lead sedentary lives, whom it would be unkind to deprive of their pleasure in the hay-field – scientific men and close students generally: so that the skilled workmen, outside those who are wanted as mowers, and foremen of the haymaking, stand aside, and take a little downright rest, which you know is good for them, whether they like it or not: or else they go to other countrysides, as I am doing here. You see, the scientific men and historians, and students generally, will not be wanted till we are fairly in the midst of the tedding, which of course will not be till the day after to-morrow.' With that he brought me out of the little field on to a kind of causeway above the riverside meadow, and thence turning to the left on to a path through the mowing grass, which was thick and very tall, led on till we came to the river above the weir and its mill. There we had a delightful swim in the broad piece of water above the lock, where the river looked much bigger than its natural size from its being dammed up by the weir.

'Now we are in a fit mood for dinner,' said Dick, when we had dressed and were going through the grass again; 'and certainly of all the cheerful meals in the year, this one of haysel is the cheerfullest; not even excepting the corn-harvest feast; for then the year is beginning to fail, and one cannot help having a feeling behind all the gaiety, of the coming of the dark days, and the shorn fields and empty gardens; and the spring is almost too far off to look forward to. It is, then, in the autumn, when one almost believes in death.'

'How strangely you talk,' said I, 'of such a constantly recurring and consequently commonplace matter as the sequence of the seasons.' And indeed these people were like children about such things, and had what seemed to me a quite exaggerated interest in the weather, a fine day, a dark night, or a brilliant one, and the like.

'Strangely?' said he. 'Is it strange to sympathize with the year and its gains and losses?'.

'At any rate,' said I, 'if you look upon the course of the year as a beautiful and interesting drama, which is what I think you do, you should be as much pleased and interested with the winter and its trouble and pain as with this wonderful summer luxury.'

'And am I not?' said Dick, rather warmly; 'only I can't look upon it as if I were sitting in a theatre seeing the play going on before me, myself taking no part of it. It is difficult,' said he, smiling good-humouredly, 'for a non-literary man like me to explain myself properly, like that dear girl Ellen would; but I mean that I am part of it all, and feel the pain as well as the pleasure in my own person. It is not done for me by somebody else, merely that I may eat and drink and sleep; but I myself do my share of it.'

In his way also, as Ellen in hers, I could see that Dick had that passionate love of the earth which was common to but few people at least, in the days I knew; in which the prevailing feeling amongst intellectual persons was a kind of sour distaste for the changing drama of the year, for the life of earth and its dealings with men. Indeed, in those days it was thought poetic and imaginative to look upon life as a thing to be borne, rather than enjoyed.

So I mused till Dick's laugh brought me back into the Oxfordshire hay-fields. 'One thing seems strange to me,' said he – 'that I must needs trouble myself about the winter and its scantiness, in the midst of the summer abundance. If it hadn't happened to me before, I should have thought it was your doing, guest; that you had thrown a kind of evil charm over me. Now, you know,' said he, suddenly, 'that's only a joke, so you mustn't take it to heart.'

'All right,' said I; 'I don't.' Yet I did feel somewhat uneasy at his words, after all.

We crossed the causeway this time, and did not turn back to the house, but went along a path beside a field of wheat now almost ready to blossom. I said: 'We do not dine in the house or garden, then? – as indeed I did not expect to do. Where do we meet, then? for I can see that the houses are mostly very small.'

'Yes,' said Dick, 'you are right, they are small in this countryside: there are so many good old houses left, that people dwell a good deal in such small detached houses. As to our dinner, we are going to have our feast in the church. I wish, for your sake, it were as big and handsome as that of the old Roman town to the west, or the forest town to the north;* but, however, it will hold us all; and though it is a little thing, it is beautiful in its way.'

This was somewhat new to me, this dinner in a church, and I thought of the church-ales of the Middle Ages;[64] but I said nothing, and presently we came out into the road which ran through the village. Dick looked up and down it, and seeing only two straggling groups before us, said: 'It seems as if we must be somewhat late; they are all gone on; and they will be sure to make a point of waiting for you, as the guest of guests, since you come from so far.'

He hastened as he spoke, and I kept up with him, and presently we came to a little avenue of lime-trees which led us straight to the church porch, from whose open door came the sound of cheerful voices and laughter, and varied merriment.

'Yes,' said Dick, 'it's the coolest place for one thing, this hot evening. Come along; they will be glad to see you.'

Indeed, in spite of my bath, I felt the weather more sultry and oppressive than on any day of our journey yet.

We went into the church, which was a simple little building with one little aisle divided from the nave by three round arches, a chancel, and a rather roomy transept for so small a building, the windows mostly of the graceful Oxfordshire fourteenth-century type. There was no modern architectural decoration in it; it looked, indeed, as if none had been attempted since the Puritans whitewashed the mediaeval saints and histories on the wall. It was, however, gaily dressed up for this latter-day festival, with festoons of flowers from arch to arch, and great pitchers of flowers standing about on the floor; while under the west window hung two cross scythes, their blades polished white, and gleaming from out of the flowers that wreathed them. But its best ornament was the crowd of handsome, happy-looking men and women that were set down to table, and who, with their bright faces and rich hair over their gay holiday raiment, looked, as the Persian poet puts it, like a bed of tulips in the sun. Though the church was a small one, there was plenty of room; for a small church makes a biggish house; and on this evening there was no need to set cross

* Cirencester and Burford he must have meant.

tables along the transepts, though doubtless these would be wanted next day, when the learned men of whom Dick had been speaking should be come to take their more humble part in the haymaking.

I stood on the threshold with the expectant smile on my face of a man who is going to take part in a festivity which he is really prepared to enjoy. Dick, standing by me, was looking round the company with an air of proprietorship in them, I thought. Opposite me sat Clara and Ellen, with Dick's place open between them: they were smiling, but their beautiful faces were each turned towards the neighbours on either side, who were talking to them, and they did not seem to see me. I turned to Dick, expecting him to lead me forward, and he turned his face to me; but strange to say, though it was as smiling and cheerful as ever, it made no response to my glance – nay, he seemed to take no heed at all of my presence, and I noticed that none of the company looked at me. A pang shot through me, as of some disaster long expected and suddenly realized. Dick moved on a little without a word to me. I was not three yards from the two women who, though they had been my companions for such a short time, had really, as I thought, become my friends. Clara's face was turned full upon me now, but she also did not seem to see me, though I know I was trying to catch her eye with an appealing look. I turned to Ellen, and she *did* seem to recognize me for an instant; but her bright face turned sad directly, and she shook her head with a mournful look, and the next moment all consciousness of my presence had faded from her face.

I felt lonely and sick at heart past the power of words to describe. I hung about a minute longer, and then turned and went out of the porch again and through the lime-avenue into the road, while the blackbirds sang their strongest from the bushes about me in the hot June evening.

Once more without any conscious effort of will I set my face toward the old house by the ford, but as I turned round the corner which led to the remains of the village cross, I came upon a figure strangely contrasting with the joyous, beautiful people I had left behind in the church. It was a man who looked old, but who I knew from habit, now half-forgotten, was really not much more than fifty. His face was rugged, and grimed rather than dirty; his eyes dull and bleared; his body bent, his calves thin and spindly, his feet dragging and limping. His clothing was a mixture of dirt and rags long over-familiar to me. As I passed him he touched his hat with some real goodwill and courtesy, and much servility.

Inexpressibly shocked, I hurried past him and hastened along the road that led to the river and the lower end of the village; but suddenly I saw as it were a black cloud rolling along to meet me, like a nightmare of my childish days; and for a while I was conscious of nothing else than being in the dark, and whether I was walking, or sitting, or lying down, I could not tell.

* * *

I lay in my bed in my house at dingy Hammersmith thinking about it all; and trying to consider if I was overwhelmed with despair at finding I had been dreaming a dream; and strange to say, I found that I was not so despairing.

Or indeed *was* it a dream? If so, why was I so conscious all along that I was really seeing all that new life from the outside, still wrapped up in the prejudices, the anxieties, the distrust of this time of doubt and struggle?

All along, though those friends were so real to me, I had been feeling as if I had no business amongst them: as though the time would come when they would reject me, and say, as Ellen's last mournful look seemed to say, 'No, it will not do; you cannot be of us; you belong so entirely to the unhappiness of the past that our happiness even would weary you. Go back again, now you have seen us, and your outward eyes have learned that in spite of all the infallible maxims of your day there is yet a time of rest in store for the world, when mastery has changed into fellowship – but not before. Go back again, then, and while you live you will see all round you people engaged in making others live lives which are not their own, while they themselves care nothing for their own real lives – men who hate life though they fear death. Go back and be the happier for having seen us, for having added a little hope to your struggle. Go on living while you may, striving, with whatsoever pain and labour needs must be, to build up little by little the new day of fellowship, and rest, and happiness.'

Yes, surely! and if others can see it as I have seen it, then it may be called a vision rather than a dream.

LECTURES

* * *

THE LESSER ARTS

* * *

Lecture given to
the Trades Guild of Learning, London 1877,
under the title 'The Decorative Arts'

Reprinted in *Hopes and Fears for Art*,
London, 1882

Hereafter I hope in another lecture to have the pleasure of laying before you an historical survey of the lesser, or as they are called the Decorative Arts, and I must confess it would have been pleasanter to me to have begun my talk with you by entering at once upon the subject of the history of this great industry; but, as I have something to say in a third lecture about various matters connected with the practice of Decoration among ourselves in these days, I feel that I should be in a false position before you, and one that might lead to confusion, or overmuch explanation, if I did not let you know what I think on the nature and scope of these arts, on their condition at the present time, and their outlook in times to come. In doing this it is like enough that I shall say things with which you will very much disagree; I must ask you therefore from the outset to believe that whatever I may blame or whatever I may praise, I neither, when I think of what history has been, am inclined to lament the past, to despise the present, or despair of the future; that I believe all the change and stir about us is a sign of the world's life, and that it will lead – by ways, indeed, of which we have no guess – to the bettering of all mankind.[1]

Now as to the scope and nature of these Arts I have to say, that though when I come more into the details of my subject I shall not meddle much with the great art of Architecture, and less still with the great arts commonly called Sculpture and Painting, yet I cannot in my own mind quite sever them from those lesser so-called Decorative Arts, which I have to speak about: it is only in latter times, and under the most intricate conditions of life, that they have fallen apart from one another; and I hold that, when they are so parted, it is ill for the Arts altogether: the lesser ones become trivial, mechanical, unintelligent, incapable of resisting the changes pressed upon them by fashion or dishonesty; while the greater, however they may be practised for a while by men of great minds and wonder-working hands, unhelped by the lesser, unhelped by each other, are sure to lose their dignity of popular arts, and become nothing but dull adjuncts to unmeaning pomp, or ingenious toys for a few rich and idle men.

However, I have not undertaken to talk to you of Architecture, Sculpture, and Painting, in the narrower sense of those words, since, most unhappily I think, these master-arts, these arts more specially of the intellect, are at the present day divorced from decoration in its narrower sense. Our subject is that great body of art, by means of which men have at all times more or less striven to beautify the familiar matters of everyday life: a wide subject, a great industry; both a great part of the history of the world, and a most helpful instrument to the study of that history.

A very great industry indeed, comprising the crafts of house-building, painting, joinery and carpentry, smiths' work, pottery and glass-making, weaving, and many others: a body of art most important to the public in general, but still more so to us handicraftsmen; since there is scarce anything that they use, and that we fashion, but it has always been thought to be unfinished till it has had some touch or other of decoration about it. True it is that in many or most cases we have got so used to this ornament, that we look upon it as if it had grown of itself, and note it no more than the mosses on the dry sticks with which we light our fires. So much the worse! for there *is* the decoration, or some pretence of it, and it has, or ought to have, a use and a meaning. For, and this is at the root of the whole matter, everything made by man's hands has a form, which must be either beautiful or ugly; beautiful if it is in accord with Nature, and helps her; ugly if it is discordant with Nature, and thwarts her; it cannot be indifferent: we, for our parts, are busy or sluggish, eager or unhappy, and our eyes are apt to get dulled to this eventfulness of form in those things which we are always looking at. Now it is one of the chief uses of decoration, the chief part of its alliance with nature, that it has to sharpen our dulled senses in this matter: for this end are those wonders of intricate patterns interwoven, those strange forms invented, which men have so long delighted in: forms and intricacies that do not necessarily imitate nature, but in which the hand of the craftsman is guided to work in the way that she does, till the web, the cup, or the knife, look as natural, nay as lovely, as the green field, the river bank, or the mountain flint.

To give people pleasure in the things they must perforce *use*, that is one great office of decoration; to give people pleasure in the things they must perforce *make*, that is the other use of it.

Does not our subject look important enough now? I say that without these arts, our rest would be vacant and uninteresting, our labour mere endurance, mere wearing away of body and mind.

As for that last use of these arts, the giving us pleasure in our work, I scarcely know how to speak strongly enough of it; and yet if I did not know the value of repeating a truth again and again, I should have to excuse myself to you for saying any more about this, when I remember how a great man now living has spoken of it: I mean my friend Professor John Ruskin, if you read the chapter in the second volume of his *Stones of Venice* entitled, 'On the Nature of Gothic, and the Office of the Workman Therein', you will read at once the truest and the most eloquent words that can possibly be said on the subject. What I have to say upon it can scarcely be more than an echo of his words, yet I repeat there is some use in reiterating a truth, lest it be forgotten; so I will say this much further: we all know what people have said about the curse of labour,[2] and what heavy and grievous nonsense are the more part of their words thereupon; whereas indeed the real curses of craftsmen have been the curse of stupidity, and the curse of injustice from within and from without: no, I cannot suppose there is anybody here who would think it either a good life, or an amusing one, to sit with one's hands before one doing nothing – to live like a gentleman, as fools call it.

Nevertheless there *is* dull work to be done, and a weary business it is setting men about such work, and seeing them through it, and I would rather do the work twice over with my own hands than have such a job: but now only let the arts which we are talking of beautify our labour, and be widely spread, intelligent, well understood both by the maker and the user, let them grow in one word *popular*, and there will be pretty much an end of dull work and its wearing slavery; and no man will any longer have an excuse for talking about the curse of labour, no man will any longer have an excuse for evading the blessing of labour. I believe there is nothing that will aid the world's progress so much as the attainment of this; I protest there is nothing in the world that I desire so much as this, wrapped up, as I am sure it is, with changes political and social, that in one way or another we all desire.

Now if the objection be made, that these arts have been the handmaids of luxury, of tyranny, and of superstition, I must needs say that it is true in a sense; they have been so used, as many other excellent things have been. But it is also true that, among some nations, their most vigorous and freest times have been the very blossoming times of art: while at the same time, I must allow that these Decorative Arts have flourished among oppressed peoples, who have seemed to have no hope of freedom: yet I do not think that we shall be wrong in thinking that at such times, among such peoples, art, at least, was free; when it has not been, when it has really been gripped by superstition, or by luxury, it has straightway begun to sicken under that grip. Nor must you forget that when men say popes, kings, and emperors built such and such buildings, it is a mere way of speaking. You look in your history-books to see who built Westminster Abbey, who built St Sophia at Constantinople, and they tell you Henry III, Justinian the Emperor. Did they? or, rather, men like you and me, handicraftsmen, who have left no names behind them, nothing but their work?

Now as these arts call people's attention and interest to the matters of everyday life in the present, so also, and that I think is no little matter, they call our attention at every step to that history, of which, I said before, they are so great a part; for no nation, no state of society, however rude, has been wholly without them: nay, there are peoples not a few, of whom we know scarce anything, save that they thought such and such forms beautiful. So strong is the bond between history and decoration, that in the practice of the latter we cannot, if we would, wholly shake off the influence of past times over what we do at present. I do not think it is too much to say that no man, however original he may be, can sit down to-day and draw the ornament of a cloth, or the form of an ordinary vessel or piece of furniture, that will be other than a development or a degradation of forms used hundreds of years ago; and these, too, very often, forms that once had a serious meaning, though they are now become little more than a habit of the hand; forms that were once perhaps the mysterious symbols of worships and beliefs now little remembered or wholly forgotten. Those who have diligently followed the delightful study of these arts are able as if through windows to look upon the life of the past:– the very first beginnings of thought among nations whom we cannot even name; the terrible empires of the ancient East; the free vigour and glory of Greece; the heavy weight, the firm grasp of Rome; the fall of her temporal Empire which spread so wide about the world all that good and evil which men can never forget, and never cease to feel; the clashing of East and West, South and North, about her rich and fruitful daughter Byzantium; the rise, the dissensions, and the waning of Islam; the wanderings of Scandinavia; the Crusades; the foundation of the States of modern Europe; the struggles of free thought with ancient dying system – with all these events and their meaning is the history of popular art interwoven; with all this, I say, the careful student of decoration as an historical industry must be familiar. When I think of this, and the usefulness of all this knowledge, at a time when history has become so earnest a study amongst us as to have given us, as it were, a new sense: at a time when we so long to know the reality of all that has happened, and are to be put off no longer with the dull records of the battles and intrigues of kings and scoundrels, – I say when I think of all this, I hardly know how to say that this interweaving of the Decorative Arts with the history of the past is of less importance than their dealings with the life of the present: for should not these memories also be a part of our daily life?

And now let me recapitulate a little before I go further, before we begin to look into the condition of the arts at the present day. These arts, I have said, are part of a great system invented for the expression of a man's delight in beauty: all peoples and times have used them; they have been the joy of free nations, and the solace of oppressed nations; religion has used and elevated them, has abused and degraded them; they are connected with all history, and are clear teachers of it; and, best of all, they are the sweeteners of human labour, both to the handicraftsman, whose life is spent in working in them, and to people in general who are influenced by the sight of them at every turn of the day's work: they make our toil happy, our rest fruitful.

And now if all I have said seems to you but mere open-mouthed praise of these arts, I must say that it is not for nothing that what I have hitherto put before you has taken that form.

It is because I must now ask you this question: All these good things – will you have them? will you cast them from you?

Are you surprised at my question – you, most of whom, like myself, are engaged in the actual practice of the arts that are, or ought to be, popular?

In explanation, I must somewhat repeat what I have already said. Time was when the mystery and wonder of handicrafts were well acknowledged by the world, when imagination and fancy mingled with all things made by man; and in those days all handicraftsmen were *artists*, as we should now call them. But the thought of man became more intricate, more difficult to express; art grew a heavier thing to deal with, and its labour was more divided among great men, lesser men, and little men; till that art, which was once scarce more than a rest of body and soul, as the hand cast the shuttle or swung the hammer, became to some men so serious a labour, that their working lives have been one long tragedy of hope and fear, joy and trouble. This was the growth of art: like all growth, it was good and fruitful for awhile; like all fruitful growth, it grew into decay; like all decay of what was once fruitful, it will grow into something new.

Into decay; for as the arts sundered into the greater and the lesser, contempt on one side, carelessness on the other arose, both begotten of ignorance of that *philosophy* of the Decorative Arts, a hint of which I have tried just now to put before you. The artist came out from the handicraftsmen, and left them without hope of elevation, while he himself was left without the help of intelligent, industrious sympathy. Both have suffered; the artist no less than the workman. It is with art as it fares with a company of soldiers before a redoubt, when the captain runs forward full of hope and energy, but looks not behind him to see if his men are following, and they hang back, not knowing why they are brought there to die. The captain's life is spent for nothing, and his men are sullen prisoners in the redoubt of Unhappiness and Brutality.

I must in plain words say of the Decorative Arts, of all the arts, that it is not so much that we are inferior in them to all who have gone before us, but rather that they are in a state of anarchy and disorganization, which makes a sweeping change necessary and certain.

So that again I ask my question, All that good fruit which the arts should bear, will you have it? will you cast it from you? Shall that sweeping change that must come, be the change of loss or of gain?

We who believe in the continuous life of the world, surely we are bound to hope that the change will bring us gain and not loss, and to strive to bring that gain about.

Yet how the world may answer my question, who can say? A man in his short life can see but a little way ahead, and even in mine wonderful and unexpected things have come to pass. I must needs say that therein lies my hope rather than in all I see going on round about us. Without disputing that if the imaginative arts perish, some new thing, at present unguessed of, *may* be put forward to supply their loss in men's lives, I cannot feel happy in that prospect, nor can I believe that mankind will endure such a loss for ever: but in the meantime the present state of the arts and their dealings with modern life and progress seem to me to point, in appearance at least, to this immediate future; that the world, which has for a long time busied itself about other matters than the arts, and has carelessly let them sink lower and lower, till many not uncultivated men, ignorant of what they once were, and hopeless of what they might yet be, look upon them with mere contempt; that the world, I say, thus busied and hurried, will one day wipe the slate, and be clean rid in her impatience of the whole matter with all its tangle and trouble.

And then – what then?

Even now amid the squalor of London it is hard to imagine what it will be. Architecture, Sculpture, Painting, with the crowd of lesser arts that belong to them, these, together with Music and Poetry, will be dead and forgotten, will no longer excite or amuse people in the least: for, once more, we must not deceive ourselves; the death of one art means the death of all; the only difference in their fate will be that the luckiest will be eaten the last – the luckiest, or the unluckiest: in all that has to do with beauty the invention and ingenuity of man will have come to a dead stop; and all the while Nature will go on with her eternal recurrence of lovely changes – spring, summer, autumn, and winter; sunshine, rain, and snow; storm and fair weather; dawn, noon, and sunset; day and night – ever bearing witness against man that he has deliberately chosen ugliness instead of beauty, and to live where he is strongest amidst squalor or blank emptiness.

You see, sirs, we cannot quite imagine it; any more, perhaps, than our forefathers of ancient London, living in the pretty, carefully whitened houses, with the famous church and its huge spire rising above them, – than they, passing about the fair gardens running down to the broad river, could have imagined a whole county or more covered over with hideous hovels, big, middle-sized, and little, which should one day be called London.

Sirs, I say that this dead blank of the arts that I more than dread is difficult even now to imagine; yet I fear that I must say that if it does not come about, it will be owing to some turn of events which we cannot at present foresee: but I hold that if it does happen, it will only last for a time, that it will be but a burning up of the gathered weeds, so that the field may bear more abundantly. I hold that men would wake up after a while, and look round and find the dulness unbearable, and begin once more inventing, imitating, and imagining, as in earlier days.

That faith comforts me, and I can say calmly if the blank space must happen, it must, and amidst its darkness the new seed must sprout. So it has been before: first comes birth, and hope scarcely conscious of itself; then the flower and fruit of mastery, with hope more than conscious enough, passing into insolence, as decay follows ripeness; and then – the new birth again.

Meantime it is the plain duty of all who look seriously on the arts to do their best to save the world from what at the best will be a loss, the result of ignorance and unwisdom; to prevent, in fact, that most discouraging of all changes, the supplying the place of an extinct brutality by a new one; nay, even if those who really care for the arts are so weak and few that they can do nothing else, it may be their business to keep alive some tradition, some memory of the past, so that the new life when it comes may not waste itself more than enough in fashioning wholly new forms for its new spirit.

To what side then shall those turn for help, who really understand the gain of a great art in the world, and the loss of peace and good life that must follow from the lack of it? I think that they must begin by acknowledging that the ancient art, the art of unconscious intelligence, as one should call it, which began without a date, at least so long ago as those strange and masterly scratchings on mammoth-bones and the like found but the other day in the drift – that this art of unconscious intelligence is all but dead; that what little of it is left lingers among half-civilized nations, and is growing coarser, feebler, less intelligent year by year; nay, it is mostly at the mercy of some commercial accident, such as the arrival of a few shiploads of European dye-stuffs or a few dozen orders from European merchants: this they must recognize, and must hope to see in time its place filled by a new art of conscious intelligence, the birth of wiser, simpler, freer ways of life than the world leads now, than the world has ever led.

I said, *to see* this in time; I do not mean to say that our own eyes will look upon it: it may be so far off, as indeed it seems to some, that many would scarcely think it worth while thinking of: but there are some of us who cannot turn our faces to the wall, or sit deedless because our hope seems somewhat dim; and, indeed, I think that while the signs of the last decay of the old art with all the evils that must follow in its train are only too obvious about us, so on the other hand there are not wanting signs of the new dawn beyond that possible night of the arts, of which I have before spoken; this sign chiefly, that there are some few at least who are heartily discontented with things as they are, and crave for something better, or at least some promise of it – this best of signs: for I suppose that if some half-dozen men at any time earnestly set their hearts on something coming about which is not discordant with nature, it will come to pass one day or other; because it is not by accident that an idea comes into the heads of a few; rather they are pushed on, and forced to speak or act by something stirring in the heart of the world which would otherwise be left without expression.

By what means then shall those work who long for reform in the arts, and who shall they seek to kindle into eager desire for possession of beauty, and better still, for the development of the faculty that creates beauty?

People say to me often enough: If you want to make your art succeed and flourish, you must make it the fashion: a phrase which I confess annoys me; for they mean by it that I should spend one day over my work to two days in trying to convince rich, and supposed influential people, that they care very much for what they really do not care in the least, so that it may happen according to the proverb: *Bell-wether took the leap, and we all went over*. Well, such advisers are right if they are content with the thing lasting but a little while; say till you can make a little money – if you don't get pinched by the door shutting too quickly: otherwise they are wrong: the people they are thinking of have too many strings to their bow, and can turn their backs too easily on a thing that fails, for it to be safe work trusting to their whims: it is not their fault, they cannot help it, but they have no chance of spending time enough over the arts to know anything practical of them, and they must of necessity be in the hands of those who spend their time in pushing fashion this way and that for their own advantage.

Sirs, there is no help to be got out of these latter, or those who let themselves be led by them: the only real help for the Decorative Arts must come from those who work in them; nor must they be led, they must lead.

You whose hands make those things that should be works of art, you must be all artists, and good artists too, before the public at large can take real interest in such things; and when you have become so, I promise you that you shall lead the fashion; fashion shall follow your hands obediently enough.

That is the only way in which we can get a supply of intelligent popular art: a few artists of the kind so-called now, what can they do working in the teeth of difficulties thrown in their way by what is called Commerce, but which should be called greed of money? working helplessly among the crowd of those who are ridiculously called manufacturers, *i.e.*, handicraftsmen, though the more part of them never did a stroke of hand-work in their lives, and are nothing better than capitalists and salesmen.[3] What can these grains of sand do, I say, amidst the enormous mass of work turned out every year which professes in some way to be decorative art, but the decoration of which no one heeds except the salesmen who have to do with it, and are hard put to it to supply the cravings of the public for something new, not for something pretty?

The remedy, I repeat, is plain if it can be applied; the handicraftsman, left behind by the artist when the arts sundered, must come up with him, must work side by side with him: apart from the difference between a great master and a scholar, apart from the differences of the natural bent of men's minds, which would make one man an imitative, and another an architectural or decorative artist, there should be no difference between those employed on strictly ornamental work; and the body of artists dealing with this should quicken with their art all makers of things into artists also, in proportion to the necessities and uses of the things they would make.

I know what stupendous difficulties, social and economical, there are in the way of this; yet I think that they seem to be greater than they are: and of one thing I am sure, that no real living decorative art is possible if this is impossible.

It is not impossible, on the contrary it is certain to come about, if you are at heart desirous to quicken the arts; if the world will, for the sake of beauty and decency, sacrifice some of the things it is so busy over (many of which I think are not very worthy of its trouble), art will begin to grow again; as for those difficulties above mentioned, some of them I know will in any case melt away before the steady change of the relative conditions of men; the rest, reason and resolute attention to the laws of nature, which are also the laws of art, will dispose of little by little: once more, the way will not be far to seek, if the will be with us.

Yet, granted the will, and though the way lies ready to us, we must not be discouraged if the journey seem barren enough at first, nay, not even if things seem to grow worse for a while: for it is natural enough that the very evil which has forced on the beginning of reform should look uglier, while on the one hand life and wisdom are building up the new, and on the other folly and deadness are hugging the old to them.

In this, as in all other matters, lapse of time will be needed before things seem to straighten, and the courage and patience that does not despise small things lying ready to be done; and care and watchfulness, lest we begin to build the wall ere the footings are well in; and always through all things much humility that is not easily cast down by failure, that seeks to be taught, and is ready to learn.

For your teachers, they must be Nature and History: as for the first, that you must learn of it is so obvious that I need not dwell upon that now: hereafter, when I have to speak more of matters of detail, I may have to speak of the manner in which you must learn of Nature. As to the second, I do not think that any man but one of the highest genius, could do anything in these days without much study of ancient art, and even he would be much hindered if he lacked it. If you think that this contradicts what I said about the death of that ancient art, and the necessity I implied for an art that should be characteristic of the present day, I can only say that, in these times of plenteous knowledge and meagre performance, if we do not study the ancient work directly and learn to understand it, we shall find ourselves influenced by the feeble work all round us, and shall be copying the better work through the copyists and *without* understanding it, which will by no means bring about intelligent art. Let us therefore study it wisely, be taught by it, kindled by it; all the while determining not to imitate or repeat it; to have either no art at all, or an art which we have made our own.[4]

Yet I am almost brought to a stand-still when bidding you to study nature and the history of art, by remembering that this is London, and what it is like: how can I ask working-men passing up and down these hideous streets day by day to care about beauty? If it were politics, we must care about that; or science, you could wrap yourselves up in the study of facts, no doubt, without much caring what goes on about you – but beauty! do you not see what terrible difficulties beset art, owing to a long neglect of art – and neglect of reason, too, in this matter? It is such a heavy question by what effort, by what dead-lift, you can thrust this difficulty from you, that I must perforce set it aside for the present, and must at least hope that the study of history and its monuments will help you somewhat herein. If you can really fill your minds with memories of great works of art, and great times of art, you will, I think, be able to a certain extent to look through the aforesaid ugly surroundings, and will be moved to discontent of what is careless and brutal now, and will, I hope, at last be so much discontented with what is bad, that you will determine to bear no longer that short-sighted, reckless brutality of squalor that so disgraces our intricate civilization.

Well, at any rate, London is good for this, that it is well off for museums – which I heartily wish were to be got at seven days in the week instead of six, or at least on the only day on which an ordinarily busy man, one of the taxpayers who support them, can as a rule see them quietly – and certainly any of us who may have any natural turn for art must get more help from frequenting them than one can well say. It is true, however, that people need some preliminary instruction before they can get all the good possible to be got from the prodigious treasures of art possessed by the country in that form: there also one sees things in a piecemeal way: nor can I deny that there is something melancholy about a museum, such a tale of violence, destruction, and carelessness, as its treasured scraps tell us.

But moreover you may sometimes have an opportunity of studying ancient art in a narrower but a more intimate, a more kindly form, the monuments of our own land. Sometimes only, since we live in the middle of this world of brick and mortar, and there is little else left us amidst it, except the ghost of the great church at Westminster, ruined as its exterior is by the stupidity of the restoring architect, and insulted as its glorious interior is by the pompous undertakers' lies, by the vainglory and ignorance of the last two centuries and a half – little besides that and the matchless Hall near it:[5] but when we can get beyond that smoky world, there, out in the country, we may still see the works of our fathers yet alive amidst the very nature they were wrought into, and of which they are so completely a part. For there indeed if anywhere, in the English country, in the days when people cared about such things, was there a full sympathy between the works of man, and the land they were made for. The land is a little land; too much shut up within the narrow seas, as it seems, to have much space for swelling into hugeness: there are no great wastes overwhelming in their dreariness, no great solitudes of forests, no terrible untrodden mountain-walls: all is measured, mingled, varied, gliding easily one thing into another: little rivers, little plains, swelling, speedily-changing uplands, all beset with handsome orderly trees; little hills, little mountains, netted over with the walls of sheep-walks: all is little; yet not foolish and blank, but serious rather, and abundant of meaning for such as choose to seek it: it is neither prison nor palace, but a decent home.

All which I neither praise nor blame, but say that so it is: some people praise this homeliness overmuch, as if the land were the very axle-tree of the world; so do not I, nor any unblinded by pride in themselves and all that belongs to them: others there are who scorn it and the tameness of it: not I any the more: though it would indeed be hard if there were nothing else in the world, no wonders, no terrors, no unspeakable beauties: yet when we think what a small part of the world's history, past, present, and to come, is this land we live in, and how much smaller still in the history of the arts, and yet how our forefathers clung to it, and with what care and pains they adorned it, this unromantic, uneventful-looking land of England, surely by this too our hearts may be touched, and our hope quickened.

For as was the land, such was the art of it while folk yet troubled themselves about such things; it strove little to impress people either by pomp or ingenuity: not unseldom it fell into commonplace, rarely it rose into majesty; yet was it never oppressive, never a slave's nightmare nor an insolent boast: and at its best it had an inventiveness, an individuality that grander styles have never overpassed: its best too, and that was in its very heart, was given as freely to the yeoman's house, and the humble village church, as to the lord's palace or the mighty cathedral: never coarse, though often rude enough, sweet, natural and unaffected, an art of peasants rather than of merchant-princes or courtiers, it must be a hard heart, I think, that does not love it: whether a man has been born among it like ourselves, or has come wonderingly on its simplicity from all the grandeur overseas. A peasant art, I say, and it clung fast to the life of the people, and still lived among the cottagers and yeomen in many parts of the country while the big houses were being built 'French and fine': still lived also in many a quaint pattern of loom and printing-block, and embroiderer's needle, while overseas stupid pomp had extinguished all nature and freedom, and art was become, in France especially, the mere expression of that successful and exultant rascality, which in the flesh no long time afterwards went down into the pit for ever.

Such was the English art, whose history is in a sense at your doors, grown scarce indeed, and growing scarcer year by year, not only through greedy destruction, of which there is certainly less than there used to be, but also through the attacks of another foe, called nowadays 'restoration'.[6]

I must not make a long story about this, but also I cannot quite pass it over, since I have pressed on you the study of these ancient monuments. Thus the matter stands: these old buildings have been altered and added to century after century, often beautifully, always historically; their very value, a great part of it, lay in that: they have suffered almost always from neglect also, often from violence (that latter a piece of history often far from uninteresting), but ordinary obvious mending would almost always have kept them standing, pieces of nature and of history.

But of late years a great uprising of ecclesiastical zeal, coinciding with a great increase of study, and consequently of knowledge of mediaeval architecture, has driven people into spending their money on these buildings, not merely with the purpose of repairing them, of keeping them safe, clean, and wind and water-tight, but also of 'restoring' them to some ideal state of perfection; sweeping away if possible all signs of what has befallen them at least since the Reformation, and often since dates much earlier: this has sometimes been done with much disregard of art and entirely from ecclesiastical zeal, but oftener it has been well meant enough as regards art: yet you will not have listened to what I have said to-night if you do not see that from my point of view this restoration must be as impossible to bring about, as the attempt at it is destructive to the buildings so dealt with: I scarcely like to think what a great part of them have been made nearly useless to students of art and history: unless you knew a great deal about architecture you perhaps would scarce understand what terrible damage has been done by that dangerous 'little knowledge' in this matter: but at least it is easy to be understood, that to deal recklessly with valuable (and national) monuments which, when once gone, can never be replaced by any splendour of modern art, is doing a very sorry service to the State.

You will see by all that I have said on this study of ancient art that I mean by education herein something much wider than the teaching of a definite art in schools of design, and that it must be something that we must do more or less for ourselves: I mean by it a systematic concentration of our thoughts on the matter, a studying of it in all ways, careful and laborious practice of it, and a determination to do nothing but what is known to be good in workmanship and design.

Of course, however, both as an instrument of that study we have been speaking of, as well as of the practice of the arts, all handicrafts-men should be taught to draw very carefully; as indeed all people should be taught drawing who are not physically incapable of learn-ing it: but the art of drawing so taught would not be the art of designing, but only a means towards *this* end, *general capability in dealing with the arts*.

For I wish specially to impress this upon you, that *designing* cannot be taught at all in a school: continued practice will help a man who is naturally a designer, continual notice of nature and of art: no doubt those who have some faculty for designing are still numerous, and they want from a school certain technical teaching, just as they want tools: in these days also, when the best school, the school of successful practice going on around you, is at such a low ebb, they do undoubtedly want instruction in the history of the arts: these two things schools of design can give: but the royal road of a set of rules deduced from a sham science of design, that is itself not a science but another set of rules, will lead nowhere; – or, let us rather say, to beginning again.

As to the kind of drawing that should be taught to men engaged in ornamental work, there is only *one best* way of teaching drawing, and that is teaching the scholar to draw the human figure: both because the lines of a man's body are much more subtle than anything else, and because you can more surely be found out and set right if you go wrong. I do think that such teaching as this, given to all people who care for it, would help the revival of the arts very much: the habit of discriminating between right and wrong, the sense of pleas-ure in drawing a good line, would really, I think, be education in the due sense of the word for all such people as had the germs of invention in them; yet as aforesaid, in this age of the world it would be mere affectation to pretend to shut one's eyes to the art of past ages: that also we must study. If other circumstances, social and economical, do not stand in our way, that is to say, if the world is not too busy to allow us to have Decorative Arts at all, these two are the *direct* means by which we shall get them; that is, general cultivation of the powers of the mind, general cultivation of the powers of the eye and hand.

Perhaps that seems to you very commonplace advice and a very roundabout road; nevertheless 'tis a certain one, if by any road you desire to come to the new art, which is my subject to-night: if you do not, and if those germs of invention, which, as I said just now, are no doubt still common enough among men, are left neglected and undeveloped, the laws of Nature will assert themselves in this as in other matters, and the faculty of design itself will gradually fade from the race of man. Sirs, shall we approach nearer to perfection by casting away so large a part of that intelligence which makes us *men*?

And now before I make an end, I want to call your attention to certain things, that, owing to our neglect of the arts for other business, bar that good road to us and are such an hindrance, that, till they are dealt with, it is hard even to make a beginning of our endeavour. And if my talk should seem to grow too serious for our subject, as indeed I think it cannot do, I beg you to remember what I said earlier, of how the arts all hang together. Now there is one art of which the old architect of Edward III's time was thinking – he who founded New College at Oxford, I mean – when he took this for his motto: 'Manners maketh man': he meant by manners the art of morals, the art of living worthily, and like a man.[7] I must needs claim this art also as dealing with my subject.

There is a great deal of sham work in the world, hurtful to the buyer, more hurtful to the seller, if he only knew it, most hurtful to the maker: how good a foundation it would be towards getting good Decorative Art, that is ornamental workmanship, if we craftsmen were to resolve to turn out nothing but excellent workmanship in all things, instead of having, as we too often have now, a very low average standard of work, which we often fall below.

I do not blame either one class or another in this matter, I blame all: to set aside our own class of handicraftsmen, of whose shortcomings you and I know so much that we need talk no more about it, I know that the public in general are set on having things cheap, being so ignorant that they do not know when they get them nasty also; so ignorant that they neither know nor care whether they give a man his due: I know that the manufacturers (so called) are so set on carrying out competition to its utmost, competition of cheapness, not of excellence, that they meet the bargain-hunters half way, and cheerfully furnish them with nasty wares at the cheap rate they are asked for, by means of what can be called by no prettier name than fraud. England has of late been too much busied with the counting-house and not enough with the workshop: with the result that the counting-house at the present moment is rather barren of orders.

I say all classes are to blame in this matter, but also I say that the remedy lies with the handicraftsmen, who are not ignorant of these things like the public, and who have no call to be greedy and isolated like the manufacturers or middlemen; the duty and honour of educating the public lies with them, and they have in them the seeds of order and organization which make that duty the easier.

When will they see to this and help to make men of us all by insisting on this most weighty piece of manners; so that we may adorn life with the pleasure of cheerfully *buying* goods at their due price; with the pleasure of *selling* goods that we could be proud of both for fair price and fair workmanship: with the pleasure of working soundly and without haste at *making* goods that we could be proud of? – much the greatest pleasure of the three is that last, such a pleasure as, I think, the world has none like it.

You must not say that this piece of manners lies out of my subject: it is essentially a part of it and most important: for I am bidding you learn to be artists, if art is not to come to an end amongst us: and what is an artist but a workman who is determined that, whatever else happens, his work shall be excellent? or, to put it in another way: the decoration of workmanship, what is it but the expression of man's pleasure in successful labour? But what pleasure can there be in *bad* work, in *un*successful labour; why should we decorate *that*? and how can we bear to be always unsuccessful in our labour?

As greed of unfair gain, wanting to be paid for what we have not earned, cumbers our path with this tangle of bad work, of sham work, so the heaped-up money which this greed has brought us (for greed will have its way, like all other strong passions), this money, I say, gathered into heaps little and big, with all the false distinction which so unhappily it yet commands amongst us, has raised up against the arts a barrier of the love of luxury and show, which is of all obvious hindrances the worst to overpass: the highest and most cultivated classes are not free from the vulgarity of it, the lower are not free from its pretence. I beg you to remember both as a remedy against this, and as explaining exactly what I mean, that nothing can be a work of art which is not useful; that is to say, which does not minister to the body when well under command of the mind, or which does not amuse, soothe, or elevate the mind in a healthy state. What tons upon tons of unutterable rubbish pretending to be works of art in some degree would this maxim clear out of our London houses, if it were understood and acted upon! To my mind it is only here and there (out of the kitchen) that you can find in a well-to-do house things that are of any use at all: as a rule all the decoration (so called) that has got there is there for the sake of show, not because anybody likes it. I repeat, this stupidity goes through all classes of society: the silk curtains in my Lord's drawing-room are no more a matter of art to him than the powder in his footman's hair; the kitchen in a country farmhouse is most commonly a pleasant and homelike place, the parlour dreary and useless.

Simplicity of life, begetting simplicity of taste, that is, a love for sweet and lofty things, is of all matters most necessary for the birth of the new and better art we crave for; simplicity everywhere, in the palace as well as in the cottage.

Still more is this necessary, cleanliness and decency everywhere, in the cottage as well as in the palace: the lack of that is a serious piece of *manners* for us to correct: that lack and all the inequalities of life, and the heaped-up thoughtlessness and disorder of so many centuries that cause it: and as yet it is only a very few men who have begun to think about a remedy for it in its widest range: even in its narrower aspect, in the defacements of our big towns by all that commerce brings with it, who heeds it? who tries to control their squalor and hideousness? there is nothing but thoughtlessness and recklessness in the matter: the helplessness of people who don't live long enough to do a thing themselves, and have not manliness and foresight enough to begin the work, and pass it on to those that shall come after them.

Is money to be gathered? cut down the pleasant trees among the houses, pull down ancient and venerable buildings for the money that a few square yards of London dirt will fetch; blacken rivers, hide the sun and poison the air with smoke and worse, and it's nobody's business to see to it or mend it: that is all that modern commerce, the counting-house forgetful of the workshop, will do for us herein.

And Science – we have loved her well, and followed her diligently, what will she do? I fear she is so much in the pay of the counting-house, the counting-house and the drill-sergeant, that she is too busy, and will for the present do nothing. Yet there are matters which I should have thought easy for her; say for example teaching Manchester how to consume its own smoke, or Leeds how to get rid of its superfluous black dye without turning it into the river, which would be as much worth her attention as the production of the heaviest of heavy black silks, or the biggest of useless guns. Anyhow, however it be done, unless people care about carrying on their business without making the world hideous, how can they care about Art? I know it will cost much both of time and money to better these things even a little; but I do not see how these can be better spent than in making life cheerful and honourable for others and for ourselves; and the gain of good life to the country at large that would result from men seriously setting about the bettering of the decency of our big towns would be priceless, even if nothing specially good befell the arts in consequence: I do not know that it would; but I should begin to think matters hopeful if men turned their attention to such things, and I repeat that, unless they do so, we can scarcely even begin with any hope our endeavours for the bettering of the arts.

Unless something or other is done to give all men some pleasure for the eyes and rest for the mind in the aspect of their own and their neighbours' houses, until the contrast is less disgraceful between the fields where beasts live and the streets where men live, I suppose that the practice of the arts must be mainly kept in the hands of a few highly cultivated men, who can go often to beautiful places, whose education enables them, in the contemplation of the past glories of the world, to shut out from their view the everyday squalors that the most of men move in. Sirs, I believe that art has such sympathy with cheerful freedom, open-heartedness and reality, so much she sickens under selfishness and luxury, that she will not live thus isolated and exclusive. I will go further than this and say that on such terms I do not wish her to live. I protest that it would be a shame to an honest artist to enjoy what he had huddled up to himself of such art, as it would be for a rich man to sit and eat dainty food amongst starving soldiers in a beleaguered fort.

I do not want art for a few, any more than education for a few, or freedom for a few.

No, rather than art should live this poor thin life among a few exceptional men, despising those beneath them for an ignorance for which they themselves are responsible, for a brutality that they will not struggle with, – rather than this, I would that the world should indeed sweep away all art for awhile, as I said before I thought it possible she might do; rather than the wheat should rot in the miser's granary, I would that the earth had it, that it might yet have a chance to quicken in the dark.

I have a sort of faith, though, that this clearing away of all art will not happen, that men will get wiser, as well as more learned; that many of the intricacies of life, on which we now pride ourselves more than enough, partly because they are new, partly because they have come with the gain of better things, will be cast aside as having played their part, and being useful no longer. I hope that we shall have leisure from war, – war commercial, as well as war of the bullet and the bayonet; leisure from the knowledge that darkens counsel; leisure above all from the greed of money, and the craving for that overwhelming distinction that money now brings: I believe that as we have even now partly achieved LIBERTY, so we shall one day achieve EQUALITY, which, and which only, means FRATERNITY, and so have leisure from poverty and all its griping, sordid cares.

Then having leisure from all these things, amidst renewed simplicity of life we shall have leisure to think about our work, that faithful daily companion, which no man any longer will venture to call the Curse of labour: for surely then we shall be happy in it, each in his place, no man grudging at another; no one bidden to be any man's *servant*, every one scorning to be any man's *master*: men will then assuredly be happy in their work, and that happiness will assuredly bring forth decorative, noble, *popular* art.

That art will make our streets as beautiful as the woods, as elevating as the mountain-sides: it will be a pleasure and a rest, and not a weight upon the spirits to come from the open country into a town; every man's house will be fair and decent, soothing to his mind and helpful to his work: all the works of man that we live amongst and handle will be in harmony with nature, will be reasonable and beautiful: yet all will be simple and inspiriting, not childish nor enervating; for as nothing of beauty and splendour that man's mind and hand may compass shall be wanting from our public buildings, so in no private dwelling will there be any signs of waste, pomp, or insolence, and every man will have his share of the *best*.

It is a dream, you may say, of what has never been and never will be; true, it has never been, and therefore, since the world is alive and moving yet, my hope is the greater that it one day will be: true, it is a dream; but dreams have before now come about of things so good and necessary to us, that we scarcely think of them more than of the daylight, though once people had to live without them, without even the hope of them.

Anyhow, dream as it is, I pray you to pardon my setting it before you, for it lies at the bottom of all my work in the Decorative Arts, nor will it ever be out of my thoughts: and I am here with you tonight to ask you to help me in realizing this dream, this *hope*.

SOME HINTS ON
PATTERN-DESIGNING

* * *

Lecture given at
the Working Men's College,
London, 1881

By the word pattern-design, of which I have undertaken to speak to you to-night, I mean the ornamentation of a surface by work that is not imitative or historical, at any rate not principally or essentially so. Such work is often not literally flat, for it may be carving or moulded work in plaster or pottery; but whatever material relief it may have is given to it for the sake of beauty and richness, and not for the sake of imitation, or to tell a fact directly; so that people have called this art ornamental art, though indeed all real art is ornamental.

Now, before we go further, we may as well ask ourselves what reason or right this so-called ornamental art has to existence? We might answer the question shortly by saying that it seems clear that mankind has hitherto determined to have it even at the cost of a good deal of labour and trouble: an answer good enough to satisfy our consciences that we are not necessarily wasting our time in meeting here to consider it; but we may furthermore try to get at the reasons that have forced men in the mass always to expect to have what to some of them doubtless seems an absurd superfluity of life.

I do not know a better way of getting at these reasons than for each of us to suppose himself to be in the room in which he will have to pass a good part of his life, the said room being quite bare of ornament, and to be there that he may consider what he can do to make the bare walls pleasant and helpful to him; I say the walls, because, after all, the widest use of pattern-designing is the clothing of the walls of a room, hall, church, or what building you will. Doubtless there will be some, in these days at least, who will say, ''Tis most helpful to me to let the bare walls alone.' So also there would be some who, when asked with what manner of books they will furnish their room, would answer, 'With none.' But I think you will agree with me in thinking that both these sets of people would be in an unhealthy state of mind, and probably of body also; in which case we need not trouble ourselves about their whims, since it is with healthy and sane people only that art has dealings.

Again, a healthy and sane person being asked with what kind of art he would clothe his walls, might well answer, 'With the best art,' and so end the question. Yet, out on it! so complex is human life, that even this seemingly most reasonable answer may turn out to be little better than an evasion.

For I suppose the best art to be the pictured representation of men's imaginings; what they have thought has happened to the world before their time, or what they deem they have seen with the eyes of the body or the soul: and the imaginings thus represented are always beautiful indeed, but oftenest stirring to men's passions and aspirations, and not seldom sorrowful or even terrible.

Stories that tell of men's aspirations for more than material life can give them, their struggles for the future welfare of their race, their unselfish love, their unrequited service: things like this are the subjects for the best art; in such subjects there is hope surely, yet the aspect of them is likely to be sorrowful enough: defeat the seed of victory, and death the seed of life, will be shown on the face of most of them.

Take note, too, that in the best art all these solemn and awful things are expressed clearly and without any vagueness, with such life and power that they impress the beholder so deeply that he is brought face to face with the very scenes, and lives among them for a time; so raising his life above the daily tangle of small things that wearies him, to the level of the heroism which they represent.

This is the best art; and who can deny that it is good for us all that it should be at hand to stir our emotions: yet its very greatness makes it a thing to be handled carefully, for we cannot always be having our emotions deeply stirred: that wearies us body and soul; and man, an animal that longs for rest like other animals, defends himself against the weariness by hardening his heart, and refusing to be moved every hour of the day by tragic emotions; nay, even by beauty that claims his attention over-much.

Such callousness is bad, both for the arts and our own selves; and therefore it is not so good to have the best art for ever under our eyes, though it is abundantly good that we should be able to get at it from time to time.

Meantime, I cannot allow that it is good for any hour of the day to be wholly stripped of life and beauty; therefore we must provide ourselves with lesser (I will not say worse) art with which to surround our common workaday or restful times; and for those times, I think, it will be enough for us to clothe our daily and domestic walls with ornament that reminds us of the outward face of the earth, of the innocent love of animals, or of man passing his days between work and rest as he does. I say, with ornament that reminds us of these things, and sets our minds and memories at work easily creating them; because scientific representation of them would again involve us in the problems of hard fact and the troubles of life, and so once more destroy our rest for us.

If this lesser art will really be enough to content us, it is a good thing; for as to the higher art there never can be very much of it going on, since but few people can be found to do it; also few can find money enough to possess themselves of any portion of it, and, if they could, it would be a piece of preposterous selfishness to shut it up from other people's eyes; while of the secondary art there ought to be abundance for all men, so much that you need but call in the neighbours, and not all the world, to see your pretty new wall when it is finished.

But this kind of art must be suggestive rather than imitative; because, in order to have plenty of it, it must be a kind of work that is not too difficult for ordinary men with imaginations capable of development; men from whom you cannot expect miracles of skill, and from whose hands you must not ask too much, lest you lose what their intelligence has to give you, by over-wearying them. Withal, the representation of this lower kind of life is pretty sure to become soulless and tiresome unless it have a soul given to it by the efforts of men forced by the limits of order and the necessities of art to think of these things for themselves, and so to give you some part of the infinite variety which abides in the mind of man.

Of course you understand that it is impossible to imitate nature literally; the utmost realism of the most realistic painter falls a long way short of that; and as to the work which must be done by ordinary men not unskilled or dull to beauty, the attempt to attain to realism would be sure to result in obscuring their intelligence, and in starving you of all the beauty which you desire in your hearts, but which you have not learned to express by means of art.

Let us go back to our wall again, and think of it. If you are to put nothing on it but what strives to be a literal imitation of nature, all you can do is to have a few cut flowers or bits of boughs nailed to it, with perhaps a blue-bottle fly or a butterfly here and there. Well, I don't deny that this may make good decoration now and then, but if all decoration had to take that form I think weariness of it would drive you to a white-washed wall; and at the best it is a very limited view to take of nature.

Is it not better to be reminded, however simply, of the close vine-trellis that keeps out the sun by the Nile side; or of the wild-woods and their streams, with the dogs panting beside them; or of the swallows sweeping above the garden boughs toward the house-eaves where their nestlings are, while the sun breaks [through] the clouds on them; or of the many-flowered summer meadows of Picardy? Is not all this better than having to count day after day a few sham-real boughs and flowers, casting sham-real shadows on your walls with little hint of anything beyond Covent Garden in them?

You may be sure that any decoration is futile, and has fallen into at least the first stage of degradation, when it does not remind you of something beyond itself, of something of which it is but a visible symbol.

Now, to sum up, what we want to clothe our walls with is (1) something that it is possible for us to get; (2) something that is beautiful; (3) something which will not drive us either into unrest or into callousness; (4) something which reminds us of life beyond itself, and which has the impress of human imagination strong on it; and (5) something which can be done by a great many people without too much difficulty and with pleasure.

These conditions I believe to have been fulfilled by the pattern-designers in all times when art has been healthy, and to have been all more or less violated when art has been unhealthy and unreal. In such evil times beauty has given place to whim, imagination to extravagance, nature to sick nightmare fancies, and finally workman-like considerate skill, which refuses to allow either the brain or the hand to be over-taxed, which, without sparing labour when necessary, refuses sternly to waste it, has given place to commercial trickery sustained by laborious botching.

Now, I have been speaking of what may be called the moral qualities of the art we are thinking of; let us try, therefore, to shorten their names, and have one last word on them before we deal with the material or technical part.

Ornamental pattern-work, to be raised above the contempt of reasonable men, must possess three qualities: beauty, imagination, and order.

'Tis clear I need not waste many words on the first of these. You will be drawing water with a sieve with a vengeance if you cannot manage to make ornamental work beautiful.

As for the second quality, imagination: the necessity for that may not be so clear to you, considering the humble nature of our art; yet you will probably admit, when you come to think of it, that every work of man which has beauty in it must have some meaning in it also; that the presence of any beauty in a piece of handicraft implies that the mind of the man who made it was more or less excited at the time, was lifted somewhat above the commonplace; that he had something to communicate to his fellows which they did not know or feel before, and which they would never have known or felt if he had not been there to force them to it.

I want you to think of this when you see, as, unfortunately, you are only too likely often to see, some lifeless imitation of a piece of bygone art, and are puzzled to know why it does not satisfy you. The reason is that the imitator has not entered into the soul of the dead artist; nay, has supposed that he had but a hand and no soul, and so has not known what he meant to do. I dwell on this, because it forces on us the conclusion that if we cannot have an ornamental art of our own, we cannot have one at all. Every real work of art, even the humblest, is inimitable. I am most sure that all the heaped-up knowledge of modern science, all the energy of modern commerce, all the depth and spirituality of modern thought, cannot reproduce so much as the handiwork of an ignorant, superstitious

Berkshire peasant of the fourteenth century; nay, of a wandering Kurdish shepherd, or of a skin-and-bone oppressed Indian ryot.[1] This, I say, I am sure of; and to me the certainty is not depressing, but inspiriting, for it bids us remember that the world has been noteworthy for more than one century and one place, a fact which we are pretty much apt to forget.

Now as to the third of the essential qualities of our art: order, I have to say of it, that without it neither the beauty nor the imagination could be made visible; it is the bond of their life, and as good as creates them, if they are to be of any use to people in general. Let us see, therefore, with what instruments it works, how it brings together the material and spiritual sides of the craft.

I have already said something of the way in which it deals with the materials which Nature gives it, and how, as it were, it both builds a wall against vagueness and opens a door therein for imagination to come in by. Now, this is done by means of treatment which is called, as one may say technically, the conventionalizing of nature. That is to say, order invents certain beautiful and natural forms, which, appealing to a reasonable and imaginative person, will remind him not only of the part of nature which, to his mind at least, they represent, but also of much that lies beyond that part. I have already hinted at some reasons for this treatment of natural objects. You can't bring a whole countryside, or a whole field, into your room, nor even a whole bush; and, moreover, only a very specially skilled craftsman can make any approach to what might pass with us in moments of excitement for an imitation of such-like things. These are limitations which are common to every form of the lesser arts; but, besides these, every material in which household goods are fashioned imposes certain special limitations within which the craftsman must work. Here again, is the wall of order against vagueness, and the door of order for imagination. For you must understand from the first that these limitations are as far as possible from being hindrances to beauty in the several crafts. On the contrary, they are incitements and helps to its attainment; those who find them irksome are not born craftsmen, and the periods of art that try to get rid of them are declining periods.

Now this must be clear to you, if you come to think of it. Give an artist a piece of paper, and say to him. 'I want a design,' and he must ask you, 'What for? What's to be done with it?' And if you can't tell him, well, I dare not venture to mention the name which his irritation will give you. But if you say, I want this queer space filled with ornament, I want you to make such and such a pretty thing out of these intractable materials, straightway his invention will be quickened, and he will set to work with a will; for, indeed, delight in skill lies at the root of all art.

Now, further, this working in materials, which is the *raison d'être* of all pattern-work, still further limits it in the direct imitation of nature, drives it still more decidedly to appeal to the imagination. For example: you have a heap of little coloured cubes of glass to make your picture of, or you have some coloured thrums of worsted wherewith to build up at once a picture and a piece of cloth;[2] well, there is a wrong and a right way of setting to work about this: if you please you may set to work with your cubes and your thrums to imitate a brush-painted picture, a work of art done in a material wherein the limitations are as few and pliable as they are many and rigid in the one you are working in; with almost invisible squares or shuttle-strokes, you may build up, square by square, or line by line, an imitation of an oil-painter's rapid stroke of the brush, and so at last produce your imitation, which doubtless people will wonder at, and say, 'How was it done? we can see neither cubes nor thrums in it.' And so also would they have wondered if you had made a portrait of the Lord Mayor in burnt sugar, or of Mr Parnell[3] in fireworks. But the wonder being over, 'tis like that some reasonable person will say, 'This is not specially beautiful; and as to its skill, after all, you have taken a year to do what a second-rate painter could have done in three days. Why have you done it at all?' An unanswerable question, I fear.

Well, such materials may be used thus, so clever are men; nay, they have been used thus, so perverse and dull are men!

On the other hand, if you will, you may thoroughly consider your glass cubes or your worsted thrums, and think what can best be done with them; but they need not fetter your imagination, for you may, with them, tell a story in a new way, even if it be not a new story; you may conquer the obstinacy of your material and make it obey you as far as the needs of beauty go, and the telling of your tale; you will be pleased with the victory of your skill, but you will not have forgotten your subject amidst mere laboriousness, and you will know that your victory has been no barren one, but has produced a beautiful thing, which nothing but your struggle with difficulties could have brought forth, and when people look at it they will be forced to say: 'Well, though it is rough, yet, in spite of the material, the workman has shown that he knows what a good line is; it is beautiful, certainly, after its fashion, and the workman has looked at things with his own eyes: and then how the tesserae gleam in this indestructible picture, how the gold glitters!' Or, 'What wealth of colour and softness of gradation there is in these interwoven thrums of worsted, that have drunk the dye so deeply! No other material conceivable could have done it just like this. And the wages are not so high; we can have plenty of this sort of work. Yes, the man is worth his keep.'

In this way, also, your materials can be used, so simple and trustful may men be that they may venture to make a work of art thus; nay, so helpful and joyous have they been, that they have so ventured, for the pleasure of many people, their own not least of all.

Now, I have tried to point out to you that the nature of the craft of pattern-designing imposes certain limitations within which it has to work, and also that each branch of it has further limitations of its own. Before saying a few words that relate to these special limitations, I will, by your leave, narrow our subject by dwelling a little on what is one of the most important parts of pattern-designing: the making of a recurring pattern for a flat surface. Let us first look a little on the construction of these, at the lines on which they are built. Now, the beauty and imagination which I have spoken of as necessary to all patterns may be, and often have been, of the very simplest kind, and their order the most obvious. So, to begin with, let us take one of these: our wall may be ornamented with mere horizontal stripes of colour; what beauty there may be in these will be limited to the beauty of very simple proportion, and in the tints and contrast of tints used, while the meaning of them will be confined to the calling people's attention to the charm of material, and due orderly construction of a wall.*

* The following notes on the construction of designs were illustrated by a series of diagrams and by drawings of historic patterns on a greatly enlarged scale. [May Morris, *Works XXII*, p. 184].

After this simplest form comes that of chequers and squares of unfoliated diaper, so to call it, which still is but a hint at the possible construction of the wall, when it is not in itself constructional. From that we get to diapers made by lines, either rectilinear or taking the form of circles touching one another. We have now left the idea of constructional blocks or curves, and are probably suggesting scoring of lines on the surface of the wall joined to inlaying, perhaps; or else there is an idea in it of some sort of hanging; at first, as in much of the ancient Egyptian work, woven of reeds or grass, but later on suggesting weaving of finer materials that do not call attention to the crossing of warp and weft.

This next becomes a floriated diaper. The lines are formed by shapes of stems, and leaves or flowers fill the spaces between the lines. This kind of ornamentation has got a long way from the original stripes and squares, and even from the cross-barred matting diapers. The first of these (when used quite simply) is commonly external work, and is used to enrich further what sunlight and shadow already enrich. The second either implies an early stage of civilization, or a persistent memory of its rudeness.

But as to this more elaborate diaper, simple as its construction is, it has never been superseded: in its richer forms it is intimately connected with the stately and vast shapes of Roman architecture; and until the great change took place, when the once-despised East began to mingle with the old decaying Western civilization, and even to dominate it, it was really the only form taken by recurring patterns, except mere chequer and scalework, though certain complications of the circle and the square were used to gain greater richness.

Now the next change, so far as mere construction goes, takes us into what is practically the last stage that recurring patterns can get to, and the change is greater than at first sight it may seem to you: it is part of that change in the master-art from late and decaying Classical into Byzantine, or, as I would rather call it, new-born Gothic art. The first places where it is seen are a few buildings of the early part of the sixth century, when architecture seems to have taken a sudden leap, and, in fact, to have passed from death to new birth.[4] As to the construction of patterns the change was simply this:

continuous growth of curved lines took the place of mere contiguity, or of the interlacement of straight lines.

All the recurring patterns of the ancient and classical world were, I repeat, founded on the diaper, square or round. All their borders or friezes were formed either by tufts of flowers growing side by side, with their tendrils sometimes touching or interlacing, or by scrolls wherein there was no continuous growth, but only a masking of the repeat by some spreading member of the pattern. But when young Gothic took the place of old Classic, the change was marked in pattern-designing by the universal acceptance of continuous growth as a necessity of borders and friezes; and in square pattern-work, as I should call it, this growth was the general rule in all the more important designs.

Of this square continuous pattern-work there are two principal forms of construction: (1) The branch formed on a diagonal line, and (2) the net framed on variously-proportioned diamonds. These main constructions were, as time went on, varied in all sorts of ways, more or less beautiful and ingenious; and they are of course only bounding or leading lines, and are to be filled up in all sorts of ways. Nay, sometimes these leading lines are not drawn, and we have left us a sort of powdering in the devices which fill up the spaces between the imaginary lines. Our Sicilian pattern of the thirteenth century gives us an example of this; and this Italian one of the fourteenth century gives us another, the leading lines of the diagonal branch being broken, and so leaving a powdering on those lines; but in all cases the net or branch lines, that is, the simple diagonal or crossing diagonal, are really there.

For clearness' sake, I will run through the different kinds of construction that I have named: (1) Horizontal stripes; (2) block diaper or chequer; (3) matting diaper, very various in form; (4) square line diaper; (5) floriated square diaper; (6) round diaper formed by contiguous circles; (7) the diagonal branch; (8) the net; (9, which is supplementary) powderings on the lines of the diagonal branch, or of the net.

These are all the elementary forms of construction for a recurring pattern, but of course there may be many varieties of each of them. Elaborate patterns may be wrought on the stripes or chequers; the

foliated diaper may be wrought interlocking; the net may be com-
plicated by net within net; the diagonal bough may be crossed
variously, or the alternate boughs may be slipped down so as to
form a kind of untied and dislocated net; the circles may intersect
each other instead of touching, or polygonal figures may be built
on them, as in the strange star patterns which are the differentia
of Arab art.

Of course, also, these constructional lines may be masked in an
infinite number of ways, and in certain periods it was most usual to
do this, and much ingenuity was spent, and not a little wasted, in
doing it.

Before I pass to the use to which these forms of pattern may be
put, I will say a little on the subject of the relief of patterns, which
may be considered as the other side of their mechanism. We have,
you see, been talking about the skeletons of them, and those skeletons
must be clothed with flesh, that is, their members must have tangible
superficial area; and by the word relief I understand the method of
bringing this out.

Of course this part of the subject is intimately connected with the
colour of designs, but of that I shall only say so much as is necessary
for dealing with their relief.

To put the matter as shortly as possible, one may say that there
are two ways of relief for a recurring surface-pattern, either that the
figure shall show light upon a dark, or dark upon a light ground; or
that the whole pattern, member by member, should be outlined by a
line of colour which both serves to relieve it from its ground, which
is not necessarily either lighter or darker than the figure, and also
prevents the colour from being inharmonious or hard.

Now, to speak broadly, the first of these methods of relief is
used by those who are chiefly thinking about form, the second by
those whose minds are most set on colour; and you will easily
see, if you come to think of it, how widely different the two methods are. Those who have been used to the first method of dark
upon light, or light upon dark, often get confused and troubled
when they have to deal with many colours, and wonder why it is
that, in spite of all their attempts at refinement of colour, their
designs still look wrong.

The fact is, that when you have many colours, when you are making up your design by contrast of hues and variety of shades, you must use the bounding line to some extent, if not through and through.

Of these two methods of relief, you must think of the first as being the relief of one plane from another, in it there is always an idea of at least more than one plane of surface, and often of several planes. The second you must think of as the relief of colour from colour, and designs treated thus both should look, and do look, perfectly flat. Again, to speak broadly, the first method is that of the West, the second that of the East; but of the later and (excuse the 'bull') the Gothic East. The idea of plane relieved on plane was always present in all the patterns of the ancient and classical world.

Now, as to the use to be made of these recurring surface patterns, the simpler of them, such as mere stripes and simpler diapers, have been, and doubtless will always be used for external decoration of walls, and also for subsidiary decoration where the scale is large and where historical art plays the chief part. On the other hand, some people may doubt as to what share, if any, the more elaborated forms of pattern-work should have in internal wall decoration. True it is that the principle of the continuous line, which led up to all that elaboration, was an invention of the later East, just as the system of relieving colour from colour was; and I believe the two things are closely connected, and sprang from this cause, that these peoples were for various reasons not much driven towards the higher pictorial art, and did not reach any great excellence in it; therefore they felt a need for developing their pattern-art to the highest degree possible, till it became something more than a little-noticed accompaniment to historical art, which was all that it used to be in the ancient or the classical world.

Perhaps the fact that the barbarians invented what the elder civilization, the great nurse of the higher arts, despised, may seem to some of you a condemnation of this more elaborate pattern-work; but before you make up your minds to that, I would ask you to remember within what narrow limits that perfection of Greece moved. It seems to me that unless you can have the whole of that severe system of theirs, you will not be bettered by taking to a minor part of it; nor, indeed, do I think that you can have that system now, for it was the servant of a perfection which is no longer attainable. The whole art of the classical ancients, while it was alive and growing, was the art of a society made up of a narrow aristocracy of citizens, waited upon by a large body of slaves, and surrounded by a world of barbarism which was always despised and never noticed till it threatened to overwhelm the self-sufficient aristocracy that called itself the civilized world.[5]

No, I think that the barbarians who invented modern Europe invented also several other things which we, their children, cannot decently disregard, or pass by wrapped up in a cloak of sham classical disguise; and that one of these things, the smallest of them if you will, was this invention of the continuous line that led to elaborate and independent pattern-work; and I believe that this was one of those things which, once invented, cannot be dropped, but must always remain a part of architecture, like the arch – like the pointed arch. Properly subordinated to architecture on the one hand, and to historic art on the other, it ought yet, I think, to play a great part in the making our houses at once beautiful and restful; an end which is one of the chief reasons for existence of all art.

As to its subordination to the greater arts, all we can say about that is that we should not have too much of it. I don't think there is any danger of its thrusting the more intellectual and historic arts out of their due place; rather, perhaps, it is like to be neglected in comparison with them. But if it makes any advance, as it may do, I can see that counsels of despair may sometimes drive us into excess in the use of surface ornament. I mean that our houses are so base and ugly, and it is hard to alter this bad condition of life, that people may be driven out of all hope of getting good architecture, and try to forget their troubles in that respect by overdoing their internal decoration. Well, you must not suppose that I object to people making the best of their ugly houses; indeed, you probably know that I personally should be finely landed if they did not. Nevertheless, noble building is the first and best and least selfish of the arts, and unless we can manage to get it somehow, we shall soon have no decoration, or, indeed, art of any kind, to put into the dog-hutches which we now think good enough for refined and educated people, to say nothing about other buildings lesser and greater.

Now, with your leave, I will go through some of the chief crafts in which surface patterns (and chiefly recurring ones) are used, and try to note some of the limitations which necessity and reason impose on them, and show how those limitations may be made helps, and not hindrances, to those crafts.

Let us take first the humble, but, as things go, useful art of paper-staining. And firstly, you must remember that it is a cheap art, somewhat easily done; elaborate patterns are easy in it; so be careful not to overdo either the elaboration in your paper or the amount of pattern-work in your rooms. I mean, by all means have the prettiest paper you can get, but don't fall in love so much with the cheapness of its prettiness as to have several patterns in one room, or even two, if you will be advised by me. Above all, eschew that bastard imitation of picture, embroidery or tapestry-work, which, under the name of dado-papers, are so common at present; even when they are well designed, as they often are, they are a mistake. They do not in the least fill the place of patterns of beautiful execution or of beautiful materials, and they weary us of those better things by simulating them. The ease with which the brushwork of an artist can be, I will not say imitated, but caricatured, in paperhangings, is a snare to this useful manufacture, and has been so from the first. In the printed wares you may have any amount of fine lines and shading by hatching, but you cannot have any colour which has not a definite outline. By disregarding these facts, you lose whatever of special pleasure is to be obtained from linear shading, and by clear relief of light upon dark or dark upon light, and you affront people's reason by trying to get the subtle gradations which the execution of handwork alone can give.

Now, again, as to paperhangings, one may accept as an axiom that, other things being equal, the more mechanical the process, the less direct should be the imitation of natural forms; on the other hand, in these wares which are stretched out flat on the wall, and have no special beauty of execution about them, we may find ourselves driven to do more than we otherwise should in masking the construction of our patterns. It gives us a chance of showing that we are pattern-designers born by accepting this apparent dilemma cheerfully, and setting our wits to work to conquer it. Let me state the difficulty again. In this craft the absence of limitations as to number of colours, and the general ease of the manufacture, is apt to tempt us into a mere twisting of natural forms into lines that may pass for ornamental; to yield to this temptation will almost certainly result in our designing a mere platitude. On the other hand is the temptation to design a pattern as we might do for a piece of woven goods, where the structure is boldly shown, and the members strongly marked; but such a pattern done in a cheap material will be apt to look over-ambitious, and, being stretched out flat on the wall, will lead the eye overmuch to its geometrical lines, and all repose will be lost.

What we have to do to meet this difficulty is to create due paper-stainers' flowers and leaves, forms that are obviously fit for printing with a block; to mask the construction of our pattern enough to prevent people from counting the repeats of our pattern, while we manage to lull their curiosity to trace it out; to be careful to cover our ground equably. If we are successful in these two last things, we shall attain a look of satisfying mystery, which is an essential in all patterned goods, and which in paperhangings must be done by the designer, since, as aforesaid, they fall into no folds, and have no special beauty of material to attract the eye.

Furthermore, we must, if we possibly can, avoid making accidental lines, which are very apt to turn up when a pattern is repeated over a wall. As to such lines, vertical lines are the worst; diagonal ones are pretty bad, and horizontal ones do not so much matter.

As to the colouring of paperhangings, it is much on the same footing as the forms of the design. The material being commonplace and the manufacture mechanical, the colour should above all things be modest; though there are plenty of pigments which might tempt us into making our colour very bright or even very rich, we shall do well to be specially cautious in their use, and not to attempt bright-ness unless we are working in a very light key of colour, and if our general tone is bound to be deep, to keep the colour grey. You understand, of course, that no colour should ever be muddy or dingy; to make goods of such sort shows inexperience, and to persist in making them, incapacity. Now, a last word about this craft. Have papers with pretty patterns if you like them, but if you don't, I beg of you, quite seriously, to have nothing to do with them, but white-wash your wall and be done with it. That, I distinctly inform you, is the way, and the only way, that you who do not care about the art can help us manufacturers.

So much for paper-staining. The craft of printing on cloth (gener-ally cotton) we may take next as a kindred art. Yet we don't meet quite the same difficulties here, for it is generally used so that it falls into folds or turns round furniture; so we need not be so anxious about masking the structure of our patterns, or so afraid of accidental lines; and as to the colour, our material is so much more interesting that we may indulge in any brightness we can get out of genuine dyes, which for the rest have always some beauty of their own.

As to the spirit of the designs for this craft, for some reason or other, I imagine because it is so decidedly an Eastern manufacture, it seems to call for specially fantastic forms. A pattern which would make a very good paperhanging would often look dull and uninterest-ing as a chintz pattern. The naïvest of flowers with which you may do anything that is not ugly; birds and animals, no less naïve, all made up of spots and stripes and flecks of broken colour, these seem the sort of thing we ask for. You cannot well go wrong so long as you avoid commonplace, and keep somewhat on the daylight side of nightmare. Only you must remember that, considering the price of the material it is done on, this craft is a specially troublesome one; so that in designing for it you must take special care that every fresh process you lay upon a poor filmy piece of cotton, worth fourpence or fivepence per yard, should really add beauty to it, and not be done for whim's sake. I really think you would be shocked if you knew how much trouble and anxiety can be thrown away on such trifles: what a stupendous weight of energy and the highest science have been brought to bear upon producing a pattern consisting of three black dots and a pink line, done in some special manner on a piece of cotton cloth. I don't quite know what excuse for this trifling a philosopher might find, but to a craftsman like myself it seems mere barbarous twaddle, and I beg of you who wish to avoid complic-ity with it never to buy a piece of patterned cotton, if you don't think the pattern pretty: that's the only way you can help us crafts-men in the matter; that is what I call patronage of art.

Now as to the pattern-designing for figured woven stuffs, which is one of the most important branches of the art. Here, as you will find yourself more limited by special material than in the branches above named, so you will not be so much beset by the dangers of commonplace. You cannot choose but make your flowers weavers' flowers. On the other hand, as the craft is a nobler one than paper-staining or cotton-printing, it claims from us a higher and more dignified style of design. Your forms must be clearer and sharper, your drawing more exquisite, your pattern must have more of meaning and history in it: in a word, your design must be more concentrated than in what we have hitherto been considering; yet again, if you have to risk more, you have some compensation in the fact that you will not be hampered by any necessity for masking the construction of your pattern, both because your stuff is pretty sure to be used falling into folds, and will be wrought in some material that is beautiful in itself, more or less; so that there will be a play of light and shade on it, which will give subordinate incident, and minimize the risk of hardness. Moreover, these last facts about woven stuffs call on you to design in a bolder fashion and on a larger scale than for stiffer and duller-surfaced goods; so we will say that the special qualities needful for a good design for woven stuff are breadth and boldness, ingenuity and closeness of invention, clear definite detail joined to intricacy of parts, and, finally, a distinct appeal to the imagination by skilful suggestion of delightful pieces of nature.

In saying this about woven stuffs I have been thinking of goods woven by the shuttle in the common looms, which produce recurring patterns; there are, however, two forms of the weaver's craft which are outside these, and on which I will say a few words: first, the art of tapestry-weaving, in which the subjects are so elaborate that, of necessity, it has thrown aside all mechanical aid, and is wrought by the most primitive process of weaving, its loom being a tool rather than a machine. Under these circumstances it would be somewhat of a waste of labour to weave recurring patterns in it, though in less mechanical times it has been done. I have said that you could scarcely bring a whole bush into a room for your wall decoration, but since in this case the mechanical imitations are so few, and the colour obtainable in its materials is so deep, rich, and varied, as to be unattainable by anything else than the hand of a good painter in a finished picture, you really may almost turn your wall into a rose-hedge or a deep forest, for its material and general capabilities almost compel us to fashion plane above plane of rich, crisp, and varying foliage with bright blossoms, or strange birds showing through the intervals. However, such designs as this must be looked upon as a sort of halting-place on the way to historical art, and may be so infinitely varied that we have not time to dwell upon it.

The second of these offshoots of the weaver's craft is the craft of carpet-making: by which I mean the real art and not the makeshift goods woven purely mechanically. Now this craft, despite its near kinship as to technical matters with tapestry, is very specially a pattern-designer's affair. As to designing for it, I must say it is mighty difficult because from the nature of it we are bound to make our carpet not only a passable piece of colour, but even an exquisite one, and, at the same time, we must get enough of form and meaning into it to justify our making it at all in these Western parts of the world; since as to the mere colour we are not likely to beat, and may well be pleased if we equal, an ordinary genuine Eastern specimen.

Once more, the necessary limitations of the art will make us, not mar us, if we have courage and skill to face and overcome them. As for a carpet-design, it seems quite clear that it should be quite flat, that it should give no more at least than the merest hint of one plane behind another; and this, I take it, not so much for the obvious reason that we don't feel comfortable in walking over what simulates high relief, but rather because in a carpet we specially desire quality in material and colour; that is, every little bit of surface must have its own individual beauty of material and colour. Nothing must thrust this necessity out of view in a carpet. Now, if in our coarse, worsted mosaic we make awkward attempts at shading and softening tint into tint, we shall dirty our colour and so degrade our material; our mosaic will look coarse, as it ought never to look; we shall expose our lack of invention, and shall be parties to the making of an expensive piece of goods for no good reason.

Now, the way to get the design flat, and at the same time to make it both refined and effective in colour, in a carpet-design, is to follow the second kind of relief I told you of, and to surround all or most of your figure by a line of another tint, and to remember while you are doing it that it is done for this end, and not to make your design look neat and trim. If this is well done, your pieces of colour will look gemlike and beautiful in themselves, your flowers will be due carpet-flowers, and the effect of the whole will be soft and pleasing. But I admit that you will probably have to go to the school of the Eastern designers to attain excellence in the art, as this in its perfection is a speciality of theirs. Now, after all, I am bound to say that when these difficulties are conquered, I, as a Western man and a picture-lover, must still insist on plenty of meaning in your patterns; I must have unmistakable suggestions of gardens and fields, and strange trees, boughs, and tendrils, or I can't do with your pattern, but must take the first piece of nonsense-work a Kurdish shepherd has woven from tradition and memory; all the more, as even in that there will be some hint of past history.

Since carpets are always bordered cloths, this will be a good place for saying a little on the subject of borders, which will apply somewhat to other kinds of wares. You may take it that there are two kinds of border: one that is merely a finish to a cloth, to keep it from looking frayed out, as it were, and which doesn't attract much notice. Such a border will not vary much from the colour of the cloth it bounds, and will have in its construction many of the elements of the construction of the filling-pattern; though it must be strongly marked enough to fix that filling in its place, so to say.

The other kind of border is meant to draw the eye to it more or less, and is sometimes of more importance than the filling; so that it will be markedly different in colour, and as to pattern will rather help out that of the filling by opposing its lines than by running with them. Of these borders, the first, I think, is the fitter when you are using a broad border; the second does best for a narrow one.

All borders should be made up of several members, even where they are narrow, or they will look bald and poor, and ruin the whole cloth. This is very important to remember.

The turning the corner of a border is a difficult business, and will try your designing skill rudely; but I advise you to face it, and not to stop your border at the corner by a rosette or what not. As a rule, you should make it run on, whereby you will at least earn the praise of trying to do your best.

As to the relative proportion of filling and border: if your filling be important in subject, and your cloth large, especially if it be long, your border is best to be narrow, but bright and sparkling, harder and sharper than the filling, but smaller in its members; if, on the contrary, the filling be broken in colour and small in subject, then have a wide border, important in subject, clear and well defined in drawing, but by no means hard in relief.

Remember on this head, once more, that the bigger your cloth is the narrower in comparison should be your border; a wide border has a most curious tendency towards making the whole cloth look small.

So much very briefly about carpet-designing and weaving in general; and, once more, those of you who don't yet know what a pretty pattern is, and who don't care about a pattern, don't be dragooned by custom into having a pattern because it is a pattern, either on your carpets or your curtains, or even your waistcoats. That's the way that you, at present, can help the art of pattern-designing.

I will finish my incomplete catalogue of the crafts that need the pattern-designer by saying a few words on designing for embroidery and for pottery-painting.

As to embroidery-designing, it stands midway between that for tapestry and that for carpets; but as its technical limits are much less narrow than those of the latter craft, it is very apt to lead people into cheap and commonplace naturalism: now, indeed, it is a delightful idea to cover a piece of linen cloth with roses and jonquils and tulips, done quite natural with the needle, and we can't go too far in that direction if we only remember the needs of our material and the nature of our craft in general: these demand that our roses and the like, however unmistakably roses, shall be quaint and naïve to the last degree, and also, since we are using specially beautiful materials, that we shall make the most of them, and not forget that we are gardening with silk and gold-thread; and lastly, that in an art which may be accused by ill-natured persons of being a superfluity of life, we must be specially careful that it shall be beautiful. and not spare labour to make it sedulously elegant of form, and every part of it refined in line and colour.

In pottery-painting we are more than ever in danger of falling into sham naturalistic platitude, since we have no longer to stamp our designs with a rough wood-block on paper or cotton, nor have we to build up our outlines by laying square by square of colour, but, pencil in hand, may do pretty much what we will. So we must be a law to ourselves, and when we get a tile or a plate to ornament remember two things; first, the confined space or odd shape we have to work in; and second, the way in which the design has to be executed. As to the first point, if we are not to miss our aim altogether, we must do something ingenious and inventive, something that will at once surprise and please people, which will take hold of their eyes as something new, and force them to look at it. Within these limits we may do as we please, so long as we do not forget, in the next place, that our design has to be pencilled by an instrument difficult to use, but delightful to handle when the difficulty is overcome, a long, sharp-pointed brush charged with heavy colour, which pencilling should be done with a firm, deliberate, and decided, but speedy hand.

I feel the more bound to insist on this in pottery-painting because of late a kind of caricature art has been going about in the shape of elaborately painted dishes of the most disastrous design and execution. Most often the designers of these have thought they have done all they need when they have drawn a bunch of flowers or a spray without any attempt at arrangement, and coloured it in imitation of a coarse daub in oils, without the least thought of what pigments were within reach of the pottery-painter. Such things teach nothing but the art of how not to do it.

Now, once more, those of you who are unconscious that there is any beauty in a pattern painted on pottery can at least help the art by utterly refusing to have any pattern on it; and I beg them earnestly and sincerely to take that amount of trouble.

You may think that I have been wandering from my point in saying so much about the various crafts for which designs have to be made, rather than treating of the designs in general; but I have not done so by accident, at any rate, but because I want you to understand that I think it of capital importance that a pattern-designer should know all about the craft for which he has to draw. Neither will knowledge only suffice him; he must have full sympathy with the craft and love it, or he can never do honour to the special material he is designing for. Without this knowledge and sympathy the cleverest of men will do nothing but provide platitudes for the public and wanton puzzles for those who execute the work to break their hearts over.

Perhaps a few words on pattern-designing generally may be of some use to some of you, though the chances are you will have heard the same thing said often enough before.

Above all things, avoid vagueness; run any risk of failure rather than involve yourselves in a tangle of poor weak lines that people can't make out. Definite form bounded by firm outline is a necessity for all ornament. If you have any inclination towards that shorthand of picture-painters, which they use when they are in a hurry, and which people call sketching, give up pattern-designing, for you have no turn for it. I repeat, do not be afraid of your design or try to muddle it up so that people can scarce see it; if it is arranged on good lines, and its details are beautiful, you need not fear its looking hard so long as it covers the ground well and is not wrong in colour.

Rational growth is necessary to all patterns, or at least the hint of such growth; and in recurring patterns, at least, the noblest are those where one thing grows visibly and necessarily from another. Take heed in this growth that each member of it be strong and crisp, that the lines do not get thready or flabby or too far from their stock to sprout firmly and vigorously; even where a line ends it should look as if it had plenty of capacity for more growth if so it would.

Again, as to dealing with nature. To take a natural spray of what not and torture it into certain lines, is a hopeless way of designing a pattern. In all good pattern-designs the idea comes first, as in all other designs, e.g., a man says, I will make a pattern which I will mean to give people an idea of a rose-hedge with the sun through it; and he sees it in such and such a way; then, and not till then, he sets to work to draw his flowers, his leaves and thorns, and so forth, and so carries out his idea.

In choosing natural forms be rather shy of certain very obviously decorative ones, e.g., bind-weed, passion-flower, and the poorer forms of ivy, used without the natural copiousness. I should call these trouble-savers, and warn you of them, unless you are going to take an extra amount of trouble over them. We have had them used so cheaply this long while that we are sick of them.

On the other hand, outlandishness is a snare. I have said that it was good and reasonable to ask for obviously natural flowers in embroidery; one might have said the same about all ornamental work, and further, that those natural forms which are at once most familiar and most delightful to us, as well from association as from beauty, are the best for our purpose. The rose, the lily, the tulip, the oak, the vine, and all the herbs and trees that even we cockneys know about, they will serve our turn better than queer, outlandish, upsidedown-looking growths. If we cannot be original with these simple things, we shan't help ourselves out by the uncouth ones.

A very few words as to style. Most true it is that if all art ought to belong specially to its time and nation, this should be, above all, the case with such a comparatively easy art as pattern-designing. Yet I am not so simple as to suppose that we can suddenly build up a style out of the wreck of inanity into which we had fallen a little while ago, without any help from the ages of art. And though I would say loudly, Don't copy any style at all, but make your own; yet you must study the history of your art, or you will be nose-led by the first bad copyist of it that you come across. Well, my advice to you in this matter is very simple. Study any or all of the styles that have real growth in them, and as for the others, don't do more than give a passing glance at them, for they can do you no good. From the days of ancient Egypt to the time of the sickness of mediaeval art the architectural arts had life and growth in them: study all that as much as you please; but, from the times of the Renaissance onwards, life, growth, and hope are gone from these, and as matters of study you have nothing to do with them. The architectural art that was in use even at the time of the great masters of the Renaissance will mislead you if you try to found any style of pattern-designing upon it, and this in spite of many splendid qualities in itself. It is not the art of hope, but of decay. As to what followed it, and culminated in the bundle of degraded whims falsely called a style, that so fitly expresses the corruption of the days of Louis XV, you need not even look at that in passing. More noble failures will serve your turn better, even for warnings.

If I am speaking to any pattern-designers here, or to those that have any influence over their lives, I should like to remind them of one thing, that the constant designing of recurring patterns is a very harassing business, and should always be supplemented with some distinctly executive work. Those who in the present unhappy state of the arts do not design for work which they carry out themselves should relieve their brain by drawing from the human figure, from flowers or landscapes or old pictures, or some such things; by doing something which is not a diagram, but is an end in itself, or they will either suffer terribly or become quite stupid. A friend of mine, who is a Manchester calico-printer told me the other day that the shifty and clever designers who draw the thousand and one ingenious and sometimes pretty patterns for garment-goods which Manchester buys of Paris, have a great tendency to go mad, and often do so; and I cannot wonder at it.

That such a caution as this should be necessary is a woeful commentary on the state of those arts on which pattern-designing lives. That the art whose office it was to give rest and pleasure to the toiling hand should now have become a torment to the wearied brain of man, is a strange inversion of the natural order of things, and, to my mind, points to matters far more serious than would at first sight seem to be wrapped up in the question of designing pretty patterns for our common household goods.

I must ask your patience for a few minutes yet while I say a word or two on these matters, for I have made a compact with myself that I will never address my countrymen on the subject of art without speaking as briefly, but also as plainly as I can, on the degradation of labour which I believe to be the great danger to civilization, as it has certainly proved itself to be the very bane of art.

Foresight and goodwill have set on foot many schemes for educating people before they come to working years: for tending them when misfortune or sickness prevents them from working, for amusing them reasonably when they are at leisure from their work: aims that are all good and some necessary to the well-being of our race.

But can they alone touch the heart of the matter, to be sedulous about what people do with their time till they are growing out of childhood into youth, to take pains to add to the pleasure of their few hours of rest, and at the same time never to give a thought to the way in which they spend their working hours (ten hours a day, and a long time it is to spend in wishing we were come to the end of it) between the ages of thirteen and seventy? This, I say, does seem to me a strange shutting of the eyes to one of the main difficulties of life, a strange turning from the great question which all well-wishers to their neighbours ought to ask: How can men gain hope and pleasure in their daily work?

I do not profess to foretell what will happen to the world if we persist in keeping our eyes shut on this point; but one thing I know will happen: the extinction of all art. I say I know it will happen, and indeed it is happening now, and unless we take the other turn before long it will soon be all done. You would not believe me if I professed to think that a light matter even by itself: the thrusting out of all beauty from the life of man; but when one knows what lies at the bottom of it, how much heavier it seems, the thrusting out of all pleasure and self-respect from man's daily work, the helplessly letting that daily work become a mere blind instrument for the over-peopling of the world, for the ceaseless multiplication of causeless and miserable lives.

Surely I am speaking to some whose lives, like mine, are blessed with pleasurable and honourable work, who cannot bear the thought that we are to go on shutting our eyes to this, and to do nothing because our time on earth is not long. Can we not face the evil and do our best to amend it our very selves? If it be a necessary evil, let us at least do our share of proving that it is so by withstanding it to the utmost. The worst that can happen to us rebels in that case is to be swept away before the flood of that necessity, which will happen to us no less if we do not struggle against it – if we are flunkies, not rebels. Indeed, you may think that the metaphor is all too true, and that we are but mere straws in that resistless flood. But don't let us strain a metaphor; for we are no straws, but men, with each one of us a will and aspirations, and with duties to fulfil; so let us see after all what we can do to prove whether it be necessary that art should perish: that is, whether men should live in an ugly world, with no work to do in it but wearisome work.

Well, first we must be conscious of the evil, as I believe some are who do not dare to acknowledge it. And next we must dare to acknowledge it, as some do who dare not act further in the matter.

And next: why, a good deal next, though it may be put into few words, for steady rebellion is a heavyish matter to take in hand; and I tell you that every one who loves art in these days and dares pursue it to the uttermost is a dangerous rebel enough; and I will finish by speaking of one or two things that we must do to fit ourselves for our troublous life of rebellion.

We ought to get to understand the value of intelligent work, the work of men's hands guided by their brains, and to take that, though it be rough, rather than the unintelligent work of machines or slaves, though it be delicate; to refuse altogether to use machine-made work unless where the nature of the thing made compels it, or where the machine does what mere human suffering would otherwise have to do: to have a high standard of excellence in wares and not to accept makeshifts for the real thing, but rather to go without; to have no ornament merely for fashion's sake, but only because we really think it beautiful, otherwise to go without it; not to live in an ugly and squalid place (such as London) for the sake of mere excitement or the like, but only because our duties bind us to it; to treat the natural beauty of the earth as a holy thing not to be rashly dealt with for any consideration; to treat with the utmost care whatever of architecture and the like is left us of the times of art. I deny that it can ever be our own to do as we like with; it is the property of the world, that we hold in trust for those that come after us.

Here is a set of things not easy to do (as it seems), which I believe to be the duty of all men taking some trouble in the art of life, and not giving in to the barbarous and cumbrous luxury, or comfort as you may please to call it, which some of us are proud of as a mark of our civilization, but which I sometimes think is really fated to stifle all art, and in the long run all intelligence, unless we grow wise in time and look to it.

I dare say that nobody but men who consciously or unconsciously care about art would think of binding themselves by these rules, but perhaps some others may join them in trying to act on these that follow. To have as little as possible to do with middlemen, but to bring together the makers and the buyers of goods as closely as possible. To do our best to further the independence and reasonable leisure of all handicraftsmen. To eschew all bargains, real or imaginary (they are mostly the latter), and to be anxious to pay and to get what a piece of goods is really worth. To that end to try to understand the difference between good and bad in wares, which will also give us an insight into the craftsman's troubles, and will tend to do away with an ignorant impatience and ill-temper which is much too common in our dealings with them nowadays.

In short, as I have said before that we must strive against barbarous luxury, so here I must say that we must strive against barbarous waste. What we have to do is to try to put co-operation in the place of competition in the dealings of men; that is, in place of commercial war, with all the waste and injustice of war, which, since men are foolish rather than malicious, has to be softened ever and anon by weak compliance and contemptuous good-nature, we must strive to put commercial peace with justice and thrift beside it.

I ask you not to think that I have been wandering from my point in saying all this: I have had to talk to you to-night about popular art, the foundation on which all art stands. I could not go through the dreary task of speaking to you of a phantom of bygone times, of a thing with no life in it; I must speak of a living thing with hope in it, or hold my peace; and most deeply am I convinced that popular art cannot live if labour is to be for ever the thrall of muddle, dishonesty, and disunion. Cheerfully I admit that I see signs about us of a coming time of order, goodwill, and union, and it is that which has given me the courage to say to you these few last words, and to hint to you what in my poor judgment we each and all of us who have the cause at heart may do to further the cause.

USEFUL WORK
versus
USELESS TOIL

* * *

Lecture given to
the Hampstead Liberal Club,
London, 1884

Reprinted in *Signs of Change*,
London, 1888

main points: the people who actually work hard & a lot (working class) don't have & the people who work little or none (rich mid class) have all the $ & dictate pay of low class

The above title may strike some of my readers as strange. It is assumed by most people nowadays that all work is useful, and by most *well-to-do* people that all work is desirable. Most people, well-to-do or not, believe that, even when a man is doing work which appears to be useless, he is earning his livelihood by it – he is 'employed', as the phrase goes; and most of those who are well-to-do cheer on the happy worker with congratulations and praises, if he is only 'industrious' enough and deprives himself of all pleasure and holidays in the sacred cause of labour. In short, it has become an article of the creed of modern morality that all labour is good in itself – a convenient belief to those who live on the labour of others. But as to those on whom they live, I recommend them not to take it on trust, but to look into the matter a little deeper.

Let us grant, first, that the race of man must either labour or perish. Nature does not give us our livelihood gratis; we must win it by toil of some sort or degree. Let us see, then, if she does not give us some compensation for this compulsion to labour, since certainly in other matters she takes care to make the acts necessary to the continuance of life in the individual and the race not only endurable, but even pleasurable.

You may be sure that she does so, that it is of the nature of man, when he is not diseased, to take pleasure in his work under certain conditions. And, yet, we must say in the teeth of the hypocritical praise of all labour, whatsoever it may be, of which I have made mention, that there is some labour which is so far from being a blessing that it is a curse; that it would be better for the community and for the worker if the latter were to fold his hands and refuse to work, and either die or let us pack him off to the workhouse or prison – which you will.

Here, you see, are two kinds of work – one good, the other bad; one not far removed from a blessing, a lightening of life; the other a mere curse, a burden to life.

What is the difference between them, then? This: one has hope in it, the other has not. It is manly to do the one kind of work, and manly also to refuse to do the other.

What is the nature of the hope which, when it is present in work, makes it worth doing?

It is threefold, I think – hope of rest, hope of product, hope of pleasure in the work itself; and hope of these also in some abundance and of good quality; rest enough and good enough to be worth having; product worth having by one who is neither a fool nor an ascetic; pleasure enough for all for us to be conscious of it while we are at work; not a mere habit, the loss of which we shall feel as a fidgety man feels the loss of the bit of string he fidgets with.

I have put the hope of rest first because it is the simplest and most natural part of our hope. Whatever pleasure there is in some work, there is certainly some pain in all work, the beast-like pain of stirring up our slumbering energies to action, the beast-like dread of change when things are pretty well with us; and the compensation for this animal pain is animal rest. We must feel while we are working that the time will come when we shall not have to work. Also the rest, when it comes, must be long enough to allow us to enjoy it; it must be longer than is merely necessary for us to recover the strength we have expended in working, and it must be animal rest also in this, that it must not be disturbed by anxiety, else we shall not be able to enjoy it. If we have this amount and kind of rest we shall, so far, be no worse off than the beasts.

As to the hope of product, I have said that Nature compels us to work for that. It remains for *us* to look to it that we *do* really produce something, and not nothing, or at least nothing that we want or are allowed to use. If we look to this and use our wills we shall, so far, be better than machines.

The hope of pleasure in the work itself: how strange that hope must seem to some of my readers – to most of them! Yet I think that to all living things there is a pleasure in the exercise of their energies, and that even beasts rejoice in being lithe and swift and strong. But a man at work, making something which he feels will exist because he is working at it and wills it, is exercising the energies of his mind and soul as well as of his body. Memory and imagination help him as he works. Not only his own thoughts, but the thoughts of the men of past ages guide his hands; and, as a part of the human race, he creates. If we work thus we shall be men, and our days will be happy and eventful.

Thus worthy work carries with it the hope of pleasure in rest, the hope of the pleasure in our using what it makes, and the hope of pleasure in our daily creative skill.

All other work but this is worthless; it is slaves' work – mere toiling to live, that we may live to toil.

Therefore, since we have, as it were, a pair of scales in which to weigh the work now done in the world, let us use them. Let us estimate the worthiness of the work we do, after so many thousand years of toil, so many promises of hope deferred, such boundless exultation over the progress of civilization and the gain of liberty.

Now, the first thing as to the work done in civilization and the easiest to notice is that it is portioned out very unequally amongst the different classes of society. First, there are people – not a few – who do no work, and make no pretence of doing any. Next, there are people, and very many of them, who work fairly hard, though with abundant easements and holidays, claimed and allowed; and lastly, there are people who work so hard that they may be said to do nothing else than work, and are accordingly called 'the working classes', as distinguished from the middle classes and the rich, or aristocracy, whom I have mentioned above.

It is clear that this inequality presses heavily upon the 'working' class, and must visibly tend to destroy their hope of rest at least, and so, in that particular, make them worse off than mere beasts of the field; but that is not the sum and end of our folly of turning useful work into useless toil, but only the beginning of it.

For first, as to the class of rich people doing no work, we all know that they consume a great deal while they produce nothing. Therefore, clearly, they have to be kept at the expense of those who do work, just as paupers have, and are a mere burden on the community. In these days there are many who have learned to see this, though they can see no further into the evils of our present system, and have formed no idea of any scheme for getting rid of this burden; though perhaps they have a vague hope that changes in the system of voting for members of the House of Commons may, as if by magic, tend in that direction. With such hopes or superstitions we need not trouble ourselves. Moreover, this class, the aristocracy, once thought most necessary to the State, is scant of numbers, and has now no power of its own, but depends on the support of the class next below it – the middle class. In fact, it is really composed either of the most success-ful men of that class, or of their immediate descendants.

As to the middle class, including the trading, manufacturing, and professional people of our society, they do, as a rule, seem to work quite hard enough, and so at first sight might be thought to help the community, and not burden it. But by far the greater part of them, though they work, do not produce, and even when they do produce, as in the case of those engaged (wastefully indeed) in the distribution of goods, or doctors, or (genuine) artists and literary men, they consume out of all proportion to their due share. The commercial and manufacturing part of them, the most powerful part, spend their lives and energies in fighting amongst themselves for their respective shares of the wealth which they *force* the genuine workers to provide for them; the others are almost wholly the hangers-on of these; they do not work for the public, but a privileged class: they are the parasites of property, sometimes, as in the case of lawyers, undisguis-edly so; sometimes, as the doctors and others above mentioned, professing to be useful, but too often of no use save as supporters of the system of folly, fraud, and tyranny of which they form a part. And all these we must remember have, as a rule, one aim in view; not the production of utilities, but the gaining of a position either for themselves or their children in which they will not have to work at all. It is their ambition and the end of their whole lives to gain, if not for themselves, yet at least for their children, the proud position of being obvious burdens on the community. For their work itself, in spite of the sham dignity with which they surround it, they care nothing: save a few enthusiasts, men of science, art, or letters, who, if they are not the salt of the earth, are at least (and oh, the pity of it!) the salt of the miserable system of which they are the slaves, which

damning society loss of hope
biblical reference

hinders and thwarts them at every turn, and even sometimes corrupts them.

Here then is another class, this time very numerous and all-powerful, which produces very little and consumes enormously, and is therefore in the main supported, as paupers are, by the real producers. The class that remains to be considered produces all that is produced, and supports both itself and the other classes, though it is placed in a position of inferiority to them; real inferiority, mind you, involving a degradation both of mind and body. But it is a necessary consequence of this tyranny and folly that again many of these workers are not producers. A vast number of them once more are merely parasites of property, some of them openly so, as the soldiers by land and sea who are kept on foot for the perpetuating of national rivalries and enmities, and for the purposes of the national struggle for the share of the product of unpaid labour. But besides this obvious burden on the producers and the scarcely less obvious one of domestic servants, there is first the army of clerks, shop-assistants, and so forth, who are engaged in the service of the private war for wealth, which, as above said, is the real occupation of the well-to-do middle class. This is a larger body of workers than might be supposed, for it includes amongst others all those engaged in what I should call competitive salesmanship, or, to use a less dignified word, the puffery of wares, which has now got to such a pitch that there are many things which cost far more to sell than they do to make.

Next there is the mass of people employed in making all those articles of folly and luxury, the demand for which is the outcome of the existence of the rich non-producing classes; things which people leading a manly and uncorrupted life would not ask for or dream of. These things, whoever may gainsay me, I will for ever refuse to call wealth: they are not wealth, but waste. Wealth is what Nature gives us and what a reasonable man can make out of the gifts of Nature for his reasonable use. The sunlight, the fresh air, the unspoiled face of the earth, food, raiment and housing necessary and decent; the storing up of knowledge of all kinds, and the power of disseminating it; means of free communication between man and man; works of art, the beauty which man creates when he is most a man, most aspiring and thoughtful – all things which serve the pleasure of people, free, manly, and uncorrupted. This is wealth. Nor can I think of anything worth having which does not come under one or other of these heads. But think, I beseech you, of the product of England, the workshop of the world, and will you not be bewildered, as I am, at the thought of the mass of things which no sane man could desire, but which our useless toil makes – and sells?

Now, further, there is even a sadder industry yet, which is forced on many, very many, of our workers – the making of wares which are necessary to them and their brethren, *because they are an inferior class*. For if many men live without producing, nay, must live lives so empty and foolish that they *force* a great part of the workers to produce wares which no one needs, not even the rich, it follows that most men must be poor; and, living as they do on wages from those whom they support, cannot get for their use the *goods* which men naturally desire, but must put up with miserable makeshifts for them, with coarse food that does not nourish, with rotten raiment which does not shelter, with wretched houses which may well make a town-dweller in civilization look back with regret to the tent of the nomad tribe, or the cave of the prehistoric savage. Nay, the workers must even lend a hand to the great industrial invention of the age – adulteration, and by its help produce for their own use shams and mockeries of the luxury of the rich; for the wage-earners must always live as the wage-payers bid them, and their very habits of life are *forced* on them by their masters.

But it is waste of time to try to express in words due contempt of the productions of the much-praised cheapness of our epoch. It must be enough to say that this cheapness is necessary to the system of exploiting on which modern manufacture rests. In other words, our society includes a great mass of slaves, who must be fed, clothed, housed and amused as slaves, and that their daily necessity compels them to make the slave-wares whose use is the perpetuation of their slavery.

To sum up, then, concerning the manner of work in civilized States, these States are composed of three classes – a class which does not even pretend to work, a class which pretends to work but which produces nothing, and a class which works, but is compelled by the other two classes to do work which is often unproductive.

Civilization therefore wastes its own resources, and will do so as long as the present system lasts. These are cold words with which to describe the tyranny under which we suffer; try then to consider what they mean.

There is a certain amount of natural material and of natural forces in the world, and a certain amount of labour-power inherent in the persons of the men that inhabit it. Men urged by their necessities and desires have laboured for many thousands of years at the task of subjugating the forces of Nature and of making the natural material useful to them. To our eyes, since we cannot see into the future, that struggle with Nature seems nearly over, and the victory of the human race over her nearly complete. And, looking backwards to the time when history first began, we note that the progress of that victory has been far swifter and more startling within the last two hundred years than ever before. Surely, therefore, we moderns ought to be in all ways vastly better off than any who have gone before us. Surely we ought, one and all of us, to be wealthy, to be well furnished with the good things which our victory over Nature has won for us.

But what is the real fact? Who will dare to deny that the great mass of civilized men are poor? So poor are they that it is mere childishness troubling ourselves to discuss whether perhaps they are in some ways a little better off than their forefathers. They are poor; nor can their poverty be measured by the poverty of a resourceless savage, for he knows of nothing else than his poverty; that he should be cold, hungry, houseless, dirty, ignorant, all that is to him as natural as that he should have a skin. But for us, for the most of us, civilization has bred desires which she forbids us to satisfy, and so is not merely a niggard but a torturer also.

Thus then have the fruits of our victory over Nature been stolen from us, thus has compulsion by Nature to labour in hope of rest, gain, and pleasure been turned into compulsion by man to labour in hope – of living to labour!

What shall we do then, can we mend it?

Well, remember once more that it is not our remote ancestors who achieved the victory over Nature, but our fathers, nay, our very selves. For us to sit hopeless and helpless then would be a strange folly indeed: be sure that we can amend it. What, then, is the first thing to be done?

We have seen that modern society is divided into two classes, one of which is *privileged* to be kept by the labour of the other — that is, it forces the other to work for it and takes from this inferior class everything that it *can* take from it, and uses the wealth so taken to keep its own members in a superior position, to make them beings of a higher order than the others: longer lived, more beautiful, more honoured, more refined than those of the other class. I do not say that it troubles itself about its members being *positively* long lived, beautiful or refined, but merely insists that they shall be so *relatively* to the inferior class. As also its cannot use the labour-power of the inferior class fairly in producing real wealth, it wastes it wholesale in the production of rubbish.

It is this robbery and waste on the part of the minority which keeps the majority poor; if it could be shown that it is necessary for the preservation of society that this should be submitted to, little more could be said on the matter, save that the despair of the oppressed majority would probably at some time or other destroy Society. But it has been shown, on the contrary, even by such incomplete experiments, for instance, as Co-operation (so-called), that the existence of a privileged class is by no means necessary for the production of wealth, but rather for the 'government' of the producers of wealth, or, in other words, for the upholding of privilege.

The first step to be taken then is to abolish a class of men privileged to shirk their duties as men, thus forcing others to do the work which they refuse to do. All must work according to their ability, and so produce what they consume — that is, each man should work as well as he can for his own livelihood, and his livelihood should be assured to him; that is to say, all the advantages which society would provide for each and all of its members.

Thus, at last, would true Society be founded. It would rest on equality of condition. No man would be tormented for the benefit of another — nay, no one man would be tormented for the benefit of Society. Nor, indeed, can that order be called Society which is not upheld for the benefit of every one of its members.

But since men live now, badly as they live, when so many people do not produce at all, and when so much work is wasted, it is clear that, under conditions where all produced and no work was wasted, not only would every one work with the certain hope of gaining a due share of wealth by his work, but also he could not miss his due share of rest. Here, then, are two out of the three kinds of hope mentioned above as an essential part of worthy work assured to the worker. When class-robbery is abolished, every man will reap the fruits of his labour, every man will have due rest – leisure, that is. Some Socialists might say we need not go any further than this; it is enough that the worker should get the full produce of his work, and that his rest should be abundant. But though the compulsion of man's tyranny is thus abolished, I yet demand compensation for the compulsion of Nature's necessity. As long as the work is repulsive it will still be a burden which must be taken up daily, and even so would mar our life, even though the hours of labour were short. What we want to do is to add to our wealth without diminishing our pleasure. Nature will not be finally conquered till our work becomes a part of the pleasure of our lives.

That first step of freeing people from the compulsion to labour needlessly will at least put us on the way towards this happy end; for we shall then have time and opportunities for bringing it about. As things are now, between the waste of labour-power in mere idleness and its waste in unproductive work, it is clear that the world of civilization is supported by a small part of its people; when *all* were working *usefully* for its support, the share of work which each would have to do would be but small, if our standard of life were about on the footing of what well-to-do and refined people now think desirable. We shall have labour-power to spare, and shall, in short, be as wealthy as we please. It will be easy to live. If we were to wake up some morning now, under our present system, and find it 'easy to live', that system would force us to set to work at once and make it hard to live; we should call that 'developing our resources', or some such fine name. The multiplication of labour has become a necessity for us, and as long as that goes on no ingenuity in the invention of machines will be of any real use to us. Each new machine will cause a certain amount of misery among the workers whose special industry it may disturb; so many of them will be reduced from skilled to unskilled workmen, and then gradually matters will slip into their due grooves, and all will work apparently smoothly again; and if it were not that all this is preparing revolution, things would be, for the greater part of men, just as they were before the new wonderful invention.

But when revolution has made it 'easy to live', when all are working harmoniously together and there is no one to rob the worker of his time, that is to say, his life; in those coming days there will be no compulsion on us to go on producing things we do not want, no compulsion on us to labour for nothing; we shall be able calmly and thoughtfully to consider what we shall do with our wealth of labour-power. Now, for my part, I think the first use we ought to make of that wealth, of that freedom, should be to make all our labour, even the commonest and most necessary, pleasant to everybody; for thinking over the matter carefully I can see that the one course which will certainly make life happy in the face of all accidents and troubles is to take a pleasurable interest in all the details of life. And lest perchance you think that an assertion too universally accepted to be worth making, let me remind you how entirely modern civilization forbids it; with what sordid, and even terrible, details it surrounds the life of the poor, what a mechanical and empty life she forces on the rich; and how rare a holiday it is for any of us to feel ourselves a part of Nature, and unhurriedly, thoughtfully, and happily to note the course of our lives amidst all the little links of events which connect them with the lives of others, and build up the great whole of humanity.

But such a holiday our whole lives might be, if we were resolute to make all our labour reasonable and pleasant. But we must be resolute indeed; for no half measures will help us here. It has been said already that our present joyless labour, and our lives scared and anxious as the life of a hunted beast, are forced upon us by the present system of producing for the profit of the privileged classes. It is necessary to state what this means. Under the present system of wages and capital the 'manufacturer' (most absurdly so called, since a manufacturer means a person who makes with his hands) having a monopoly of the means whereby the power to labour inherent in every man's body can be used for production, is the master of those who are not so privileged; he, and he alone, is able to make use of this labour-power, which, on the other hand, is the only commodity by means of which his 'capital', that is to say, the accumulated product of past labour, can be made productive to him. He therefore buys the labour-power of those who are bare of capital and can only live by selling it to him; his purpose in this transaction is to increase his capital, to make it breed. It is clear that if he paid those with whom he makes his bargain the full value of their labour, that is to say, all that they produced, he would fail in his purpose. But since he is the monopolist of the means of productive labour, he can *compel* them to make a bargain better for him and worse for them than that; which bargain is that after they have earned their livelihood, estimated according to a standard high enough to ensure their peaceable submission to his mastership, the rest (and by far the larger part as a matter of fact) of what they produce shall belong to him, shall be his *property* to do as he likes with, to use or abuse at his pleasure; which property is, as we all know, jealously guarded by army and navy, police and prison; in short, by that huge mass of physical force which superstition, habit, fear of death by starvation – IGNORANCE, in one word, among the propertyless masses, enables the propertied classes to use for the subjection of – their slaves.

Now, at other times, other evils resulting from this system may be put forward. What I want to point out now is the impossibility of our attaining to attractive labour under this system, and to repeat that it is this robbery (there is no other word for it) which wastes the available labour-power of the civilized world, forcing many men to do nothing, and many, very many more to do nothing useful; and forcing those who carry on really useful labour to most burdensome overwork. For understand once for all that the 'manufacturer' aims primarily at producing, by means of the labour he has stolen from others, not goods but profits, that is, the 'wealth' that is produced over and above the livelihood of his workmen, and the wear and tear of his machinery. Whether that 'wealth' is real or sham matters nothing to him. If it sells and yields him a 'profit' it is all right. I have said that, owing to there being rich people who have more money than they can spend reasonably, and who therefore buy sham wealth, there is waste on that side; and also that, owing to there being poor people who cannot afford to buy things which are worth making, there is waste on that side. So that the 'demand' which the capitalist 'supplies' is a false demand. The market in which he sells is 'rigged' by the miserable inequalities produced by the robbery of the system of Capital and Wages.

It is this system, therefore, which we must be resolute in getting rid of, if we are to attain to happy and useful work for all. The first step towards making labour attractive is to get the means of making labour fruitful, the Capital, including the land, machinery, factories, etc., into the hands of the community, to be used for the good of all alike, so that we might all work at 'supplying' the real 'demands' of each and all – that is to say, work for livelihood, instead of working to supply the demand of the profit market – instead of working for profit – i.e., the power of compelling other men to work against their will.

When this first step has been taken and men begin to understand that Nature wills all men either to work or starve, and when they are no longer such fools as to allow some the alternative of stealing, when this happy day is come, we shall then be relieved from the tax of waste, and consequently shall find that we have, as aforesaid, a mass of labour-power available, which will enable us to live as we please within reasonable limits. We shall no longer be hurried and driven by the fear of starvation, which at present presses no less on the greater part of men in civilized communities than it does on mere savages. The first and most obvious necessities will be so easily provided for in a community in which there is no waste of labour, that we shall have time to look round and consider what we really do want, that can be obtained without over-taxing our energies; for the often-expressed fear of mere idleness falling upon us when the force supplied by the present hierarchy of compulsion is withdrawn, is a fear which is but generated by the burden of excessive and repulsive labour, which we most of us have to bear at present.

I say once more that, in my belief, the first thing which we shall think so necessary as to be worth sacrificing some idle time for, will be the attractiveness of labour. No very heavy sacrifice will be required for attaining this object, but some *will* be required. For we may hope that men who have just waded through a period of strife and revolution will be the last to put up long with a life of mere utilitarianism, though Socialists are sometimes accused by ignorant persons of aiming at such a life. On the other hand, the ornamental part of modern life is already rotten to the core, and must be utterly swept away before the new order of things is realized. There is nothing of it – there is nothing which could come of it that could satisfy the aspirations of men set free from the tyranny of commercialism.

We must begin to build up the ornamental part of life – its pleasures, bodily and mental, scientific and artistic, social and individual – on the basis of work undertaken willingly and cheerfully, with the consciousness of benefiting ourselves and our neighbours by it. Such absolutely necessary work as we should have to do would in the first place take up but a small part of each day, and so far would not be burdensome; but it would be a task of daily recurrence, and therefore would spoil our day's pleasure unless it were made at least endurable while it lasted. In other words, all labour, even the commonest, must be made attractive.

How can this be done? – is the question the answer to which will take up the rest of this paper. In giving some hints on this question, I know that, while all Socialists will agree with many of the suggestions made, some of them may seem to some strange and venturesome. These must be considered as being given without any intention of dogmatizing, and as merely expressing my own personal opinion.

From all that has been said already it follows that labour, to be attractive, must be directed towards some obviously useful end, unless in cases where it is undertaken voluntarily by each individual as a pastime. This element of obvious usefulness is all the more to be counted on in sweetening tasks otherwise irksome, since social morality, the responsibility of man towards the life of man, will, in the new order of things, take the place of theological morality, or the responsibility of man to some abstract idea. Next, the day's work will be short. This need not be insisted on. It is clear that with work unwasted it *can* be short. It is clear also that much work which is now a torment, would be easily endurable if it were much shortened. Variety of work is the next point, and a most important one. To compel a man to do day after day the same task, without any hope of escape or change, means nothing short of turning his life into a prison-torment. Nothing but the tyranny of profit-grinding makes this necessary. A man might easily learn and practise at least three crafts, varying sedentary occupation with outdoor – occupation calling for the exercise of strong bodily energy for work in which the mind had more to do. There are few men, for instance, who would not wish to spend part of their lives in the most necessary and pleasantest of all work – cultivating the earth. One thing which will make this variety of employment possible will be the form that education will take in a socially ordered community. At present all education is directed towards the end of fitting people to take their places in the hierarchy of commerce – these as masters, those as workmen. The education of the masters is more ornamental than that of the workmen, but it is commercial still; and even at the ancient universities learning is but little regarded, unless it can in the long run be made *to pay*. Due education is a totally different thing from this, and concerns itself in finding out what different people are fit for, and helping them along the road which they are inclined to take. In a duly ordered society, therefore, young people would be taught such handicrafts as they had a turn for as a part of their education, the discipline of their minds and bodies; and adults would also have opportunities of learning in the same schools, for the development of individual capacities would be of all things chiefly aimed at by education, instead, as now, the subordination of all capacities to the great end of 'money-making' for oneself – or one's master. The amount of talent, and even genius, which the present system crushes, and which would be drawn out by such a system, would make our daily work easy and interesting.

Under this head of variety I will note one product of industry which has suffered so much from commercialism that it can scarcely be said to exist, and is, indeed, so foreign from our epoch that I fear there are some who will find it difficult to understand what I have to say on the subject, which I nevertheless must say, since it is really a most important one. I mean that side of art which is, or ought to be, done by the ordinary workman while he is about his ordinary work, and which has got to be called, very properly, Popular Art. This art,

I repeat, no longer exists now, having been killed by commercialism. But from the beginning of man's contest with Nature till the rise of the present capitalistic system, it was alive, and generally flourished. While it lasted, everything that was made by man was adorned by man, just as everything made by Nature is adorned by her. The craftsman, as he fashioned the thing he had under his hand, ornamented it so naturally and so entirely without conscious effort, that it is often difficult to distinguish where the mere utilitarian part of his work ended and the ornamental began. Now the origin of this art was the necessity that the workman felt for variety in his work, and though the beauty produced by this desire was a great gift to the world, yet the obtaining variety and pleasure in the work by the workman was a matter of more importance still, for it stamped all labour with the impress of pleasure. All this has now quite disappeared from the work of civilization. If you wish to have ornament, you must pay specially for it, and the workman is compelled to produce ornament, as he is to produce other wares. He is compelled to pretend happiness in his work, so that the beauty produced by man's hand, which was once a solace to his labour, has now become an extra burden to him, and ornament is now but one of the follies of useless toil, and perhaps not the least irksome of its fetters.

Besides the short duration of labour, its conscious usefulness, and the variety which should go with it, there is another thing needed to make it attractive, and that is pleasant surroundings. The misery and squalor which we people of civilization bear with so much complacency as a necessary part of the manufacturing system, is just as necessary to the community at large as a proportionate amount of filth would be in the house of a private rich man. If such a man were to allow the cinders to be raked all over his drawing-room, and a privy to be established in each corner of his dining-room, if he habitually made a dust and refuse heap of his once beautiful garden, never washed his sheets or changed his tablecloth, and made his family sleep five in a bed, he would surely find himself in the claws of a commission *de lunatico*. But such acts of miserly folly are just what our present society is doing daily under the compulsion of a supposed necessity, which is nothing short of madness, I beg you to bring your commission of lunacy against civilization without more delay.

For all our crowded towns and bewildering factories are simply the outcome of the profit system. Capitalistic manufacture, capitalistic landowning, and capitalistic exchange force men into big cities in order to manipulate them in the interests of capital; the same tyranny contracts the due space of the factory so much that (for instance) the interior of a great weaving-shed is almost as ridiculous a spectacle as it is a horrible one. There is no other necessity for all this, save the necessity for grinding profits out of men's lives, and of producing cheap goods for the use (and subjection) of the slaves who grind. All labour is not yet driven into factories; often where it is there is no necessity for it, save again the profit-tyranny. People engaged in all such labour need by no means be compelled to pig together in close city quarters. There is no reason why they should not follow their occupations in quiet country homes, in industrial colleges, in small towns, or, in short, where they find it happiest for them to live.

As to that part of labour which must be associated on a large scale, this very factory system, under a reasonable order of things (though to my mind there might still be drawbacks to it), would at least offer opportunities for a full and eager social life surrounded by many pleasures. The factories might be centres of intellectual activity also, and work in them might well be varied very much: the tending of the necessary machinery might to each individual be but a short part of the day's work. The other work might vary from raising food from the surrounding country to the study and practice of art and science. It is a matter of course that people engaged in such work, and being the masters of their own lives, would not allow any hurry or want of foresight to force them into enduring dirt, disorder, or want of room. Science duly applied would enable them to get rid of refuse, to minimize, if not wholly to destroy, all the inconveniences which at present attend the use of elaborate machinery, such as smoke, stench, and noise; nor would they endure that the buildings in which they worked or lived should be ugly blots on the fair face of the earth. Beginning by making their factories, buildings, and sheds decent and convenient like their homes, they would infallibly go on to make them not merely negatively good, inoffensive merely, but even beautiful, so that the glorious art of architecture, now for some time slain by commercial greed, would be born again and flourish.

So, you see, I claim that work in a duly ordered community should be made attractive by the consciousness of usefulness, by its being carried on with intelligent interest, by variety, and by its being exercised amidst pleasurable surroundings. But I have also claimed, as we all do, that the day's work should not be wearisomely long. It may be said, 'How can you make this last claim square with the others? If the work is to be so refined, will not the goods made be very expensive?'

I do admit, as I have said before, that some sacrifice will be necessary in order to make labour attractive. I mean that, if we *could* be contented in a free community to work in the same hurried, dirty, disorderly, heartless way as we do now, we might shorten our day's labour very much more than I suppose we shall do, taking all kinds of labour into account. But if we did, it would mean that our new-won freedom of condition would leave us listless and wretched, if not anxious, as we are now, which I hold is simply impossible. We should be contented to make the sacrifices necessary for raising our condition to the standard called out for as desirable by the whole community. Nor only so. We should, individually, be emulous to sacrifice quite freely still more of our time and our ease towards the raising of the standard of life. Persons, either by themselves or associated for such purposes, would freely, and for the love of the work and for its results – stimulated by the hope of the pleasure of creation – produce those ornaments of life for the service of all, which they are now bribed to produce (or pretend to produce) for the service of a few rich men. The experiment of a civilized community living wholly without art or literature has not yet been tried. The past degradation and corruption of civilization may force this denial of pleasure upon the society which will arise from its ashes. If that must be, we will accept the passing phase of utilitarianism as a foundation for the art which is to be. If the cripple and the starveling disappear from our streets, if the earth nourish us all alike, if the sun shine for all of us alike, if to one and all of us the glorious drama of the earth – day and night, summer and winter – can be presented as a thing to understand and love, we can afford to wait awhile till we are purified from the shame of the past corruption, and till art arises again amongst people freed from the terror of the slave and the shame of the robber.

Meantime, in any case, the refinement, thoughtfulness, and deliberation of labour must indeed be paid for, but not by compulsion to labour long hours. Our epoch has invented machines which would have appeared wild dreams to the men of past ages, and of those machines we have as yet *made no use.*

They are called 'labour-saving' machines – a commonly used phrase which implies what we expect of them; but we do not get what we expect. What they really do is to reduce the skilled labourer to the ranks of the unskilled, to increase the number of the 'reserve army of labour' – that is, to increase the precariousness of life among the workers and to intensify the labour of those who serve the machines (as slaves their masters). All this they do by the way, while they pile up the profits of the employers of labour, or force them to expend those profits in bitter commercial war with each other. In a true society these miracles of ingenuity would be for the first time used for minimizing the amount of time spent in unattractive labour, which by their means might be so reduced as to be but a very light burden on each individual. All the more as these machines would most certainly be very much improved when it was no longer a question as to whether their improvement would 'pay' the individual, but rather whether it would benefit the community.

So much for the ordinary use of machinery, which would probably, after a time, be somewhat restricted when men found out that there was no need for anxiety as to mere subsistence, and learned to take an interest and pleasure in handiwork which, done deliberately and thoughtfully, could be made more attractive than machine work.

Again, as people freed from the daily terror of starvation found out what they really wanted, being no longer compelled by anything but their own needs, they would refuse to produce the mere inanities which are now called luxuries, or the poison and trash now called cheap wares. No one would make plush breeches when there were no flunkies to wear them, nor would anybody waste his time over making oleo-margarine when no one was *compelled* to abstain from real butter. Adulteration laws are only needed in a society of thieves – and in such a society they are a dead letter.

Socialists are often asked how work of the rougher and more repulsive kind could be carried out in the new condition of things.

To attempt to answer such questions fully or authoritatively would be attempting the impossibility of constructing a scheme of a new society out of the materials of the old, before we knew which of those materials would disappear and which endure through the evolution which is leading us to the great change. Yet it is not difficult to conceive of some arrangement whereby those who did the roughest work should work for the shortest spells. And again, what is said above of the variety of work applies specially here. Once more I say, that for a man to be the whole of his life hopelessly engaged in performing one repulsive and never-ending task, is an arrangement fit enough for the hell imagined by theologians, but scarcely fit for any other form of society. Lastly, if this rougher work were of any special kind, we may suppose that special volunteers would be called on to perform it, who would surely be forthcoming, unless men in a state of freedom should lose the sparks of manliness which they possessed as slaves.

And yet if there be any work which cannot be made other than repulsive, either by the shortness of its duration or the intermittency of its recurrence, or by the sense of special and peculiar usefulness (and therefore honour) in the mind of the man who performs it freely – if there be any work which cannot be but a torment to the worker, what then? Well, then, let us see if the heavens will fall on us if we leave it undone, for it were better that they should. The produce of such work cannot be worth the price of it.

Now we have seen that the semi-theological dogma that all labour, under any circumstances, is a blessing to the labourer, is hypocritical and false; that, on the other hand, labour is good when due hope of rest and pleasure accompanies it. We have weighed the work of civilization in the balance and found it wanting, since hope is mostly lacking to it, and therefore we see that civilization has bred a dire curse for men. But we have seen also that the work of the world might be carried on in hope and with pleasure if it were not wasted by folly and tyranny, by the perpetual strife of opposing classes.

It is Peace, therefore, which we need in order that we may live and work in hope and with pleasure. Peace so much desired, if we may trust men's words, but which has been so continually and steadily rejected by them in deeds. But for us, let us set our hearts on it and win it at whatever cost.

What the cost may be, who can tell? Will it be possible to win peace peaceably? Alas, how can it be? We are so hemmed in by wrong and folly, that in one way or other we must always be fighting against them: our own lives may see no end to the struggle, perhaps no obvious hope of the end. It may be that the best we can hope to see is that struggle getting sharper and bitterer day by day, until it breaks out openly at last into the slaughter of men by actual warfare instead of by the slower and crueller methods of 'peaceful' commerce. If we live to see that, we shall live to see much; for it will mean the rich classes grown conscious of their own wrong and robbery, and consciously defending them by open violence; and then the end will be drawing near.

But in any case, and whatever the nature of our strife for peace may be, if we only aim at it steadily and with a singleness of heart, and ever keep it in view, a reflection from that peace of the future will illumine the turmoil and trouble of our lives, whether the trouble be seemingly petty, or obviously tragic; and we shall, in our hopes at least, live the lives of men: nor can the present times give us any reward greater than that.

THE HOPES
OF CIVILIZATION

* * *

Lecture given to
the Hammersmith Branch
of the Socialist League,
Hammersmith, 1885.

Published in *Signs of Change*,
London, 1888

Every age has had its hopes, hopes that look to something beyond the life of the age itself, hopes that try to pierce into the future; and, strange to say, I believe that those hopes have been stronger not in the heyday of the epoch which has given them birth, but rather in its decadence and times of corruption: in sober truth it may well be that these hopes are but a reflection in those that live happily and comfortably of the vain longings of those others who suffer with little power of expressing their sufferings in an audible voice: when all goes well the happy world forgets these people and their desires, sure as it is that their woes are not dangerous to them the wealthy: whereas when the woes and grief of the poor begin to rise to a point beyond the endurance of men, fear conscious or unconscious falls upon the rich, and they begin to look about them to see what there may be among the elements of their society which may be used as palliatives for the misery which, long existing and ever growing greater among the slaves of that society, is now at last forcing itself on the attention of the masters. Times of change, disruption, and revolution are naturally times of hope also, and not seldom the hopes of something better to come are the first tokens that tell people that revolution is at hand, though commonly such tokens are no more believed than Cassandra's prophecies, or are even taken in a contrary sense by those who have anything to lose; since they look upon them as signs of the prosperity of the times, and the long endurance of that state of things which is so kind to them. Let us then see what the hopes of civilization are like to-day: for indeed I purpose speaking of our own times chiefly, and will leave for the present all mention of that older civilization which was destroyed by the healthy barbarism out of which our present society has grown.

Yet a few words may be necessary concerning the birth of our present epoch and the hopes it gave rise to, and what has become of them: that will not take us very far back in history; as to my mind our modern civilization begins with the stirring period about the time of the Reformation in England, the time which in the then more important countries of the Continent is known as the period of the Renaissance, the so-called new birth of art and learning.

And first remember that this period includes the death-throes of feudalism, with all the good and evil which that system bore with it. For centuries past its end was getting ready by the gradual weakening of the bonds of the great hierarchy which held men together: the characteristics of those bonds were, theoretically at least, personal rights and personal duties between superior and inferior all down the scale; each man was born, so to say, subject to these conditions, and the mere accidents of his life could not free him from them: commerce, in our sense of the word, there was none; capitalistic manufacture, capitalistic exchange was unknown: to buy goods cheap that you might sell them dear was a legal offence (forestalling): to buy goods in the market in the morning and to sell them in the afternoon in the same place was not thought a useful occupation and was forbidden under the name of regrating;[1] usury, instead of leading as now directly to the highest offices of the State, was thought wrong, and the profit of it mostly fell to the chosen people of God: the robbery of the workers, thought necessary then as now to the very existence of the State, was carried out quite crudely without any concealment or excuse by arbitrary taxation or open violence: on the other hand, life was easy, and common necessaries plenteous; the holidays of the Church were holidays in the modern sense of the word, downright play-days, and there were ninety-six obligatory ones: nor were the people tame and sheep-like, but as rough-handed and bold a set of good fellows as ever rubbed through life under the sun.

I remember three passages, from contemporary history or gossip, about the life of those times which luck has left us, and which illustrate curiously the change that has taken place in the habits of Englishmen. A lady writing from Norfolk four hundred years ago to her husband in London, amidst various commissions for tapestries, groceries, and gowns, bids him also not to forget to bring back with him a good supply of cross-bows and bolts, since the windows of their hall were too low to be handy for long-bow shooting.[2] A German traveller, writing quite at the end of the mediaeval period, speaks of the English as the laziest and proudest people and the best cooks in Europe. A Spanish ambassador about the same period says, 'These English live in houses built of sticks and mud,* but therein they fare as plenteously as lords.'

Indeed, I confess that it is with a strange emotion that I recall these times and try to realize the life of our forefathers, men who were named like ourselves, spoke nearly the same tongue, lived on the same spots of earth, and therewithal were as different from us in manners, habits, ways of life and thought, as though they lived in another planet. The very face of the country has changed; not merely I mean in London and the great manufacturing centres, but through the country generally; there is no piece of English ground, except such places as Salisbury Plain, but bears witness to the amazing change which four hundred years has brought upon us.

Not seldom I please myself with trying to realize the face of mediaeval England; the many chases and great woods, the stretches of common tillage and common pasture quite unenclosed; the rough husbandry of the tilled parts, the unimproved breeds of cattle, sheep, and swine; especially the latter, so lank and long and lathy, looking so strange to us; the strings of packhorses along the bridle-roads, the scantiness of the wheel-roads, scarce any except those left by the Romans, and those made from monastery to monastery: the scarcity of bridges, and people using ferries instead, or fords where they could; the little towns, well bechurched, often walled; the villages just where they are now (except for those that have nothing but the church left to tell of them), but better and more populous; their churches, some big and handsome, some small and curious, but all crowded with altars and furniture, and gay with pictures and ornament; the many religious houses, with their glorious architecture; the beautiful manor-houses, some of them castles once, and survivals from an earlier period; some new and elegant; some out of all proportion small for the importance of their lords. How strange it

* I suppose he was speaking of the frame houses of Kent.

would be to us if we could be landed in fourteenth-century England! Unless we saw the crest of some familiar hill, like that which yet bears upon it a symbol of an English tribe, and from which, looking down on the plain where Alfred was born,[3] I once had many such ponderings, we should not know into what country of the world we were come: the name is left, scarce a thing else.

And when I think of this it quickens my hope of what may be: even so it will be with us in time to come; all will have changed, and another people will be dwelling here in England, who, although they may be of our blood and bear our name, will wonder how we lived in the nineteenth century.

Well, under all that rigidly ordered caste society of the fourteenth century, with its rough plenty, its sauntering life, its cool acceptance of rudeness and violence, there was going on a keen struggle of classes which carried with it the hope of progress of those days: the serfs gradually getting freed, and becoming some of them the town population, the first journeymen, or 'free-labourers,' so called, some of them the copyholders of agricultural land: the corporations of the towns gathered power, the craft-gilds grew into perfection and corruption, the power of the Crown increased, attended with nascent bureaucracy; in short, the middle class was forming underneath the outward show of feudalism still intact: and all was getting ready for the beginning of the great commercial epoch in whose *latter* days I would fain hope we are living. That epoch began with the portentous change of agriculture which meant cultivating for profit instead of for livelihood, and which carried with it the expropriation of the *people* from the land, the extinction of the yeoman, and the rise of the capitalist farmer;[4] and the growth of the town population, which, swelled by the drift of the landless vagabonds and masterless men, grew into a definite proletariat or class of free-workmen; and their existence made that of the embryo capitalist-manufacturer also possible; and the reign of commercial contract and cash payment began to take the place of the old feudal hierarchy, with its many-linked chain of personal responsibilities. The latter half of the seventeenth century, the reign of Charles II, saw the last blow struck at this feudal system, when the landowners' military service was abolished, and they became simple owners of property that had no duties attached to it save the payment of a land-tax.

The hopes of the early part of the commercial period may be read in almost every book of the time, expressed in various degrees of dull or amusing pedantry, and show a naïf arrogance and contempt of the times just past through which nothing but the utmost simplicity of ignorance could have attained to. But the times were stirring, and gave birth to the most powerful individualities in many branches of literature, and More and Campanella,[5] at least from the midst of the exuberant triumph of young commercialism, gave to the world prophetic hopes of times yet to come when that commercialism itself should have given place to the society which we hope will be the next transform of civilization into something else: into a new social life.

This period of early and exuberant hopes passed into the next stage of sober realization of many of them, for commerce grew and grew, and moulded all society to its needs: the workman of the sixteenth century worked still as an individual with little co-operation, and scarce any division of labour: by the end of the seventeenth he had become only a part of a group which by that time was in the handicrafts the real unit of production; division of labour even at that period had quite destroyed his individuality, and the worker was but part of a machine: all through the eighteenth century this system went on progressing towards perfection, till to most men of that period, to most of those who were in any way capable of expressing their thoughts, civilization had already reached a high stage of perfection, and was certain to go on from better to better.

These hopes were not on the surface of a very revolutionary kind, but nevertheless the class struggle still went on, and quite openly too; for the remains of feudality, aided by the mere mask and grimace of the religion which was once a real part of the feudal system, hampered the progress of commerce sorely, and seemed a thousand-fold more powerful than it really was; because in spite of the class struggle there was really a covert alliance between the powerful middle classes who were the children of commerce and their old masters the aristocracy; an unconscious understanding between them rather, in the midst of their contest, that certain matters were to be respected even by the advanced party. The contest and civil war between the king and the commons in England in the seventeenth century illustrate this well: the caution with which privilege was attacked in the beginning of the struggle, the unwillingness of all the leaders save a few enthusiasts to carry matters to their logical consequences, even when the march of events had developed the antagonism between aristocratic privilege and middle-class freedom of contract (so called); finally, the crystallization of the new order conquered by the sword of Naseby into a mongrel condition of things between privilege and bourgeois freedom, the defeat and grief of the purist Republicans, and the horror at and swift extinction of the Levellers, the pioneers of Socialism in that day, all point to the fact that the 'party of progress', as we should call it now, was determined after all that privilege should not be abolished further than its own standpoint.[6]

The seventeenth century ended in the great Whig revolution in England, and, as I said, commerce throve and grew enormously, and the power of the middle classes increased proportionately and all things seemed going smoothly with them, till at last in France the culminating corruption of a society still nominally existing for the benefit of the privileged aristocracy, forced their hand: the old order of things, backed as it was by the power of the executive, by that semblance of overwhelming physical force which is the real and only cement of a society founded on the slavery of the many – the aristocratic power – seemed strong and almost inexpugnable: and since any stick will do to beat a dog with, the middle classes in France were forced to take up the first stick that lay ready to hand if they were not to give way to the aristocrats, which indeed the whole evolution of history forbade them to do.[7] Therefore, as in England in the seventeenth century, the middle classes allied themselves to religious and republican, and even communistic enthusiasts, with the intention, firm though unexpressed, to keep them down when they had mounted to power by their means, so in France they had to ally themselves with the proletariat: which, shamefully oppressed and degraded as it had been, now for the first time in history began to feel its power, the power of numbers: by means of this help they triumphed over aristocratic privilege, but, on the other hand, although the proletariat was speedily reduced again to a position not much better than that it had held before the revolution, the part it played therein gave a new and terrible character to that revolution, and from that time forward the class struggle entered on to a new phase; the middle classes had gained a complete victory, which in France carried with it all the outward signs of victory, though in England they chose to consider a certain part of themselves an aristocracy, who had indeed little signs of aristocracy about them either for good or for evil, being in very few cases of long descent, and being in their manners and ideas unmistakably *bourgeois*.

So was accomplished the second act of the great class struggle with whose first act began the age of commerce; as to the hopes of this period of the revolution we all know how extravagant they were; what a complete regeneration of the world was expected to result from the abolition of the grossest form of privilege; and I must say that, before we mock at the extravagance of those hopes, we should try to put ourselves in the place of those that held them, and try to conceive how the privilege of the old noblesse must have galled the respectable well-to-do people of that time. Well, the reasonable part of those hopes were realized by the revolution; in other words, it accomplished what it really aimed at, the freeing of commerce from the fetters of sham feudality; or, in other words, the destruction of aristocratic privilege. The more extravagant part of the hopes expressed by the eighteenth-century revolution were vague enough, and tended in the direction of supposing that the working classes would be benefited by what was to the interest of the middle class in some way quite unexplained – by a kind of magic, one may say – which welfare of the workers, as it was never directly aimed at, but only hoped for by the way, so also did not come about by any such magical means, and the triumphant middle classes began gradually to find themselves looked upon no longer as rebellious servants, but as oppressive masters.

The middle class had freed commerce from her fetters of privilege, and had freed thought from her fetters of theology, at least partially; but it had not freed, nor attempted to free, labour from its fetters. The leaders of the French Revolution, even amidst the fears, suspicions, and slaughter of the Terror, upheld the rights of 'property' so called, though a new pioneer or prophet appeared in France, analogous in some respects to the Levellers of Cromwell's time, but, as might be expected, far more advanced and reasonable than they were. Gracchus Babeuf[8] and his fellows were treated as criminals, and died or suffered the torture of prison for attempting to put into practice those words which the Republic still carried on its banners, and Liberty, Fraternity, and Equality were interpreted in a middle-class, or if you please a Jesuitical, sense, as the rewards of success for those who could struggle into an exclusive class; and at last property had to be defended by a military adventurer, and the Revolution seemed to have ended with Napoleonism.

Nevertheless, the Revolution was not dead, nor was it possible to say thus far and no further to the rising tide. Commerce, which had created the propertyless proletariat throughout civilization, had still another part to play, which is not yet played out; she had and has to teach the workers to know what they are; to educate them, to consolidate them, and not only to give them aspirations for their advancement as a class, but to make means for them to realize those aspirations. All this she did, nor loitered in her work either; from the beginning of the nineteenth century the history of civilization is really the history of the last of the class struggles which was inaugurated by the French Revolution; and England, who all through the times of the Revolution and the Cae-sarism[9] which followed it appeared to be the steady foe of Revolution, was really as steadily furthering it; her natural conditions, her store of coal and minerals, her temperate climate, extensive sea-board and many harbours, and lastly her position as the outpost of Europe looking into America across the ocean, doomed her to be for a time at least the mistress of the commerce of the civilized world, and its agent with barbarous and semi-barbarous countries. The necessities of this destiny drove her into the implacable war with France, a war which, nominally waged on behalf of monarchical principles, was really, though doubtless unconsciously, carried on for the possession of the foreign and colonial markets. She came out victorious from that war, and fully prepared to take advantage of the industrial revolution which had been going on the while, and which I now ask you to note.

I have said that the eighteenth century perfected the system of labour which took the place of the mediaeval system, under which a workman individually carried his piece of work all through its various stages from the first to the last.

This new system, the first change in industrial production since the Middle Ages, is known as the system of division of labour, wherein, as I said, the unit of labour is a group, not a man; the individual workman in this system is kept life-long at the performance of some task quite petty in itself, and which he soon masters, and having mastered it has nothing more to do but to go on increasing his speed of hand under the spur of competition with his fellows, until he has become the perfect machine which it is his ultimate duty to become, since without attaining to that end he must die or become a pauper.[10] You can well imagine how this glorious invention of division of labour, this complete destruction of individuality in the workman, and his apparent hopeless enslavement to his profit-grinding master, stimulated the hopes of civilization; probably more hymns have been sung in praise of division of labour, more sermons preached about it, than have done homage to the precept, 'do unto others as ye would they should do unto you'.

To drop all irony, surely this was one of those stages of civilization at which one might well say that, if it was to stop there, it was a pity that it had ever got so far. I have had to study books and methods of work of the eighteenth century a good deal, French chiefly;[11] and I must say that the impression made on me by that study is that the eighteenth-century artisan must have been a terrible product of civilization, and quite in a condition to give rise to *hopes* – of the torch, the pike, and the guillotine.

However, civilization was not going to stop there; having turned the man into a machine, the next stage for commerce to aim at was to contrive machines which would widely dispense with human labour; nor was this aim altogether disappointed.

Now, at first sight it would seem that having got the workman into such a plight as he was, as the slave of division of labour, this new invention of machines which should free him from a part of his labour at least, could be nothing to him but an unmixed blessing. Doubtless it will prove to have been so in the end, when certain institutions have been swept away which most people now look on as eternal; but a longish time has passed during which the workman's hopes of civilization have been disappointed, for those who invented the machines, or rather who profited by their invention, did not aim at the saving of labour in the sense of reducing the labour which every man had to do, but, first taking it for granted that every workman would have to work as long as he could stand up to it, aimed, under those conditions of labour, at producing the utmost possible amount of goods which they could sell at a profit.

Need I dwell on the fact that, under these circumstances, the invention of the machines has benefited the workman but little even to this day?

Nay, at first they made his position worse than it had been: for, being thrust on the world very suddenly, they distinctly brought about an industrial revolution, changing everything suddenly and completely; industrial productiveness was increased prodigiously, but so far from the workers reaping the benefits of this, they were thrown out of work in enormous numbers, while those who were still employed were reduced from the position of skilled artisans to that of unskilled labourers: the aims of their masters being, as I said, to make a profit, they did not trouble themselves about this as a class, but took it for granted that it was something that couldn't be helped and didn't hurt *them*: nor did they think of offering to the workers that compensation for harassed interests which they have since made a point of claiming so loudly for themselves.

This was the state of things which followed on the conclusion of European peace, and even that peace itself rather made matters worse than better, by the sudden cessation of all war industries, and the throwing on to the market many thousands of soldiers and sailors: in short, at no period of English history was the condition of the workers worse than in the early years of the nineteenth century.

There seem during this period to have been two currents of hope that had reference to the working classes: the first affected the masters, the second the men.

In England, and, in what I am saying of this period, I am chiefly thinking of England, the hopes of the richer classes ran high; and no wonder; for England had by this time become the mistress of the markets of the world, and also, as the people of that period were never weary of boasting, the workshop of the world: the increase in the riches of the country was enormous, even at the early period I am thinking of now – prior to '48,[12] I mean – though it increased much more speedily in times that we have all seen: but part of the jubilant hopes of this newly rich man concerned his servants, the instruments of his fortune: it was hoped that the population in general would grow wiser, better educated, thriftier, more industrious, more comfortable; for which hope there was surely some foundation, since man's mastery over the forces of Nature was growing yearly towards completion; but you see these benevolent gentlemen supposed that these hopes would be realized perhaps by some unexplained magic as aforesaid, or perhaps by the working classes, *at their own expense*, by the exercise of virtues supposed to be specially suited to their condition, and called, by their masters, 'thrift' and 'industry'. For this latter supposition there was no foundation: indeed, the poor wretches who were thrown out of work by the triumphant march of commerce had perforce worn thrift threadbare, and could hardly better their exploits in *that* direction; while as to those who worked in the factories, or who formed the fringe of labour elsewhere, industry was no new gospel to them, since they already worked as long as they could work without dying at the ioom, the spindle, or the stithy. They for their part had their hopes, vague enough as to their ultimate aim, but expressed in the passing day by a very obvious tendency to revolt: this tendency took various forms, which I cannot dwell on here, but settled down at last into Chartism:[13] about which I must speak a few words. But first I must mention, I can scarce do more, the honoured name of Robert Owen,[14] as representative of the nobler hopes of his day, just as More was of his, and the lifter of the torch of Socialism amidst the dark days of the confusion consequent on the reckless greed of the early period of the great factory industries.

That the conditions under which man lived could affect his life and his deeds infinitely, that not selfish greed and ceaseless contention, but brotherhood and co-operation were the bases of true society, was the gospel which he preached and also practised with a single-heartedness, devotion, and fervour of hope which have never been surpassed: he was the embodied hope of the days when the advance of knowledge and the sufferings of the people thrust revolutionary hope upon those thinkers who were not in some form or other in the pay of the sordid masters of society.

As to the Chartist agitation, there is this to be said of it, that it was thoroughly a working-class movement, and it was caused by the simplest and most powerful of all causes – hunger. It is noteworthy that it was strongest, especially in its earlier days, in the Northern and Midland manufacturing districts – that is, in the places which felt the distress caused by the industrial revolution most sorely and directly; it sprang up with particular vigour in the years immediately following the great Reform Bill; and it has been remarked that disappointment of the hopes which that measure had cherished had something to do with its bitterness. As it went on, obvious causes for failure were developed in it; self-seeking leadership; futile discussion of the means of making the change, before organization of the party was perfected; blind fear of ultimate consequences on the part of some, blind disregard to immediate consequences on the part of others; these were the surface reasons for its failure: but it would have triumphed over all these and accomplished revolution in England, if it had not been for causes deeper and more vital than these. Chartism differed from mere Radicalism in being a class movement; but its aim was after all political rather than social. The Socialism of Robert Owen fell short of its object because it did not understand that, as long as there is a privileged class in possession of the executive power, they will take good care that their economical position, which enables them to live on the unpaid labour of the people, is not tampered with: the hopes of the Chartists were disappointed because they did not understand that true political freedom is impossible to people who are economically enslaved: there is no first and second in these matters, the two must go hand in hand together: we cannot live as we will, and as we should, as long as we allow people to *govern* us whose interest it is that we should live as *they* will, and by no means as we should; neither is it any use claiming the right to manage our own business unless we are prepared to have some business of our own: these two aims united mean the furthering of the class struggle till all classes are abolished – the divorce of one from the other is fatal to any hope of social advancement.

Chartism therefore, though a genuine popular movement, was incomplete in its aims and knowledge; the time was not yet come and it could not triumph openly; but it would be a mistake to say that it failed utterly: at least it kept alive the holy flame of discontent; it made it possible for us to attain to the political goal of democracy, and thereby to advance the cause of the people by the gain of a stage from whence could be seen the fresh gain to be aimed at.

I have said that the time for revolution had not then come: the great wave of commercial success went on swelling, and though the capitalists would if they had dared have engrossed the whole of the advantages thereby gained at the expense of their wage slaves, the Chartist revolt warned them that it was not safe to attempt it. They were *forced* to try to allay discontent by palliative measures. They had to allow Factory Acts to be passed regulating the hours and conditions of labour of women and children, and consequently of men also in some of the more important and consolidated industries; they were *forced* to repeal the ferocious laws against combination among the workmen; so that the Trades Unions won for themselves a legal position and became a power in the labour question, and were able by means of strikes and threats of strikes to regulate the wages granted to the workers, and to raise the standard of livelihood for a certain part of the skilled workmen and the labourers associated with them: though the main part of the unskilled, including the agricultural workmen, were no better off than before.

Thus was damped down the flame of a discontent vague in its aims, and passionately crying out for what, if granted, it could not have used: twenty years ago any one hinting at the possibility of serious class discontent in this country would have been looked upon as a madman; in fact, the well-to-do and cultivated were quite unconscious (as many still are) that there was any class distinction in this country other than what was made by the rags and cast clothes of feudalism, which in a perfunctory manner they still attacked.

There was no sign of revolutionary feeling in England twenty years ago: the middle class were so rich that they had no need to hope for anything – but a heaven which they did not believe in: the well-to-do working men did not hope, since they were not pinched and had no means of learning their degraded position: and lastly, the drudges of the proletariat had such hope as charity, the hospital, the workhouse, and kind death at last could offer them.

In this stock-jobbers' heaven let us leave our dear countrymen for a little, while I say a few words about the affairs of the people on the continent of Europe. Things were not quite so smooth for the fleecer there: Socialist thinkers and writers had arisen about the same time as Robert Owen; St Simon, Proudhon, Fourier[15] and his followers kept up the traditions of hope in the midst of a *bourgeois* world. Amongst these Fourier is the one that calls for most attention: since his doctrine of the necessity and possibility of making labour attractive is one which Socialism can by no means do without. France also kept up the revolutionary and insurrectionary tradition, the result of something like hope still fermenting amongst the proletariat: she fell at last into the clutches of a second Caesarism[16] developed by the basest set of sharpers, swindlers, and harlots that ever insulted a country, and of whom our own happy *bourgeois* at home made heroes and heroines: the hideous open corruption of Parisian society, to which, I repeat, our respectable classes accorded heartfelt sympathy, was finally swept away by the horrors of a race war: the defeats and disgraces of this war developed, on the one hand, an increase in the wooden implacability and baseness of the French *bourgeois*, but on the other made way for revolutionary hope to spring again, from which resulted the attempt to establish society on the basis of the freedom of labour, which we call the Commune of Paris of 1871. Whatever mistakes or imprudences were made in this attempt, and all wars blossom thick with such mistakes, I will leave the reactionary enemies of the people's cause to put forward: the immediate and obvious result was the slaughter of thousands of brave and honest revolutionists at the hands of the respectable classes, the loss in fact of an army for the popular cause. But we may be sure that the results of the Commune will not stop there: to all Socialists that heroic attempt will give hope and ardour in the cause as long as it is to be won; we feel as though the Paris workman had striven to bring the day-dawn for us, and had lifted us the sun's rim over the horizon, never to set in utter darkness again: of such attempts one must say, that though those who perished in them might have been put in a better place in the battle, yet after all brave men never die for nothing, when they die for principle.

Let us shift from France to Germany before we get back to

England again, and conclude with a few words about our hopes at the present day. To Germany we owe the school of economists, at whose head stands the name of Karl Marx, who have made modern Socialism what it is: the earlier Socialist writers and preachers based their hopes on man being taught to see the desirableness of co-operation taking the place of competition, and adopting the change voluntarily and consciously, and they trusted to schemes more or less artificial being tried and accepted, although such schemes were necessarily constructed out of the materials which capitalistic society offered: but the new school, starting with an historical view of what had been, and seeing that a law of evolution swayed all events in it, was able to point out to us that the evolution was still going on, and that, whether Socialism be desirable or not, it is at least inevitable. Here then was at last a hope of a different kind to any that had gone before it; and the German and Austrian workmen were not slow to learn the lesson founded on this theory; from being one of the most backward countries in Europe in the movement, before Lassalle started his German workman's party in 1863, Germany soon became the leader in it: Bismarck's repressive law has only acted on opinion there, as the roller does to the growing grass – made it firmer and stronger; and whatever vicissitudes may be the fate of the party as a party, there can be no doubt that Socialistic opinion is firmly established there, and that when the time is ripe for it that opinion will express itself in action.[17]

Now, in all I have been saying, I have been wanting you to trace the fact that, ever since the establishment of commercialism on the ruins of feudality, there has been growing a steady feeling on the part of the workers that they are a class dealt with as a class, and in like manner to deal with others; and that as this class feeling has grown, so also has grown with it a consciousness of the antagonism between their class and the class which employs it, as the phrase goes; that is to say, which lives by means of its labour.

Now it is just this growing consciousness of the fact that as long as there exists in society a propertied class living on the labour of a propertyless one, there *must* be a struggle always going on between those two classes – it is just the dawning knowledge of this fact which should show us what civilization can hope for – namely, transformation into true society, in which there will no longer be classes with their necessary struggle for existence and superiority: for the antagonism of classes which began in all simplicity between the master and the chattel slave of ancient society, and was continued between the feudal lord and the serf of mediaeval society, has gradually become the contention between the capitalist developed from the workmen of the last-named period, and the wage-earner: in the former struggle the rise of the artisan and villeinage tenant created a new class, the middle class, while the place of the old serf was filled by the propertyless labourer, with whom the middle class, which has absorbed the aristocracy, is now face to face: the struggle between the classes therefore is once again a simple one, as in the days of the classical peoples; but since there is no longer any strong race left out of civilization, as in the time of the disruption of Rome, the whole struggle in all its simplicity between those who have and those who lack is *within* civilization.

Moreover, the capitalist or modern slave-owner has been forced by his very success, as we have seen, to organize his slaves, the wage-earners, into a co-operation for production so well arranged that it requires little but his own elimination to make it a foundation for communal life: in the teeth also of the experience of past ages, he has been compelled to allow a modicum of education to the propertyless, and has not even been able to deprive them wholly of political rights; his own advance in wealth and power has bred for him the very enemy who is doomed to make an end of him.

But will there be any new class to take the place of the present proletariat when that has triumphed, as it must do, over the present privileged class? We cannot foresee the future, but we may fairly hope not: at least we cannot see any signs of such a new class forming. It is impossible to see how destruction of privilege can stop short of absolute equality of condition; pure Communism is the logical deduction from the imperfect form of the new society, which is generally differentiated from it as Socialism.

Meantime, it is this simplicity and directness of the growing contest which above all things presents itself as a terror to the conservative instinct of the present day. Many among the middle class who are sincerely grieved and shocked at the condition of the proletariat which civilization has created, and even alarmed by the frightful inequalities which it fosters, do nevertheless shudder back from the idea of the class struggle, and strive to shut their eyes to the fact that it is going on. They try to think that peace is not only possible, but natural, between the two classes, the very essence of whose existence is that each can only thrive by what it manages to force the other to yield to it. They propose to themselves the impossible problem of raising the inferior or exploited classes into a position in which they will cease to struggle against the superior classes, while the latter will not cease to exploit them. This absurd position drives them into the concoction of schemes for bettering the condition of the working classes at their own expense, some of them futile, some merely fantastic; or they may be divided again into those which point out the advantages and pleasures of involuntary asceticism, and reactionary plans for importing the conditions of the production and life of the Middle Ages (wholly misunderstood by them, by the way) into the present system of the capitalist farmer, the great industries, and the universal world-market. Some see a solution of the social problem in sham co-operation, which is merely an improved form of joint-stockery: others preach thrift to (precarious) incomes of eighteen shillings a week, and industry to men killing themselves by inches in working overtime, or to men whom the labour-market has rejected as not wanted: others beg the proletarians not to breed so fast; an injunction the compliance with which might be at first of advantage to the proletarians themselves in their present condition, but would certainly undo the capitalists, if it were carried to any lengths, and would lead through ruin and misery to the violent outbreak of the very revolution which these timid people are so anxious to forgo.

Then there are others who, looking back on the past, and perceiving that the workmen of the Middle Ages lived in more comfort and self-respect than ours do, even though they were subjected to the class rule of men who were looked on as another order of beings than they, think that if those conditions of life could be reproduced under our better political conditions the question would be solved for a time at least. Their schemes may be summed up in attempts, more or less preposterously futile, to graft a class of independent peasants on our system of wages and capital. They do not understand that this system of independent workmen, producing almost entirely for the consumption of themselves and their neighbours, and exploited by the upper classes by obvious taxes on their labour, which was not otherwise organized or interfered with by the exploiters, was what in past times took the place of our system, in which the workers sell their labour in the competitive market to masters who have in their hands the whole organization of the markets, and that these two systems are mutually destructive.

Others again believe in the possibility of starting from our present workhouse system, for the raising of the lowest part of the working population into a better condition, but do not trouble themselves as to the position of the workers who are fairly above the condition of pauperism, or consider what part they will play in the contest for a better livelihood. And, lastly, quite a large number of well-intentioned persons belonging to the richer classes believe, that in a society that compels competition for livelihood, and holds out to the workers as a stimulus to exertion the hope of their rising into a monopolist class of non-producers, it is yet possible to 'moralize' capital (to use a slang phrase of the Positivists): that is to say, that a sentiment imported from a religion which looks upon another world as the true sphere of action for mankind, will override the necessities of our daily life in this world. This curious hope is founded on the feeling that a sentiment antagonistic to the full development of commercialism exists and is gaining ground, and that this sentiment is an independent growth of the ethics of the present epoch. As a matter of fact, admitting its existence, as I think we must do, it is the birth of the sense of insecurity which is the shadow cast before by the approaching dissolution of modern society founded on wage-slavery.

The greater part of these schemes aim, though seldom with the consciousness of their promoters, at the creation of a new middle class out of the wage-earning class, and at their expense, just as the present middle class was developed out of the serf-population of the early Middle Ages. It may be possible that such a *further* development of the middle class lies before us, but it will not be brought about by any such artificial means as the above-mentioned schemes. If it comes at all, it must be produced by events, which at present we cannot foresee, acting on our commercial system, and revivifying for a little time, maybe, that Capitalist Society which now seems sickening towards its end.

For what is visible before us in these days is the competitive commercial system killing itself by its own force: profits lessening, businesses growing bigger and bigger, the small employer of labour thrust out of his function, and the aggregation of capital increasing the numbers of the lower middle class from above rather than from below, by driving the smaller manufacturer into the position of a mere servant to the bigger. The productivity of labour also increasing out of all proportion to the capacity of the capitalists to manage the market or deal with the labour supply: lack of employment therefore becoming chronic, and discontent therewithal.

All this on the one hand. On the other, the workman claiming everywhere political equality, which cannot long be denied; and education spreading, so that what between the improvement in the education of the working class and the continued amazing fatuity of that of the upper classes, there is a distinct tendency to equalization here; and, as I have hinted above, all history shows us what a danger to society may be a class at once educated and socially degraded: though, indeed, no history has yet shown us – what is swiftly advancing upon us – a class which, though it shall have attained knowledge, shall lack utterly the refinement and self-respect which come from the union of knowledge with leisure and ease of life. The growth of such a class may well make the 'cultured' people of to-day tremble

Whatever, therefore, of unforeseen and unconceived-of may lie in the womb of the future, there is nothing visible before us but a decaying system, with no outlook but ever-increasing entanglement and blindness, and a new system, Socialism, the hope of which is ever growing clearer in men's minds – a system which not only sees how labour can be freed from its present fetters, and organized unwastefully, so as to produce the greatest possible amount of wealth for the community and for every member of it, but which bears with it its own ethics and religion and aesthetics: that is the hope and promise of a new and higher life in all ways. So that even if those unforeseen economical events above spoken of were to happen, and put off for a while the end of our Capitalist system, the latter would drag itself along as an anomaly cursed by all, a mere clog on the aspirations of humanity.

It is not likely that it will come to that: in all probability the logical outcome of the latter days of Capitalism will go step by step with its actual history: while all men, even its declared enemies, will be working to bring Socialism about, the aims of those who have learned to believe in the certainty and beneficence of its advent will become clearer, their methods for realizing it clearer also, and at last ready to hand. Then will come that open acknowledgment for the necessity of the change (an acknowledgment coming from the intelligence of civilization) which is commonly called Revolution. It is no use prophesying as to the events which will accompany that revolution, but to a reasonable man it seems unlikely to the last degree, or we will say impossible, that a moral sentiment will induce the propriety classes – those who live by *owning* the means of production which the unprivileged classes must needs *use* – to yield up this privilege uncompelled; all one can hope is that they will see the implicit threat of compulsion in the events of the day, and so yield with a good grace to the terrible necessity of forming part of a world in which all, including themselves, will work honestly and live easily.

GOTHIC
ARCHITECTURE

* * *

Lecture given to
the Arts and Crafts Exhibition Society,
London 1889

Published by the Kelmscott Press, 1893

By the word Architecture is, I suppose, commonly understood the art of ornamental building, and in this sense I shall often have to use it here. Yet I would not like you to think of its productions merely as well-constructed and well-proportioned buildings, each one of which is handed over by the architect to other artists to finish, after his designs have been carried out (as we say) by a number of mechanical workers, who are not artists. A true architectural work rather is a building duly provided with all necessary furniture, decorated with all due ornament, according to the use, quality, and dignity of the building, from mere mouldings or abstract lines, to the great epical works of sculpture and painting, which, except as decorations of the nobler form of such buildings, cannot be produced at all. So looked on, a work of architecture is a harmonious co-operative work of art, inclusive of all the serious arts, all those which are not engaged in the production of mere toys, or of ephemeral prettinesses.

Now, these works of art are man's expression of the value of life, and also the production of them makes his life of value: and since they can only be produced by the general goodwill and help of the public, their continuous production, or the existence of the true Art of Architecture, betokens a society which, whatever elements of change it may bear within it, may be called stable, since it is founded on the happy exercise of the energies of the most useful part of its population.[1]

What the absence of this Art of Architecture may betoken in the long run it is not easy for us to say: because that lack belongs only to these later times of the world's history, which as yet we cannot fairly see, because they are too near to us; but clearly in the present it indicates a transference of the interest of civilized men from the development of the human and intellectual energies of the race to the development of its mechanical energies. If this tendency is to go along the logical road of development, it must be said that it will destroy the arts of design and all that is analogous to them in literature; but the logical outcome of obvious tendencies is often thwarted by the historical development; that is, by what I can call by no better name than the collective will of mankind; and unless my hopes deceive me, I should say that this process has already begun, that there is a revolt on foot against the utilitarianism which threatens to destroy the Arts; and that it is deeper rooted than a mere passing fashion.[2] For myself I do not indeed believe that this revolt can effect much, so long as the present state of society lasts; but as I am sure that great changes which will bring about a new state of society are rapidly advancing upon us, I think it a matter of much importance that these two revolts should join hands, or at least should learn to understand one another. If the New society when it comes (itself the result of the ceaseless evolution of countless years of tradition) should find the world cut off from all tradition of art, all aspiration towards the beauty which man has proved that he can create, much time will be lost in running hither and thither after the new thread of art; many lives will be barren of a manly pleasure which the world can ill afford to lose even for a short time. I ask you, therefore, to accept what follows as a contribution toward the revolt against utilitarianism, toward the attempt at catching-up the slender thread of tradition before it be too late.

Now, that Harmonious Architectural unit, inclusive of the arts in general, is no mere dream. I have said that it is only in these later times that it has become extinct: until the rise of modern society, no Civilization, no Barbarism has been without it in some form; but it reached its fullest development in the Middle Ages, an epoch really more remote from our modern habits of life and thought than the older civilizations were, though an important part of its life was carried on in our own country by men of our own blood. Nevertheless, remote as those times are from ours, if we are ever to have architecture at all, we must take up the thread of tradition there and nowhere else, because that Gothic Architecture is the most completely organic form of the art which the world has seen; the break in the thread of tradition could only occur there: all the former developments tended thitherward, and to ignore this fact and attempt to catch up the thread before that point was reached, would be a mere piece of artificiality, betokening, not new birth, but a corruption into mere whim of the ancient traditions.

In order to illustrate this position of mine, I must ask you to allow me to run very briefly over the historical sequence of events which led to Gothic Architecture and its fall, and to pardon me for stating familiar and elementary facts which are necessary for my purpose. I must admit also that in doing this I must mostly take my illustrations from works that appear on the face of them to belong to the category of ornamental building, rather than that of those complete and inclusive works of which I have spoken. But this incompleteness is only on the surface; to those who study them they appear as belonging to the class of complete architectural works; they are lacking in completeness only through the consequences of the lapse of time and the folly of men, who did not know what they were, who, pretending to use them, marred their real use as works of art; or in a similar spirit abused them by making them serve their turn as instruments to express their passing passion and spite of the hour.

We may divide the history of the Art of Architecture into two periods, the Ancient and the Mediaeval: the Ancient again may be divided into two styles, the barbarian (in the Greek sense) and the classical. We have, then, three great styles to consider: the Barbarian, the Classical, and the Mediaeval. The two former, however, were partly synchronous, and at least overlapped somewhat. When the curtain of the stage of definite history first draws up, we find the small exclusive circle of the highest civilization, which was dominated by Hellenic thought and science, fitted with a very distinctive and orderly architectural style. That style appears to us to be, within its limits, one of extreme refinement, and perhaps seemed so to those who originally practised it. Moreover, it is ornamented with figure-sculpture far advanced towards perfection even at an early period of its existence, and swiftly growing in technical excellence; yet for all that, it is, after all, a part of the general style of architecture of the Barbarian world, and only outgoes it in the excellence of its figure-sculpture and its refinement. The bones of it, its merely architectural part, are little changed from the Barbarian or primal building, which is a mere piling or jointing together of material, giving one no sense of growth in the building itself and no sense of the possibility of growth in the style.

The one Greek form of building with which we are really familiar, the columnar temple, though always built with blocks of stone, is clearly a deduction from the wooden god's-house or shrine, which was a necessary part of the equipment of the not very remote ancestors of the Periclean Greeks; nor had this god's-house changed so much as the city had changed from the Tribe, or the Worship of the City (the true religion of the Greeks) from the Worship of the Ancestors of the Tribe. In fact, rigid conservatism of form is an essential part of Greek architecture as we know it. From this conservatism of form there resulted a jostling between the building and its higher ornament. In early days, indeed, when some healthy barbarism yet clung to the sculpture, the discrepancy is not felt; but as increasing civilization demands from the sculptors more naturalism and less restraint, it becomes more and more obvious, and more and more painful; till at last it becomes clear that sculpture has ceased to be a part of architecture and has become an extraneous art bound to the building by habit or superstition. The form of the ornamental building of the Greeks, then, was very limited, had no capacity in it for development, and tended to divorce from its higher or epical ornament. What is to be said about the spirit of it which ruled that form? This I think: that the narrow superstition of the form of the Greek temple was not a matter of accident, but was the due expression of the exclusiveness and aristocratic arrogance of the ancient Greek mind, a natural result of which was a demand for pedantic perfection in all the parts and details of a building; so that the inferior parts of the ornament are so slavishly subordinated to the superior, that no invention or individuality is possible in them, whence comes a kind of bareness and blankness, a rejection in short of all romance, which does not indeed destroy their interest as relics of past history, but which puts the style of them aside as any possible foundation for the style of the future architecture of the world. It must be remembered also that this attempt at absolute perfection soon proved a snare to Greek architecture; for it could not be kept up long. It was easy indeed to ensure the perfect execution of a fret or a dentil[3]; not so easy to ensure the perfection of the higher ornament: so that as Greek energy began to fall back from its high-water mark, the demand for absolute perfection became rather a demand for absolute plausibility, which speedily dragged the architectural arts into mere Academicism.

But long before classical art reached the last depths of that degradation, it had brought to birth another style of architecture, the Roman style, which to start with was differentiated from the Greek by having the habitual use of the arch forced upon it. To my mind, organic Architecture, Architecture which must necessarily grow, dates from the habitual use of the arch, which, taking into consideration its combined utility and beauty, must be pronounced to be the greatest invention of the human race. Until the time when man not only had invented the arch, but had gathered boldness to use it habitually, architecture was necessarily so limited, that strong growth was impossible to it. It was quite natural that a people should crystallize the first convenient form of building they might happen upon, or, like the Greeks, accept a traditional form without aspiration towards anything more complex or interesting. Till the arch came into use, building men were the slaves of conditions of climate, materials, kind of labour available, and so forth. But once furnished with the arch, man has conquered Nature in the matter of building; he can defy the rigours of all climates under which men can live with fair comfort: splendid materials are not necessary to him; he can attain a good result from shabby and scrappy materials. When he wants size and span he does not need a horde of war-captured slaves to work for him; the free citizens (if there be any such) can do all that is needed without grinding their lives out before their time. The arch can do all that architecture needs, and in turn from the time when the arch comes into habitual use, the main artistic business of architecture is the decoration of the arch; the only satisfactory style is that which never disguises its office, but adorns and glorifies it. This the Roman architecture, the first style that used the arch, did not do. It used the arch frankly and simply indeed, in one part of its work, but did not adorn it; this part of the Roman building must, however, be called engineering rather than architecture, though its massive and simple dignity is a wonderful contrast to the horrible and restless nightmare of modern engineering. In the other side of its work, the ornamental side, Roman building used the arch and adorned it, but disguised its office, and pretended that the structure of its buildings was still that of the lintel, and that the arch bore no weight worth speaking of. For the Romans had no ornamental building of their own (perhaps we should say no art of their own) and therefore fitted their ideas of the ideas of the Greek sculpture-architect on to their own massive building; and as the Greek plastered his energetic and capable civilized sculpture on to the magnified shrine of his forefathers, so the Roman plastered sculpture, shrine, and all, on to his magnificent engineer's work. In fact, this kind of front-building or veneering was the main resource of Roman ornament; the construction and ornament did not interpenetrate; and to us at this date it seems doubtful if he gained by hiding with marble veneer the solid and beautiful construction of his wall of brick or concrete; since others have used marble far better than he did, but none have built a wall or turned an arch better. As to the Roman ornament, it is not in itself worth much sacrifice of interest in the construction: the Greek ornament was cruelly limited and conventional; but everything about it was in its place, and there was a reason for everything, even though that reason were founded on superstition. But the Roman ornament has no more freedom than the Greek, while it has lost the logic of the latter: it is rich and handsome, and that is all the reason it can give for its existence; nor does its execution and its design interpenetrate. One cannot conceive of the Greek ornament existing apart from the precision of its execution; but well as the Roman ornament is executed in all important works, one almost wishes it were less well executed, so that some mystery might be added to its florid handsomeness. Once again, it is a piece of necessary history, and to criticize it from the point of view of work of to-day would be like finding fault with a geological epoch: and who can help feeling touched by its remnants which show crumbling and battered amidst the incongruous mass of modern houses, amidst the disorder, vulgarity and squalor of some modern town? If I have ventured to call your attention to what it was as architecture, it is because of the abuse of it which took place in later times and has even lasted into our own anti-architectural days; and because it is necessary to point out that it has not got the qualities essential to making it a foundation for any possible new-birth of the arts. In its own time it was for centuries the only thing that redeemed the academical period of classical art from mere nothingness, and though it may almost be said to have perished before the change came, yet in perishing it gave some token of the coming change, which indeed was as slow as the decay of imperial Rome herself. It was in the height of the tax-gathering period of the Roman Peace, in the last days of Diocletian (died 313) in the palace of Spalato which he built himself to rest in after he was satiated with rule, that the rebel, Change, first showed in Roman art, and that the builders admitted that their false lintel was false, and that the arch could do without it.

This was the first obscure beginning of Gothic or organic Architecture; henceforth till the beginning of the modern epoch all is growth uninterrupted, however slow. Indeed, it is slow enough at first: Organic Architecture took two centuries to free itself from the fetters which the Academical ages had cast over it, and the Peace of Rome had vanished before it was free. But the full change came at last, and the architecture was born which logically should have supplanted the primitive lintel-architecture, of which the civilized style of Greece was the last development. Architecture was become organic; henceforth no academical period was possible to it, nothing but death could stop its growth.

The first expression of this freedom is called Byzantine art, and there is nothing to object to in the name. For centuries Byzantium was the centre of it, and its first great work in that city (the Church of the Holy Wisdom,[4] built by Justinian in the year 540) remains its greatest work. The style leaps into sudden completeness in this most lovely building: for there are few works extant of much importance of earlier days. As to its origin, of course buildings were raised all through the sickness of classical art, and traditional forms and ways of work were still in use, and these traditions, which by this time included the forms of Roman building, were now in the hands of the Greeks. This Romano-Greek building in Greek hands met with traditions drawn from many sources. In Syria, the borderland of so many races and customs, the East mingled with the West, and

Byzantine art was born. Its characteristics are simplicity of structure and outline of mass; amazing delicacy of ornament combined with abhorrence of vagueness: it is bright and clear in colour, pure in line, hating barrenness as much as vagueness; redundant, but not florid, the very opposite of Roman architecture in spirit, though it took so many of its forms and revivified them. Nothing more beautiful than its best works has ever been produced by man, but in spite of its stately loveliness and quietude, it was the mother of fierce vigour in the days to come, for from its first days in St Sophia, Gothic architecture has still one thousand years of life before it. East and West it overran the world wherever men built with history behind them. In the East it mingled with the traditions of the native populations, especially with Persia of the Sassanian period, and produced the whole body of what we, very erroneously, call Arab art (for the Arabs never had any art) from Ispahan to Granada. In the West it settled itself in the parts of Italy that Justinian had conquered, notably Ravenna, and thence came to Venice. From Italy, or perhaps even from Byzantium itself, it was carried into Germany and pre-Norman England, touching even Ireland and Scandinavia. Rome adopted it, and sent it another road through the south of France, where it fell under the influence of provincial Roman architecture, and produced a very strong orderly and logical substyle, just what one imagines the ancient Romans might have built, if they had been able to resist the conquered Greeks who took them captive. Thence it spread all over France, the first development of the architecture of the most architectural of peoples, and in the north of that country fell under the influence of the Scandinavian and Teutonic tribes, and produced the last of the round-arched Gothic styles (named by us Norman), which those energetic warriors carried into Sicily, where it mingled with the Saracenic Byzantine and produced lovely works. But we know it best in our own country; for Duke William's intrusive monks used it everywhere, and it drove out the native English style derived from Byzantium through Germany.[5]

Here on the verge of a new change, a change of form important enough (though not a change of essence), we may pause to consider once more what its essential qualities were. It was the first style since the invention of the arch that did due honour to it, and instead of concealing it decorated it in a logical manner. This was much; but the complete freedom that it had won, which indeed was the source of its ingenuousness, was more. It had shaken off the fetters of Greek superstition and aristocracy, and Roman pedantry, and though it must needs have had laws to be a style at all, it followed them of free will, and yet unconsciously. The cant of the beauty of simplicity (*i.e.*, bareness and barrenness) did not afflict it; it was not ashamed of redundancy of material, or super-abundance of ornament, any more than nature is. Slim elegance it could produce, or sturdy solidity, as its moods went. Material was not its master, but its servant: marble was not necessary to its beauty; stone would do, or brick, or timber. In default of carving it would set together cubes of glass or whatso-ever was shining and fair-hued, and cover every portion of its interiors with a fairy coat of splendour; or would mould mere plaster into intricacy of work scarce to be followed, but never wearying the eyes with its delicacy and expressiveness of line. Smoothness it loves, the utmost finish that the hand can give; but if material or skill fail, the rougher work shall so be wrought that it also shall please us with its inventive suggestion. For the iron rule of the classical period, the acknowledged slavery of every one but the great man, was gone, and freedom had taken its place; but harmonious freedom. Subordination there is, but subordination of effect, not uniformity of detail; true and necessary subordination, not pedantic.

The full measure of this freedom Gothic Architecture did not gain until it was in the hands of the workmen of Europe, the gildsmen of the Free Cities, who on many a bloody field proved how dearly they valued their corporate life by the generous valour with which they risked their individual lives in its defence. But from the first, the tendency was towards this freedom of hand and mind subordinated to the co-operative harmony which made the freedom possible. That is the spirit of Gothic Architecture.

Let us go on a while with our history: up to this point the progress had always been from East to West, *i.e.*, the East carried the West with it; the West must now go the East to fetch new gain thence. A revival of religion was one of the moving causes of energy in the early Middle Ages in Europe, and this religion (with its enthusiasm for visible tokens of the objects of worship) impelled people to visit the East, which held the centre of that worship. Thence arose the warlike pilgrimages of the crusades amongst races by no means prepared to turn their cheeks to the smiter. True it is that the tendency of the extreme West to seek East did not begin with the days just before the crusades. There was a thin stream of pilgrims setting eastward long before, and the Scandinavians had found their way to Byzantium, not as pilgrims but as soldiers, and under the name of Voerings a bodyguard of their blood upheld the throne of the Greek Kaiser,[6] and many of them, returning home, bore with them ideas of art which were not lost on their scanty but energetic populations. But the crusades brought gain from the East in a far more wholesale manner; and I think it is clear that part of that gain was the idea of art that brought about the change from round-arched to pointed Gothic. In those days (perhaps in ours also) it was the rule for conquerors settling in any country to assume that there could be no other system of society save that into which they had been born; and accordingly conquered Syria received a due feudal government, with the King of Jerusalem for Suzerain, the one person allowed by the heralds to bear metal on metal in his coat-armour. Nevertheless, the Westerners who settled in this new realm, few in number as they were, readily received impressions from the art which they saw around them, the Saracenic Byzantine art, which was, after all, sympathetic with their own minds: and these impressions produced the change. For it is not to be thought that there was any direct borrowing of forms from the East in the gradual change from the round-arched to the pointed Gothic: there was nothing more obvious at work than the influence of a kindred style, whose superior lightness and elegance gave a hint of the road which development might take.

Certainly this change in form, when it came, was a startling one: the pointed-arched Gothic, when it had grown out of its brief and most beautiful transition, was a vigorous youth indeed. It carried combined strength and elegance almost as far as it could be carried: indeed, sometimes one might think it overdid the lightness of effect, as *e.g.*, in the interior of Salisbury Cathedral. If some abbot or monk of the eleventh century could have been brought back to his rebuilt church of the thirteenth, he might almost have thought that some miracle had taken place: the huge cylindrical or square piers transformed into clusters of slim, elegant shafts; the narrow round-headed windows supplanted by tall wide lancets showing the germs of the elaborate traceries of the next century, and elegantly glazed with pattern and subject; the bold vault spanning the wide nave instead of the flat wooden ceiling of past days; the extreme richness of the mouldings with which every member is treated; the elegance and order of the floral sculpture, the grace and good drawing of the imagery: in short, a complete and logical style with no longer anything to apologize for, claiming homage from the intellect, as well as the imagination of men; the developed Gothic Architecture which has shaken off the trammels of Byzantium as well as of Rome, but which has, nevertheless, reached its glorious position step by step with no break and no conscious effort after novelty from the wall of Tiryns and the Treasury of Mycenae.[7]

This point of development was attained amidst a period of social conflict, the facts and tendencies of which, ignored by the historians of the eighteenth century, have been laid open to our view by our modern school of evolutionary historians. In the twelfth century the actual handicraftsmen found themselves at last face to face with the development of the earlier associations of freemen which were the survivals from the tribal society of Europe: in the teeth of these exclusive and aristocratic municipalities the handicraftsmen had associated themselves into guilds of craft, and were claiming their freedom from legal and arbitrary oppression, and a share in the government of the towns; by the end of the thirteenth century they had conquered the position everywhere and within the next fifty or sixty years the governors of the free towns were the delegates of the craft guilds, and all handicraft was included in their associations. This period of their triumph, marked amidst other events by the Battle of Courtray,[8] where the chivalry of France turned their backs in flight before the Flemish weavers, was the period during which Gothic Architecture reached its zenith. It must be admitted, I think, that during this epoch, as far as the art of beautiful building is concerned, France and England were the architectural countries par excellence; but all over the intelligent world was spread this bright, glittering, joyous art, which had now reached its acme of elegance and beauty;

and moreover in its furniture, of which I have spoken above, the excellence was shared in various measure betwixt the countries of Europe. And let me note in passing that the necessarily ordinary conception of a Gothic interior as being a colourless whitey-grey place dependent on nothing but the architectural forms, is about as far from the fact as the corresponding idea of a Greek temple standing in all the chastity of white marble. We must remember, on the contrary, that both buildings were clad, and that the noblest part of their raiment was their share of a great epic, a story appealing to the hearts and minds of men. And in the Gothic building, especially in the half century we now have before us, every part of it, walls, windows, floor, was all looked on as space for the representation of incidents of the great story of mankind, as it had presented itself to the minds of men then living; and this space was used with the greatest frankness of prodigality, and one may fairly say that wherever a picture could be painted there it was painted.

For now Gothic Architecture had completed its furniture: Dante, Chaucer, Petrarch, the German Hero ballad-epics, the French Romances, the English Forest-ballads, that epic of revolt, as it has been called, the Icelandic Sagas, Froissart and the Chroniclers, represent its literature. Its painting embraces a host of names (of Italy and Flanders chiefly), the two great realists Giotto and Van Eyck at their head: but every village has its painter, its carvers, its actors even; every man who produces works of handicraft is an artist. The few pieces of household goods left of its wreckage are marvels of beauty; its woven cloths and embroideries are worthy of its loveliest building, its pictures and ornamented books would be enough in themselves to make a great period of art, so excellent they are in epic intention, in completeness of unerring decoration, and in marvellous skill of hand. In short, those masterpieces of noble building, those specimens of architecture, as we call them, the sight of which makes the holiday of our lives to-day, are the standard of the whole art of those times, and tell the story of all the completeness of art in the heyday of life, as well as that of the sad story which follows. For when anything human has arrived at quasi-completion there remains for it decay and death, in order that the new thing may be born from it; and this wonderful joyous art of the Middle Ages could by no means escape its fate.

In the middle of the fourteenth century Europe was scourged by that mysterious terror the Black Death (a terror similar to which perhaps waylays the modern world) and, along with it, the no less mysterious pests of Commercialism and Bureaucracy attacked us. This misfortune was the turning point of the Middle Ages; once again a great change was at hand.

The birth and growth of the coming change was marked by art with all fidelity. Gothic Architecture began to alter its character in the years that immediately followed on the Great Pest; it began to lose its exaltation of style and to suffer a diminution in the generous wealth of beauty which it gave us in its heyday. In some places, *e.g.*, England, it grew more crabbed, and even sometimes more common-place; in others, as in France, it lost order, virility, and purity of line. But for a long time yet it was alive and vigorous, and showed even greater capacity than before for adapting itself to the needs of a developing society: nor did the change of style affect all its furniture injuriously; some of the subsidiary arts as *e.g.*, Flemish tapestry and English wood-carving, rather gained than lost for many years.

At last, with the close of the fifteenth century, the Great Change became obvious; and we must remember that it was no superficial change of form, but a change of spirit affecting every form inevitably. This change we have somewhat boastfully, and as regards the arts quite untruthfully, called the New Birth. But let us see what it means.

Society was preparing for a complete recasting of its elements: the Mediaeval Society of Status was in process of transition into the modern Society of Contract. New classes were being formed to fit the new system of production which was at the bottom of this; political life began again with the new birth of bureaucracy; and political, as distinguished from natural, nationalities were being hammered together for the use of that bureaucracy, which was itself a necessity to the new system. And withal a new religion was being fashioned to fit the new theory of life: in short, the Age of Commercialism was being born.

Now some of us think that all this was a source of misery and degradation to the world at the time, that it is still causing misery and degradation, and that as a system it is bound to give place to a better one. Yet we admit that it had a beneficent function to perform; that amidst all the ugliness and confusion which it brought with it, it was a necessary instrument for the development of freedom of thought and the capacities of man; for the subjugation of nature to his material needs. This Great Change, I say, was necessary and inevitable, and on this side, the side of commerce and commercial science and politics, was a genuine new birth. On this side it did not look backward but forward: there had been nothing like it in past history; it was founded on no pedantic model; necessity, not whim, was its crafts-master.[9]

But, strange to say, to this living body of social, political, religious, scientific New Birth was bound the dead corpse of a past art. On every other side it bade men look forward to some change or other, were it good or bad: on the side of art, with the sternest pedagogic utterance, it bade men look backward across the days of the 'Fathers and famous men that begat them', and in scorn of them, to an art that had been dead a thousand years before. Hitherto, from the very beginning the past was past, all of it that was not alive in the present, unconsciously to the men of the present. Henceforth the past was to be our present, and the blankness of its dead wall was to shut out the future from us. There are many artists at present who do not sufficiently estimate the enormity, the portentousness of this change, and how closely it is connected with the Victorian Architecture of the brick box and the slate lid, which helps to make us the dullards that we are. How on earth could people's ideas of beauty change so? you may say. Well, was it their ideas of beauty that changed? Was it not rather that beauty, however unconsciously, was no longer an object of attainment with the men of that epoch?

This used once to puzzle me in the presence of one of the so-called masterpieces of the New Birth, the revived classical style, such a building as St Paul's in London, for example. I have found it difficult to put myself in the frame of mind which could accept such a work as a substitute for even the latest and worst Gothic building. Such taste seemed to me like the taste of a man who should prefer his lady-love bald. But now I know that it was not a matter of choice on the part of any one then alive who had an eye for beauty: if the change had been made on the grounds of beauty it would be wholly inexplicable; but it was not so. In the early days of the Renaissance there were artists possessed of the highest qualities; but those great men (whose greatness, mind you, was only in work not carried out by co-operation, painting, and sculpture for the most part) were really but the fruit of the blossoming-time, the Gothic period; as was abundantly proved by the succeeding periods of the Renaissance, which produced nothing but inanity and plausibility in all the arts. A few individual artists were great truly; but artists were no longer the masters of art, because the people had ceased to be artists: its masters were pedants. St Peter's in Rome, St Paul's in London, were not built to be beautiful, or to be beautiful and convenient. They were not built to be homes of the citizens in their moments of exaltation, their supreme grief or supreme hope, but to be proper, respectable, and therefore to show the due amount of cultivation and knowledge of the only peoples and times that in the minds of their ignorant builders were not ignorant barbarians. They were built to be the homes of a decent unenthusiastic ecclesiasticism, of those whom we sometimes call Dons now-a-days. Beauty and romance were outside the aspirations of their builders. Nor could it have been otherwise in those days; for, once again, architectural beauty is the result of the harmonious and intelligent co-operation of the whole body of people engaged in producing the work of the workman; and by the time that the changeling New Birth was grown to be a vigorous imp, such workmen no longer existed. By that time Europe had begun to transform the great army of artist-craftsmen, who had produced the beauty of her cities, her churches, manor-houses and cottages, into an enormous stock of human machines, who had little chance of earning a bare livelihood if they lingered over their toil to think of what they were doing: who were not asked to think, paid to think, or allowed to think. That invention we have, I should hope, about perfected by this time, and it must soon give place to a new one. Which is happy; for as long as the invention is in use you need not trouble yourselves about architecture, since you will not get it, as the common expression of our life, that is as a genuine thing.

But at present I am not going to say anything about direct remedies for the miseries of the New Birth; I can only tell you what you ought to do if you can. I want you to see that from the brief historic review of the progress of the Arts it results that to-day there is only one style of Architecture on which it is possible to found a true living art, which is free to adapt itself to the varying conditions of social life, climate, and so forth, and that that style is Gothic architecture. The greater part of what we now call architecture is but an imitation of an imitation of an imitation, the result of a tradition of dull respectability, or of foolish whims without root or growth in them.

Let us look at an instance of pedantic retrospection employed in the service of art. A Greek columnar temple when it was a real thing, was a kind of holy railing built round a shrine: these things the people of that day wanted, and they naturally took the form of a Greek Temple under the climate of Greece and given the mood of its people. But do we want those things? If so, I should like to know what for. And if we pretend we do and so force a Greek Temple on a modern city, we produce such a gross piece of ugly absurdity as you may see spanning the Lochs at Edinburgh. In these islands we want a roof and walls with windows cut in them; and these things a Greek Temple does not pretend to give us.

Will a Roman building allow us to have these necessaries? Well, only on the terms that we are to be ashamed of wall, roof and windows, and pretend that we haven't got either of them, but rather a whimsical attempt at the imitation of a Greek Temple.

Will a neo-classical building allow us these necessities? Pretty much on the same terms as the Roman one; except when it is rather more than half Gothic. It will force us to pretend that we have neither roof, walls, nor windows, nothing but an imitation of the Roman travesty of a Greek Temple.

Now a Gothic building has walls that it is not ashamed of; and in those walls you may cut windows wherever you please; and, if you please, may decorate them to show that you are not ashamed of them; your windows, which you must have, become one of the great beauties of your house, and you have no longer to make a lesion in logic in order not to sit in pitchy darkness in your own house, as in the sham sham-Roman style: your window, I say, is no longer a concession to human weakness, an ugly necessity (generally ugly enough in all conscience) but a glory of the Art of Building. As for the roof in the sham style: unless the building is infected with Gothic common sense, you must pretend that you are living in a hot country which needs nothing but an awning, and that it never rains or snows in these islands. Whereas in a Gothic building the roof both within and without (especially within, as is most meet) is the crown of its beauties, the abiding place of its brain.

Again, consider the exterior of our buildings, that part of them that is common to all passers-by, and that no man can turn into private property unless he builds amidst an inaccessible park. The original of our neo-classic architecture was designed for marble in a bright dry climate, which only weathers it to a golden tone. Do we really like a neo-classic building weather-beaten by the roughness of hundreds of English winters from October to June? And on the other hand, can any of us fail to be touched by the weathered surface of a Gothic building which has escaped the restorers' hands? Do we not clearly know the latter to be a piece of nature, that more excellent mood of nature that uses the hands and wills of men as instruments of creation?

Indeed time would fail me to go into the many sides of the contrast between the Architecture which is a mere pedantic imitation of what was once alive, and that which after a development of long centuries has still in it, as I think, capacities for fresh developments, since its life was cut short by an arbitrary recurrence to a style which had long lost all elements of life and growth. Once for all, then, when the modern world finds that the eclecticism of the present is barren and fruitless, and that it needs and will have a style of architecture which, I must tell you once more, can only be as part of a change as wide and deep as that which destroyed Feudalism; when it has come to that conclusion, the style of architecture will have to be historic in the true sense; it will not be able to dispense with tradition; it cannot begin at least with doing something quite different from anything that has been done before; yet whatever the form of it may be, the spirit of it will be sympathy with the needs and aspirations of its own time, not simulation of needs and aspirations passed away. Thus it will remember the history of the past, make history in the present, and teach history in the future. As to the form of it, I see nothing for it but that the form, as well as the spirit, must be Gothic;

an organic style cannot spring out of an eclectic one, but only from an organic one. In the future, therefore, our style of architecture must be Gothic Architecture.

And meanwhile of the world demanding architecture, what are we to do? Meanwhile? After all, is there any meanwhile? Are we not now demanding Gothic Architecture and crying for the fresh New Birth? To me it seems so. It is true that the world is uglier now than it was fifty years ago; but then people thought that ugliness a desirable thing, and looked at it with complacency as a sign of civilization, which no doubt it is. Now we are no longer complacent, but are grumbling in a dim unorganized manner. We feel a loss, and unless we are very unreal and helpless we shall presently begin to try to supply that loss. Art cannot be dead so long as we feel the lack of it, I say: and though we shall probably try many roundabout ways for filling up the lack; yet we shall at last be driven into the one right way of concluding that in spite of all risks, and all losses, unhappy and slavish work must come to an end. In that day we shall take Gothic Architecture by the hand, and know it for what it was and what it is.

OCCASIONAL
PROSE

* * *

'LOOKING BACKWARD'

* * *

—

A review of
Looking Backward by Edward Bellamy,
published in the *Commonweal*,
22 June 1889

We often hear it said that the signs of the spread of Socialism among English-speaking people are both abundant and striking. This is true; six or seven years ago the word Socialism was known in this country, but few even among the educated classes knew more about its meaning than Mr Bradlaugh, Mr Gladstone, or Admiral Maxse[1] know now – *i.e.* nothing. Whereas at present it is fashionable for even West-end dinner-parties to affect an interest in and knowledge of it, which indicates a wide and deep public interest. This interest is more obvious in literature perhaps than in anything else, quite outside the propagandist tracts issued by definitely Socialist societies. A certain tincture of Socialism, for instance (generally very watery), is almost a necessary ingredient nowadays in a novel which aims at being at once serious and life-like, while more serious treatment of the subject at the hands of non-Socialists is common enough. In short the golden haze of self-satisfaction and content with the best of all possible societies is rolling away before the sun-heat bred of misery and aspiration, and all people above the lowest level of intelligence (which I take to be low gambling and statesmanship) are looking towards the new development, some timorously, some anxiously, some hopefully.

It seems clear to me from the reception which Mr Bellamy's *Looking Backward* has received that there are a great many people who are hopeful in regard to Socialism. I am sure that ten years ago it would have been very little noticed if at all: whereas now several editions have been sold in America, and it is attracting general attention in England, and to anyone not deeply interested in the social question it could not be at all an attractive book. It is true that it is cast into the form of a romance, but the author states very frankly in his preface that he has only given it this form as a sugarcoating to the pill, and the device of making a man wake up in a new world has now grown so common, and has been done with so much more care and art than Mr Bellamy has used, that by itself this would have done little for it; it is the serious essay and not the slight envelope of romance which people have found interesting to them.

Since, therefore, both Socialists and non-Socialists have been so much impressed with the book, it seems to me necessary that the *Commonweal* should notice it. For it is a 'Utopia'. It purports to be written in the year 2000, and to describe the state of society at that period after a gradual and peaceable revolution has realized the Socialism which to us is but in the beginning of its militant period. It requires notice all the more because there is a certain danger in such books as this: a twofold danger; for there will be some temperaments to whom the answer given to the question, How shall we live then? will be pleasing and satisfactory, others to whom it will be displeasing and unsatisfactory. The danger to the first is that they will accept it with all its necessary errors and fallacies (which such a book *must* abound in) as conclusive statements of facts and rules of action, which will warp their efforts into futile directions. The danger to the second, if they are but enquirers or very young Socialists, is that they also accepting its speculations as facts will be inclined to say, If *that* is Socialism, we won't help its advent, as it holds out no hope to us.

The only safe way of reading a Utopia is to consider it as the expression of the temperament of its author. So looked at, Mr Bellamy's Utopia must be still called very interesting as it is constructed with due economical knowledge, and with much adroitness; and of course his temperament is that of many thousands of people. This temperament may be called the unmixed modern one, unhistoric and unartistic; it makes its owner (if a Socialist) perfectly satisfied with modern civilization, if only the injustice, misery, and waste of class society could be got rid of; which half-change seems possible to him. The only ideal of life which such a man can see is that of the industrious *professional* middle-class men of to-day purified from their crime of complicity with the monopolist class, and become independent instead of being, as they now are, parasitical. It is not to be denied that if such an ideal could be realized, it would be a great improvement on the present society. But can it be realized? It means in fact the alteration of the machinery of life in such a way that all men shall be allowed to share in the fulness of that life, for the production and upholding of which the machinery was instituted. There are clear signs to show us that that very group whose life is thus put forward as an ideal for the future are condemning it in the present, and that they also demand a revolution. The pessimistic revolt of the latter end of this century led by John Ruskin against the philistinism of the triumphant *bourgeois*, halting and stumbling as it necessarily was, shows that the change in the life of civilization had begun, before any one seriously believed in the possibility of altering its machinery.

It follows naturally from the author's satisfaction with the best part of modern life that he conceives of the change to Socialism as taking place without any breakdown of that life, or indeed disturbance of it, by means of the final development of the great private monopolies which are such a noteworthy feature of the present day. He supposes that these must necessarily be absorbed into one great monopoly which will include the whole people and be worked for its benefit by the whole people. It may be noted in passing that by this use of the word monopoly he shows unconsciously that he has his mind fixed firmly on the mere *machinery* of life: for clearly the only part of their system which the people would or could take over from the monopolists would be the machinery of organization, which monopoly is forced to use, but which is not an essential part of it. The essential of monopoly is, I warm myself by the fire which you have made, and you (very much the plural) stay outside in the cold.

To go on. This hope of the development of the trusts and rings to which the competition for privilege has driven commerce, especially in America, is the distinctive part of Mr Bellamy's book; and it seems to me to be a somewhat dangerous hope to rest upon, too uncertain to be made a sheet-anchor of. It may be indeed the logical outcome of the most modern side of commercialism – *i.e.*, the outcome that *ought* to be; but then there is its historical outcome to be dealt with – *i.e.*, what *will* be; which I cannot help thinking may be after all, as far as this commercial development is concerned, the recurrence of breaks-up and re-formations of this kind of monopoly, under the influence of competition for privilege, or war for the division of plunder, till the flood comes and destroys them all. A far better hope to trust to is that men having once got it into their heads that true life implies free and equal life, and that is now possible of attainment, they will consciously strive for its attainment at any cost. The economical semi-fatalism of some Socialists is a deadening and discouraging view, and may easily become more so, if events at present unforeseen bring back the full tide of 'commercial prosperity'; which is by no means unlikely to happen.

The great change having thus peaceably and fatalistically taken place, the author has to put forward this scheme of the organization of life; which is organized with a vengeance. His scheme may be described as State Communism,[2] worked by the very extreme of national centralization. The underlying vice in it is that the author cannot conceive, as aforesaid, of anything else than the *machinery* of society, and that, doubtless naturally, he reads in to the future of a society, which he tells us is unwastefully conducted, that terror of starvation, which is the necessary accompaniment of a society in which two-thirds or more of its labour-power *is* wasted: the result is that though he *tells* us that every man is free to choose his occupation and that work is no burden to anyone, the impression which he produces is that of a huge standing army, tightly drilled, compelled by some mysterious fate to unceasing anxiety for the production of wares to satisfy every caprice, however wasteful and absurd, that may cast up amongst them.

As an illustration it may be mentioned that everybody is to begin the serious work of production at the age of twenty-one, work three years as a labourer, and then choose his skilled occupation and work till he is forty-five, when he is to knock off his work and amuse himself (improve his mind, if he has one left him). Heavens! think of a man of forty-five changing all his habits suddenly and by compulsion! It is a small matter after this that the said persons past work should form a kind of aristocracy (how curiously old ideas cling) for the performance of certain judicial and political functions.

Mr Bellamy's ideas of life are curiously limited; he has no idea beyond existence in a great city; his dwelling of man in the future is Boston (USA) beautified. In one passage, indeed, he mentions villages, but with unconscious simplicity shows that they do not come into his scheme of economical equality, but are mere servants of the great centres of civilization. This seems strange to some of us, who cannot help thinking that our experience ought to have taught us that such aggregations of population afford the worst possible form of dwelling-place, whatever the second-worst might be.

In short, a machine-life is the best which Mr Bellamy can imagine for us on all sides; it is not to be wondered at then that his only idea of making labour tolerable is to decrease the amount of it by means of fresh and ever fresh developments of machinery. This view I know he will share with many Socialists with whom I might otherwise agree more than I can with him; but I think a word or two is due to this important side of the subject. Now surely this ideal of the great reduction of the hours of labour by the mere means of machinery is a futility. The human race has always put forth about as much energy as it could in given conditions of climate and the like, though that energy has had to struggle against the natural laziness of mankind: and the development of man's resources, which has given him greater power over nature, has driven him also into fresh desires and fresh demands on nature, and thus made his expenditure of energy much what it was before. I believe that this will be always so, and the multiplication of machinery will just – multiply machinery; I believe that the ideal of the future does not point to the lessening of men's energy by the reduction of labour to a minimum, but rather to the reduction of *pain in labour* to a minimum, so small that it will cease to be a pain; a gain to humanity which can only be dreamed of till men are even more completely equal than Mr Bellamy's Utopia would allow them to be, but which will most assuredly come about when men are really equal in condition; although it is probable that much of our so-called 'refinement', our luxury – in short, our civilization – will have to be sacrificed to it. In this part of his scheme, therefore, Mr Bellamy worries himself unnecessarily in seeking (with obvious failure) some incentive to labour to replace the fear of starvation, which is at present our only one, whereas it cannot be too often repeated that the true incentive to useful and happy labour is and must be pleasure in the work itself.

I think it necessary to state these objections to Mr Bellamy's

Utopia, not because there is any need to quarrel with a man's vision of the future of society, which, as above said, must always be more or less personal to himself; but because this book, having produced a great impression on people who are really enquiring into Socialism, will be sure to be quoted as an authority for what Socialists believe, and that, therefore, it is necessary to point out that there are some Socialists who do not think that the problem of the organization of life and necessary labour can be dealt with by a huge national centralization, working by a kind of magic for which no one feels himself responsible; that on the contrary it will be necessary for the unit of administration to be small enough for every citizen to feel himself responsible for its details, and be interested in them; that individual men cannot shuffle off the business of life on to the shoulders of an abstraction called the State, but must deal with it in conscious association with each other: that variety of life is as much an aim of a true Communism as equality of condition, and that nothing but an union of these two will bring about real freedom: that modern nationalities are mere artificial devices for the commercial war that we seek to put an end to, and will disappear with it. And, finally, that art, using that word in its widest and due signification, is not a mere adjunct of life which free and happy men can do without, but the necessary expression and indispensable instrument of human happiness.

On the other hand, it must be said that Mr Bellamy has faced the difficulty of economical reconstruction with courage, though he does not see any other sides to the problem, such, *e.g.*, as the future of the family; that at any rate he sees the necessity for the equality of the reward of labour, which is such a stumbling-block for incomplete Socialists; and his criticism of the present monopolist system is forcible and fervid. Also up and down his pages there will be found satisfactory answers to many ordinary objections. The book is one to be read and considered seriously, but it should not be taken as the Socialist bible of reconstruction; a danger which perhaps it will not altogether escape, as incomplete systems impossible to be carried out but plausible on the surface are always attractive to people ripe for change, but not knowing clearly what their aim is.

UNDER AN ELM-TREE;

or,

Thoughts in the Countryside

* * *

Published in the *Commonweal*,
6 July 1889

Midsummer in the country; here you may walk between the fields and hedges that are as it were one huge nosegay for you, redolent of bean-flowers and clover and sweet hay and elder-blossom. The cottage-gardens are bright with flowers, the cottages themselves mostly models of architecture in their way. Above them towers here and there the architecture proper of days bygone, when every crafts-man was an artist and brought definite intelligence to bear upon his work. Man in the past, nature in the present, seem to be bent on pleasing you and making all things delightful to your senses; even the burning dusty road has a look of luxury as you lie on the strip of roadside green, and listen to the blackbirds singing, surely for your benefit, and, I was going to say, as if they were paid to do it, but I was wrong, for as it is they seem to be doing their best.

And all, or let us say most, things are brilliantly alive. The shadowy bleak in the river down yonder, which – ignorant of the fate that Barking Reach is preparing for its waters – is sapphire blue under this ruffling wind and cloudless sky, and barred across here and there with the pearly white-flowered water-weeds, every yard of its banks a treasure of delicate design, meadowsweet and dewberry, and comfrey and bed-straw: from the bleak in the river, among the labyrinth of grasses, to the starlings busy in the new-shorn fields, or about the grey ridges of the hay, all is eager, and I think all is happy that is not anxious.

What is that thought that has come into one's head as one turns round in the shadow of the roadside elm? A countryside worth fighting for, if that were necessary, worth taking trouble to defend its peace. I raise my head, and betwixt the elm-boughs I see far off a grey buttressed down rising over the sea of green and blue-green meadows and fields, and dim on the flank of it over its buttresses I can see a quaint figure made by cutting the short turf away from the chalk of the hillside; a figure which represents a White Horse according to the heraldry of the period, eleven hundred years ago.[1] Hard by the hillside the country people of the day did verily fight for the peace and loveliness of this very country where I lie, and coming back from their victory scored the image of the White Horse as a token of their valour, and, who knows? perhaps as an example for their descendants to follow.

For a little time it makes the blood stir in me as I think of that; but as I watch the swallows flitting past me betwixt hedge and hedge, or mounting over the hedge in any easy sweep and hawking over the bean-field beyond, another thought comes over me. These live things I have been speaking of, bleak and swallows and starlings and blackbirds, are all after their kind beautiful and graceful, not one of them is lacking in its due grace and beauty; but yesterday as I was passing by a hay-field there was an old red-roan cart-horse looking seriously but good-humouredly at me from a gap in the hedge, and I stopped to make his acquaintance, and I am sorry to say that in spite of his obvious merits he was ugly, Roman-nosed, shambling, ungainly: yet how useful had he been – for others. Also the same day (but not in the same field) I saw some other animals, male and female, with whom also I made acquaintance, for the male ones at least were thirsty. And these animals, both male and female, were ungraceful, unbeautiful, for they were making hay before my eyes. Then I bethought me that as I had seen starlings in Hertfordshire that were of the same race as the Thames-side starlings, so I had seen or heard of featherless, two-legged animals of the same race as the thirsty creatures in the hay-field; they had been sculptured in the frieze of the Parthenon, painted on the ceiling of the Sistine Chapel, imagined in literature as the heroes and heroines of romance; nay, when people had created in their minds a god of the universe, creator of all that was, is, or shall be, they were driven to represent him as one of that same race to which the thirsty haymakers belonged; as though supreme intelligence and the greatest measure of gracefulness and beauty and majesty were at their highest in the race of those ungainly animals.

Under the elm-tree these things puzzle me, and again my thoughts return to the bold men of that very countryside who, coming back from Ashdown field, scored that White Horse to look down for ever on the valley of the Thames; and I thought it likely that they had this much in common with the starlings and the bleak, that there was more equality among them than we are used to now, and that there would have been more models available amongst them for Woden than one would be like to find in the Thames-side meadows.

Under the elm-tree I don't ask myself whether that is owing to the greater average intelligence of men at the present day, and to the progress of humanity made since the time of the only decent official that England ever had: Alfred the Great, to wit; for indeed the place and time are not favourable to such questions, which seem sheer nonsense amidst of all that waste of superabundant beauty and pleasure held out to men who cannot take it or use it, unless some chance rich idler may happen to stray that way. My thoughts turn back to the haymakers and their hopes, and I remember that yesterday morning I said to a bystander, 'Mr So-and-so (the farmer) is late in sending his men into the hay-field.'

Quoth he, 'You see, sir, Mr So-and-so is short-handed.'

'How's that?' said I, pricking up my Socialist ears.

'Well, sir,' said he, 'these men are the old men and women bred in the village, and pretty much past work; and the young men with more work in them, they do think that they ought to have more wages than them, and Mr So-and-so he won't pay it. So you see, he be short-handed.'

As I turned away, thinking over all the untold, untellable details of misery that lay within this shabby sordid story, another one met my ears. A labourer of the village comes to a farmer and says to him that he really can't work for 9s. a week any more, but must have 10s.[2] Says the farmer, 'Get your 10s. somewhere else then.' The man turns away to two months' lack of employment, and then comes back begging for his 9s. slavery.

Commonplace stories of unsupported strikes, you will say. Indeed they are, if not they would be easily remedied; the casual tragedy cut short; the casual wrong-doer branded as a person out of humanity. But since they are so commonplace—

What will happen, say my gloomy thoughts to me under the elm-tree, with all this country beauty so tragically incongruous in its richness with the country misery which cannot feel its existence? Well, if we must still be slaves and slave-holders, it will not last long:

the Battle of Ashdown will be forgotten for the last commercial crisis: Alfred's heraldry will yield to the lions on the half crown. The architecture of the crafts-gildsmen will tumble down, or be 'restored' for the benefit of hunters of the picturesque, who, hopeless themselves, are incapable of understanding the hopes of past days, or the expression of them. The beauty of the landscape will be exploited and artificialized for the sake of villa-dwellers' purses where it is striking enough to touch their jaded appetites; but in quiet places like this it will vanish year by year (as indeed it is now doing) under the attacks of the most grovelling commercialism.

Yet think I to myself under the elm-tree, whatever England, once so beautiful, may become, it will be good enough for us if we set no hope before us but the continuance of a population of slaves and slave-holders for the country which we pretend to love, while we use it and our sham love for it as a stalking-horse for robbery of the poor at home and abroad. The worst outward ugliness and vulgarity will be good enough for such sneaks and cowards.

Let me turn the leaf and find a new picture, or my holiday is spoilt; and don't let some of my Socialist friends with whom I have wrangled about the horrors of London say, 'This is all that can come of your country life.' For as the round of the seasons under our system of landlord, farmer and labourer produces in the country pinching parsimony and dulness, so does the 'excitement of intellectual life'[3] in the cities produce the slum under the capitalist system of turning out and selling market wares not for use but for waste. Turn the page, I say. The hay-field is a pretty sight this month seen under the elm, as the work goes forward on the other side of the way opposite to the bean-field, till you look at the haymakers closely. Suppose the haymakers were friends working for friends on land which was theirs, as many as were needed, with leisure and hope ahead of them instead of hopeless toil and anxiety, need their useful labour for themselves and their neighbours cripple and disfigure them and knock them out of the shape of men fit to represent the Gods and Heroes? If under such conditions a new Ashdown had to be fought (against *capitalist* robbers this time), the new White Horse would look down on the home of men as wise as the starlings, in their *equality*, and so perhaps as happy.

Preface to
THE NATURE OF GOTHIC
A chapter from *The Stones of Venice*
by John Ruskin

* * *

Kelmscott Press, 1892

The Chapter which is here put before the reader can be well considered as a separate piece of work, although it contains here and there references to what has gone before in *The Stones of Venice*. To my mind, and I believe to some others, it is one of the most important things written by the author, and in future days will be considered as one of the very few necessary and inevitable utterances of the century.

To some of us when we first read it, now many years ago, it seemed to point out a new road on which the world should travel. And in spite of all the disappointments of forty years, and although some of us, John Ruskin amongst others, have since learned what the equipment for that journey must be, and how many things must be changed before we are equipped, yet we can still see no other way out of the folly and degradation of Civilization.

For the lesson which Ruskin here teaches us is that art is the expression of man's pleasure in labour; that it is possible for man to rejoice in his work, for, strange as it may seem to us to-day, there have been times when he did rejoice in it; and lastly, that unless man's work once again becomes a pleasure to him, the token of which change will be that beauty is once again a natural and necessary accompaniment of productive labour, all but the worthless must toil in pain, and therefore live in pain.[1] So that the result of the thousands of years of man's effort on the earth must be general unhappiness and universal degradation; unhappiness and degradation, the conscious burden of which will grow in proportion to the growth of man's intelligence, knowledge, and power over material nature.

If this be true, as I for one most firmly believe, it follows that the hallowing of labour by art is the one aim for us at the present day.

If Politics are to be anything else than an empty game, more exciting but less innocent than those which are confessedly games of skill or chance, it is toward this goal of the happiness of labour that they must make.

Science has in these latter days made such stupendous strides, and is attended by such a crowd of votaries, many of whom are doubtless single-hearted, and worship in her not the purse of riches and power, but the casket of knowledge, that she seems to need no more than a little humility to temper the insolence of her triumph, which has taught us everything except how to be happy. Man has gained mechanical victory over nature, which in time to come he may be able to enjoy, instead of starving amidst of it. In those days science also may be happy; yet not before the second birth of Art, accompanied by the happiness of labour, has given her rest from the toil of dragging the car of Commerce.

Lastly it may well be that the human race will never cease striving to solve the problem of the reason for its own existence; yet it seems to me that it may do this in a calmer and more satisfactory mood when it has not to ask the question, Why were we born to be so miserable? but rather, Why were we born to be so happy?

At least it may be said that there is time enough for us to deal with this problem, and that it need not engross the best energies of mankind, when there is so much to do otherwhere.

But for this aim of at last gaining happiness through our daily and necessary labour, the time is short enough, the need so urgent, that we may well wonder that those who groan under the burden of happiness can think of anything else; and we may well admire and love the man who here called the attention of English-speaking people to this momentous subject, and that with such directness and clearness of insight, that his words could not be disregarded.

I know indeed that Ruskin is not the first man who has put forward the possibility and the urgent necessity that men should take pleasure in Labour; for Robert Owen[2] showed how by companionship and goodwill labour might be made at least endurable; and in France Charles Fourier[3] dealt with the subject at great length, and the whole of his elaborate system for the reconstruction of society is founded on the certain hope of gaining pleasure in labour. But in their times neither Owen nor Fourier could possibly have found the key to the problem with which Ruskin was provided. Fourier depends, not on art for the motive power of the realization of pleasure in labour, but on incitements, which, though they would not be lacking in any decent state of society, are rather incidental than essential parts of pleasurable work; and on reasonable arrangements, which would certainly lighten the burden of labour, but would not procure for it the element of sensuous pleasure, which is the essence of all true art. Nevertheless, it must be said that Fourier and Ruskin were touched by the same instinct, and it is instructive and hopeful to note how they arrived at the same point by such very different roads.

Some readers will perhaps wonder that in this important Chapter of Ruskin I have found it necessary to consider the ethical and political, rather than what would ordinarily be thought, the artistic side of it. I must answer, that, delightful as is that portion of Ruskin's work which describes, analyses, and criticizes art, old and new, yet this is not after all the most characteristic side of his writings. Indeed from the time at which he wrote this chapter here reprinted, those ethical and political considerations have never been absent from his criticism of art; and, in my opinion, it is just this part of his work, fairly begun in the 'Nature of Gothic' and brought to its culmination in the great book *Unto this Last*,[4] which has had the most enduring and beneficent effect on his contemporaries, and will have through them on succeeding generations.

John Ruskin the critic of art has not only given the keenest pleasure to thousands of readers by his life-like descriptions, and the ingenuity and delicacy of his analysis of works of art, but he has let a flood of daylight into the cloud of sham-technical twaddle which was once the whole substance of 'art-criticism', and is still its staple, and that is much. But it is far more that John Ruskin, the teacher of morals and politics (I do not use this word in the newspaper sense), has done serious and solid work towards that new-birth of Society, without which genuine art, the expression of man's pleasure in his handiwork, must inevitably cease altogether, and with it the hopes of the happiness of mankind.

Foreword to
UTOPIA
by Sir Thomas More

* * *

Kelmscott Press, 1893

Ralph Robinson's translation of More's *Utopia*[1] would not need any foreword if it were to be looked upon merely as a beautiful book embodying the curious fancies of a great writer and thinker of the period of the Renaissance. No doubt till within the last few years it has been considered by the moderns as nothing more serious than a charming literary exercise, spiced with the interest given to it by the allusions to the history of the time, and by our knowledge of the career of its author.

But the change of ideas concerning 'the best state of a publique weale',[2] which, I will venture to say, is the great event of the end of this century, has thrown a fresh light upon the book; so that now to some it seems not so much a regret for days which might have been, as (in its essence) a prediction of a state of society which will be. In short this work of the scholar and Catholic, of the man who resisted what has seemed to most the progressive movement of his own time,[3] has in our days become a Socialist tract familiar to the meetings and debating rooms of the political party which was but lately like 'the cloud as big as a man's hand'.[4] Doubtless the *Utopia* is a necessary part of a Socialist's library; yet it seems to me that its value as a book for the study of sociology is rather historic than prophetic, and that we Socialists should look upon it as a link between the surviving Communism of the Middle Ages[5] (become hopeless in More's time, and doomed to be soon wholly effaced by the advancing wave of Commercial Bureaucracy), and the hopeful and practical progressive movement of to-day. In fact I think More must be looked upon rather as the last of the old than the first of the new.

Apart from what was yet alive in him of mediaeval Communist tradition, the spirit of association, which amongst other things produced the Gilds, and which was strong in the Mediaeval Catholic

Church itself, other influences were at work to make him take up his parable against the new spirit of his Age. The action of the period of transition from Mediaeval to Commercial Society, with all its brutalities, was before his eyes; and though he was not alone in his time in condemning the injustice and cruelty of the revolution which destroyed the peasant life of England, and turned it into a grazing farm for the moneyed gentry; creating withal at one stroke the propertyless wage-earner, and the masterless vagrant (bodie 'pauper'),[6] yet he saw deeper into its root-causes than any other man of his own day, and left us little to add to his views on this point except a reasonable hope that those 'causes' will yield to a better form of society before long.

Moreover the spirit of the Renaissance, itself the intellectual side of the very movement which he strove against, was strong in him, and doubtless helped to create his *Utopia*, by means of the contrast which it put before his eyes of the ideal free nations of the ancients, and the sordid welter of the struggle for power in the days of dying feudalism, of which he himself was a witness. This Renaissance enthusiasm has supplanted in him the chivalry feeling of the age just passing away. To him war is no longer a delight of the well born, but rather an ugly necessity, to be carried on, if so it must be, by ugly means. Hunting and hawking are no longer the choice pleasures of Knight and Lady, but are jeered at by him as foolish and unreasonable pieces of butchery: his pleasures are in the main the reasonable ones of learning and music. With all this, his imaginations of the past he must needs read into his ideal vision, together with his own experiences of his time and people. Not only are there bondslaves and a king, and priests almost adored, and cruel punishments for the breach of the marriage contract, in that happy island, but there is throughout an atmosphere of asceticism, which has a curiously blended savour of Cato the Censor[7] and a mediaeval monk.

On the subject of war; on capital punishment; the responsibility to the public of kings and other official personages and such-like matters, More speaks words that would not be out of place in the mouth of an eighteenth-century Jacobin;[8] and at first sight this seems rather to show sympathy with what is now mere Whigism[9] than with Communism; but it must be remembered that opinions which have become (in words) the mere commonplace of ordinary *bourgeois* politicians, were then looked on as pieces of startling new and advanced thought, and do not put him on the same plane with the mere radical of the last generation.

In More, then, are met together the man instinctively sympathetic with the Communistic side of Mediaeval society; the protester against the ugly brutality of the earliest period of Commercialism; the enthusiast of the Renaissance, ever looking toward his idealized ancient society as the type and example of all really intelligent human life; the man tinged with the asceticism at once of the classical philosopher and of the monk: an asceticism indeed which he puts forward not so much as a duty, but rather as a kind of stern adornment of life.

These are we may say, the moods of the man who created Utopia for us; and all are tempered and harmonized by a sensitive clearness and delicate beauty of style, which make the book a living work of art.

But lastly we Socialists cannot forget that these qualities and excellencies meet to produce a steady expression of the longing for a society of equality of condition; a society in which the individual man can scarcely conceive of his existence apart from the Commonwealth of which he forms a portion. This, which is the essence of his book, is the essence also of the struggle in which we are engaged. Though doubtless it was the pressure of circumstances in his own days that made More what he was, yet that pressure forced him to give us, not a vision of the triumph of the new-born capitalistic society, the element in which lived the new learning and the new freedom of thought of his epoch; but a picture (his own indeed, not ours) of the real New Birth[10] which many men before him had desired; and which now indeed we may well hope is drawing near to realization, though after such a long series of events which at the time of their happening seemed to nullify his hopes completely.

HOW I BECAME
A SOCIALIST

* * *

Published in *Justice*,
16 July 1894

I am asked by the Editor to give some sort of a history of the above conversion, and I feel that it may be of some use to do so, if my readers will look upon me as a type of a certain group of people, but not so easy to do clearly, briefly and truly. Let me, however, try. But first, I will say what I mean by being a Socialist, since I am told that the word no longer expresses definitely and with certainty what it did ten years ago. Well, what I mean by Socialism is a condition of society in which there should be neither rich nor poor, neither master nor master's man, neither idle nor overworked, neither brain-sick brain workers nor heart-sick hand workers, in a word, in which all men would be living in equality of condition, and would manage their affairs unwastefully, and with the full consciousness that harm to one would mean harm to all – the realization at last of the meaning of the word COMMONWEALTH.

Now this view of Socialism which I hold to-day, and hope to die holding, is what I began with; I had no transitional period, unless you may call such a brief period of political radicalism during which I saw my ideal clear enough, but had no hope of any realization of it. That came to an end some months before I joined the (then) Democratic Federation,[1] and the meaning of my joining that body was that I had conceived a hope of the realization of my ideal. If you ask me how much of a hope, or what I thought we Socialists then living and working would accomplish towards it, or when there would be effected any change in the face of society, I must say, I do not know. I can only say that I did not measure my hope, nor the joy that it brought me at the time. For the rest, when I took that step I was blankly ignorant of economics; I had never so much as opened Adam Smith, or heard of Ricardo, or of Karl Marx. Oddly enough, I *had* read some of Mill, to wit, those posthumous papers of his (published, was it in the *Westminster Review* or the *Fortnightly*?) in which he attacks Socialism in its Fourierist guise.[2] In those papers he put the arguments, as far as they go, clearly and honestly, and the result, so far as I was concerned, was to convince me that Socialism was a necessary change, and that it was possible to bring it about in our own days. Those papers put the finishing touch to my conversion to Socialism. Well, having joined a Socialist body (for the Federation soon became definitely Socialist), I put some conscience into trying to learn the economical side of Socialism, and even tackled Marx, though I must confess that, whereas I thoroughly enjoyed the historical part of *Capital*, I suffered agonies of confusion of the brain over reading the pure economics of that great work. Anyhow, I read what I could, and will hope that some information stuck to me from my reading; but more, I must think, from continuous conversation with such friends as Bax and Hyndman and Scheu,[3] and the brisk course of propaganda meetings which were going on at the time, and in which I took my share. Such finish to what of education in practical Socialism as I am capable of I received afterwards from some of my Anarchist friends, from whom I learned, quite against their intention, that Anarchism was impossible, much as I learned from Mill against *his* intention that Socialism was necessary.

But in this telling how I fell into *practical* Socialism I have begun, as I perceive, in the middle, for in my position of a well-to-do man, not suffering from the disabilities which oppress a working man at every step, I feel that I might never have been drawn into the practical side of the question if an ideal had not forced me to seek towards it. For politics as politics, *i.e.*, not regarded as a necessary if cumbersome and disgustful means to an end, would never have attracted me, nor when I had become conscious of the wrongs of society as it now is, and the oppression of poor people, could I have ever believed in the possibility of a *partial* setting right of those wrongs. In other words, I could never have been such a fool as to believe in the happy and 'respectable' poor.

If, therefore, my ideal forced me to look for practical Socialism, what was it that forced me to conceive of an ideal? Now, here comes in what I said (in this paper) of my being a type of a certain group of mind.

Before the uprising of *modern* Socialism almost all intelligent people either were, or professed themselves to be, quite contented with the civilization of this century. Again, almost all of these really were thus contented, and saw nothing to do but to perfect the said civilization by getting rid of a few ridiculous survivals of the barbarous ages. To be short, this was the *Whig* frame of mind, natural to the modern prosperous middle-class men, who, in fact, as far as mechanical progress is concerned, have nothing to ask for, if only Socialism would leave them alone to enjoy their plentiful style.

But besides these contented ones there were others who were not really contented, but had a vague sentiment of repulsion to the triumph of civilization, but were coerced into silence by the measureless power of Whiggery. Lastly, there were a few who were in open rebellion against the said Whiggery – a few, say two, Carlyle and Ruskin. The latter, before my days of practical Socialism, was my master towards the ideal aforesaid, and, looking backward, I cannot help saying, by the way, how deadly dull the world would have been twenty years ago but for Ruskin! It was through him that I learned to give form to my discontent, which I must say was not by any means vague. Apart from the desire to produce beautiful things, the leading passion of my life has been and is hatred of modern civilization. What shall I say of it now, when the words are put into my mouth, my hope of its destruction – what shall I say of its supplanting by Socialism?

What shall I say concerning its mastery of and its waste of mechanical power, its commonwealth so poor, its enemies of the commonwealth so rich, its stupendous organization – for the misery of life! Its contempt of simple pleasures which everyone could enjoy but for its folly? Its eyeless vulgarity which has destroyed art, the one certain solace of labour? All this I felt then as now, but I did not know why it was so. The hope of the past times was gone, the struggles of mankind for many ages had produced nothing but this sordid, aimless, ugly confusion; the immediate future seemed to me likely to intensify all the present evils by sweeping away the last survivals of the days before the dull squalor of civilization had settled down on the world. This was a bad look-out indeed, and, if I may mention myself as a personality and not as a mere type, especially so to a man of my disposition, careless of metaphysics and religion, as well as of scientific analysis, but with a deep love of the earth and the life on it, and a passion for the history of the past of mankind. Think of it! Was it all to end in a counting-house on the top of a cinder-heap, with Podsnap's drawing-room[4] in the offing, and a Whig committee dealing out champagne to the rich and margarine to the poor in such convenient proportions as would make all men contented together, though the pleasure of the eyes was gone from the world, and the place of Homer was to be taken by Huxley?[5] Yet, believe me, in my heart, when I really forced myself to look towards the future, that is what I saw in it, and, as far as I could tell, scarce anyone seemed to think it worth while to struggle against such a consummation of civilization. So there I was in for a fine pessimistic end of life, if it had not somehow dawned on me that amidst all this filth of civilization the seeds of a great chance, what we others call Social-Revolution, were beginning to germinate. The whole face of things was changed to me by that discovery, and all I had to do then in order to become a Socialist was to hook myself on to the practical movement, which, as before said, I have tried to do as well as I could.

To sum up, then, the study of history and the love and practice of art forced me into a hatred of the civilization which, if things were to stop as they are, would turn history into inconsequent nonsense, and make art a collection of the curiosities of the past which would have no serious relation to the life of the present.

But the consciousness of revolution stirring amidst our hateful modern society prevented me, luckier than many others of artistic perceptions, from crystallizing into a mere railer against 'progress' on the one hand, and on the other from wasting time and energy in any of the numerous schemes by which the quasi-artistic of the middle classes hope to make art grow when it has no longer any root, and thus I became a practical Socialist.

A last word or two. Perhaps some of our friends will say, what have we to do with these matters of history and art? We want by means of Social-Democracy to win a decent livelihood, we want in some sort to live, and that at once. Surely any one who professes to think that the question of art and cultivation must go before that of the knife and fork (and there are some who do propose that) does not understand what art means, or how that its roots must have a soil of a thriving and unanxious life. Yet it must be remembered that civilization has reduced the workman to such a skinny and pitiful existence, that he scarcely knows how to frame a desire for any life much better than that which he now endures perforce. It is the province of art to set the true ideal of a full and reasonable life before him, a life to which the perception and creation of beauty, the enjoyment of real pleasure that is, shall be felt to be as necessary to man as his daily bread, and that no man, and no set of men, can be deprived of this except by mere opposition, which should be resisted to the utmost.

A NOTE
BY WILLIAM MORRIS
ON HIS AIMS IN FOUNDING
THE KELMSCOTT PRESS

* * *

Published by
the Kelmscott Press,
1896

I began printing books with the hope of producing some which would have a definite claim to beauty, while at the same time they should be easy to read and should not dazzle the eye, or trouble the intellect of the reader by eccentricity of form in the letters. I have always been a great admirer of the calligraphy of the Middle Ages, and of the earlier printing which took its place. As to the fifteenth-century books, I had noticed that they were always beautiful by force of the mere typography, even without the added ornament, with which many of them are so lavishly supplied. And it was the essence of my undertaking to produce books which it would be a pleasure to look upon as pieces of printing and arrangement of type. Looking at my adventure from this point of view then, I found I had to consider chiefly the following things: the paper, the form of the type, the relative spacing of the letters, the words, and the lines; and lastly the position of the printed matter on the page.

It was a matter of course that I should consider it necessary that the paper should be hand-made, both for the sake of durability and appearance. It would be a very false economy to stint in the quality of the paper as to price: so I had only to think about the kind of hand-made paper. On this head I came to two conclusions: first, that the paper must be wholly of linen (most hand-made papers are of cotton today), and must be quite 'hard' *i.e.*, thoroughly well sized; and second, that, though it must be 'laid' and not 'wove' (*i.e.*, made on a mould made of obvious wires), the lines caused by the wires of the mould must not be too strong, so as to give a ribbed appearance. I found that on these points I was at one with the practice of the papermakers of the fifteenth century; so I took as my model a Bolognese paper of about 1473. My friend Mr Batchelor, of Little Chart, Kent, carried out my views very satisfactorily, and produced from the first the excellent paper which I still use.[1]

Next as to type. By instinct rather than by conscious thinking it over, I began by getting myself a fount of Roman Type. And here what I wanted was letter pure in form; severe, without needless excrescences; solid, without the thickening and thinning of the line, which is the essential fault of the ordinary modern type, and which makes it difficult to read;[2] and not compressed laterally, as all later type has grown to be owing to commercial exigencies. There was only one source from which to take examples of this perfected Roman type, to wit, the works of the great Venetian printers of the fifteenth century, of whom Nicholas Jenson[3] produced the completest and most Roman characters from 1470 to 1476. This type I studied with much care, getting it photographed to a big scale, and drawing it over many times before I began designing my own letter; so that though I think I mastered the essence of it, I did not copy it servilely; in fact, my Roman type,[4] especially in the lower-case, tends rather more to the Gothic than does Jenson's.

After a while I felt that I must have a Gothic as well as a Roman fount; and herein the task I set myself was to redeem the Gothic character from the charge of unreadableness which is commonly brought against it. And I felt that this charge could not be reasonably brought against the types of the first two decades of printing: that Schoeffer at Mainz, Mentelin at Strassburg, and Günther Zainer at Augsburg,[5] avoided the spiky ends and undue compression which lay some of the later type open to the above charge. Only the earlier printers (naturally following therein the practice of their predecessors the scribes) were very liberal of contractions, and used an excess of 'tied' letters,[6] which, by the way, are very useful to the compositor. So I entirely eschewed contractions, except for the '&', and had very few tied letters, in fact none but the absolutely necessary ones. Keeping my end steadily in view, I designed a black-letter type[7] which I think I may claim to be as readable as a Roman one, and to say the truth I prefer it to the Roman. This type is of the size called Great Primer (the Roman type is of 'English' size); but later on I was driven by the necessities of the Chaucer (a double-columned book) to get a smaller Gothic type of Pica size.[8]

The punches for all these types, I may mention, were cut for me with great intelligence and skill by Mr E. P. Prince,[9] and render my designs most satisfactorily.

Now as to the spacing: First, the 'face' of the letter should be as nearly conterminous with the 'body' as possible,[10] so as to avoid undue whites between the letters. Next, the lateral spaces between the words should be (*a*) no more than is necessary to distinguish clearly the division into words, and (*b*) should be as nearly equal as possible. Modern printers, even the best, pay very little heed to these two essentials of seemly composition, and the inferior ones run riot in licentious spacing, thereby producing, *inter alia*, those ugly rivers of lines running about the page which are such a blemish to decent printing. Third, the whites between the lines should not be excessive; the modern practice of 'leading'[11] should be used as little as possible, and never without some definite reason, such as marking some special piece of printing. The only leading I have allowed myself is in some cases a 'thin' lead between the lines of my Gothic Pica type: in the Chaucer and the double-columned books I have used a 'hair' lead, and not even this in the 16mo books.[12] Lastly, but by no means least, comes the position of the printed matter on the page. This should always leave the inner margin the narrowest, the top somewhat wider, the outside (fore-edge) wider still, and the bottom widest of all. This rule is never departed from in mediaeval books, written or printed. Modern printers systematically transgress against it; thus apparently contradicting the fact that the unit of a book is not one page, but a pair of pages. A friend, the librarian of one of our most important private libraries, tells me that after careful testing he has come to the conclusion that the mediaeval rule was to make a difference of twenty per cent from margin to margin. Now these matters of spacing and position are of the greatest importance in the production of beautiful books; if they are properly considered they will make a book printed in quite ordinary type at least decent and pleasant to the eye. The disregard of them will spoil the effect of the best designed type.

It was only natural that I, a decorator by profession, should attempt to ornament my books suitably: about this matter I will only say that I have always tried to keep in mind the necessity for making my decoration a part of the page of type. I may add that in designing the magnificent and inimitable woodcuts which have adorned several of my books, and will above all adorn the Chaucer which is now drawing near completion, my friend Sir Edward Burne-Jones has never lost sight of this important point, so that his work will not only give us a series of most beautiful and imaginative pictures, but form the most harmonious decoration possible to the printed book.

LETTERS

* * *

[THE EASTERN QUESTION]

* * *

From the *Daily News*,
26 October 1876

I cannot help noting that a rumour is about in the air that England is
going to war;[1] and from the depths of my astonishment I ask, On
behalf of whom? Against whom? And for what end? Some three
weeks ago, if such a rumour had arisen, my questions would, I
imagine, have been answered in this way: – 'The English nation has
been roused to a sense of justice (for at heart they are a generous
people) by a story of horrors that no man has been able to gainsay;
so they are going to war against the Turkish Government on behalf
of certain subject peoples, whom the Turks conquered long ago but
have never assimilated, and whom now, in their decrepitude, insol-
vency, and terror, they have been torturing and oppressing in the
vilest manner, while they claim to be considered and treated as a
civilized government and a part of the comity of Europe. The end
and aim of the war is to force the Turkish Government (who, to
speak the downright truth, are a gang of thieves and murderers) to
give these subject peoples, who are quite orderly and industrious,
some chance for existence; to force the Turkish Government to agree
to give these peoples some security for life, limb, and property, and
to take order that they shall carry out their agreement (by occupying
their territory or otherwise) – this is the end and aim of the war; and
we and all Europe think it is a just and honourable aim, and that we
are the right people to see it carried through; for we, a peaceful
people, not liars (except in trade), we have nothing to gain by
helping these luckless folks to live; and, though we are only their
neighbours, in the sense that the Samaritan was to him who fell
among thieves, yet w. are in a kind of way responsible for their
usage, for we have before this waged a great war to keep the Turks,
their jailors, alive,[2] thinking that we could make them a respectable

and even a progressive people – so sanguine, and, to say the truth, such fools we were! However, except that we are still paying for it out of pocket, all that is past; we meant no harm then, and now we mean good and will do it.'

If I had fallen asleep three weeks ago, and woke up yesterday, I should have expected some such answer to my questions of – For whom? Against whom? and Why?[3] And I, a mere sentimentalist, should have rejoiced in such a war, and thought it wholly good: the people to be helped worthy of helping, the enemy thieves and murderers, all Europe our friends, no mouth to gainsay us but the mouths of thieves and murderers. Yes, I should have thought I had lived for something at last: to have seen all England just, and in earnest, the Tories converted or silenced, and our country honoured throughout all the world. In very truth, all this seemed on the point of happening three weeks ago, though without the terrible expense of a war; but alas, though I have not slept, I have awakened, and find the shoe quite on the other foot. The Tories are not converted; England is pretty much mocked throughout all the world. I must sorrowfully say, justly mocked, if, as I fear, we were not in earnest when we held all those meetings, and passed all those resolutions full of just anger, as it seemed. I say, not in earnest, because, to put all conventionalities aside, we know well that, in matters of peace or war, no government durst go against the expressed will of the English people, when it has a will and can find time to express it; and, on the other hand, again setting aside conventionalities of 'deliberation', 'calm', 'statesmanship', and the like, we know well that our Tory Government has determined to disregard, as utterly as if it had not happened, the seeming enthusiasm of repentance which the dreadful facts stated by your Correspondent and Mr Schuyler, and confirmed by Mr Baring, seemed to awake,[4] and which Mr Gladstone's noble and generous rhetoric,[5] and Mr Freeman's manly and closely-reasoned letters,[6] fanned into a seeming fire. We know, to speak plainly, that the new-made 'brave' earl,[7] to whom 'nothing is difficult', has at all events found it easy to see through a ladder, and is determined to drag us into a shameful and unjust war – how shameful and unjust no words can say. I say it would be impossible for even that clever trickster to do this, not only if united England were in earnest to gainsay him, but even if a large minority were but half in earnest and spoke, and said 'No'. And now, not even the wretched packed Parliament we have got is sitting. The cry for that was not believed; the members are too busy shooting in the country, and the nation is dumb, if it were not for the 2,000 working men who met last Sunday at Clerkenwell,[8] and who took it for granted, as every-body I come across does, that the crossing of the Turkish boundaries by Russian troops would be followed at a greater or less time by England's declaration of war against Russia. And do you suppose the Turks do not take the same thing for granted?

I appeal to the Liberal party, and ask if it is not worth while their making some effort to avoid this shame. I appeal to the working men, and pray them to look to it that if this shame falls upon them they will certainly remember it and be burdened by it when their day clears for them, and they attain all, and more than all, they now are striving for: to the organizers of both these bodies I specially appeal, to set their hands to the work before it is too late, to drop all other watch-words that this at least may be heard – No war on behalf of Turkey; no war on behalf of the thieves and murderers! I appeal to all men of sense and feeling of all parties, and bid them think what war means, and to think if only perhaps this were an unjust war! What, then, could come of it but shame in defeat and shame in victory, and in the end ignominious undoing of all that the war should seem to do. I who am writing this am one of a large class of men – quiet men, who usually go about their own business, heeding public matters less than they ought, and afraid to speak in such a huge concourse as the English nation, however much they may feel, but who are now stung into bitterness by thinking how helpless they are in a public matter that touches them so closely. To these also I appeal to break silence at last, if they in any wise can, and to be as little hopeless as may be, for that all may perhaps help, and perhaps they as much as people more busy in such things; for the old proverb is true now as ever – 'Like people, like priest.' If this monstrous shame and disaster – if this curse – has to fall upon us, we cannot make Lord Beaconsfield or Lord Derby,[9] the Tory party or the House of Commons, our scapegoats; we must, our very selves, bear the curse, and make the best of it, for we put these men where they sit over us, and do their own will, such as it is; and we can put them down again if we choose. And, meanwhile till that happy day comes round, I say again that I firmly believe that a large minority, or even not so very large a minority of the English people, expressing their earnest will, would be enough to prevent any war; for, surely, even the Earl of Beaconsfield must hesitate before signing the death-warrant of so many men, if he has an excuse given him for it; since they say he is human, though, indeed, I scarce believe it. Any war could be stayed, much more, surely, such a cynically unjust and shameful one as this would be – nay, such a monstrously laughable one, if the world could laugh for shame and grief. This is the last word. I call on all those who attended those many-thronged and enthusiastic meetings throughout the country the other day to meet again. Let their organizers see to it. For I assure them that not the less because they have forgotten it were those babies murdered in Bulgaria – there were more, I believe, slain in Scio a while ago,[10] but that is more utterly forgotten than these last – not the less were the poor souls robbed to their very shirts, it seems; not the less because they no longer heed it are people dying hundreds a day of cold and hunger out there; let those who attended those meetings, now they have rested, once more bring their imaginations to bear upon it all, and to take note that we have refused to help these poor people, that we have refused to take order that the like desolation shall not happen again, and have forced the Russians to do our share and their own of the business – for which we propose to go to war with them, after all we have said in our thronged and enthusiastic meetings! Can history show a greater absurdity than this, or greater fools than the English people will be if they do not make it clear to the Ministry and the Porte[11] that they will wage no war on behalf of the Turks, no war on behalf of thieves and murderers?

I beg with humility to be allowed to inscribe myself, in the company of Mr Gladstone and Mr Freeman, and all men that I esteem, as an hysterical sentimentalist; and I am, Sir, your obedient servant,

William Morris
Author of *The Earthly Paradise*

[ANTI-SCRAPE]

* * *

From the *Athenaeum*,
10 March 1877

My eye just now caught the word 'restoration' in the morning paper, and, on looking closer, I saw that this time it is nothing less than the Minster of Tewkesbury that is to be destroyed by Sir Gilbert Scott.[1] Is it altogether too late to do something to save it – it and whatever else of beautiful or historical is still left us on the sites of the ancient buildings we were once so famous for? Would it not be of some use once for all, and with the least delay possible, to set on foot an association for the purpose of watching over and protecting these relics, which, scanty as they are now become, are still wonderful treasures, all the more priceless in this age of the world, when the newly-invented study of living history is the chief joy of so many of our lives?

Your paper has so steadily and courageously opposed itself to those acts of barbarism which the modern architect, parson, and squire call 'restoration',[2] that it would be waste of words to enlarge here on the ruin that has been wrought by their hands; but, for the saving of what is left, I think I may write a word of encouragement, and say that you by no means stand alone in the matter, and that there are many thoughtful people who would be glad to sacrifice time, money, and comfort in defence of those ancient monuments: besides, though I admit that the architects are, with very few exceptions, hopeless, because interest, habit and ignorance bind them, and that the clergy are hopeless, because their order, habit, and an ignorance yet grosser, bind them; still there must be many people whose ignorance is accidental rather than inveterate, whose good sense could surely be touched if it were clearly put to them that they were destroying what they, or, more surely still, their sons and sons' sons, would one day fervently long for, and which no wealth or energy could ever buy again for them.

What I wish for, therefore, is that an association should be set on foot to keep a watch on old monuments, to protest against all 'restoration' that means more than keeping out wind and weather, and, by all means, literary and other, to awaken a feeling that our ancient buildings are not mere ecclesiastical toys, but sacred monuments of the nation's growth and hope.

William Morris

[ST MARK'S, VENICE]

* * *

From the *Daily News*,
1 November 1879

Sir   31 October 1879

I have just received information, on the accuracy of which I can rely, that the restoration of the west front of St Mark's at Venice, which has long been vaguely threatened, is to be taken in hand at once.[1] A commission is called for next month, to examine its state and to determine whether it is to be pulled down immediately or to be allowed to stand till next year. The fate of such a building seems to me a subject important enough to warrant me in asking you to grant me space to make an appeal to your readers to consider what a disaster is threatened hereby to art and culture in general. Though this marvel of art and treasure of history has suffered some disgraces, chiefly in the base mosaics that have supplanted the earlier ones, it is in the main in a genuine and untouched state, and to the eye of anyone not an expert in building looks safe enough from anything but malice or ignorance. But anyhow, if it be in any way unstable, it is impossible to believe that a very moderate exercise of engineering skill would not make it as sound as any building of its age can be. Whatever pretexts may be put forward, therefore, the proposal to rebuild it can only come from those that suppose that they can renew and better (by imitation) the workmanship of its details, hitherto supposed to be unrivalled; by those that think that there is nothing distinctive between the thoughts, and expression of the thoughts, of the men of the twelfth and of the nineteenth century; by those that prefer gilding, glitter, and blankness, to the solemnity of tone, and the incident that hundreds of years of wind and weather have given to the marble, always beautiful, but from the first meant to grow more beautiful by the lapse of time; in short, those only can think the 'restoration' of St Mark's possible who neither know nor care that it has now become a work of art, a monument of history, and a piece of nature. Surely I need not enlarge on the pre-eminence of St Mark's in all these characters, for no one who even pretends to care about art, history, or nature, would call it in question; but I will assert that, strongly as I may have seemed to express myself, my words but feebly represent the feelings of a large body of cultivated men who will feel real grief at the loss that seems imminent – a loss which may be slurred over, but which will not be forgotten, and which will be felt ever deeper as cultivation spreads. That the outward aspect of the world should grow uglier day by day in spite of the aspirations of civilization, nay, partly because of its triumphs, is a grievous puzzle to some of us who are not lacking in sympathy for those aspirations and triumphs, artists and craftsmen as we are. So grievous it is that sometimes we are tempted to say, 'Let them make a clean sweep of it all then: let us forget it all, and muddle on as best we may, unencumbered with either history or hope!' But such despair is, we well know, a treason to the cause of civilization and the arts, and we do our best to overcome it, and to strengthen ourselves in the belief that even a small minority will at last be listened to, and its reasonable opinions be accepted. In this belief I have troubled you with this letter, and I call on all those who share it to join earnestly in any attempt that may be made to save us from an irreparable loss – a loss which only headlong rashness could make possible. Surely it can never be too late to pull down St Mark's at Venice, the wonder of the civilized world? – I am, Sir, yours obediently,

William Morris

NOTES

* * *

ROMANCE

A King's Lesson

1. *Matthias Corvinus, king of Hungary*: Reigned from 1458 to 1490. He was the ideal Renaissance prince: scholar, soldier and statesman. Like Alfred the Great, he was elected to the throne before he reached his majority. Long after his death it was said among the Hungarian peasants: 'King Matthias is dead; justice is perished.'
2. *carles*: A carle is a man, freeman, man of the people (Old Norse, but found in Old English from the time of the Danish Kings).
3. *For you must know ... he were a king's son*: János Hunyadi (*c.* 1387–1456), Hungarian general, statesman and national hero. Regarded as the champion of Christendom, he successfully repelled several Turkish invasions. He was at one time rumoured to have been the illegitimate son of the Emperor Sigismund.

Two extracts from A Dream of John Ball

1. *delator*: Informer.
2. *St Martin, and St Francis, and St Thomas of Canterbury*: All saints with whom Ball might be expected to identify. St Thomas à Becket defied a king and was martyred as a result; tradition holds, moreover, that he championed the oppressed Saxons against their Norman masters. St Francis of Assisi espoused poverty. St Martin of Tours was the soldier who is said to have cut his cloak in half to clothe a beggar. (A painting of the incident is described later in this extract.)
3. *Our dead*: i.e., those on the rebel side who had fallen in the day's battle.

4. *as thou thyself saidst at the cross*: The dreamer had heard Ball preaching at the village cross before the battle.

5. *villein*: A serf. The villeinage was the lowest and most populous class in the feudal system.

6. *the men of the Canterbury gilds*: i.e., the cradle of Wat Tyler's rebellion in 1381. Morris saw the medieval craftsman's gild (or guild) as a forerunner of the modern trades union.

The words 'shuttle', 'spring-staves', 'sley' and 'shed' refer to parts of the old hand-weaver's loom, which Morris had taught himself how to use. In 1879 he designed and wove a whole high-warp tapestry single-handed. In this passage the narrator is explaining to Ball the principle of the spinning-jenny and the other innovations in weaving that launched the Industrial Revolution.

7. *the hundred*: Division of a county in medieval England.

8. *forestalling and regrating*: See 'The Hopes of Civilization', p. 310, for Morris's own definitions of these terms, central to his understanding of the feudal economy.

9. *dortoir*: Dormitory. Under feudalism, it was only through the Church that churls (i.e., peasants) could rise in society.

10. *St Alban's ... Merton*: Immensely wealthy abbeys that, since the Dissolution of the Monasteries, have disappeared almost without trace. The Morris & Co. print-works, as it happens, were near the site of Merton Abbey.

11. *poll-groat bailiffs*: Poll tax collectors ('poll' means 'head'; a groat was a coin worth fourpence). The introduction of a poll tax was one of the main causes of the revolt.

12. *quit-rent*: 'A rent ... paid by a freeholder or copyholder in lieu of services that might be required of him' (OED).

13. *I got up presently ... against my will*: A Dream of John Ball ends where News from Nowhere begins: at Morris's London home, Kelmscott House, which overlooks the Thames at Hammersmith.

The Thames Conservancy Board was responsible for maintaining the river. Because they took maintenance to include clearing the river-banks of wild flowers and cutting down trees on the tow-paths, Morris often came into conflict with them.

the 'Great Wen': London. The phrase is from *Rural Rides* by William Cobbett (1763–1835). Morris was much influenced by the directness of

Cobbett's prose, as well as by the anarchic tinge to his radical politics.

14. *John Ruskin ... would call 'play'*: Ruskin (1819–1900) was a major influence on every aspect of Morris's work. (See Introduction, pp. xii, xxv, xxxiii–xxxiv.) Morris is presumably thinking of 'The Nature of Gothic' (see pp. 365–9). For instance: 'It is not that men are ill-fed, but that they have no pleasure in the work by which they make their bread, and therefore look to wealth as the only means of pleasure.' Since Morris's work was a pleasure to him, he thought of it as 'play' by comparison with that of a factory-worker. There is also a rich meditation on play in art in 'Grotesque Renaissance', a chapter from the third volume of Ruskin's *The Stones of Venice*.

News from Nowhere

The text used here is that of the first British edition, published by Reeves & Turner (London, 1891) and subsequently followed by May Morris in *The Collected Works*. For this edition Morris revised and enlarged the text that had appeared in the *Commonweal* and in the first US edition, published by Roberts Bros. (Boston, 1890). A further edition was published by Morris himself at the Kelmscott Press in 1892. In the following notes I am often indebted to the only previous annotated edition, edited by James Redmond, London (Routledge & Kegan Paul) 1970; I refer to this edition as 'Redmond'. In the interests of consistency and readability, I have made a few adjustments to spelling, capitalization and punctuation. This is especially the case with *News from Nowhere*, there being so many early editions, but I have also taken a few such liberties with other texts as well.

1. *Up at the League*: The 'friend' has just attended an executive meeting of the Socialist League at Farringdon Street in the City. As *News from Nowhere* was serialized in the League's weekly paper, the *Commonweal*, it is explicitly addressed to Morris's fellow 'Leaguers', as the end of this chapter makes clear.

2. *For the rest ... Anarchist opinions*: See Introduction, p. xix.

3. *a carriage of the underground railway*: The London Tube was opened in 1863. The Metropolitan and District lines, which run

through Hammersmith (where Morris lived), were already in operation in 1890. The steam locomotives then in use were causing serious ventilation problems and overcrowding was regarded as normal.

4. *his own house ... suspension bridge*: Morris bought Kelmscott House in Hammersmith in 1878. A Georgian building, it takes its name from Kelmscott Manor, the sixteenth-century house he rented in Oxfordshire, which provides the setting for the book's conclusion. Hammersmith Bridge was built in 1887.

5. *2003*: In the *Commonweal* this date was 1971.

6. *Colney Hatch*: An asylum for the mentally ill in north London, now Friern Hospital.

7. *Crosby Hall*: The hall of a fifteenth-century house built in Bishopsgate for Sir John Crosby, a wool merchant, and subsequently the home of Sir Thomas More. In 1908 it was demolished and reconstructed near the Thames at Chelsea, where it still stands. According to Sir Nikolaus Pevsner, 'Crosby Hall is invaluable as evidence of how sumptuously C15 merchants built in London' (*The Buildings of England*).

8. *clearing of houses in 1955*: Walthamstow was a village in the Essex countryside when Morris was born there in 1834. By the 1890s it was beginning to be absorbed into London.

9. *High Beech*: Queen Elizabeth's Lodge was a hunting lodge at Chingford, which now survives as a museum of natural history. High Beech was a village in the forest noted for its beauty and the height of its church spire.

10. *as Scott says*: Morris was a passionate devotee of Sir Walter Scott's novels. His set of them can still be found on his bookshelves at Kelmscott Manor.

11. Ne quid nimis: Latin motto: 'Nothing in excess'.

12. *Boffin*: From Charles Dickens's *Our Mutual Friend*. Boffin is nicknamed 'the Golden Dustman' because he has unexpectedly inherited a fortune from his employer, a wealthy dust-contractor. Morris was a great admirer of Dickens and was especially fond of Boffin, a warmhearted humorous character, whose catch-phrases he liked to imitate.

13. *King Street*: A major road, now part of the A315. It runs into Hammersmith Broadway, a busy road junction at the centre of the suburb, where the Tube station is situated.

14. *Gothic of northern Europe ... and Byzantine*: Morris did not admire much Gothic Revival architecture. In *News from Nowhere* he praises design that has roots in ancient traditions but without any purist attachment to particular styles or periods. 'Saracenic' is the term Morris uses for the architecture of medieval Islam.

15. *Mote-House*: A *moot* or *mote* (Old English and Old Norse) is 'an assembly of people, *esp*. one forming a court of judicature' (OED). The language of *News from Nowhere* includes fewer archaisms than the historical romances do, but Morris's love of English and Norse in their older forms occasionally led him to borrow appropriate words – partly for historical resonance, partly as ornaments. The democratic institutions of Nowhere owe much to the Norse *Thing*, as described in the sagas (see *The Story of Grettir the Strong*, which Morris translated, and *Burnt Njal*).

16. *Do you still use them?*: For the Socialist League's opposition to Parliament, see Introduction, pp. xix–xx.

17. *a queer antiquarian society ... public nuisances*: Morris anticipates the survival into post-revolutionary times of his own Society for the Protection of Ancient Buildings (see Introduction, pp. xvii–xviii). He loathed the 'wedding-cake' Gothic of the Houses of Parliament, but in practice he sometimes campaigned through the Society to preserve old buildings of historic value that he disliked (e.g., Wren's City churches; St Paul's Cathedral is one of the buildings Dick goes on to disparage).

18. *Blue-devils ... Mulleygrubs*: Traditional nicknames for depression or hypochondria.

19. *too ridiculous to be true*: The old man is referring to the event Guest has just recalled, the dispersal of free-speech demonstrators by violent police action in Trafalgar Square, 13 November 1887 (see Introduction, pp. xx–xxi). The 'great battle' of 1952, clearly modelled on Morris's memories of that confrontation, is described in Chapter XVII.

20. *We came just here on a gang ... Again I pondered silently*: Added in 1891.

21. *For this the Gods ... the tale and the lay*: From Homer's *Odyssey*, Bk VIII. The nineteenth-century translation is in fact by William Morris. Hammond does indeed quote roughly – which is to say he misquotes!

22. *no bed of Procrustes*: In the Greek myth, a robber named Procrustes forced his victims into one or other of two beds. He stretched their bodies to fit the big bed and chopped off their extremities to fit the small one. In Morris's view the centralization of modern society similarly deforms our humanity in the interests of social control. Where sexual relations are concerned, social convention is as rigid and oppressive as the rule of law.

23. *How the Man minded the House*: A Norwegian folk-tale which Morris found in George Webb Dasent's *Popular Tales from the Norse* (1858).

24. *a pretty good cook myself*: As Morris himself was proud of being.

25. *respectable commercial marriage bed*: Redmond comments: 'Here, as so often in *News from Nowhere*, Morris is elaborating one of the central points of *The Manifesto of the Socialist League*, which he successfully presented for adoption ... on 5 July 1885.' Redmond quotes this sentence:

Our modern bourgeois property-marriage, maintained as it is by its necessary complement, universal venal prostitution, would give place to kindly and human relations between the sexes.

He adds this note from the second edition of the *Manifesto*:

Under a Socialist system contracts between individuals would be voluntary and unenforced by the community. This would apply to the marriage contract as well as others, and it would become a matter of simple inclination. Women also would share in the certainty of livelihood which would be the lot of all: and children would be treated from their birth as members of the community entitled to share in all its advantages; so that economical compulsion could no more be brought to bear on the contract than legal compulsion could be. Nor would a truly enlightened public opinion, freed from mere theological views as to chastity, insist on its permanently binding nature in the face of any discomfort or suffering that might come of it.

This cannot have been uninfluenced by Morris's own unhappy experience of the married state.

26. *Fourierist phalangsteries*: François Charles Marie Fourier (1772–1837) was a French Socialist thinker. He argued that the capitalist emphasis on self-interest had twisted human instincts and desires and that the

consequent deformity was embodied in the social arrangements of modern life – in marriage, in the family and in housing. He therefore proposed that a Socialist society would be divided into *phalanges*, each consisting of about 1,600 people, who would live in communal buildings called *phalanstères*. To Morris, though he esteemed Fourier (see Chapter XV), this smacked of the regimentation he disliked in Bellamy's *Looking Backward* and in many aspects of 'scientific' Socialism. As Hammond here suggests, such communes might have been useful as 'refuge[s] from mere destitution', but Socialism (so Morris thought) should ultimately aspire to humaner, more natural forms of social organization.

27. *towards the east*: The dockland district of London, the East End, was until recently the poorest part of the city. Most of the places referred to in the next few pages are in this district.

28. *Hood's Song of the Shirt*: A popular ballad of 1843 which protests against the notoriously unjust conditions of labour that prevailed in the clothing industry at that time. The poet, Thomas Hood (1799–1845), is mainly known for light and humorous verse, but he also wrote several 'protest poems' that had some social effect.

29. *the Swindling Kens*: '[Vagabonds' slang.] A house; *esp.* a house where thieves, beggars, or disreputable characters meet or lodge' (*OED*).

30. *Isaak Walton used to fish*: Walton (1593–1683) was a Londoner and wrote a book about fishing, *The Compleat Angler* (1653). Stratford is a suburb of London on the river Lea, which joins the Thames four miles east of the City. Fishing was Morris's favourite relaxation.

31. *It is now a garden*: Morris's writings, including *News from Nowhere*, influenced the Garden City movement in the United States and Britain. He also affected modern ideas about gardening, notably through the work of Gertrude Jekyll.

32. *no tumble-down picturesque . . . drawing architecture*: 'Picturesque' artists in the late eighteenth and nineteenth centuries tended to paint scenes that were wild, disordered and associated with poverty. They particularly favoured humble dwellings in a state of decay.

33. *old Horrebow's snakes in Iceland*: Chapter LXXII of *The Natural History of Iceland* by Niels Horrebow (1752) is entitled 'Concerning Snakes' and consists of one sentence only: 'No snakes of any kind are to be met with throughout the whole island.'

34. *Said I: 'How about ... Do you assert that there are none?'*: Added in 1891.

35. *But do you know ... very like democracy*: Guest is presumably referring to the direct democracy of ancient Athens.

36. *the tyranny of society should be abolished*: i.e., Anarchism. Morris agreed with most of the *aims* of Anarchism, but he thought they could be achieved only through the evolution of Socialism.

37. *Fourier ... understood the matter better*: For Fourier, see note 26 above. Fourier was the only major Socialist thinker to advocate 'the necessity and possibility of making labour attractive', which, as Morris says in 'The Hopes of Civilization' (p. 322), 'Socialism can by no means do without'. Morris's theory of pleasurable labour is the most original part of his thought. It derives largely from Ruskin but is modified by Fourier and by Marx's theory of alienation. In his preface to *The Nature of Gothic* (pp. 368–9) Morris compares Ruskin with Fourier to the latter's disadvantage. For a fuller account of these matters, see Paul Meier, *William Morris: The Marxist Dreamer*, Hassocks (Harvester Press) 1978.

38. *to the time when Africa ... named Stanley*: Henry Morton Stanley (1841–1904), journalist and explorer, encouraged and inspired the colonization of Africa. In 1890, after a successful trip to Africa, Stanley was being lionized in London. Though the hero of the national press, he was attacked week by week in the *Commonweal*, in the same issues as these instalments of *News from Nowhere*. Morris saw him as a bandit and murderer, who was pillaging Africa to prop up English capitalism.

39. *State Socialism*: See Introduction, pp. xix–xx.

40. *At the end of the nineteenth ... had to yield to it*: A reference to the successful trades union campaign, supported by the SDF, for an eight-hour day. The Socialist League regarded it as a 'palliative' – for the reasons Hammond goes on to give.

41. *To explain this you must understand ... the crash aforesaid*: Added in 1891.

42. *for the last sixty years*: In the *Commonweal*, twenty years. Thus, in 1890, Morris had thought of the 'change' as coming in about 1910. A year later he altered this to 1952.

43. *it seemed as if the end ... from yesterday*: Redmond points out that

Morris is affected here not only by the Marxist idea of historical determinism – the inevitability of the revolution – but also by the Norse myth of Ragnarök, the twilight of the gods. In Icelandic and Old Norse literature the destruction of the world is envisaged as a cleansing process leading to renewal.

44. *The exceptions were one ... fads of Socialism*: This reflects Morris's disillusionment with the Liberal Party and middle-class radicalism. He had been especially angered by the Liberal press, which, for all its talk of fundamental freedoms, had been silent about the violence of Bloody Sunday.

45. *That remedy was ... every man who produces*: A very Ruskinian passage. In his later work Ruskin treats the words 'work' and 'art' as synonyms.

46. *All this was much helped ... common amongst us*: Another Ruskinian passage, though note the reference to a well-known phrase from *The Communist Manifesto*: 'the idiocy of rural life' (see note 3, pp. 423–4). This was an aspect of Marx's thought with which Morris must have had some difficulty.

47. *cockney*: Not used in the modern sense. It refers to the cocksure tastelessness of the *nouveau riche*. Morris was especially fond of the word.

48. *sele*: Happiness or good fortune: another archaism from the Old English *sael* and the Icelandic *saell*.

49. *I came to the hurdles ... was not amongst them*: Added in 1891.

50. *I turned round ... beautiful girl again*: Added in 1891.

51. *his rather natural blunder*: Eton College was founded by Henry VI, 1440–41.

52. *I understood pretty well ... steam-power carrying*: One of the few moments where Morris envisages the value of modern technology for his new society. As this passage illustrates, he was not opposed to labour-saving machinery, though he is unenthusiastic about it. (For a fuller account of his view of machinery, see 'Useful Work *versus* Useless Toil', p. 304.)

53. *the ancient house of the Blunts*: i.e., Mapledurham House, built by Sir Richard Blount, *c.* 1585. The Blounts were a prominent family from the fourteenth to the seventeenth centuries.

54. *Chapter XXVI*: The whole chapter was added in 1891.

55. *ashlar*: Built of square hewn stone.

56. *the little plain of Basildon.* Again, the whole of this chapter reflects Morris's lifelong admiration for Ruskin's 'The Nature of Gothic'.

Morris has been criticized for the subservient roles performed by most of the women in *News from Nowhere*. It is therefore noteworthy that he here gives the main creative role to a woman in what might have been thought a man's job. Interestingly, there is also a female stone carver in his very first tale, 'The Story of the Unknown Church', p. 7–8.

57. *the foot-hills of the White Horse*: See 'Under an Elm-tree', pp. 361–4, and note 1, p. 423. From his schooldays at Marlborough College, Morris had been deeply attached to this region of England, with its many prehistoric remains and its association with the one English monarch he wholly admired, Alfred the Great (reigned 871–901). The ancient road known as the Ridgeway begins near Marlborough. It passes the stone circle at Avebury, the megalithic tomb known as Wayland's Smithy, the White Horse carved in the turf of the chalk downs near Uffington and the site of Alfred's victory at Ashdown. The road ends near the Thames beyond Wantage, not far from where Walter is set ashore.

58. *a hatred of civilization impressed upon them*: In his lectures Morris continually emphasized the view that art would need to die before it could be reborn. (See for example 'The Lesser Arts', p. 253.)

59. *the Lotos-Eaters' land ... where it was always afternoon*: A reference to Tennyson's poem 'The Lotos-Eaters' (1833). The poem is based on the incident in the *Odyssey* when Odysseus visits an island inhabited by a people who live in a permanent state of drugged trance. In this way they escape the realities of a harsh world. In *News from Nowhere*, however, the dream is not an escape but an opening on to a possible reality.

60. mamelon: 'A rounded eminence or hummock' (OED). Presumably a prehistoric earthwork.

61. *passed a mill ... as a Gothic cathedral*: Cf. Morris's praise of the thirteenth-century tithe-barn at Great Coxwell, near Kelmscott: 'unapproachable in its dignity, as beautiful as a cathedral, yet with no ostentation of the builder's art' (quoted in J. W. Mackail, *The Life of William Morris*).

62 *So then they turned ... and let things alone*: A reference to the Thames Conservancy Board. (See note 13, p. 408.)

63. *And the house itself... this heart of summer*: Kelmscott Manor, which remains as Morris described it to this day. (The church in the following chapter is Kelmscott Church, where Morris is buried with his wife and daughters.)

64. *and I thought of the church-ales of the Middle Ages*: Added in 1891. A church-ale was a village festival, so called because ale was the main beverage. In medieval times they were held in village churches.

LECTURES

The Lesser Arts

1. *the bettering of all mankind*: Morris was soon to react against this ingenuous optimism. At the time of this lecture, he was still a Liberal.

2. *the curse of labour*: Adam's punishment in Genesis 3:19: 'In the sweat of thy face shalt thou eat bread, till thou return unto the ground.' Commenting on this verse, Ruskin writes: 'It may be proved, with much certainty, that God intends no man to live in this world without working: but it seems to me no less evident that He intends every man to be happy in his work' (*Pre-Raphaelitism*). For 'The Nature of Gothic', see Introduction, p. xii, and Morris's preface, pp. 367–9.

3. *the crowd of those ... capitalists and salesmen*: Morris alludes to the Latin roots of 'manufacturer' – 'maker-by-hand'.

4. *Let us therefore study it ... which we have made our own*: This shows clearly that Morris was not a mere 'historicist'. It was only through study of the past – in design as in politics – that one could envisage a better future.

5. *there is little else left ... the matchless Hall near it*: Westminster Abbey was founded in the eleventh century, but the main part of the present building dates from the reign of Henry III – i.e., the thirteenth century. Morris often bemoaned the countless monuments (mainly from the seventeenth to nineteenth centuries) that clutter up the building, disrupting the lines and proportions of the design. (See *News from Nowhere*, p. 69.)

Westminster Hall, the only part of the old Palace of Westminster that survives intact, was incorporated into the nineteenth-century Houses of Parliament built after the fire. It dates from 1090, though its most noted feature, the hammerbeam roof, was built in 1399.

6. *'restoration'*: The present lecture was given partly in order to earn funds for the Society for the Protection of Ancient Buildings.

7. *Now there is one art ... and like a man*: William of Wykeham (1324–1404), bishop, statesman and public benefactor, founded New College in 1379, two years after the death of Edward III. In Morris's day he was credited with the invention of Perpendicular Gothic and does seem to have had some architectural experience.

Some Hints on Pattern-designing

1. *ryot*: Peasant (Hindi).

2. *For example ... a piece of cloth*: The cubes of glass used in mosaic are usually called 'tesserae'. In this context, 'thrums' are odds and ends of thread to be used in weaving. All Morris says on the innate limitations of any medium derives from Ruskin, though it is much enriched by his own experience as a craftsman. For instance, Ruskin writes:

if you don't want the qualities of the substance you use, you ought to use some other substance: it can only be affectation, and desire to display your skill, that lead you to employ a refractory substance, and therefore your art will be base. Glass, for instance, is eminently, in its nature, transparent. If you don't want transparency, let the glass alone. Do not try to make a window look like an opaque picture, but take an opaque ground to begin with. (*The Two Paths*)

Morris's own stained glass is living proof of how well he learnt this lesson.

3. *Mr Parnell*: Charles Stewart Parnell (1846–91), the controversial leader of the Irish Parliamentary Party: i.e., a prominent public figure.

4. *The first places ... from death to new birth*: Morris is probably thinking mainly of St Sophia in Istanbul, a building he had not seen but had studied in books. He frequently refers to it, notably in 'Gothic Architecture', pp. 337–8, where he gives a fuller account of the developments outlined in the present passage.

5. *Perhaps the fact that ... the civilized world*: This derives, again, from 'The Nature of Gothic', where Ruskin categorizes architectural ornament in terms of the kind of labour needed to produce it. He calls Greek ornamentation 'servile' because, as he sees it, the classical insistence on 'perfection' requires the suppression of the workman's personality. Modern machine-made work, he argues, takes this form of enslavement even further. The greatest art, which is 'naturalist' and 'revolutionary', gives freedom of expression to each individual workman or artist, a freedom which confesses to human imperfection.

The Hopes of Civilization

1. *to buy goods cheap ... the name of regrating*: Cf. *A Dream of John Ball*, p. 34.
2. *A lady writing ... long-bow shooting*: From the earliest collection of family letters in English, *The Paston Letters*. The letter in question, from Margaret Paston to her husband John, is dated 1448.
3. *Unless we saw ... where Alfred was born*: The White Horse of Uffington. (See 'Under an Elm-tree', pp. 361–4, and note 1, p. 423.)
4. *That epoch began ... the capitalist farmer*: Social changes satirized in More's *Utopia*. (See Morris's foreword to the Kelmscott Press edition, pp. 373–5.)
5. *Campanella*: Tommaso Campanella (1538–1639) was a Dominican friar of humanistic convictions and also a notable poet in his native Italian. His utopian fable, *The City of the Sun*, proposes the abolition of private property. It was written in the Neapolitan prison where he was held for a time by the Spanish Inquisition.
6. *finally, the crystallization ... its own standpoint*: Naseby (1645) was the decisive battle of the English Civil War. Once he had defeated the king, Cromwell suppressed all the radically egalitarian elements on the Parliamentary side. The Levellers, led by John Lilburne (1614–57), were an ultra-republican group in the Parliamentary army. Lilburne was imprisoned for his criticisms of the Protectorate, and a mutiny by his followers was put down soon afterwards in 1649. With the phrase 'party of progress' Morris implies a comparison between Cromwell's suppression of his radical followers and, in Morris's own day, the Liberal Party's betrayal of the working-class movement.

7. *the whole evolution of history forbade them to do*: i.e., according to the Marxist theory of historical determinism. The whole lecture shows the influence of Marx, notably in its use of the phrase 'class struggle' and in the tribute to Marx with which it ends.

8. *Gracchus Babeuf*: François Noël Babeuf (1760–97) was a radical journalist who urged the transformation of the French Revolution into a movement for economic and social communism. He criticized all the leading parties, including the Jacobins, and in 1796 conspired to overthrow the Directory. The conspiracy was discovered, however, and Babeuf guillotined the following year.

9. *Caesarism*: P. J. Proudhon's expression for the rule of Napoleon.

10. *This new system ... became a pauper*: Adam Smith's *The Wealth of Nations* (1776), the first great work of classical economics, begins with these words: 'The greatest improvement in the productive powers of labour, and the greater part of the skill, dexterity, and judgement with which it is anywhere directed, or applied, seem to have been the effects of the division of labour.' That is to say, without division of labour and the consequent destruction of personal creativity in the workman, there could have been no factory system and so no Industrial Revolution. The part played by this method in the workman's alienation is identified by Ruskin as well as Marx.

11. *I have had to study ... French chiefly*: In 1879 Morris taught himself the forgotten art of high-warp tapestry weaving from 'a very good little eighteenth-century book, one of the series of *Arts et Métiers*'. He also visited the famous Gobelins factory in France to study their methods, but he despised the work produced there – largely copies of Neo-classical oil paintings – and wrote that 'a more idiotic waste of human labour and skill it is impossible to conceive'.

12. *prior to '48*: 1848 was throughout Europe the 'year of Revolutions'. In England there was much agitation by the Chartists (see below).

13. *Chartism*: Working-class movement for the democratic reform of Parliament. The Chartists were active between 1836 and 1848. They were named after the People's Charter, presented as a petition to Parliament in 1838.

14. *Robert Owen*: Socialist and philanthropist (1771–1858), founder of model industrial communities at New Lanark in Scotland and New Harmony in the United States. He pioneered the Co-operative move-

ment and was a major influence on the Factory Act of 1819. His view of the role of work in an ideal society is to be found in his book *A New View of Society* (1813), which influenced Morris's conception of Socialism. Owen is often thought of as typifying the English 'ethical' tradition of Socialism, by contrast with Marx and his 'scientific' school.

15. *St Simon, Proudhon, Fourier*: The founding fathers of French Socialism.

Henri de Saint-Simon (1760–1825), the first systematic Socialist, was also the father of Positivism. In opposition to the destructive spirit of the French Revolution, he advocated a new social order based on industry, science and secularized Christian values.

Pierre Joseph Proudhon (1809–65) was one of the inspirations behind the Paris Commune of 1871. He argued that 'property is theft', in that it appropriates the value created by the labour of others in the form of profit, rent or interest without restoring an equivalent by way of exchange. In his view that laws, the police and the machinery of government are merely the signs of an undeveloped society, he shares some ground with Anarchism.

For Fourier, see note 26, pp. 412–13 and note 37, p. 414.

16. *a second Caesarism*: i.e., the Second Empire of Napoleon III (1851–70). The Emperor fell as a result of French defeat in the Franco-Prussian War, which Morris refers to as 'a race war'. His fall was followed by the brief flowering of the Paris Commune in 1871, the subject of Morris's poem *The Pilgrims of Hope* (1885–6).

17. *from being one of the most backward ... express itself in action*: Ferdinand Lassalle (1825–64) founded the General Working Men's Association, the main component of what was soon to become the Social Democratic Party of Germany. The conservative Prussian Prime Minister, Bismarck, at first attempted to compromise with Lassalle, whom he admired, in an attempt to foil the Liberal opposition. After German unification, however, Bismarck (now Imperial Chancellor) changed tack and, in response to an assassination attempt on the Kaiser in 1878, introduced a series of repressive anti-Socialist measures.

Gothic Architecture

1. *useful part of its population*: 'Gothic Architecture' is possibly the

most Ruskinian of all Morris's writings. Two quotations from Ruskin will indicate what Morris adds to his master's vision. Architecture, says Ruskin in 'The Nature of Gothic', is a social art: 'born of man's necessities and expressive of his nature'. And in his *Lectures on Architecture and Painting* he writes: '*Ornamentation is the principal part of architecture.* That is to say, the highest nobility of a building does not consist in its being well built, but in its being nobly sculptured or painted.' In this view Morris and Ruskin are at odds with the architects and designers of the Modern movement in architecture, many of whom they influenced.

2. *there is a revolt ... passing fashion*: Morris is probably thinking mainly of his audience, members of the Arts and Crafts movement, whose work he had inspired. He must also be thinking of his own masters, the Pre-Raphaelites and their associates, and perhaps too of the Aesthetic movement and Art Nouveau, anti-utilitarian currents with which he was less in sympathy.

3. *a fret or a dentil*: Fretwork is a form of ceiling decoration consisting of intersecting lines in relief. Dentils are the small square blocks arranged in series which decorate classical cornices.

4. *the Church of the Holy Wisdom*: i.e., St Sophia, Istanbul (sixth century).

5. *Byzantium through Germany*: What Morris calls Arab art and Saracenic Byzantine would now tend to be classed as Islamic, thus bringing together Persian, Turkish and Moorish elements. The style originating in the South of France under Roman and Byzantine influence is the Romanesque, to which Norman architecture belongs, while 'the native English style' is Anglo-Saxon.

6. *the Greek Kaiser*: i.e., the Byzantine Emperor.

7. *the wall of Tiryns and the Treasury of Mycenae*: The fortress and palace of Tiryns and the monumental tomb in Mycenae known as 'the Treasury of Atreus'. Both are outstanding buildings of the Mycenaean civilization, dating from the fourteenth century BC – i.e., from the very beginning of European architecture.

8. *the Battle of Courtray*: In 1302: sometimes known as the Battle of the Spurs. Courtrai is in Flanders and was one of the free cities referred to.

9. *Yet we admit ... was its crafts-master*: This acknowledgement of the

importance of capitalism in the process of historical evolution is not unprecedented in Morris's work but it is hardly characteristic. The phrase, 'the subjugation of nature', is strikingly un-Morrisian. The whole paragraph is plainly indebted to Karl Marx and his doctrine of historical determinism (cf. 'The Hopes of Civilization', pp. 323–8).

OCCASIONAL PROSE

'Looking Backward'

1. *Mr Bradlaugh, Mr Gladstone, or Admiral Maxse*: Charles Bradlaugh (1833–91) was a working-class Liberal MP, well known to be a free-thinker; Frederick Maxse (1833–1900) was a radical polemicist on a wide range of social issues. All three would have been thought of as typifying the most progressive of contemporary attitudes.

2. *State Communism*: i.e., by analogy with State Socialism, which is common ownership by means of State control. A Communist society, in the Marxist system, would be one in which the State, having performed the Socialist task of transforming society, had withered away. This aspect of Marxist theory is fundamental to *News from Nowhere*. In Bellamy's novel, Morris suggests, Communism has been attained without the disappearance of the centralized State.

Under an Elm-tree; or, Thoughts in the Countryside

1. *a figure which represents ... eleven hundred years old*: The White Horse of Uffington in Berkshire was one of the prehistoric artefacts Morris learned to love during his time at Marlborough College. It is a gigantic horse (360 ft long by 160 ft high) that was cut into the turf of the chalk downs between 2,000 and 4,000 years ago. In Morris's day, however, it was thought to commemorate King Alfred's victory over the Danes at nearby Ashdown in 871.

2. *9s....10s.*: Nine shillings, ten shillings – equivalent to 45 and 50 pence in today's coinage.

3. *'excitement of intellectual life'*: Presumably alluding to *The Communist Manifesto*:

The bourgeoisie has subjected the country to the rule of the towns. It has created enormous cities, has greatly increased the urban population as compared with the rural, and has thus rescued a considerable part of the population from *the idiocy of rural life* [Editor's italics].

Preface to The Nature of Gothic

1. *For the lesson . . . therefore live in pain*: For instance:

And now, reader, look round this English room of yours, about which you have been proud so often, because the work of it was so good and strong, and the ornaments of it so finished . . . Alas! if read rightly, these perfectnesses are signs of a slavery in our England a thousand times more bitter and more degrading than that of the scourged African, or helot Greek . . . there might be more freedom in England, though her feudal lords' lightest words were worth men's lives . . . than there is while the animation of her multitudes is sent like fuel to feed the factory smoke, and the strength of them is given daily to be wasted into the fineness of a web, or racked into the exactness of a line.

And, on the other hand, go forth again to gaze upon the old cathedral front . . . examine once more those ugly goblins, and formless monsters, and stern statues, anatomiless and rigid; but do not mock at them, for they are signs of the life and liberty of every workman who struck the stone, a freedom of thought, and rank in the scale of being, such as no laws, no charters, no charities can secure; but which it must be the first aim of all Europe at this day to regain for her children.

'The Nature of Gothic' was published in book form by Morris's Kelmscott Press as a kind of tribute. It is printed in Golden Type, which was also used for *News from Nowhere*.

2. *Robert Owen*: See note 14, p. 420.

3. *Charles Fourier*: See note 26, pp. 412–13 and note 37, p. 414.

4. Unto this Last: Ruskin's most rigorous and impassioned attack on nineteenth-century free-market economics and the social evils it was used to justify. First published 1860.

Foreword to Utopia

1. *Ralph Robinson's ... More's* Utopia: Sir Thomas More (1478–1535), humanist, statesman and saint, composed his great satire in Latin. It was published at Louvain in 1516; a book so critical of the English state was not publishable in England, even though its author was admired and favoured by the English King.

Robinson's fine English translation was first published in 1551, but Morris used the revised text of 1566 for the Kelmscott Press edition, to which he wrote this foreword. The edition is printed in Troy, Morris's small-scale adaptation of Gothic type.

2. *'the best state of a publique weale'*: From the title-page of Robinson's translation.

3. *the progressive movement of his own time*: i.e., the Protestant Reformation.

4. *'the cloud as big as a man's hand'*: Probably a reference to I Kings 18: 44. The little cloud is the first sign of an approaching storm.

5. *the surviving Communism of the Middle Ages*: Several communistic or egalitarian movements arose in Europe during the Middle Ages. Most of them were violently suppressed. Among the leaders Morris had in mind would have been John Ball, of course, and the Christian reformer who inspired him, the Lollard John Wycliffe (1320–84). For a somewhat Morrisian essay on such movements, see Bede Jarrett, *Medieval Socialism*, London and Edinburgh (The People's Books) 1913. A well-known modern study is Norman Cohn, *The Pursuit of the Millennium*, London (Secker & Warburg) 1957.

6. *and though he was not alone ... (bodie 'pauper')*: More explicitly attacks the enclosure of common land by powerful landowners wishing to make sheep farms. Countless peasant farmers were dispossessed in the early sixteenth century as a result of this innovation.

7. *Cato the Censor*: Roman statesman and orator (234–149 BC), noted for his rigorously conservative morality. He introduced a tax on luxury.

8. *Jacobin*: The radical party in the French Revolution.

9. *Whigism*: Morris's contemptuous term for liberalism. The Liberal Party had its roots largely in the old Whig Party. Though the more radical of the two main political traditions, the Whigs were always more oligarchical than democratic.

10. *New Birth*: Translating 'Renaissance'.

How I Became a Socialist

1. *the (then) Democratic Federation*: Founded in 1881 in an attempt to organize radical clubs of working men. It changed its name to Social Democratic Federation in 1883 on adopting an unambiguously Socialist programme. In Morris's day the term Social Democracy tended to be synonymous with Marxism.

2. *some of Mill ... in its Fourierist guise*: John Stuart Mill (1806–73), Utilitarian philosopher, economist and radical politician, wrote three 'Chapters on Socialism', which were published in the *Fortnightly Review*, February to April 1879. They are reprinted in vol. V of his *Collected Works*, ed. J. M. Robson. As a Liberal, Mill was opposed to Socialism but sympathized with its objectives. Mill, Adam Smith (1723–90) and David Ricardo (1772–1823) are regarded as the three great 'classical' economists.

3. *Bax and Hyndman and Scheu*: E. Belfort Bal (1854–1926) met Morris in the SDF and followed him into the Socialist League. For a time they co-edited the *Commonweal* and collaborated on a book, *Socialism: Its Growth and Outcome* (1893).

For H. M. Hyndman (1842–1921), see Introduction, p. xix.

Andreas Scheu (1844–1927) was a Viennese furniture-designer and Socialist, who came to Britain as a political refugee. His book of reminiscences, *Seeds of Revolution* (1923), includes a chapter on Morris, with whom he felt much in sympathy.

4. *Podsnap's drawing-room*: Podsnap is the type of the self-satisfied, self-important bourgeois in Dickens's novel *Our Mutual Friend* (1865).

5. *Huxley*: T. H. Huxley (1825–95), scientist and essayist, best known for his polemics on behalf of Darwin and the agnostic outlook. Morris seems somewhat unjustly to have thought him the type of the unimaginative materialist.

A Note by William Morris on His Aims in Founding the Kelmscott Press

1. *My friend Mr Batchelor ... which I still use*: Morris discovered the

firm of Joseph Batchelor & Son in 1890. Once he was satisfied with Batchelor's paper, he designed a watermark for it and used no other paper at the Press. In 1895 Batchelor secured Morris's permission to distribute his product commercially under the name 'Kelmscott Hand-made'. It was soon adopted by other private presses, notably the Ashendene, Doves and Essex House fine presses.

2. *without the thickening ... difficult to read*: Morris detested the so-called 'modern' style of typography, which derives mainly from the work of Giambattista Bodoni (1740–1813).

3. *of whom Nicholas ... from 1470 to 1476*: Nicolas Jenson (1420?–1481) was a French printer who studied under Gutenberg and developed the Roman style typeface. He established a press at Venice in 1470.

4. *my Roman type*: i.e., Morris's Golden type, named after the Kelmscott edition of *The Golden Legend* of Jacobus de Voragine (1892). Versions of this type were quite common in some commercially produced books of the earlier twentieth century, notably the Temple Classics, published by Dent.

5. *Schoeffer at Mainz ... Zainer at Augsburg*: Peter Schöffer (1425?–1502) acquired Gutenberg's printing equipment with Johann Fust. Johann Mentelin (fl. 1468–78) and his follower Günther Zainer (fl. 1460–78) were German printers of the same period noted for their use of splendid woodcuts. All three developed simpler Gothic types to some extent influenced by Roman.

6. *contraction ... 'tied' letters*: The use in early printing of standard abbreviations; the pairing of overlapped letters on one piece of type.

7. *a black-letter type*: i.e., a Gothic one. This is the Troy type, first used for *The Recuyell of the Historyes of Troye* (1892).

8. *a smaller Gothic type of Pica size*: The Chaucer type – so-called because of its employment in the most famous of all Kelmscott books, *The Works of Geoffrey Chaucer* (1896). Pica is a type-size, about six lines to the inch.

9. *Mr E. P. Prince*: 'Edward Prince ... was a sober, old-fashioned craftsman destined to cut the punches for many of the most celebrated private presses of the following generation, including the Doves, Ashendene, and Vale Presses. Indeed, at the time of his death in 1923 he was the last living independent punch-cutter in England, for by then the process of engraving punches had become thoroughly

mechanized.' William S. Peterson, *The Kelmscott Press*, Oxford (Clarendon Press) 1991.

10. *First, the 'face' ... the 'body' as possible*: The 'body' is a rectangular piece of metal having a raised type image on one end; the 'face' is the type image, the printing surface.

11. *'leading'*: Using thin strips of metal, less than type-high, to separate lines of type.

12. *16mo books*: Sextodecimo – based on sixteen leaves, thirty-two pages, to the sheet.

LETTERS

[*The Eastern Question*]

1. *that England is going to war*: Morris's letter was written in response to a threat by the Conservative government that Britain would declare war on Russia if she invaded the Ottoman Empire (see Introduction, p. xvi). The *Daily News* was a prominent Liberal newspaper.

2. *for we have before this waged ... jailors, alive*: i.e., the Crimean War (1854–56).

3. *If I had fallen asleep ... whom? and Why*: For Morris's use of the dream motif, see Introduction, p. xxix.

4. *the dreadful facts ... seemed to awake*: Eugene Schuyler, the US Consul-General at Constantinople, had published a report on Turkish atrocities in Bulgaria. Walter Baring was a Foreign Office envoy sent to investigate the same atrocities. He denounced the Turkish action as 'the most heinous crime of the century'.

5. *Mr Gladstone's ... rhetoric*: The former Liberal Prime Minister, supposedly in retirement, had recently published a pamphlet on the Eastern Question and, at a huge open-air rally of his constituents, denounced the Turkish action in inspiring language. Morris's enthusiasm for Gladstone was to cool soon after the latter resumed his political career.

6. *Mr Freeman's ... letters*: E. A. Freeman, a historian, had denounced the massacres in a series of letters to the *Daily News*.

7. *the new-made 'brave' earl*: The Prime Minister, Benjamin Disraeli,

had just been elevated to the peerage, taking the title Earl o~ ~acons-
field.

8. *if it were not for ... Sunday at Clerkenwell*: The Patriotic Club, a
body of working-class democrats, had demonstrated against the proposed war. It is significant that Morris, entirely new to politics, was
already investing hope in the working class.

9. *Lord Derby*: i.e., the Foreign Secretary.

10. *there were more ... in Scio a while ago*: An allusion to the massacre
by Turkish troops of 25,000 Greeks on the Aegean island of Chios in
1822. This was in the early stages of the Greek War of Independence
and it touched the conscience and sympathy of people all over
Europe, among them Lord Byron, who may be in Morris's mind
here. The Italian name Scio, which derives from a period of Genoese
rule, is the name Byron uses in *Don Juan* when he deplores the massacre.

11. *the Porte*: The Turkish government was officially known as the
Sublime Porte.

[*Anti-Scrape*]

1. *My eye just now ... Sir Gilbert Scott*: This is the earliest known letter
in which Morris proposes the foundation of a pressure group to keep
a watch on the preservation of ancient buildings: what was to become
'Anti-Scrape' (see Introduction, p. xvii). Sir George Gilbert Scott
(1811–78), architect of the St Pancras Hotel and the Albert Memorial,
was the most successful of Gothic Revival architects. As such, he was
often entrusted with the 'restoration' of major ecclesiastical buildings.
Morris despised Scott's work for its arrogance and superficiality; he
particularly deplored its indifference to the surviving texture and
substance of medieval building.

2. *Your paper has so steadily ...'restoration'* The opposition had been
largely conducted by F. G. Stephens, art critic of the *Athenaeum*, who
as a young painter had been a minor member of the Pre-Raphaelite
Brotherhood.

[St Mark's, Venice]

1. *the restoration of ... St Mark's at Venice ... at once*: A proposal was made in 1879 to rebuild the eleventh-century façade of St Mark's, Venice. This would have involved replacing the mosaics, the best of which date from the twelfth and thirteenth centuries (the 'base mosaics' which Morris goes on to mention are of the seventeenth century). With this letter Morris sparked off a large-scale campaign to save the basilica. He drafted a petition to the Italian Minister of Works, which was signed by Disraeli, Gladstone, Browning, Ruskin and other eminent figures of the day. How influential the campaign was remains unclear, for the 'restoration' plan was dropped before the petition arrived.